ROCK is HARD

by
Max Kay

Grosvenor House
Publishing Limited

This book is published by
Grosvenor House Publishing Ltd
28-30 High Street, Guildford, Surrey, GU1 3EL.
www.grosvenorhousepublishing.co.uk

A CIP record for this book
is available from the British Library

ISBN 978-1-78148-368-8

Contents

To Stanley & Hap
The Mandolin Brothers

Tattoo design by Benjamin Davies at
Madam Butterfly's, Hastings.

Design and artwork
by Sally Geeve www.sallygeeve.com

Side

A

CHAPTER ONE

"Testing, one, two. Testing, one, two. Testing, two, two. Test......"

"Get on with it. We haven't got all fucking week."

"Listen, arsehole," a voice boomed out of the PA system. "If nobody can hear themselves in the monitor mixes, you'll be the first to complain – and I'll be the first to hear about it. So just shut the fuck up, will you?"

The PA first arrived late then refused to function. Now, to top it all, the band's keyboard player was being insulted by his roadie.

A big man, weighing in around 17 stone, built like a brick shithouse, Basil Spence was an ardent fan of the 'rhythm read'. Exceedingly well versed in his field, he took inordinate pride in his ability to name every top-shelf publication available in Europe.

"Where the hell have you been?" David demanded of the late arrivals.

"Oooh, touchy," opined the man who played guitar when he wasn't busy winding people up. "I know we may seem late, but Basil did call the flat earlier. He left a message saying the PA hadn't arrived and not to bother rushing over. Don't tell me he didn't call you?"

"Jay, you know damn well he didn't. What's more, when that fat arsehole finishes pissing around with the PA system, I may kill him."

"You take it all so personally."

"Let's see how personally you take it next time your amp blows a fuse and Basil stuffs it with silver paper."

"Always good to know you have my best interests at heart."

David was in no mood for confrontation. He wanted to plough on with the rehearsal and nail the three songs they planned to record as soon as possible to avoid wasting time and money in the studio. He'd travelled down that well-worn avenue with other bands he'd played in.

"Anyone had a visit from the coke fairy?" asked the singer.

"I've got some hash if you want," Brian shouted, from behind a stack of flight cases.

"You know my joints are twice as nice – built by angels in paradise."

"Wow! Are those new lyrics you're working on, Calum?"

"No, Simon," Basil interrupted him. "They're not. They're the words we're going to put on his tombstone if he doesn't hurry up and roll one."

After one joint lead to another, then another, they eventually decided the local pub might be a better place to discuss the songs they were planning to rehearse.

"Good tune, no doubt about it," reasoned Jay, nodding his approval to Calum, who'd written the song. "But don't you think the lyrics are a bit near the knuckle?"

"I suppose I could remove the second 'fuck' in the first verse if you like."

"That and the first 'piss on you' from the last chorus if you don't mind." Jay had a point. "If a record company decided to release it you can bet we'd have to tone down some of the lyrics if we're to stand any chance of airplay."

"I disagree. By the time the lyrics are buried in the mix, nobody will be able to hear them anyway."

"Calum, the song's bursting to the seams with expletives. It's riddled with profanity."

"That's right," chipped in Basil, whom nobody would mistake for the church-going type. "And it's fucking blasphemous. What's more, I think 'Lord suck my cock' might offend some folk. Even if they don't take offence to the eight fucks I counted last time I heard it."

"How many?" Calum blinked.

"Anyway, I personally think it's overkill repeating 'piss on you' twelve times before the fadeout," Basil assured him. "And this pub is such a shithole," he added, surveying the tired-looking décor of the boozer's saloon bar that the band referred to fondly as The Whore & Handbag.

"I couldn't agree more," said Jay. "But if you hadn't tried to strangle the barmaid at The Nags Head, if you hadn't walked around the Queens with your dick hanging out of your trousers, and if you'd refrained from asking that new bartender at the Archers Tavern if she banged like a shithouse door in the wind, we wouldn't be sitting here now. Would we Basil?"

Wandering back to their rehearsal space with the others, past crumbling brick walls plastered with torn fly posters, David pointed towards the series of huge gasometers that interrupted the Kings Cross skyline.

"They're so unremittingly ugly. This whole area is – including the disgusting place we rent from that vile landlord."

"It's cheap, David."

"It's nasty, Jay."

On their return, Jay was surprised to find the girlfriend he'd met at Stringfellows waiting for him, perched on top of a flight case. At parties she'd introduce herself as an ecdysiast. A euphemism for stripper, it was a word she could pronounce but had never been asked to spell.

"Have you heard the news?" she asked.

"Chicks aren't allowed at rehearsals?"

"Shut up, Basil. What news my love?"

"Collected Thoughts have gone to number one," she grimaced.

"What did you say?"

"I think she said, 'We're fucked,' Simon." Rooted to the spot, he surveyed the dank rehearsal room, peeled paint tumbling down on to their equipment as another train sped past overhead. "I suppose we could chuck it in."

Collected Thoughts had been their main rivals since both bands formed towards the end of 1996. When Q Magazine had tipped the Manchester-based Collected Thoughts to reach the top, NME had come down firmly on the side of the London-based SSB. All in their mid-twenties, determined to reach the pinnacle of their chosen profession, SSB comprised five members.

Calum James, the band's vocalist and resident heartbreaker, was a man who thought with his dick and rarely pretended otherwise. Positively dripping charisma, the tall, blond, former drama student was the owner of looks most guys would kill for. Piercing pale blue eyes apart, he possessed the kind of sculpted cheekbones women would trample over each other to stroke before yielding to him.

A rock 'n' roller at heart, Jay Jackson was his song-writing partner and natural foil in the band. He was also the man who was forever digging the singer out of the shit when the latter's tangled love life took one of its frequent turns for the worst. He'd already had a minor hit in the UK with a song he'd written and recorded with a previous band. Disappointingly, both his record label and distributor filed for voluntary liquidation within weeks of each other.

A snappy dresser and owner of a sassy mouth, keyboard player David Edwards was SSB's diva in waiting and the band's gay icon. Listing his hobbies as bitching, moaning and whining without the dining, this highly strung individual had earned his living previously as a graphic designer before turning to music to fulfil his dreams of stardom.

Bassist Brian Lang had worked for two years as a session player appearing twice on Top of the Pops – the second time dressed as a turkey.

Their drummer, Simon Harding, had spent three years playing in pit bands for West End musicals. While this undoubtedly improved his percussive skills and increased his range considerably, the work had proved too soul destroying to contemplate any real future in. Rock solid as a drummer, he was the musical anchor of the band.

The real unknown quantity was Calum. Never having sung a note before he joined them, he was the most inexperienced member of SSB. He wasn't the best singer they'd auditioned and he'd been nowhere near the worst. But since he could act the part, he got the job. To convince the others he was serious about the gig, he'd been taking singing lessons for a year and, as a result, was beginning to sound impressive.

"Tight as a duck's arse," declared Jay, strolling out into the cool night air, the session finally over.

"No doubt about it," nodded Brian, zipping up his leather biker's jacket to fend off the cold before lighting the joint he was holding.

"The monitor mixes were so clear," beamed Calum.

"Much as I'm loathe to admit it, tonight's sound was the best I've ever heard in the shithole we call a rehearsal room."

"Why thank you, kind sir," Basil acknowledged David's comment. "Does that count as a compliment?"

CHAPTER TWO

"It's Pamela at Konk," said Alannah, passing the phone to Jay before hobbling back towards the bed, wondering how she'd trapped both legs in one side of her knickers.

"Hello."

"Oh, hi Jay. We'd planned to make twenty copies of the demo you asked for," said the studio employee, clearly embarrassed at having to make this call on its behalf.

"What's stopping you?"

"We can't find your master tape."

"What do you mean, you can't find the fucking master?"

"Don't you swear at me," snapped Pamela Johnson, intolerant of bad manners.

"We left the master in the studio with the engineer last night. Didn't he make a backup copy?"

"I hope so. I'll ask and call you back. Is that OK?"

"No, it's not OK," he spat, positively seething as he slammed down the receiver. "I can't believe those wankers," he continued to vent. "I don't know about you, but I'm off to the bloody pub. D'ya wanna come sweetie?"

"Already did. Right before the phone disturbed us."

"I could use a drink," ventured Calum, appearing from nowhere.

"Can you bring your mobile with you in case Pamela calls?"

"Haven't got one, have I?"

"Yes you do."

"Lost it last week."

"You dozy bastard. You're worse than those fuckers at Konk. Let's get out of here before anyone loses anything else. See you later darling," he called out, before slamming the front door shut behind him.

Outside of the pub the pair watched in amusement as an inebriate lurched into the hairdressing salon next door, mistaking it for the pub. It happened all the time. Once inside, comfortably ensconced at the bar, Calum's eyes began to roam.

"Whoa! I couldn't half slip her a crippler," he leered, pointing to a slim blonde deep in conversation with another girl over in the far corner of the room. "I wonder why she came in here?"

"She's probably just moved into the area. Why else would she drink in a place only fit for losers?"

"True enough."

"Still got a dose of the dawn horn, have we?"

"Certainly have my friend," the singer reassured him. "Hey Basil. What's happening?" he asked the man who'd joined the table without them noticing.

"Pamela called back as soon as you'd walked out of the door."

"And?" Jay prompted him, waving his hands in the air for encouragement.

"They found the master tape and she said you can collect your twenty copies at two o'clock."

"Thank you, my man." As Calum spoke, the girl he'd been admiring flashed him a smile as she walked past the table. Immediately, he downed the remainder of his pint in one mighty gulp and rose to follow her out of the door. "I'll see you guys later."

"I think you're on a winner there," Basil encouraged him. "Save some for me."

"For God's sake give it up, will you?"

"She was a good-looking tart, wasn't she?"

"Basil, why do you always have to bring things down to the lowest common denominator whenever the subject of women arises? They're human beings, too, you know?"

"I bet you wouldn't say that if you'd met this bird I once pulled in Southampton. That girl used to perform miracles with lemonade bottles. How she got one all the way up north without breaking sweat, I'll never know. And one up the jacksie."

"Basil, I do not want to be having this depraved conversation with you. Do we understand each other? Now just shut the fuck up and get another round in, will you?"

Owned by The Kinks' legendary front man, Ray Davies, Konk Studios was, if anything, beginning to look a tad on the tired side. Décor aside, the studio boasted analogue and digital mixing consoles, which allowed them to capture the live atmosphere of their performance on analogue before mixing down on a modern automated digital console. It took them three days to record three songs with a fourth day set aside for mixing. In Ray Davies' day, all of this would have taken place in the space of three hours.

"Happy now?" asked Pamela.

Jay's face lit up as she handed him twenty freshly labelled compact discs, all labelled neatly in their jewels.

"If there's anything I can do for you," he offered, "don't hesitate to ask."

She jammed an envelope with the bill poking out of it into his top pocket. "You can pay this for a start."

"Perfect timing. It just so happens we're on our way to see the management and I'll give them the bill as soon as we arrive. And I'll ask them to put yours at the top of the pile."

"Is that right?" she sneered, as Jay began to descend the stairwell. "And will that be before Shirley the receptionist grows a willy? Or after I join the Foreign Legion?"

"Promises, promises," Jay replied, blowing her a kiss from the bottom of the stairs.

After a quick pit stop at the rehearsal room to retrieve some cannabis he'd dropped down the back of a sofa, Basil parked the band's Mercedes truck in a leafy side turning in Primrose Hill.

"It's such a nice day. Why don't we walk to the curb?" he sniggered, before they both legged it the last hundred yards.

Andrew Symes was committed to making his first million by the time he was thirty. Thin-lipped and somewhat vain, he wore his sandy hair with a side parting and shoes with a lift to make up for his lack of stature. Showing little or no interest in women, he showed even less in anything that didn't involve making money. The twenty-eight-year-old who loathed small talk had formed his company, Tangent Productions, after leaving the booking agency where he'd looked after the interests of SSB.

"Did you come by taxi?" he asked.

"By truck, if you must know. The same one you're supposed to give me petrol money for."

"Thank you for reminding me of my obligations, Basil. Might I remind you I still haven't had the VAT invoices for the last two services, which, as I recall, I did pay you for. More importantly, I'm a little perturbed about your showcase gig at Ronnie's," he said, nostrils twitching as he grappled with the window latch.

"It's got some of the best load-in facilities in London. It's ideal."

"That's absolutely correct, Basil. Ronnie Scott's is a marvellous place to play: a wonderful, venerable institution. However, due to budget restrictions, we'll be showcasing at Ronnie's Upstairs this time around."

"You're having me on. Upstairs? I'm not humping all that gear up that steep flight of stairs on my own. Last time I worked there one of the guys humping equipment fell down them with a flight case for company. Bloke broke three ribs, his left arm and dislocated his shoulder. And you're telling me…"

"Calm down Basil. I'll get Kenny to help you do the load in."

"But…"

"And out."

"I thought Kenny was on the road with Quo," Jay cut in.

"He was," said Symes, totting up the commission he was losing while one of his roadies remained out of action. "They caught him snorting a couple of lines in one of the dressing rooms and fired him on the spot."

"Bit rich considering the huge amounts of charlie they put up their noses."

"Used to, Jay. Quit years ago. Now they're almost evangelical about it all. As only born-again drug users can be. Amusing isn't it?" smirked Symes, his nose still struggling to cope with Basil's presence in the room.

He stared vacantly out of the window overlooking Regent's Park, allowing his mind to wander for a moment. One of the new breed of managers, Symes relied on the services of solicitors not thugs.

"The time has come," he said, referring to Friday's showcase gig for the record companies and the opportunities it would present.

"Time to take a piss," said Basil, squeezing past on the way to relieve himself.

Symes flung open the window immediately, as far as it would go, and began to gulp down fresh air as if his life depended upon it. "Where did you find him?"

"Long story. Sad in places, sordid in others. But what I can tell you is he's got a good heart, he's incredibly loyal and he works his balls off for this band. What more could anybody ask for?"

"Deodorant."

"What?"

"Surely he could use a deodorant once in a while?"

"You try telling him. Whenever I do he says it's for pillow biters and players of the pink oboe."

Symes shuddered. "Do you mind if I burn some incense?"

"Do whatever you like," Jay shrugged. "We're off now. You won't forget to bike those CDs over to the record companies this afternoon, will you?"

"Whatever you wish."

"I bet you wish we'd fuck off," chuckled Basil, his seventeen-stone frame blocking the doorway.

"Precisely," said Symes. "Have a nice day."

CHAPTER THREE

"Rather tacky, don't you think?"

David grimaced, taking his first look at the dimly lit room with its tiers of small circular tables covered with matching red gingham checked tablecloths. After Calum and Jay had complained bitterly, Symes had relented. The showcase was now taking place in Ronnie Scott's main room instead of the Upstairs club as originally intended.

"You've got a point."

Seated at one of the tables in front of the stage, he couldn't understand how Ronnie Scott's club on Frith Street in Soho, the heart of London's West End, had earned its huge reputation when it was so frigging tiny. The jazz club's sound booth, not much bigger than a telephone box, was shoehorned into one corner of the room.

"Do you think they bought the light fittings in a car boot sale?"

"Looks that way, doesn't it?" acknowledged David, glancing around the room at the distinctly naff wicker lampshades, a hangover from the sixties. "But, to be fair to them, the place does look like a typical jazz club."

"All I can think of is Hendrix," mused the guitarist. "I can almost feel his presence here."

"What's Hendrix got to do with the place?"

"Jimi Hendrix," returned the guitarist, about to give his fellow musician a history lesson, "played his last ever gig in this very room, on that very stage. In fact, he played here the night he died."

"You don't say," marvelled the ivory tickler.

After a shaky start, Jay's beloved 50-watt Marshall valve amplifier died on him during the first number of a meticulously planned forty-five minute set. Mensch that he was, Basil had insisted on keeping a second amp on standby. The mid-song changeover was almost seamless and the audience failed to notice anything untoward.

Over by the bar, watching not the band but the audience itself, was Andrew Symes. It was comprised of journalists and the all-important A&R (artist & repertoire) men, supplemented by the usual complement of freeloaders, girlfriends and hangers-on.

Indecisive by nature and often referred to as 'Um & Ah', these men had just one thing in common – literally. All those Symes had met shared the honour of having signed just one act apiece. Mission accomplished, they'd be shunted off into the sidings to make way for the next whiz kid in short pants who'd inevitably hold down the job for an even shorter term than his predecessor.

"Is it true?" asked the journalist standing behind him.

Wheeling around, Symes found himself face to face with Harvey Robertson. Dressed in white jeans, T-shirt and regulation Nike trainers, he was the hack from Q Magazine who championed their rivals at every available opportunity.

"Is what true?"

Aiming to destabilise the opponent with his opening gambit, Robertson had been trained to go straight for the jugular.

"A lot of people in the industry say you're gay. Are you Andrew?"

"Harvey. Let me ask you something, you gutless little bastard. Have you any idea why you will never die by drowning?"

"No. But I'm sure you're going to tell me."

"Because scum," Symes lowered his voice, jabbing his inquisitor in the ribs, "will always float to the surface."

The subsequent record company interest and resulting press coverage, much of it ecstatic, meant the showcase gig had been an unqualified success. If band and manager were elated by the response, one person in particular had taken an entirely different view of the proceedings. Once again the venomous pen of Harvey Robertson had been working overtime.

Though it's widely known cream floats to the top, as I was reminded throughout SSB's lacklustre performance, scum performs in identical fashion. Intended as a showcase gig for the record company A&R men in attendance, who reminded me of flies descending on a freshly laid turd, it provided an opportunity to examine in detail the exceedingly limited range of talents of a band who've managed to combine and distil the very worst aspects of The Verve and Coldplay.

Between spouting polemic that would shame Bono, vocalist Calum Jones pouted, preened and posed throughout a performance that failed to impress. Desperate to shine, desperate to please, or just plain desperate as the case turned out to be, guitarist Jay Jackson spent his entire time on stage playing to an entirely different soundtrack to the rest of the band. The rhythm section, which audibly danced to the beat of two metronomes, neither in sync with the other, was risible. While the end of this dreary presentation couldn't have arrived soon enough, it's my guess keyboard player David Edwards, the newest member of the band, will rue the day he joined them.

"I will kill that snivelling little shit," quaked the normally placid Symes. "What gives that pompous arsehole the right to walk into our gig and write crap like this? The slimy little bastard couldn't even spell Calum's fucking name right!"

"Did you invite him?" his secretary asked.

"No Jane, I did not!" he fumed. "I need you to do something for me," he said, feverishly lighting a cigar before issuing her with instructions to take a taxi into Camden Town.

By the time Jane, stuck in traffic for much of her return journey, arrived back at the office with the parcel she was carrying, the hot summer sun streaming in through the taxi windows had begun to wreak havoc inside the black cab.

"Jesus effing Christ – you got a license for that?" gasped the driver as he threw back the glass partition. "The back of my taxi stinks of bloody fish!"

"I'm terribly sorry, please accept this," she apologised, thrusting him a £10 tip. Blood money for the guilt she felt perpetrating such an unspeakably awful act upon the unsuspecting cabbie. "Have a nice day," she said, grateful to get out into the fresh air.

"I bloody well was until you got into the back of my cab," he replied, head hanging out of the window, his expression indicating he may puke at any given moment.

"I'm sorry," she called out.

"Brand new this week," he announced to the oncoming traffic, wondering how long it would take for the stench coming from the back of his taxi to abate.

Following the instructions, back inside the building Jane had triple-wrapped the parcel now containing decomposing fish heads before placing it on a windowsill in another part of the building. "As far away from my office as possible," Symes had instructed her. An hour later, her face a sickly shade of green, she could take no more.

"I'm sorry, Andrew, but this foul smell is getting worse by the minute. Can we please have it removed before I throw up?"

Symes grinned. "Put an address label on it and call our courier. I think a bike would suit our purposes admirably in this instance."

"No sane taxi driver would take it. Ask the last one who dropped me off here. Poor man. So tell me: who are we sending it to?"

"Harvey Robertson. And thank you for your help Jane."

"Don't mention it. If you like I'll send a horse's head to Harvey Goldsmith while I'm at it?"

"That won't be necessary. But could you call the band and ask them to be here by twelve midday tomorrow."

"Basil too?"

Her boss, eyes narrowing, recalled the other distinctly unpleasant odour that had lingered in his office following the roadie's previous visit.

"Certainly not. Quite frankly, I'd be grateful if he never set foot in this office again."

The following morning, the band minus Basil, who had business to attend to elsewhere, followed Symes into the boardroom. Certain he had everybody's full attention, tea and coffee ordered, he closed the door before taking his seat at the head of the grand zebrawood table.

"Today marks the beginning of a new era," Symes started. "I was going to say we've been offered a record deal. But that's not strictly true. We," he continued, clearly enjoying himself, "have been offered two deals."

"You're joking."

"David, you should know one thing I never joke about is money. Both Platinum Records and Epic Records have made firm offers. Both have contracts prepared and ready for your signatures."

"What exactly are they offering?"

"Epic's offer is a three-album deal worth a guaranteed £1.1 million. That, and an advance of £350,000 for signing along the dotted line."

"Fucking hell," whooped Calum, who let out a shrill whistle.

"Platinum Records has also put a serious deal on the table. They're offering a guarantee of £1.5 million with the added inducement of £500,000 in advance if we sign with them."

At lunchtime the following day the entire band was sat around the first-floor flat they all shared apart from David. The lounge facing Crouch End's reservoir was dominated by a huge L-shaped sofa draped with Moroccan throws and plump velvet cushions. Although the flat had seen better days, the ornate cornices and ceiling rose were still in decent condition and highlighted dramatically by rag-rolled, Wedgwood blue walls. Lacking the feminine touch, it was typically littered with ashtrays full to the brim, beer cans that were empty and an assortment of pizza boxes that fell somewhere in between. Assorted guitars, amplifiers, microphones and recording equipment just added to the general chaos and untidiness.

"I'm sure we'd all like the money Platinum's offering," Jay reasoned, circling the room as he spoke. "But if we sign to Epic," he continued to argue, "they're willing to guarantee us complete artistic control."

"Won't Platinum do that?" asked Simon, drumming away on the arm of the sofa.

"Doubtful."

"I don't think we should sign with another record label that's owned by Sony," insisted Brian.

"Is Epic owned by Sony?"

"Ye...es," said Calum, dragging the word out as he began to lose patience with the drummer who was still tapping away on the furniture. "The same Sony that signed your favourite band."

"Collected Thoughts?"

"Jesus Christ. How many more times? Ye...ess," he repeated, making the word sound even longer the second time. "Maybe if you quit hammering on the furniture you'd stand a better chance of hearing what's being said." And on it went for most of the weekend.

They discussed artistic integrity. They discussed green issues. They discussed human rights. And although they weighed up the pros and cons of each deal, in truth not one of them had a clue how the royalty rates would pan out. What was really occupying their minds that weekend was something of a more pressing nature: how each of them would spend their share of the advance.

CHAPTER FOUR

It was a fairly warm early autumn afternoon when Symes and his charges trooped into reception at Platinum Records' West London corporate HQ. No expense had been spared to impress those who crossed its threshold.

Turquoise Italian leather sofas sat alongside gilded glass coffee tables strewn with industry magazines. These vied for attention with antique Persian rugs and vases that reached two metres high standing guard in each corner of the lobby.

It was a moment to savour. They'd worked hard and waited years for this. And knowing their peers were consumed by jealousy the moment they heard that SSB had landed a recording contract with Platinum only added to that enjoyment.

Calum, examining the gold records adorning the walls, had never seen so many in one place at the same time.

"Pretty impressive, huh Jay?"

"I should say so. We might even have one of our own up here in the future if we can stop Simon falling off his drum seat."

"I heard you," said Simon, tripping arse over tit that very moment on the priceless red Persian rug beneath his feet.

"Was I right?"

"Always, Jay. Simon, you're a clumsy fucker. No doubt about it."

"No I'm not."

"Yes you are."

"No I'm not."

"Are."

"Not."

"Hi everybody. I'm Richard Holdsworth and I'd like to extend a big warm welcome to you all on behalf of Platinum Records."

The suntanned figure standing by the doorway, the owner of thinning blond hair and a smile a mile wide, was the company's A&R man.

"A pleasure to meet you again, Mr. Holdsworth," said Symes, stepping forward to shake his hand.

"Please, call me Richard," insisted the man who loathed being called Dick. "Now, if you'd like to follow me into the boardroom, we can sign the contract before sealing the deal with Bollinger I already have chilling on ice."

"Where do I sign?" asked Simon, grabbing a pen upside down before attempting to scribble his name in plastic.

"Just here," advised Holdsworth, turning the pen the right way up. "Where the others have signed," he added, wondering why it was always the drummers who were thick. "Great. Thank you very much, gentlemen. Perhaps now we can get on with some rather more serious business. Champagne everybody?"

"Absolutely," beamed Symes, formalities over.

As they toasted their success and drank nothing but Bollinger's finest, glasses swiftly turned into bottles, which usually became cases – empty ones. Posing for pictures, happy to oblige the in-house photographer, this was turning into one of the best days of their lives.

While the bubbly flowed, a succession of marketing men, lawyers, press officers, record pluggers and secretaries were wheeled in to 'press the flesh' with the band. One of the latter, a long-legged secretary who'd caught Calum's roving eye in reception, even asked for autographs. What she hadn't revealed was that massaging their egos in this fashion was standard company policy: a greeting extended to all new signings.

With a signed contract poking out of his pocket, a half empty glass of champers in has hand, Symes, having spent three hours availing himself of Platinum's hospitality, was ready to express his true feelings.

"Genklemen, Richard," he began. "We, EshEshBee intend to become the biggesht shelling act in the hishtory of thish label. We will make thish the proudesht moment for EMI shince they shined the Beatlsh."

"But this isn't EMI," Holdsworth reminded him. "It's Platinum Records."

"Preshishly," slurred Symes, now holding aloft his empty glass. "Shir Josheph," he proposed a toast to Sir Joseph Lockwood, the long deceased Chairman of EMI Records, who ran the company in the Beatles heyday. "Thish ish for you," he said, before crashing to the floor in an undignified manner and landing in a crumpled heap at the feet of the A&R man.

"I can't believe you did that to us."

Sat up in the front of the truck next to Basil, the disgust was written all over Brian's face. Symes, cowering in the back on the return journey to Primrose Hill, was already regretting his uncharacteristic outburst.

"You're a fucking embarrassment! A liability," Jay scolded him. "That's what you are."

Reclined in an aircraft seat, Symes suddenly regretted his didn't benefit from the regulation waxed sick bag.

"Correct me if I'm wrong," said David, "but aren't you the one supposed to be setting us a good example?"

"Even Basil wouldn't get that pissed," insisted Calum.

"My mum would kill me if she caught me acting like that," protested the drummer. "Honest. She would."

"Look," Symes exhorted them all, struggling to find words to explain his abominable performance. "I know my behaviour was beyond reprehensible. Bordering on the unforgivable. But I promise I'll never do it again," he said, taking on the air of a small child caught with its hand in the cookie jar.

With rush-hour traffic causing maximum chaos on the roads, Symes had to endure the band's jibes for another hour before they pitched up outside Tangent. On arrival, Basil offered his paymaster some sound advice.

"Never drink on an empty head," he admonished the queasy-looking manager who'd managed to stumble out of the truck. "Oh and, by the way Andrew, I love the smell of your deodorant," he cackled, watching as Symes struggled to get his key into the lock. Still drunk, Symes failed to hear the accompanying gales of laughter.

"I want receipts for everything – and I mean for everything," Symes shouted after them in the street.

"We can hear you," Basil shouted back before they all piled into the truck en route to 'Tin Pan Alley', or Denmark Street to give it its proper name.

When the dust had settled at last, Symes had ingratiated himself by agreeing to front the band with part of their advance. One that had yet to land in Tangent's depleted coffers.

"The street's full. Where are we going to park, Basil?"

"Fuck it, Calum. I'll park around the corner and if we get a ticket I'll…"

"Give it to Andrew?" Jay chortled from the back of the vehicle.

Once parked, they spilt into two groups. Calum, Jay and Simon headed towards Andy's Guitar Workshop at one end of the street, while David, Brian and Basil made Rose Morris their first port of call at the other end.

"Does this thing bark?" Basil asked the acne-scarred youth manning the counter.

"It does. But the one over there..." grinned the salesman, pointing to the sampler racked up beside it, "does it far better. With the over-sampling features of the newer model, the sound quality will make you think you're actually standing next to a barking dog. You'll positively jump out of your skin when you hear the sound of breaking glass. And when you hear the sound of sheep this thing produces, you'll imagine yourself in the middle of a field in empty countryside on a hot summer's day."

"Is that a fact?"

"Aha."

"We'll take ten of them," said Basil. "Wrap 'em up sonny."

"Uh?"

"For the time being, if you really want to score in the public services sector, do me a favour and direct me to your toilets, my good man."

"The toilets?"

"Yeah. You know: the things people shit in."

Easily the scruffiest store on the street, Andy's Guitar Workshop was also the only emporium to offer their customers the chance to contract twenty-five different tropical diseases by touching the handrail on the journey to the store's upper level. It was up in the high-end room, where the shop hung its more exotic and other ludicrously overpriced instruments, that Jay was feverishly examining a 1958 Gibson Les Paul Standard.

"Can I try it?"

"Only if you've got £150,000 in your pocket," replied the sales assistant.

"How much?"

"A hundred and fifty thousand pounds. Although I believe the owner's willing to haggle a bit."

"I'll bet he is," said Jay, taking an instant dislike to the young American with spiky hair and a sneer on his face.

"I have another question."

"Yes?"

"Do you take luncheon vouchers?"

"No we don't," snapped the salesman, getting irritated by Jay's whimsical negotiating skills.

"Then how about cash? Would you take that?"

"Of course we would," nodded the American, who'd been taught at an early age to worship the dollar bill. "Are you interested?"

"Of course I'm not. I'm not insane either," he deadpanned, to accompanying gales of laughter from the others.

He'd visited Andy's on many occasions, mainly to purchase strings and buy leads. He'd never bought a guitar. Never had the kind of money they charged. Today was different.

"Tell you what: I'm going to let you into a little secret," Jay confided. "We, as in me and the gentlemen you can see in the far corner trying to put a dent in that Fender Stratocaster so we can get a better price on it, have just signed a deal with Platinum Records."

"Whoa. Are you guys Collected Thoughts?"

"No, we're fucking not," spat the guitarist.

"So who are you?" No sooner had he uttered the words than he realised who he was addressing. "I know. You're the Soft Southern Bastards."

"SSB will do," Calum shot him the kind of glance that would kill.

"And if you play ball with us," Jay continued to negotiate, "we might just spend some of the £20,000 we have at our disposal with you this afternoon. "So, are you going to be nice to us today or nasty?"

"Oh, nice," the salesman nodded. "Definitely nice. My name's Brad by the way."

"Well, pleased to meet you, Brad."

"Is there anything in particular you're looking for?"

"I'm interested in a Gibson Les Paul Custom. Stripped down to the wood. Like the one Mick Ronson played with David Bowie in the Spiders from Mars."

"Might be difficult to find but I could put out a few feelers for you. Was there anything else that might interest you?"

"An Epiphone like Noel Gallagher's. But not one with a Union Jack plastered all over the front of it like his. It makes him look like he's promoting the National Front or those other Nazi bastards, the BNP."

"I haven't got one of those either, but that doesn't mean to say one won't turn up as soon as you walk out of the door. I got this piece in yesterday," he said, still trying to figure out if he was being messed around or about to make a sale. "They say it used to belong to Jimi Hendrix," he revealed, before opening the case bearing a stencilled JHE sitting behind the counter. "This is awesome dude."

Being new in town, Brad hadn't realised this acronym was stamped on anything emanating from London's leading musical equipment hire company, John Henry Enterprises. More commonly known as JHE. Or maybe he did.

"Jesus," exclaimed the guitarist, surveying the battered old Fender Stratocaster on the counter in front him. He pointed to the hand-painted psychedelic mini-mural adorning the front of the instrument. "Who the fuck's responsible for this abortion?"

"Jimi?"

He leant in closer to examine the series of images showing the deceased star performing a selection of the trickier positions as depicted in the Kama Sutra. "Are you telling me Hendrix painted this guitar?"

"I really don't know who did it, man."

"How much are you asking for it?"

"Eight thousand pounds. Which is relatively cheap."

"Cheap!" Jay visibly choked on the word. "Cheap? How is it cheap?"

"If we had any serious provenance for the guitar we'd be asking probably twice that amount."

"Forget it. Got anything else I might be interested in?"

"How about one of the new limited-edition Fenders? The one with the green, red and gold finish?"

"Sounds very Jamaican."

"Yeah. I call it the Rastacaster."

"You know what?" Jay grinned. "You're a very funny guy, Brad."

By the end of a very expensive afternoon, the entire £20,000 had been disposed of. Suffice to say they were thrilled with their purchases. Symes wasn't.

"How much did you spend on cymbals?" he shrieked at Simon, who as usual had his mobile phone pressed up against his ear.

"Two thousand quid," he replied nonchalantly, as if he spent that kind of money on cymbals every day of the week.

Symes groaned, examining the receipt again, unable to comprehend how anybody could pay that much for something they were going to thrash the living daylights out of.

"You'd better have a look at this," said Basil, passing him a cellophane envelope.

"What is it?"

Symes stared at it then groaned again. It was the parking ticket the band had collected for outstaying their welcome on Denmark Street.

CHAPTER FIVE

"Hurry up with that fucking joint, Calum! We need you in here to check all the balances again."

"Keep your shirt on, Basil... 'Hello?'" he said, responding to a bleep from his mobile in the middle of skinning up.

Both he and the others were delighted at the outcome of their efforts in setting up a small recording studio in their rehearsal space. The results, gratifying in the extreme, were there to hear. After working steadily from noon till nine, they had over a period of two months rehearsed and recorded demos of all the songs for their debut album. It was tentatively titled *Hearts & Souls*.

"Calum! We need you! Now!"

"I'll be right there."

After deftly ramming home a roach into his latest masterpiece, he wrapped up the call and walked into the control room.

"I just spoke with Andrew."

"Did he say whether it was OK for me to buy that eighteen-inch crash cymbal?"

"No Simon, he didn't. He said Platinum wants us all in the studio to start work on the album this coming Monday."

"Great. Which studio are we booked into?"

"The Church," revealed the singer. "And if it's good enough for the likes of Mick Jagger and Bob Dylan, it's good enough for me."

Bang in the middle of Crouch End, The Church formerly owned by the Eurythmics before Dave Stewart bought out his business partner and former lover, Annie Lennox. Now it belonged to David Gray.

"Remember the time I narrowly avoided mowing him down?" chuckled Basil. "He was munching a sticky iced bun when he should have been paying more attention crossing a busy road with buses running up and down it."

"He also told me it's likely we'd be mixing in a different studio."

"Did he mention any names?"

"Yes Calum. Abbey Road."

"Wow!" said Jay, clearly excited. "Any others?"

"Perhaps Air Studios in Hampstead."

Any one of them would have given a limb for the opportunity to record at Abbey Road. Neither was Air to be sneezed at. It was the studio complex developed and formerly owned by Beatles' producer George Martin.

The following Monday both band and producer Jonathan Storey had begun to settle in to what would be their new home for the next two months. As in demand for his remix work as he was for major album projects, the producer knew additional studio time would send costs spiralling out of control if they overran – something he and his paymasters at Platinum planned to avoid.

Seated at the massive 48-channel SSL mixing console parked in the middle of the control room, the balding producer was already viewed by his peers as a veteran at the age of twenty-six.

"Here we go, guys." He pressed play and settled back to listen. Midway through the first track he stopped the machine. "We have a problem right there." Selecting rewind then play for a second time, Storey registered the look of horror on the singer's face. "Can you hear it?"

"Fucking arsehole!" Calum screamed. "I'll kill that fat bastard."

In his eagerness to help overdub a new last-minute guitar solo Jay had come up with, Basil had accidentally erased the entire vocal track.

"Relax," insisted the most experienced man in the room. "You're in a recording studio. And that's what we do here. Record. So, why don't you grab a cup of coffee, zip up a joint and then when you're ready, we'll replace the vocals and problem solved. Happy with that Calum?"

"Yeah. Fine by me." The singer breathed a sigh of relief. "I'm glad somebody's in control."

By the middle of October the band's confidence had received a terrific boost knowing they already had six great tracks in the bag. Naturally, there were problems along the way.

Storey had trouble synchronising the band's DAT demo with the studio's Mitsubishi 48-track digital recorder. Then Simon tipped a can of Coca-Cola into the faders of the SSL console. Easily the worst possible punishment anybody could inflict on such a delicate, not to mention extremely expensive, piece of equipment. To cap it all, Calum broke a pre-war vintage Neumann valve microphone. While the studio was able to claim on its insurance policy, Storey doubted they'd find a replacement. He certainly didn't intend to sell them his.

"Unbelievable."

David was sat with the others in the pub next door to The Church after a particularly gruelling day in the studio.

"What's wrong with the décor this time?"

"This place is frightful. I find it hard to believe somebody of Bob Dylan's stature would frequent a dive like this. It astounds me. I know it's right next door to the studio, but really?"

"If you must know, he stopped coming here."

"And why was that?"

"He started to get hassled – you know, recognised – and that was the end of that. Takes his business elsewhere now."

"Calum, most of the people who drink in this place wouldn't recognise their own face if you put a mirror in front of it – let alone Bob Dylan's."

"He did used to come in here, though."

"You say."

"Guys," Brian interjected. "I thought this meeting was convened to discuss the artwork for our record."

"Will the record company let Jay do it?"

"If it involves saving money, Simon, I'm sure they'd consider most things," said Symes, setting down the drinks and crisps. "Anyway, what have you come up with so far?"

Jay reached under the table to retrieve his portfolio. "Take a look Andrew. In fact, all of you take a look."

Unlike the Rolling Stones' Ron Wood and many others in the business, Jay wasn't a former art student. That said, those who'd seen his work regarded him as talented. Certainly compared to Ron Wood.

"What do you think?" he asked Symes, the latter's face impassive as he examined the contents of the portfolio.

"I'm impressed."

"Really?"

"Painting by numbers never looked so easy – or professional," he added with a wink. "No. They're very good. And I mean every single piece. You have a talent. I must get you to do something for me."

"My pleasure. It would be an honour to portray you counting money."

"Now there's an idea! Meanwhile, if you don't mind I'd like to hang on to these so I can show them to Richard Holdsworth when I see him tomorrow.'

"No problem. I trust you'll be fighting my corner."

"Of course."

"Thank you Andrew. I really appreciate your input."

"Ahem!" Basil was holding aloft an empty glass as if admiring its transparent quality. "Now we've sorted that problem out, whose turn is it to get them in?"

CHAPTER SIX

With mixing for the album scheduled to take place early in the New Year, by mid-December SSB had completed all twelve tracks that would appear on their debut disc for Platinum Records: *Hearts & Souls*. And with Christmas on the horizon there would be plenty of time to recover from the ordeal of being denied all daylight, locked in a studio for weeks on end.

"What a strange year it's been," mused Calum, stretched out on the sofa, staring up at the ceiling. "The year started with the Press banging on about Dolly the sheep. And it finished with them bleating on about the death of a princess."

"Truly weird," concurred Jay, who for the life of him couldn't understand the outpouring of grief surrounding the death of Princess Diana. "Whereas this year, the most insane thing that's happened is Radiohead taking the number one spot. I love *OK Computer*. I wish we'd recorded it. Still, mustn't get too despondent, must we?"

"You're right. Of course we mustn't. But it has been quiet of late," said Calum. "I'll tell you what: why don't we throw a New Year's Eve Party to thank all of our friends and the people who've supported us?"

"Excellent idea."

"We could make it fancy dress if you like."

"Another cracking idea. What do you reckon the theme should be?"

"Tarts and vicars?"

"Surely we can think of something a bit more original."

"Well, I can't think of anything. How about you?" he asked the man in a world of his own, tapping away on the table.

"What about a musical slant?"

"Not bad. Not bad at all, Simon. In fact, I think it's a brilliant idea. Let's face it, most of our friends are musicians. And if they're stoned when they read the invitation and inadvertently come as themselves, they won't look out of place, will they?"

"What I was actually thinking," said the drummer, "was everybody should come dressed as Elvis."

"Fuck off Simon," the others said.

Although Basil had been repeatedly asked to 'tone it down', after the ensuing fiasco at the previous party where he'd shown up wearing just his underpants, he had other ideas. This year he turned up at the front door wearing a seedy-looking overcoat that hadn't been near a dry-cleaning establishment in years. The garment in question, rank in the extreme and unbuttoned at the front, revealed urine-stained woollen long-john combinations. Complementing his unseemly apparel he was sporting a flat cap and fingerless gloves, one hand clutching a bag of sticky toffees. With four teeth blacked out in strategic places and judicious application of rouge to his cheeks, Basil to most guests was the genuine article.

Consequently, on New Year's Eve, with the party already in full swing, Basil, dressed as Uncle Ernie, the perverted character portrayed by The Who's Keith Moon in *Tommy*, was ready to ply his trade. Staying in character the entire evening, he was quick to take advantage of his disguise.

"That's a lovely pair of tits you've got there," he leered, obligingly groping a startled female guest. "I make no apologies for what I am, madam."

Fuelled by a constant supply of Special Brew, still clutching his toffees, he moved through the heaving throng of sweating bodies in search of fresh victims, confidence growing with every successive grope.

"Piss off you dirty old bugger!" the woman who lived two doors away scolded him. "Go on. Piss off you dirty old man!"

Aroused from his slumbers the following afternoon, Calum rubbed the sleep from his eyes as he surveyed the wreckage behind him. Nursing the mother of all hangovers, he stretched out his hand and picked up the phone.

"Hello," was all he could manage.

"Who was that bloody obnoxious person handing out toffees at your party last night?"

"Basil."

"Basil? I would never have recognised him. Anyway, what time did you guys quit drinking last night?" The very mention of the word 'drink' made Calum want to heave. And when he turned to face the other side of the bed, he almost did.

"Jesus Christ!"

Clearly startled, visibly wincing, he rubbed his eyes again. Another pair of eyes stared back at him. They belonged to Camilla Morse. Slowly it dawned on him: he might conceivably have spent a very small part of the previous night inside the most neurotic person it had ever been his misfortune to shag.

"Are you listening to me?" said Symes.

"I am now," said someone who'd rather have been facing his bank manager than the person lying next to him.

"Richard Holdsworth wants you in the studio on Tuesday to start mixing. We're at Abbey Road, which I thought would please you."

"Terrific," croaked the singer.

"Let's all meet there at midday. And please don't be late."

"Don't worry. We won't be," he promised.

"Well?" exclaimed his ex, retrieving her knickers and other assorted clothes she'd scattered around the room in the heat of the moment. "Explain yourself."

"What is there to explain?"

"Your pathetic performance last night."

"We didn't, did we?"

"No," she announced tartly, much to his subsequent relief. "We bloody well did not. And do you want to know why?"

"Carry on," he said, as if he had any choice in the matter.

"Because you, Calum fucking James, pop-star extraordinaire and self-styled stallion, couldn't get it up."

"I couldn't?"

"No, you couldn't and I can honestly say I've had more intimate moments with sex toys," she roared in his face.

"Thank Christ for that," he muttered.

"What did you just say?"

"You'd need batteries for that."

"What fucking batteries you snivelling sack of shit?" she reprimanded him, before slamming the bedroom door behind her.

"Do you want to do it with your socks off like McCartney did?" asked Eddie. A professional photographer and friend of the band, he'd agreed to take pictures of them standing on the same zebra crossing as The Beatles had on the Abbey Road album sleeve.

"A bit cold for that today," said Brian. "Can't you think of a more gratifying way of emulating my hero without my having to catch pneumonia?"

"Suit yourself," nodded the snapper, a notorious stickler for detail.

He'd reasoned that showing up very early in the morning would enable him to orchestrate the shoot without having to contend with the rush-hour traffic. Unfortunately for them, while they'd waited for daylight to break, traffic movement in the area had begun to build significantly.

"I think we should knock it on the head now," Eddie advised after shooting for only half an hour. "It's getting too dangerous. We've probably got what we need."

"Just one more," Simon pleaded. "Please."

"OK. Just one more," he agreed, a move he would soon come to regret. Twenty minutes after the accident had happened, as Eddie packed away the assorted cameras and lenses into their brushed aluminium cases, Brian was still apologising to the cyclist.

"Truly mate, we really are sorry about what just happened. I know it shouldn't have. But it did. And I apologise profusely. Unreservedly." Seemingly appearing out of nowhere, the cyclist had ploughed into Simon on the legendary crossing before hurtling into the air, his fall broken, ironically, by the bonnet of a parked Volkswagen Beetle. "These are for you."

In an effort to pacify the poor guy, Brian handed him a signed photograph of the band, a T-shirt and the promise of two free tickets to their next gig. After much hand shaking, honour restored, the band returned to the warmth of the studio to continue the lengthy process of mixing the album.

While many entertain the notion of a band standing around a single microphone to record, before the producer gets out of his chair to say, "It's in the can," at the end of the first take, this is not the case. As Jonathan Storey was aware, modern recordings are painstakingly constructed. Layering each instrument separately, a track at a time, he would build up anything from sixteen to forty-eight parallel tracks of sound, which then had to be mixed. And since most human beings don't possess the aural ability to balance forty-eight sound sources into one meaningful whole, the process, as SSB were beginning to find out, could go on forever.

Like too many other producers, Storey would prove his worth by filling up every available track with sound. His particular trademark was layer after layer of tubular bells. These he combined with layer upon layer of angelic vocals. Ever on the lookout for new sounds to record, he would have sampled his cleaning lady's vacuum cleaner had he thought it would add something unique to one of his epic productions.

By early February the overdubs had been completed. All but two tracks had been mixed and they'd also agreed a new revised running order for the album. At this point, the exhausted musicians elected to leave the ship in Storey's capable hands. Meanwhile, they all took a well-earned break for two weeks before buckling down to the serious challenge of promoting *Hearts & Souls*.

CHAPTER SEVEN

United in their love of all things American, Calum and Jay made the most of their two-week break taking Alannah and Suzanne on holiday to New York. On their first day they'd gazed out at New Jersey in the distance from the top of the Empire State Building before taking lunch even higher up in the sky at a restaurant in one of the Twin Towers at the World Trade Center. In addition, all confessed to enjoying the Staten Island Ferry, from which they were able to take a closer look at the Statue of Liberty. And while the girls indulged themselves with a spot of retail therapy at Saks, Bloomingdale's and Macy's, Calum and Jay made a beeline for the musical instrument stores off Times Square. Evenings were spent wining and dining in Greenwich Village before hitting the clubs and returning to their hotel in the early hours of the morning. New York, as they soon discovered, never sleeps. While the visit to the Big Apple proved to be an unqualified success, the red-eye flight back to London proved otherwise.

Jay showed his boarding pass to the obese fellow sat next to him taking up half his seat.

"The point I'm trying to make is this: since I paid for the entire seat, would you mind if I have back the part of 67D you're currently occupying?"

Remaining silent, the twenty-five-stone American shifted his bulky frame further into the aisle. Now he'd be annoying the stewardesses.

Seated across the aisle from him, Calum was faring little better.

"Do you really have to keep doing that?" he asked the little old Japanese lady sat next to him who hadn't stop fidgeting since the moment she sat down. She either wouldn't or couldn't stop twitching her spindly elbows, repeatedly jabbing them into his throughout the flight.

"I don't think I can take much more of this," he confided in Jay while they were stretching their legs in one of the tiny areas airlines still allowed passengers to stand up in. "First I get this slit-eyed old crackpot trying to stab me to death for hours, and whenever she stops, which isn't often, the Hassidic Jew on the other side keeps letting rip with his prayer book every half hour on the hour. That and my seat-back entertainment packed up half way across the pond."

"I'll swap my fat bastard for your cranky old Jap and the Jew if you fancy a change," suggested Jay. "I loathe travelling economy. Loathe it."

Although Alannah and Suzanne were lucky enough to have been allocated adjoining seats, all thoughts of intimate conversation were dashed after their stewardess seated the family from hell in the row in front. The product of years of inbreeding, the youngest member of this family of mountain dwellers, a six-month-old baby, bawled its eyes out for almost the entire journey.

"God, Alannah, they're so ugly," Suzanne whispered, after catching her first glimpse of the baby's infant brothers.

Her friend locked eyes with the three-year-old boy, who sported the ears of a rabbit and teeth that could gnaw an apple through a tennis racket. "You can say that again."

While their parents snoozed, these genetic freaks of nature played peek-a-boo, their heads appearing at regular intervals over the seat back.

"Check this one out," Suzanne whispered, pointing discreetly to the four-year-old member of the family, who was looking decidedly queasy.

Taking after his father, the eldest possessed a nose that pointed north and a lazy eye that, unable to focus naturally alongside the other, stared wildly to the right.

"Jesus Christ," shrieked Alannah, when the eldest of the pair threw up directly over the seat back and into her lap.

"What are you going to tell them if they stop you with the guitar?" asked Calum, as he and Jay stretched their legs at the back of the plane.

"Some old crap or other."

"I see some signs of fret wear," noted the sole customs officer manning the green channel that morning. "How long have you owned it?"

"Ten years or thereabouts," lied Jay. "Is that right Calum?"

"About nine or ten," he motioned towards the vintage Gibson acoustic guitar Jay had purchased in New York.

"Mmmm," the officer deliberated, a fellow player who regarded himself as something of an expert in these matters. Stroking his chin, he examined the guitar more closely.

"It's been in a lot of scrapes," confessed the guitarist, continuing to make it up as he went along.

"Both fret wear and lacquer cracking are, I would say, commensurate with an instrument of that age, which would suggest this is not a brand new guitar." And on that basis he waved them on their way.

"What a fucking plonker," said Jay, striding towards the exit, hoping the guy hadn't changed his mind but thinking better of turning round to check.

"How much did you save on that little exercise?"

"I would say if you take into account the duty, the VAT and hiring the services of a customs agent to clear it, somewhere in the region of four hundred pounds."

"No flies on you, are there boy?"

Still recovering from the after effects of jet lag, Calum and Jay and the others had been summoned to Tangent to discuss the all-important video to accompany the release of their first single.

Long gone were the days when record companies would splash out upwards of £100,000 on what amounted to making a mini-movie. For most bands that figure had been slashed to around £10,000. In the case of SSB, Platinum relented and were prepared to cough up in the region of £35,000.

"Who's directing?"

"An Italian guy. Piero Pini. The label claims he's really interested in working with you."

"Have you actually met him?"

"Just the once, Jay. And like so many Italians he's a dedicated chain-smoker. He's got this long, silver and yellow nicotine-stained hair greased back into a plait. Never stops talking. Waves his arms in the air whenever he speaks. Neither can he pronounce the album's title. After he's mixed his vowels and mangled his consonants it comes out of his mouth sounding like 'arseholes'. Strange fellow."

"What's his CV like?"

"Hardly impressive if you eliminate the tampon commercials."

"Tampon commercials?" queried Calum.

"Quite," replied Symes, not entirely satisfied himself with Platinum's choice of director.

"What else has he done?"

"A string of obscure movies that enjoyed major critical success at a number of minor European film festivals. Hardly the stuff that translates into bums on seats and box office success."

"Have you any idea what this video might wind up looking like?"

"The usual cliché-ridden plot. Damsels in distress, knights on white chargers and clowns, I should think. Plus the obligatory sole juggler and a couple of dwarves thrown in for good measure. One of whom you can be certain will be in drag."

"I'll do it," David insisted. "Me, me, me."

"And that's before you all wake up and realise it was a dream."

Unlikely though it sounded, this was a fairly accurate description of the video Piero Pini finally delivered to them.

"What is all this crap they throw into duty frees? Looks like wood chippings." Jay was examining the contents of a cigarette he'd split open at the seam.

"Why don't you write and complain," suggested Basil, casting an eye over the strange-looking shrapnel the guitarist was flicking into the ashtray.

"What a great idea. And while I'm at it, I'll dash off another to the people who make the rolling papers.

"Dear Mr. Rizla, on the occasions I've found it necessary to bulk buy, purchasing ten or more packets at a time, I've often found the papers don't stick together quite as well as they normally do, but have been too embarrassed to return them to the shop where I bought them. Can you help?"

"Excellent. Someone ought to tell them and put their customer complaints department to the test."

"Well, it won't be me. Quite frankly, I doubt if Rizla has a customer complaints department. More like a customer relations helpline doubling as a hotline that automatically connects all callers to the local drug squad."

"Mmmm. Shall we get on with the interviews?"

Taking tea and spliffs that afternoon with Basil, the band had convened with the sole purpose of honing their interview skills in preparation for those they'd be giving to the press later that same week. Following Symes' instructions, Basil, acting as quizmaster, would grill each member in turn while recording the proceedings.

"Ready everybody?"

"Ready."

He hit record before launching into the first question.

"What is your opinion on drugs?"

Jay smirked. "Depends what you've got."

"Your honest opinion," pressed the roadie, unwilling to let his prey off the hook that easily.

Jay pondered this loaded question. "I think the authorities are fighting a losing battle. Just take a look at how much taxpayers' money that America's Drugs Enforcement Agency has spent on dealing with the problem. And what has the DEA achieved? Nothing, if we're being honest about it. What they already know, but refuse to admit, is that it's impossible to contain the situation. Frankly, it's hard to see how the DEA can win this battle. Don't they know it's far easier to score drugs in prison than it is in the outside world? Because everybody else seems to, including those who've never even been there."

"Not bad," said Basil. "Not bad at all. Impressive, even."

The guitarist had acquitted himself rather well. He'd avoided answering the question he'd been asked. Then he'd raised a couple of his own accompanied by a series of facts. These he discussed in an articulate, intelligent manner, while managing to avoid admitting he'd dabbled in just about every illegal substance known to mankind. In addition, armed with the knowledge he'd gained from previous interviews, Jay knew from bitter experience the golden rule was never to say anything you wouldn't want to read in print in the cold, sobering light of day.

"OK David, it's your turn now," said Basil, punching record again. "Do you think gays should have the same rights as everyone else? And that includes rug-munchers, in case you wondered."

"What kind of question is that supposed to be?"

"One you may be asked."

"Are you suggesting I'm gay?"

"I know damn well you are. So just answer the bloody question."

"I think," said David, gritting his teeth, "that gays should be accorded the same respect as everybody else on the planet. Not that you know the first thing about gays. Or respect, for that matter."

"Ah, now there you're wrong. I've seen dozens of videos on the subject."

"I don't doubt it. And I'm sure we can all take an educated guess what was in them."

"On top of that," the roadie continued, "I've borrowed books on the subject from the library, I know what KY Jelly is for, I know what cottage trotting is and, equally important, I know you."

"But you don't know anything about respect. Do you?"

"Respect? I'm still working on that aspect. Anyway, I thought I was supposed to be interviewing you. If you're going to rise to the bait every time you're asked a penetrating question, excuse my pun, they'll make mincemeat out of you. Only trying to help, mate."

"Let's get one thing straight: you are not my mate. Do you understand me?" thundered David, thoroughly pissed off by Basil's tactless line of questioning.

"A despatch rider just delivered this."

"Thank you." Symes examined the package containing the tape Jane had handed him.

Lighting up his first Montecristo of the day, he slipped the cassette into the machine before engaging play. Taking a long pull on the cigar, he sat back to listen to the question/answer session the band had recorded with Basil the previous day.

"Is it true that drummers have a greater sex drive than the other members of a band?" he heard Basil ask Simon.

"Not in ours. The keyboard player's far more promiscuous than I am. He goes cruising on Clapham Common," he confided, to accompanying gales of laughter in the background.

"Jesus," Symes groaned.

"And he likes teenage boys. So he says."

Almost choking on his cigar at this point, Symes screwed up his eyes, compelled to listen to what was rapidly turning into an essay on how not to conduct an interview.

"Said he gets the biggest kick of all from cottage trotting. So compared to him, most drummers must seem like angels."

"Christ Almighty!" spluttered Symes, removing the stogey that was threatening to choke him. "The imbecile. What a bloody fool." There was a tap at the door.

"These are for your attention, too," said Jane, handing him an armful of documents.

"Have you listened to this tape?"

"Enough of it," divulged the secretary, who'd stopped by the band's flat the previous day when they were midway through recording.

"And?"

"Simon hasn't got a clue."

"You don't say."

"David sounds defensive. And Brian comes across as paranoid."

"Enough. I don't want to hear any more."

"I think I understand why."

"Could you bring me some coffee? A double espresso maybe?"

"Right away boss."

Fast-forwarding through the tape, he stumbled upon gem after gem. Nugget after nugget of gold waiting to be mined by a hungry tabloid press and fed to a salivating public. His worst nightmare, come true. The press would have had a field day.

Prepared to hear the sound of Simon Harding hanging himself on magnetic tape, Symes pressed play again.

"What are your thoughts on record companies?" Basil asked him.

"Off the record?"

"If you like."

"They suck. Most of them are bloody thieves. The rest are parasites if you ask me – and that includes ours." This was followed by a short pause. "You won't print that, will you?" asked Simon.

CHAPTER EIGHT

With Simon barred from sharing his thoughts with the press, none of the others had screwed up their interviews. Even Q Magazine wrote glowingly of the band. The journalist who'd conducted the interview with Jay openly admitted that few, if any, of his fellow scribes on the magazine shared Harvey Robertson's opinions. Most were big fans of the band. Few, it transpired, were fans of Robertson.

"The press coverage we've received so far is phenomenal," Symes addressed the band. For this we must thank the Platinum press office. They've done a fantastic job. And you've all done a fantastic job." He continued the pep talk, jabbing an index finger in the air to hammer home his point. "But, before all this positive coverage goes to your heads, there's more work to be done."

"More work?"

"Yes Jay. The label wants you to do more interviews. All of you except Simon, that is." He glanced at the drummer.

"And when's this likely to be?"

"Next week." He averted his gaze from Simon. "They've lined up a series of regional radio interviews for you."

"I promised to take my girlfriend shopping."

"No Calum. You were going to take your girlfriend shopping. Not anymore. As I was saying, Platinum has lined up a series of regional radio slots, only this time you'll be working in pairs. Jane?"

"Yes, Andrew?"

"Could you hand out the itineraries please?"

They each studied the schedules she'd presented them with in complete silence.

ITINERARY – I (JAY & DAVID)

Monday	- March 1st	- Norwich Broadland FM
Tuesday	- March 2nd	- Exeter Gemini
Wednesday	- March 3rd	- Cardiff Galaxy (AM)
		- Bristol BBC Radio (PM)
Thursday	- March 4th	- Birmingham BRMB (AM)
		- Oxford Oasis FM (PM)
Friday	- March 5th	- London Capital Radio

ITINERARY – II (BRIAN & CALUM)

Monday	- March 1st	- Edinburgh Forth FM
Tuesday	- March 2nd	- Glasgow Scott FM
Wednesday	- March 3rd	- Liverpool radio City FM (AM)
		- Manchester Piccadilly Radio (PM)
Thursday	- March 4th	- Newcastle Metro FM
Friday	- March 5th	- Leeds Magic 828 (AM)
		- Sheffield Hallam FM (PM)

"Jay and David will be taking care of the South of England and Wales. Brian and Calum will cover Scotland and the North of England. Any questions?"

"I can't see any holes in this schedule. When do we get a day off?"

"Good question," acknowledged Symes. "And the reason you can't see any gaps in the schedule, Calum, is because there aren't any. So, no, you won't be getting a day off."

"Will we need passports for Scotland?"

"Very funny. Any more questions? Yes, Jay?"

"Do you know I'm cartographically dyslexic?"

"I confess I do not. Is it that annoying Pogues record they're always playing on the radio?"

"No, Andrew. It means I can't read a map."

"You won't need to read a bloody map," replied an exasperated Symes. "Platinum's press office will supply two minibuses with drivers whose sole purpose is to ferry you around. In addition, each pair has been assigned a PR who'll be on hand to check you in and out of hotels. They will be there to ensure you arrive on time and you don't say anything stupid." He glared at Simon. "Believe me, you won't even have to think for yourselves. These people will be there to do it for you. All you have to do is show up. That, and act like rock stars. Not too much to ask, is it?"

Inedible breakfast apart, the early morning flight up to Edinburgh was uneventful.

"Pretty soon they'll be handing you a selection of tubes when you board," opined Brian. "Then you'll be able to squeeze the shit they give you on to a piece of bread."

As Symes had promised, PR Debbie Cameron and their driver were there to meet Calum and Brian when they stepped into the arrivals lounge at Edinburgh Airport. A good-humoured fellow by the name of Hamish, he regaled them with countless amusing tales of other bands he'd worked for to fill in the boring hours spent on the bus.

"Did you know rap was originally white man's music?" he asked Calum during the drive to their interview at Glasgow's Scott FM. The singer was baffled.

"How do you make that out?"

"Years ago," revealed Hamish, "when I was a kid, there was a TV series called *The Beverley Hillbillies*. And the words to the theme tune were spoken not sung by a white guy, the star of the show who played Jed Clampett."

"You're a complete hoot, Hamish. Bet you didn't know 'Strangers in the Night' was one of the earliest recordings to feature a reference to drugs. Even Frank didn't cotton on all those years he was singing it."

"Really?" laughed the Scot, visibly enjoying this round of rock trivia.

"Listen to the chorus. What's Frank singing?"

"Doobie, doobie, doo," cackled Hamish, almost losing control of the vehicle.

Down in the South West of England, Jay and David were warming up for their interview on air at Exeter's Gemini Radio. The previous day, when Brian and Calum had talked to Edinburgh Forth FM, they'd been doing exactly the same at Norwich Broadland FM. Although they'd struggled to comprehend the Norfolk accent, they were ill prepared for what assaulted their ears on arrival at Gemini.

"Put 'e over there boy," the Exeter station's engineer suggested when Jay handed him a three-track sampler from their CD. Unsurprisingly, the guitarist failed to comprehend he'd been asked to place the CD on the shelf opposite. Delivered in a rich Devonian burr, his next comment went right over Jay's head, too. "'Er's a priddy maid," the engineer remarked when he saw Platinum's attractive PR lady.

By the time they reached their destinations on day four of their respective schedules, all were firmly into the rhythm of interview mode. With Calum and Brian doing the honours at Newcastle's Metro FM, Jay and David played rock stars at Birmingham's BRMB. But while everything went according to plan in Newcastle, Jay didn't fare too well with the cocky young upstart intent on making a name for himself at BRMB.

"Dievid," the jock asked in that irritating Black Country yawl that passes for a dialect. "Is it true what people are saying? By which I mean, is it true that yow put the band together purely as a cynical exercise to make money?"

"Not at all," he assured him, wisely refusing to rise to the bait this time. "In fact, years ago, long before I joined this band, I had a successful career in graphic design. If all I'd wanted to do was make money I think I'd have stayed in graphic design. Don't you?"

"Fairynuff," the jock responded disingenuously, clearly determined to make a kill live on air. "But what I've heard on the grapevine is that none of yow actually played on the new CD," the last word pronounced as 'seedy'.

"What did you say?" Jay retaliated, hackles rising.

Seated behind the mixing console in the control room, the station's engineer grew increasingly anxious, sensing trouble brewing on the other side of the glass. His right hand hovered over the fader controlling Jay's microphone, ready to act should the situation escalate.

"I said, 'Was is it true none of yow actually played on the new record?'"

In less time than it takes to say 'you're off the play list', the guitarist exploded live on air. "Fuck you!"

Immediately, the engineer pulled down the fader to risk further embarrassment to the station. Then, utilising a sleight of hand rarely seen outside The Magic Circle, he slipped in a jingle cartridge as he cued up the next record. This man was one smooth operator.

Simon took great pleasure in attending the post-mortem on his fellow band members' radio debut the following week. He was grinning like a Cheshire cat seeing his band mate torn into for a change. Finding nothing to laugh about when he'd learned of the fiasco at BRMB, Symes reprimanded Jay in front of the others for his outrageous behaviour on air.

"Jay, I can assure you that your record label was not amused. Neither am I. And I'm going to tell you why. Due to your outburst on air, the station director at BRMB is threatening to remove your record from its play list. This has pissed off Platinum big-time because its market research suggests sales of your record could be huge in the Midlands. Now do you understand what this fuss is all about? Why people are so upset?"

"I'm really sorry," offered the guitarist, already regretting his outburst on the radio waves. "I can assure you it won't happen again."

"Andrew. Does that mean I can do interviews now?"

"You know, Simon, I'm thinking about it. I am actually thinking about it."

Later that week, celebrating the good fortune of having his artwork for the new record accepted by Platinum, Jay was in sparkling form hosting dinner at a favourite restaurant on Crouch End Broadway.

Hipper than a Hooray Henry's coke dealer, it was crammed with badly dressed locals eager to experience a new dining experience before ditching it in search of an even newer one. Crammed in cheek by jowl while paying for the privilege, the people sat at the tables talked animatedly into their mobile phones, but noticeably, not too much to each other.

"Don't look now," Jay commanded his fellow diners. "But I believe we're all about to have a religious experience."

Tilting his head sideways, he indicated a man and his friends seated at another table. Instantly, the other five craned their necks to get a better view, in that infuriating way people always do when urged not to.

"Who is it?" asked Brian.

"Jesus," the guitarist responded between clenched teeth, somehow making it sound like they were old friends.

"Jesus?"

"Christ!" muttered Suzanne, realising it was him.

"Well, if it is Jesus, I can't see any holes in his hands," said Brian.

"Who the hell is it?" asked Alannah, someone who had difficulty identifying anyone who didn't appear in one of the trashy magazines she was always engrossed in.

"It's Robert Powell," Suzanne whispered, employing the kind of exaggerated lip movements that could be heard by the hard of hearing, or read by the partially sighted, from the opposite side of a crowded room. "The A-C-T-O-R," she mimed.

"The one who played Jesus Christ in the television series," revealed Calum. At this point Jay's phone rang.

"Hi Andrew. What's up? Really? Where? Wow! When? Interesting. Yes, I'll tell the others. OK. You too. Bye."

"What was that all about?"

"Andrew spoke with Holdsworth this afternoon. Says Platinum wants to hold a combined press conference and reception to launch the record. Luckily for us they want to hype it to the max."

"Where do they intend to hold it?"

"Andrew said we'll be doing it on a boat. While we're all floating down the River Thames."

"Face down if you're unlucky," suggested Tania, eyebrows raised in mock horror. "It sounds like one of those drink 'n' drown excursions if you ask me."

CHAPTER NINE

"That," observed David, pointing out of the window, "is no boat."

He looked towards the Embankment as they stepped out on to a pavement sodden with the mulch of autumn leaves.

"Here we go again. What's bothering you this time? What is it you don't like about the boat?"

"I already told you, Brian. It's not a boat."

"What is it then?"

"A tug. One that looks like it might stink of fish."

"Not fish again," Jane gulped.

"Fish, piss and oil," announced Calum, stepping aboard the pleasure craft christened Hope. "I wonder if they've got a lifeboat."

Timed to coincide with the release of Hearts & Souls, the press conference featured the usual scrum with snappers from the tabloids in their element making the most of the free-for-all. All feet, elbows and mouth, combined with the morals of a money launderer, somebody should have been taking pictures of them.

"Stick your tits out darling!" shouted one of them as the band squared up to a multitude of lenses.

"I'm not in the bloody band," the well-endowed Platinum PR hissed at the gormless smudge who hadn't done his homework.

"Say c-h-e-e-s-e."

"Pussy," another yelled.

And so it went on until the paparazzi had the photos they needed to make a sale. Since most were nothing special, the photographers, all hoping to get a scoop, stayed on to attend the press conference that had just begun inside the boat where it was warmer.

Seated behind a long trestle table behind five microphones, SSB were ready to field questions from the house. Simon, sporting a T-shirt bearing the slogan DRUMMERS ARE THICK on the front and AS THIEVES on the back, had been told to remain silent wherever possible. Before introducing the band to the audience, Symes had a few words of his own to say on their behalf.

"Apart from thanking you all for coming here today, I'd like to tell you something about SSB, a band I believe is going to be the biggest band the world has ever seen. Not only do they have the talent to succeed, they all have the determination and character needed to achieve their goals. I have never known five individuals like them."

"Is he talking about us?" Calum quipped.

"So without further ado, ladies and gentlemen, may I present on bass guitar, Brian Lang; on drums, Simon Harding; on keyboards, David Edwards; on guitar, Jay Jackson; and finally, on vocals, the inimitable Calum James."

A smattering of polite applause from the assembled media hacks was offset by the over-enthusiastic applause emanating from the roped-off area reserved for executives from their record label.

"Thank you," Symes acknowledged them. "Please feel free to ask any questions you might have."

"There's a rumour," a man from the gutter press called out.

"One you've heard or one you're about to spread?" Jay yanked his chain.

"Yes?" said Calum, pointing to another outstretched hand.

"What does SSB stand for? Because according to another rumour I've heard going the rounds, it's an acronym for Soft Southern Bastards."

"Bollocks."

"Soft Southern Bollocks?" the reporter repeated to gales of laughter.

"I'll tell you what it stands for: Sex Sounds Better," said Calum, who hadn't a clue what it stood for.

"You made that up."

"Did I? Next question. Lady over there," he said, pointing to a diminutive Japanese girl.

Where others reported on earthquakes, floods, famine, forest fires and all manner of tragedies, her readers wanted the inside story on something far more important.

"Carum. Wo ar yaw favit cowar sox?"

"Red today," replied the singer, after checking under the table. "Tomorrow it'll probably be blue," he confided. "Then again, the day after I'll probably be back to wearing red again."

"So, wo ar yaw favit cowar sox?" the oriental female fuckwit persisted, determined to get a straight answer out of him.

"Probably the pink and black ones with little teddy bears on them. I wear those at weekends," he added helpfully.

None the wiser, his Japanese interrogator gave up. Now she'd have to explain to her editor why she'd wound up with none of the real information her readers craved. That and why they'd paid her round-trip ticket.

"Man over there," said Jay, pointing to an arm he could see, attached to a face he couldn't.

"Is it true none of you actually played a note on the record?" asked Harvey Robertson, who'd somehow managed to get onboard without alerting security to his presence.

"Ah, that old chestnut again," said Jay, suddenly recognising the perpetrator of this question he was getting sick of answering. "You are, of course, entirely correct Harvey."

"Oh! So now we get the truth."

"I'm not going to lie to you. Why should I? Laa-Laa played bass, we had Dipsy on drums, Po on keyboard, and Tink-Winky did all the vocals. We had the Teletubbies do the bloody lot."

"Yeah, course you did," said Robertson, realising he was being wound up but still spoiling for a fight. "Who played guitar then?"

"We tried to get Kermit the Frog, Harvey. But as you probably already know, having done all your in-depth research, he was unavailable at the time. So I fucking well played guitar," Jay swore at him, as the room howled its approval. "Next question. Man over there."

As the afternoon wore on, a member of the party lost his balance whilst arguing vociferously with a group of revellers standing close to the guardrail. A light-hearted slap on the back was all it had taken to help him on his way.

"Bastards!" shouted the figure below, flailing about in the murky water. "You fucking bastards!" he screamed up at the crowd he'd been arguing with. "I fucking hate you" he bellowed, gulping down half a pint of recycled piss for his troubles. "Bastards!" he yelled again as a life belt landed in the water feet from where he was bobbing up and down. Paddling frantically, he watched his prized Collected Thoughts baseball cap float away downriver.

"Remember what I told you," Symes shouted over the side of the craft.

"Who's that?" asked Jay, after he'd threaded his way through the crowd that had gathered to watch.

"Our old friend," grinned Symes.

Minutes later, an angry face covered in flotsam appeared at the top of the rope ladder that had been suspended hurriedly over the side of the boat. Pausing only to remove a piece of driftwood lodged in one of the pockets of his

Collected Thoughts tour jacket, the sodden figure spat out the remains of a crisp packet as he wiped the slime away from his face.

"Now do you remember what I told you?"

The journalist coughed, almost choking.

"Scum," Symes reminded Harvey Robertson once more, "will always float to the surface."

CHAPTER TEN

"It's almost as bad as clocking on," grumbled David.

Examining his recently manicured fingernails, he and the others had convened in Primrose Hill at ten o'clock on a drizzly Monday morning for yet another meeting.

"I agree," said Symes, noting the musician's ever expanding waistline. "Pretty soon you'll wish you'd joined the army instead. And perhaps, David, this is as good a time as any to get those tired old tits of yours in shape ready for the razzmatazz of rock 'n' roll."

"Thanks a bunch," acknowledged the keyboard player, somewhat affronted. Still waiting for tangible results that might prompt the odd compliment, he'd been working out in the gym of late.

"Exactly what has the label got planned for us this week?" asked Jay, eager to get the meeting over with.

"Something that should come fairly naturally to all of you."

"Would that be farting?"

"Basil. Please be quiet when I'm addressing the band. Platinum wants you to inflate your egos and act like the stars you are for a meet and greet at Tower Records in Piccadilly Circus."

"When?"

"In ten days' time, Brian, they want you to pump the flesh, sign autographs, pose for pictures, pander to your public and generally cater to the whims of your fawning fans. Shouldn't be too difficult. And they're laying on a Cadillac stretch limousine for the occasion."

"More stretch limousines? This is getting beyond the pale."

"What do you mean, Brian?"

"What I'm saying is this, Andrew. We do interviews. We do radio appearances. We make videos. We do photo-shoots. And when we're asked to, we attend press conferences to answer streams of fucking stupid questions. What I would like to know is this: when exactly do we get to play?"

"I'm working on it."

"Working on it? What happened to the fucking music? Remember the music? The reason why we're all doing this, Andrew?"

"Of course I remember."

"Sometimes I wonder."

"Listen, I'm sorry if you're finding things a bit tough at present. And though you may find little in the way of consolation, I do understand how you feel. But try to understand that what the record company is asking you to do is all part of the fame game."

"So you keep telling us."

"We're getting strong airplay on the single all across the UK right now. And if we don't go out and promote the product, we'll be doing ourselves a disservice."

"Did you say 'product'?"

"Indeed I did."

"Is that the best you can come up with? Calling our art fucking 'product'."

"I'm sorry, Brian. I do apologise. I can be insensitive at times. What I really meant to say was if we don't go out and promote the record, we can't blame Platinum's marketing department when it stiffs. Right now you're in the First Division. But I know in your heart of hearts what all of you really want is to be at the top of the Premier League. And for this we need to go the extra nine yards."

"I didn't know you were a big soccer fan," said Simon, taking a break from beating the table to death. "You've never mentioned it before."

"That's because I'm not a bloody soccer fan." Symes glared at him. "I was merely trying to illuminate my point employing a sporting metaphor – several, in fact."

"What's a 'meta' for?"

"For God's sake, Simon. Will you just shut up?"

"So what are you suggesting here?" Brian continued to probe. "That we spend the next ten days practising our autographs and developing an attitude problem in time for the signing?"

"Why not? I suppose some bands do."

Unable to offer any real help on the subject, he wished he could send his charges to rock school. Somewhere they would learn everything they'd need to know in their quest for stardom. Unfortunately, they still hadn't built the school yet.

"Maybe I should have a few tattoos done," the bassist sneered.

"I did."

"You did, Andrew?"

"Absolutely. Pretty soon people are going to think you're odd if you don't have one," he added.

He rolled back the neck of his cashmere jumper to reveal a blue and green butterfly tattooed on his right shoulder.

"I agree," said David. "I have a dolphin tattooed on my left buttock."

Brian winced.

"You know, even genital piercing is pretty straightforward these days. A quick pinch, and it's all over."

"Fucking hell," said Basil. "That's disgusting."

"Thank you for sharing that priceless information with us," acknowledged Symes. "Perhaps a little more than most of us will ever need to know. In the meantime, I'll be speaking to your agent about potential dates for the UK tour. And the small matter of contract riders."

"And when is this mythical tour likely to begin?"

"Could be as little as four or five weeks away, Brian. It all depends on whether we can get the right venues."

"What size halls will we be playing?"

"Probably medium size – bigger halls if we go top ten. Excuse me," he said when the telephone on his desk rang.

"I'm sorry to interrupt," said Jane, calling from the adjacent office, "but I've got Seymour Levy on line one. He wants to talk to you."

"Just say I'm in a meeting and take his number. Tell him I'll get back when I'm finished up here."

"Was that good news by any chance?" asked Jay.

"Another band manager I know."

"What does he want to talk to you about?"

"Maybe he thinks he can do a better job of managing us than you can," Brian sneered.

"That's terribly loyal of you. Perhaps for the time being you could show a little courtesy and put the revolution on hold until after the Tower Records signing. Yes, Basil, what is it?"

"Can I have some petty cash for petrol?"

Symes' phone rang again. "Pardon me for a moment Basil. Yes, Jane?"

"I've just had a call from Richard at Platinum. I thought you might like to hear what he said."

"Go on."

"Congratulations. The single's gone top twenty."

"Wow!"

"He sounded pretty certain the album would do the same."

"Did he say when?"

"Later this week maybe."

"Fuck me! I mean, thank you very much, Jane."

"Everything OK?"

"Absolutely, Brian. Never been better, in fact."

"And why's that?"

"Your single," he announced, "has just gone top twenty."

The room exploded into a blur of high fives and the type of hugging, hair ruffling and backslapping normally associated with football matches.

"Andrew," beamed the singer. "The meeting's over. We're off to the pub. Will you be joining us?"

"I will but I need to make a phone call first. Brian, doesn't this make all the hassle worthwhile?"

"Suppose so," mumbled the bass player, left with little to argue about.

"I think you all deserve to get horribly pissed. Just give me ten minutes and I'll join you."

Airplay for the single now sat at number eight in the charts and was approaching saturation point. The whole of London was flyposted with ads for the record. The media had been alerted. On a roll, Symes prayed their appearance at Tower Records and the resulting publicity would ensure they moved another step closer to conquering the charts.

Mariah Carey had made headlines at the store by showing up with more bodyguards than the Pope and the US President put together. More disturbingly, the mighty Shabba Ranks made headlines there when his fans used his appearance as an excuse to loot the store. What, Symes wondered, would SSB have to do to make the front pages?

CHAPTER ELEVEN

As the white stretch limousine carrying the band swung around Hyde Park Corner on its last leg of the journey down Piccadilly, David cast a practised eye around its interior.

"Pray tell me what's pissing off your lordship today?" asked Brian.

"Tacky," bitched the keyboard player.

He gazed at the red plastic interior, button-down vinyl upholstery and the abundance of chrome coloured plastic knobs. Then he winced.

"Bet you'd love a bit of slap and tickle on the love log down here," smirked Jay, pointing to the raised transmission shaft area running all the way from the mini bar to the back seat.

The queue, three deep in places, began to form as soon as the store opened. By eleven o'clock it snaked all the way from the front entrance down along Piccadilly. Around two thousand fans had besieged Tower Records that day. Hoping to spend precious minutes in the company of their idols, a number were clutching the new CD for signing. Others, eager to have their picture taken with the band, were toting cheap point-and-shoot cameras or their digital cousins.

In the main, the crowd was made up of followers from the early days and fan club members. Inevitably, there were one or two who would turn up to the opening of a cigarette packet. The rest were star-struck American teenagers on holiday and the curious out and about during the lunch hour.

As their fans surged forwards, the limousine pulled up outside Tower Records and one of them thrust a scrap of paper and a pen in front of Simon's face as he emerged.

"Can I have your autograph?"

Unbeknown to each other, they'd all dedicated at least an hour a day to practising their respective autographs. At first glance, Simon Harding looked like Semen Hardening. David's wouldn't have looked out of place on a doctor's prescription. Brian's resembled that of an accountant signing off a tax return. Only Calum and Jay's autographs looked like a rock star's autograph should. Impressive.

Pausing momentarily at the front door to sign more autographs, they were led down to the store's lower ground floor by Tower Records' in-house security team. After negotiating their way through the heaving crowd gathered in the large basement room, they found themselves surrounded by boisterous fans on three sides. Eventually they were seated on the fourth side of the room behind a raised counter covered in red baize. Symes tapped the microphone set up in front of him.

"Thank you for coming here today, don't forget to buy the record. Now give a huge, warm London welcome to the five guys who're about to become the biggest rock band on the planet. Will you please give it up for ESS ESS BEE."

Instantly both fans and the press let rip with a thousand-flashgun salute, obligatory rock star shades their only protection against temporary blindness. Shielded by security men who let fans through the crash barriers two at a time, they all began to revel in the limelight.

"Beats signing-on," said Simon, watching the crowd surge forwards.

"Sure does," Calum agreed, his gaze otherwise engaged by the statuesque brunette approaching him.

Standing around five feet eleven tall in stiletto heels and wearing a tiny crimson leather mini skirt, she was accompanied by two girlfriends.

"Calum," she said. "Such a pleasure to meet you in person at last."

"No, no. The pleasure's all mine," he assured her, hoping it would be.

"I l-o-v-e your music. It's s-o sexy."

Removing his sunglasses for closer inspection, he found it impossible to wrench his eyes from her long jet-black hair and the breasts it couldn't hide.

"Are you willing to sign anything?" she asked him, as her friends giggled mischievously in the background.

"Whatever you like. Anything at all. Just name it."

The girl, who couldn't have been more than nineteen, knowing she had his undivided attention, made her move.

"So you don't mind autographing this then?"

Slowly, purposefully, she peeled back her black Lycra top to reveal one half of the most perfectly formed 36C breasts the gawping singer had clapped eyes on.

"Sign anywhere you like," she added, offering up her naked breast, seemingly unworried at being the centre of attention.

Swallowing hard, he admired the curve of her exquisitely proportioned appendage. "Any particular colour?"

"Red," she answered, lasciviously licking glossy red lips. "My favourite colour."

"Mine too," Calum revealed, hoping their joint obsessions would extend to oral sex.

"What's your name?"

"Katrina," trilled the brown-eyed beauty.

As a hail of flashguns exploded around them, Calum picked up a red felt-tip pen. Supporting her left breast with one hand, he drew a heart shape on it before signing his name, followed by hers.

Not unexpectedly, all autograph signing came to a halt during this interlude as the other heterosexual members of the band anticipated their turn to sign various parts of her anatomy eagerly. As the pictures would testify, she'd had little difficulty in accommodating the singer's signature. Or the Mickey Mouse cartoon he'd thoughtfully added as a bonus. This featured her nipple masquerading as the cartoon character's nose.

"Will you call me?" she asked.

"I would if I had your number."

"Will you really?" she fluttered her eyelashes.

"I will if you give it to me," he assured her, allowing his manhood to rule his mind. He was infatuated.

"Of course I will," she replied, pouting through bee-stung lips, about to play her ace card.

Brazenly she lowered the right side of her black stretch top to reveal another equally astounding breast. Absolutely identical to the left one, her mobile phone number had been scrawled on it.

"You are just the wildest thing," said Calum, looking away momentarily to tap the precious digits into his phone.

When he looked up, she'd gone. "Where is she?"

"Missing her already are we?" Jay taunted him.

The singer scanned the crowds on the other side of the barriers. "I was about to give her a record."

"Really?" countered Jay. "Is that all you were going to give her?"

"OK! Time to travel. Let's hit the high road."

Basil, a welcome sight in his ever-present black T-shirt, placed a firm hand on Jay's shoulder. This was the pre-arranged signal for the rest of the band to follow him up in the lift and along the stairway that would lead them out on to the roof of the building. Surrounded by security personnel, they moved as one through the seething crowd as a boxer would approaching the ring before a title fight.

"Stand back," Basil exhorted, dodging the pawing and clawing of the more enthusiastic fans who were trying to get at the band.

Upon reaching the top of the building, they emerged into bright sunlight and were rewarded with a raucous reception from those lucky enough to secure tickets for this one-off performance. The applause, the whistling and the stomping carried on for a full five minutes.

"Thank you for buying the record," Jay acknowledged the crowd as the band took their respective places in front of a row of amplifiers set up beneath a small marquee. "And don't forget to buy the next one," he urged, much to the amusement of the suits from Platinum, out in force to gauge public reaction to their latest investment.

"Hello, Piccadilly Circus," Calum screamed into a Shure SM58.

'Hello, Piccadilly Circus," the same voice boomed back from the buildings directly opposite.

Clicking his sticks together in 4/4 time, Simon then began to thrash and flail at his kit like a dervish possessed as Calum launched into their opening number, 'Part Of A Plan'.

Down in the streets below, passers-by craned their necks trying to locate the source of the music. Others were stopped in their tracks by the sheer power of it all. With an insidious Cajun-style beat and a penetrating lick, the song, delivered at ear-splitting volume, was impossible to ignore. Complete strangers slowed down to smile at each other. For some it was the most subversive lunch hour they'd had in years. From his vantage point up on the roof, Symes spotted two pen pushers in their mid-fifties openly smoking a joint.

When SSB launched into their second song, crowds of onlookers had gathered outside the shops flanking Regent Street and Piccadilly. As they thronged around the statue of Eros, spilling off the pavement outside the Criterion Theatre, they were soon joined by a number of TV crews who'd materialised out of the ether to film the event. At the end of the song, waving frantically from the side of the stage, Symes finally caught Jay's attention.

"It's gone crazy," he shouted, pointing down below. "They're going absolutely mental down there."

"I can't hear you," the guitarist yelled back, ears ringing from the damage inflicted by the tremendous sound pressure levels they were generating. "What did you say?"

"I said it's gone crazy. The fans are going barmy down there. There are people hanging out of windows and dangling off traffic signs. Frankly, I've never seen anything to match it. Providing the Queen doesn't pop her clogs in the next couple of hours we're bound to make the late edition of the Evening Standard. And if it doesn't make the front page," he gabbled excitedly, "I'll eat my hat."

"But you don't wear a hat, Andrew."

"Then I'll bloody buy one. Just keep it going. Basil," he shouted to the roadie who was standing behind the mixing console at the side of the makeshift stage area.

"Yes, Boss."

"Turn it up."

"You can't do that," said the employee from Tower Records standing behind him.

"Says who?"

"The police. They've threatening to shut you down."

"Fuck them," spat Symes, his comment drowned out by the PA. "And the horse they rode in on," he added as an afterthought.

With adrenaline levels soaring, the band was firing on all cylinders as they launched into the third song of their mini set. *Hearts & Souls* never sounded better.

"Jesus, these guys are good," said the head honcho from Platinum.

Witnessing the band's live performance for the very first time, he and the others from the record label agreed SSB exuded that intangible star quality that separates the best from the rest. More importantly, it was proof his team had done their homework. For the time being, their investment was safe.

After making minor tweaks to the EQ, Basil cranked up the faders another notch as the band launched into the fourth and final song of the set. A reworking of The Beatles' classic, 'Come Together'.

Down in the streets it was mayhem as the massed spectators began to clap. First a few, then a hundred, then hundreds, then a thousand, before ten thousand hands attempted to clap in time. A solid, if incredibly sloppy, wall of sound, it was the audio equivalent of the Mexican Wave.

The traffic on Piccadilly and Regent Street had stopped altogether. Unable to get any of its patrol cars through grid locked traffic, West End Central, its switchboard flooded with complaints, despatched a small number of police officers on foot to investigate. When the first of them arrived he was accosted by a dreadlocked crusty attached to a dog via the customary length of rope.

"Take a hit on this," he instructed the man from the Met, a gleam in his eyes as he offered the constable the joint he was brandishing. "Gold Lebanese, man. Rare as rocking horse shit," he added, before taking another toke. "I bet even you guys have trouble getting hold of stuff this good."

"Fortunately for you," the policeman informed him as he brushed past, "I'm busy right now."

The young copper removed his helmet and began to issue instructions into the walkie-talkie attached to his shoulder. He headed towards the lift that would take him out on to the roof. He'd indulged in the odd puff himself in his own misspent youth and he still couldn't see what the fuss was all about.

"*One thing I can tell you is you got to be free,*" they chanted down in the streets below. As twenty thousand hands clapped in unison, ten thousand wage slaves missed the irony. "*Come Together, Right Now,*" they sang, collected voices rising to a crescendo that reverberated around Piccadilly Circus. "*OVER ME.*"

"And I thought this sort of stuff only ever happened in the movies," observed an amazed Holdsworth, convinced his paymasters really had struck platinum. "I've never experienced anything like it," he grinned, the roar of the music now deafening.

"*Hold him in his armchair you can feel his disease*, COME TOGETHER, RIGHT NOW, OVER ME."

CHAPTER TWELVE

"Name?"

"Is this really necessary? I've already said I'm sorry."

"Name?" "And I've apologised to the PC who arrested me."

"Name?"

"Surely we can leave it at that?"

"Name?" the desk sergeant kept repeating, his eyes riveted to the paperwork in front of him.

Seated opposite, the resignation in his voice clearly audible, the dejected figure in the black linen suit replied.

"Andrew Tarquin Symes."

Stroking his squirrel red beard, the bemused officer looked up from the paperwork he was engrossed in.

"Would that be with a hyphen, or without?"

"Without."

"Occupation?"

"Rock group manager," he responded.

"Once again?"

"Manager."

"Almost sounds respectable when you put it like that," said the sergeant.

And so it continued until he had all the information he needed before he marched Symes off to have his picture and fingerprints taken. Then, at twelve thirty in the morning with the business end taken care of, stripped of all dignity, he was allowed to call his solicitor.

After the call was taken by a message service and all efforts to raise bail failed him, it was a thoroughly demoralised Symes who spent the night banged up in the cells at West End Central. Humiliated and abandoned, with the spirit all but knocked out of him, he eventually drifted off to sleep on the hard padded bench that passed for a bed.

Early the following morning the prisoner was transported to court caged in the back of a paddy wagon. He silently prayed this would be his first and last appearance before Marlborough Street Magistrates Court.

The unshaven Symes entered the hushed courtroom from the cells below. He was still wearing his crumpled linen suit as he was led into the mahogany panelled dock, forced to suffer the indignity of having the charges against him read out aloud. Hoping for the best, he listened impassively as the magistrate began to speak.

"Andrew Symes," the baritone voice rang out across the courtroom, its sheer gravitas unnerving. "You have been charged with a number of offences relating to an appearance by SSB, a group of artists you represent, which took place yesterday on the roof of Tower Records in Piccadilly Circus. Those charges," he continued, peering over the top of half-moon tortoiseshell spectacles, "I am about to read out to you. They are: obstructing a police officer in the course of his duties; flagrantly breaking the agreed maximum sound pressure level limits set down by law; and, of a more serious nature, incitement to riot."

Symes, biting his lip hard enough to draw blood, looked visibly shaken as the last three words were read out.

"On a separate charge," he noted rather jovially, "it is also alleged you attempted to pervert the course of justice by trying to bribe a police officer."

Symes winced again. The magistrate, having met and dealt with more than a few bent coppers in his time, merely smiled benevolently.

"I am, of course, referring to the first police officer who arrived at the scene of the incident. Do you understand the charges, Mr. Symes?"

"Yes, I do."

Looking up at the bench from the best seat in the house, he momentarily fixed his gaze on the policeman he'd foolishly tried to bribe with two hundred pounds. Something he now bitterly regretted.

"And how do you plead?"

His head hung in shame, Symes replied. "Guilty."

The sitting magistrate, secretly a Freemason and a fan of autoerotic asphyxiation, was also a huge fan of The Beatles, which may have played a part in his decision to pursue a course of leniency. Dropping all but one of the charges, he eventually fined Symes one thousand eight hundred pounds for noise pollution.

It wasn't all bad news. Under the headline, 'MANAGERIAL DISPUTE', a reference to Symes' unceremonious exit from Tower Records when he was bundled into the back of a police car, the band, if not their manager, had benefited from front-page and inside coverage in the late edition of the Evening Standard. In addition, footage of the event had appeared on Sky News the previous evening. Expertly edited to show the negative side of what had purportedly happened, most of it dwelt on the mayhem that took place in the streets outside Tower Records, largely ignoring the band's rooftop perfor-mance.

Far from upset, the accounts department at Platinum was delighted at the outcome. The resulting publicity alone was worth in the region of one hundred and twenty five thousand pounds. On this basis they happily agreed to pay the fine, which they promptly offset against *Hearts & Souls'* promotional and advertising budget – money they would recoup against royalties accruing from SSB's record sales.

"Can I speak to Katrina?"

"Who may I say is calling?"

"It's Mario. Mario from the Chippendales," he said.

"Here she is," the girl giggled, passing the phone to her friend.

"Hello. Katrina speaking."

"Hi sweetie."

"Who's that?"

"Guess."

"Why don't you just tell me?"

"Have you taken a peek at your breasts recently?"

"Calum," she squealed, thrilled to be taking the call from him in the presence of a female friend.

"How are you, Katrina?"

"I saw your picture in the paper. And I saw you on TV," she gushed.

"Have you washed it off yet?" he enquired.

"Actually," she sighed, her voice reduced to a whimper ready to set back the feminist movement a full thirty years, "I thought I'd wait until you came over to help me."

"That would be great," he replied, desperate for another peek at his own handiwork. "By the way, where did you disappear to that afternoon?"

"I'll tell you when you come over," she purred, knowing her action, drastic though it may have seemed at the time, had made him hot to trot.

"I'm free this evening," he said, hot to trot.

"Me too."

"You'd better give me your address, then."

"It's one eight five Elgin Avenue, Maida Vale, W9, flat D, top bell. Do you know Maida Vale?"

"Yeah. Used to rehearse there with a band. What time would you like me to show up?"

"How about seven thirty?"

"Sounds fine."

"Maybe we could go for a drink."

"Great idea," he enthused, the prospect of other far more hands-on activity involving this tantalising beauty occupying his mind. "Will you be wearing something sexy?"

"Why not let me worry about that? Ciao," she cooed down the line before she blew him a kiss and hung up.

"Who was that?" asked Suzanne, poking her head around the door.

Wrapped in a thick terry-towelling robe, her hair tucked into a white towel, she'd spent the last hour locked in the bathroom pampering her long, slender body. While he admired her natural beauty, he couldn't fail to miss the stray tufts of blonde pubic hair clearly visible as she bent over to kiss him.

"Aren't you going to tell me?" she asked, enveloping him with the scent of sandalwood.

"Andrew," he lied, wondering how much of the conversation she'd heard.

"About what?"

"He wants us to meet in the West End tonight. Just the two of us."

"Why?"

"To discuss the tour bus we're hiring."

"But you said you were going to take me out for dinner tonight."

"Sorry babe."

"Cal…um."

"I said I'm sorry, babe."

"Couldn't somebody else go?"

"No, they can't."

"Why not?"

"Because," he replied, unsure exactly what to say, "I drew the short straw."

"I guess that's alright then," she sulked, not entirely convinced by talk of buses. "So long as you're not meeting up with another woman."

Bang on the dot of seven thirty, Calum, reeking of Chanel aftershave, emerged from the back of a black taxi outside the house on Elgin Avenue. He glanced up at the door of number one eight five painted a bright shade of red. He guessed this gigantic house had recently benefited from the services of a firm of bespoke decorators. It looked seriously swanky.

He climbed the steep flight of steps leading up to the front door where he spoke into the voice entry phone. "It's Calum, sweetheart."

"Come on up." The door opened.

Once inside the building, he breathed in the smell of fresh gloss paint as he made the long ascent up four flights of newly carpeted stairs. Arriving on the fourth floor he saw three doors leading off the landing. He headed for the one marked 'D'. As he grasped the knocker firmly in hand, the door, which had already been unlocked from the inside, swung open to reveal Katrina standing there. Framed by the architrave, backlit by the sunlight, she'd left very little to Calum's imagination.

Clothed in a diaphanous creation split to the thigh, a silken spider's web of peach gauze barely hid the matching flesh coloured bra and panties she'd carefully selected. Standing mere feet away, his eyes were magnetically attracted by the daylight factor, that inherently sexy little triangle of light that few women can boast of located in the area where crotch meets thigh.

"You can put your tongue back now."

Still transfixed, he was already dreaming of paradise. A whiff of it at the very least.

"You look absolutely fabulous," he complimented her after regaining the power of speech. "I mean it."

"Well," she beckoned, resisting the temptation to physically drag him inside. "Are you coming in or not?"

Pole-vaulting through the door, he fell on her like a man with a long story to tell and very little time in which to tell it.

"You don't waste any time, do you?" she observed, as they repaired to the bedroom before locking the door behind them.

She began unbuttoning the fly of his very expensive jeans. "Now it's my turn to take a peek. Oh my God!" she shrieked. "Calum, you're hung like a horse my darling. I don't think I've ever seen a cock as big as yours before." She held his throbbing, fully erect penis in her hand. "How long is it?" she giggled. "Eight inches?"

"Eight and a half," he replied nonchalantly, knowing it was he who had her attention now.

"I've never been fucked by such a large one. Will it hurt?"

"In the nicest possible way," he reassured her.

They didn't go out for the drink after all. There wasn't time. Mad for it, and each other, they were soon engaged in every conceivable sexual position known to mankind. The two lovers licked, sucked, fondled and fucked for five glorious hours.

Meanwhile, working on female intuition, Suzanne had visited a number of bars Calum often frequented. The following day, determined to get to the bottom of what had happened the night before, she paid a visit to the flat in Mountview Road.

"So tell me more about this bus," she asked, eyes boring holes into the back of his head as he stared out of the window looking for inspiration.

"What exactly is it you want to know?" he asked, turning to face her.

"What's it like," she probed, wondering if she'd jumped the gun.

"Basically," he explained, after screwing up the courage to make eye contact, "Andrew wants to rent a purpose-built coach with all mod cons for this tour. From Berryhurst," he added.

"Never heard of them."

"Haven't you?"

"No. I haven't," she announced tartly.

"They've done tours with the Commodores. Them, Simply Red, Santana, Michael Jackson, Madonna."

"What's the coach like inside?" she challenged someone who'd have difficulty describing the layout of his own kitchen.

"Two bunks high, air conditioning and climate controlled throughout. The lower deck has a well-equipped kitchen, so I'm told. Not that we're ever likely to use it. On top of that there's a washroom/toilet, an eight-seat lounge…"

"Really!" she exclaimed, listening to the detailed description emerging from the lips of a man who, until this afternoon, had possessed the memory of a sieve.

"Upstairs," he continued, "there are twelve bunk beds, each with its own porthole window. Added to that are two lounge areas: one large, one small. Both levels have surround sound music systems wired up to plasma-screen TVs and DVD systems. If that isn't enough, there's satellite phone, fax and internet connection. Best of all, the coach has…"

"Don't tell me: wall-to-wall groupies?"

"A Sony PlayStation," her boyfriend marvelled, refusing to rise to the bait.

Suzanne didn't know what to believe. He definitely seemed to know his stuff. He certainly sounded like he'd listened attentively to Andrew. And yet.

"Three hundred thousand pounds a shot they cost. Robbie Williams had them install a snooker table on the one we're hiring," he added, heading for information overload.

"Amazing. Truly amazing," she agreed, angry with herself for having doubted him in the first place.

She wasn't aware that the previous day Calum had immersed himself in a trade paper he'd borrowed from Basil. And while scanning its pages he'd stumbled on an article about

Berryhurst Showtours, who supplied luxury coaches for the rock 'n' roll touring market. Neither was she aware that after memorising whole chunks of the text, he'd gleaned enough information to convince her he wasn't the complete and utter bastard she thought he was.

CHAPTER THIRTEEN

"I must say it's rather magnanimous of you to invite me here." Symes had acknowledged Seymour Levy's offer to lunch with him at the much fêted, Michelin-starred Le Gavroche. "Have you ever brought Collected Thoughts here?"

"You must be joking," said Levy. "And no plans to do so in the foreseeable future."

"Why is that?"

"Andrew, these Manchester lads of mine wouldn't know the difference between a whore and an hors d'oeuvre. McDonald's? Maybe. Michelin? Not on my money."

While Symes had never visited this gourmet's paradise in the past, he knew they fielded a waiter for every single customer. He also knew that two businessmen lunching there had racked up a bill that would induce a heart attack in all but the filthy stinking rich. But as he wouldn't be paying for this jolly, why should he care?

"We could eat à la carte today. Or, if you'd prefer, the set menu."

"Ooh, I don't know," Symes deliberated in that annoying way the English do when they don't want to appear greedy. "What are you going to have?"

"I think I'll choose from the à la carte. Care to join me?"

Symes dithered, all the while wondering how much cash they could work their way through in the space of the next three hours. "Do you think I should?"

"It would be rude not to," replied his munificent host, nose buried deep in the wine list.

Dressed today in a three-button grey suit, Seymour Levy was, at thirty five, the eldest and more experienced of the pair. To his credit, the former record company lawyer could read a contract at twenty paces and hold his own in the company of bean counters. Having inherited half a million pounds on his twenty-fifth birthday, he'd invested wisely in the property market. By the age of thirty, he'd turned that into two million. Unlike Symes, he was already a rich man.

"While I can't deny this is jolly decent of you, both of us know there's no such thing as a free…."

"…Lunch?" ventured Levy.

"Precisely."

Having exhausted all options the menu had to offer, the duo had retired to the lounge area.

"What did you say that last wine was called again?"

"Château d'Yquem. It's the world's most desirable wine. Certainly the best dessert wine money can buy."

"And the most expensive," added Symes, acknowledging the hefty £4,500 plus service charge his host would be asked to cough up for the half bottle they'd just drunk with dessert. "Indescribably delicious, Seymour."

"Glad you approve, Andrew."

Relaxing on a pair of leather Chesterfield sofas with a freshly made pot of Kenyan coffee and a mound of petits fours, they both puffed away contentedly on Cohibas the size of Canary Wharf. Finally, over a 1963 Armagnac as smooth as any he'd tasted, Levy revealed why he'd invited Symes to lunch.

"I suppose it could feasibly work," agreed Symes.

"I don't see how it can fail," argued Levy. "The tabloids are gagging for the kind of story I've outlined. They can't get enough."

"True. I find it unbelievable some of the shit they print."

"But don't you see, Andrew? You're the very best there is in that department."

"What department?"

"The unbelievable."

"Am I?"

"You certainly are. You orchestrated that Tower Records launch brilliantly."

"Did I?" retorted Symes, still suffering from nightmares after his run in with the Met.

"Listen," advised the older man. "There's no hurry. Why don't you give it some thought and call me back on it? Do you have my new number?"

"Better give it to me again just to be on the safe side."

"So you'll think about it?"

"Leave it with me and I'll call you next week."

"Excellent. And how was lunch?" he asked, as the bill arrived at the table.

"Possibly the finest I've ever tasted."

Levy placed an American Express Platinum card inside the leather wallet the bill had arrived in. "And probably the most expensive," he grinned. "Still, it beats baked beans any day," he laughed, scrutinising a bill whose final tally was a breathtaking fifteen thousand pounds.

Plus service charge.

With SSB's first UK tour one week away, they'd all gathered to iron out last minute details.

"Anymore ideas?" asked Symes, still unsure himself which song the band would pick to precede their entrance on stage.

"How about 'Come Together'?" Calum suggested.

"It certainly wouldn't be my first choice," shuddered Symes, who now found it only served to remind him of his arrest, incarceration and subsequent court appearance.

"Blur once played something by Oasis before they went on stage," remarked Simon.

"And what's that supposed to mean? That we play one by Collected Thoughts?

"Why not, Jay?"

"Why not? Listen, dickhead. If our single's at number five and they can only manage number eighteen, they can kiss my arse. They should be playing our fucking record for their stage entrance."

"Simon has a point," reasoned their manager, unsure how to broach the subject he'd discussed over lunch with the competition's manager. "I'll grant you Collected Thoughts have slipped down the singles charts this week. However, according to the latest albums charts they're at number seven, while we're still stuck at fifteen. So I can sort of see where Simon's coming from on this one."

"Well, I can't see what either of you are driving at," Jay continued to argue. "I think that lunch with their manager turned your head, that's what I fucking think. Anyway, tell us: what exactly was it you discussed with him? Or can't you remember?"

"Yeah. What was that all about?" Calum probed. "Did you sell us down the river after one too many vintage ports?"

"I didn't drink any vintage port at all, if you must know," he replied huffily, naming one of the few alcoholic beverages he hadn't poured down his throat that memorable afternoon.

"But you don't deny selling us down the river?" Brian pressed him, having remained tight-lipped until now. "I think you've got some explaining to do."

"As you're probably aware, last month Collected Thoughts moved down south from Manchester. Now they're based here in London. So they're out and about all the time."

"What's all this got to do with anything?"

"I'm about to tell you, if you'll listen. Their manager, Seymour Levy, had an idea he felt would benefit both you and Collected Thoughts," he revealed, concealing the rest of their discussion, which might have earned him a lynching.

"You mean benefit you and him," snapped Brian.

"No, I mean you and them. But like Seymour, I do feel both bands could benefit massively."

"How?"

"By creating interesting situations."

"Such as?"

"Such as getting yourselves in the papers by manufacturing a feud for the benefit of the press. It would give the tabloids something to write about. That way both bands will wind up selling more records, more concert tickets, more T-shirts, more posters and more everything else if we're lucky."

"And if we're unlucky?"

"Well, Brian, much as I hate to even think about it, I suppose I could wind up in jail again. But let's not dwell on the negative."

"Who's a naughty boy then?"

"David. Please don't remind me. Now, if everybody's agreed, we're all going to meet for a drink on Wednesday evening at a hotel bar in the West End. Seymour has booked two tables. One for each band. Not next to each other, of course."

"So what do you expect to happen while we're there?"

Symes shrugged his shoulders.

"Well, that all rather depends on you." He had no intention of getting his own hands dirty. "I suppose what would be ideal is... how can I put it? 'A spot of bother'. Yes, a spot of bother. Nothing too major," he added flippantly.

"Why?" asked Simon, still completely in the dark regarding his manager's intentions.

"Good question, Simon."

At this point they should have smelt a rat.

"Key members of the paparazzi have been tipped off to expect some kind of incident that evening. Something they can use. Photographs they can all sell to the hungry tabloids. Seymour will be arranging all of this, so don't worry."

"Isn't that called 'colluding with the enemy'?" Brian asked.

"Something like that," agreed his manager.

CHAPTER FOURTEEN

"Don't leave the guitar lying on the fucking floor Calum. I paid good money for it."

"Less all that duty, VAT and whatever else you screwed Her Majesty's Government out of at the airport," his friend reminded him. "Anyway, where's Simon?"

"At the bloody doctor again."

"Not good."

"I hope this recurring problem he has with carpal tunnel syndrome isn't going to affect the tour."

"What exactly is carpal tunnel syndrome?" Calum asked.

Jay reached for the medical dictionary Simon had been looking at earlier. He knew the ailment affected the wrist bones and was common amongst rock drummers who attacked their kits hard – just like Simon. Cradling the heavy tome in his lap, he began to quote from the British Medical Association's Complete Family Health Encyclopaedia.

"It's described here as 'numbness, tingling and pain in the thumb, index and middle fingers, likely to get worse at night'."

"Sounds like a dose of wanker's cramp, if you ask me."

"It goes on to say 'the condition may affect one or both hands, sometimes accompanied by weakness in the thumb'."

"In the head, in Simon's case," guffawed the singer, compassion failing to get the better of him.

"Listen to the next bit. 'Carpal tunnel syndrome occurs most commonly among middle-aged women.'"

"Well, there's a surprise. He acts like one half the time, doesn't he? What else does it say?"

"'It also occurs more commonly than average during pregnancy in women who've just started using oral contraceptives, or those suffering from pre-menstrual syndrome.'"

"Simon to a bloody T. He has been acting a bit strange of late, when I think about it. Have you noticed the way he keeps dropping things and getting those hot flushes?"

"People who live in glasshouses shouldn't throw stones. And if I were you, I'd keep my head down. While you were still in bed, the man you've just been lampooning took a very interesting phone call from your newest best friend."

"Which one?"

"The cock hound, Calum."

"Who are we talking about?"

"Have you forgotten already? It was the titty fairy. Katrina left a message saying she'd like to see you."

"Why?"

"How would I know? Maybe she wants you to redecorate her place."

"It was just done a few weeks ago."

"Ah. So you admit to visiting her pad and bonking her?"

"I admit to nothing of the sort."

"Maybe this time she wants you to paint an entire mural on her enormous breasts."

"Has anybody told Suzanne about this?" asked Calum, worried Jay had already broadcast the news throughout the whole of North London.

"No. Simon thought you might like to do that."

"So what do you think of the place Jay?"

Palms outstretched, Symes surveyed the room languidly from the red banquette they were occupying at one end of the massive semicircular bar.

"Atmospheric."

Completely oblivious to his new surroundings, Simon kept pounding away on the banquette. Keeping time to Sly and the

Family Stone playing in the background, he was doing little to help alleviate his carpal tunnel syndrome problem.

"You're right about the atmosphere," Calum agreed.

"These are delicious," remarked David, tucking into the olives. "What time did you say they're likely to arrive Andrew?"

"About nine thirty, so I'd give them fifteen minutes or so."

"So what time is it now?"

"Nine o'clock," said Brian. "By the way, Andrew, how are ticket sales going?"

"Edinburgh, Manchester, Newcastle, Birmingham, Sheffield, Reading, Oxford and Cardiff are all sell- outs. Glasgow, Liverpool and Leeds look like doing the same."

"Excellent. And the rest?"

"Sales in Exeter and Bristol are sluggish. Slower still in Norwich."

"Norwich!" the guitarist hooted. "That doesn't surprise me in the slightest. They're probably having trouble reading the fly posters. Would you agree?"

"I would, as it happens," said David.

"Remember when we were doing that radio interview a few weeks ago at Norwich Broadland FM?"

"Hard to forget."

"We saw some of the local dorks wearing T-shirts with 'DON'T RUSH ME I'M SUFFOLK' emblazoned across them.

"That's right," concurred David. "Frankly I doubt they could chew gum and walk, let alone read a poster."

"So, what's happening with the London gig?" asked Jay.

"We're holding Shepherd's Bush Empire in the event the single goes to number one."

"Good stuff."

"We've also got the Jazz Café booked in case it stiffs."

"Are you joking?"

"For a change," beamed Symes. "No, it looks as though you might be playing at the Kentish Town Forum instead.

That said, if we can generate enough interest and ticket sales, we could wind up playing both venues. We'll just have to wait and see."

They were about to order more drinks when they all heard a kerfuffle accompanied by the sound of loud drunken voices coming from the other end of the bar.

"Christ! What was that?" said Jay.

This was followed by the unmistakeable sound of glass exploding on a tiled floor.

"What are you looking at you fat bastard?" one of the new arrivals threatened a customer who'd been minding his own business.

Craning their necks as one, the band caught sight of Collected Thoughts with Seymour Levy in tow, trailed by a posse of young women and two bodyguards.

"Move out the way," the larger of the two commanded a terrified woman standing close by as they scythed their way through the crowded bar.

With practised belligerence, scattering all before them, the party made a beeline for the restaurant area, where an identical banquette had been reserved for them.

"What an ugly looking bunch of criminals," said David, making sure to keep his voice down.

"They could only look attractive behind bars," said Calum, no fan of thugs who made their living as musicians.

"According to Seymour they spent the last ten years behind them or drinking in them," confided Symes.

"Now who's a bitch?" grinned David. "Calum, did you notice those trollops who waltzed in with them?"

"Why? Anybody I might recognise?"

"I think you might know at least one of them."

"I don't know what you're droning on about."

"Katrina. The one you met at Tower Records."

Calum turned his head only to see the person in question. "Aw fuck! I may have to leave."

"Bit late for that," said Brian, as Katrina, dressed to kill, headed towards their table.

"Hi Calum."

Standing before them all she presented an arresting sight. The tight black leather outfit she was wearing incorporated enough zips and pockets to accommodate a year's supply of lottery tickets for an entire housing estate.

"Cat got your tongue?" she flashed her dazzling smile.

"Oh, hello," he replied, feigning surprise.

Clearly embarrassed, he introduced her to Andrew and the others before leading her over to the cloakroom area on the pretext of buying cigarettes from the kiosk.

"What the fuck's going on?" he demanded, as soon as they were out of earshot.

"Calm down! The only reason I'm here tonight is because Seymour happens to be a friend of my brother."

"Is that so? Well, Melinda Messenger's a friend of Simon's big sister but we didn't invite her here tonight."

"Calum, the only reason he invited me here tonight was to add a little glamour to the proceedings."

"Well, your lot could certainly use a sprinkling of that."

"I don't want you causing any trouble. Do you hear me? Besides, they all know me here."

"You mean in the biblical sense?"

"Don't be such a wanker, Calum. Just because you slept with me once doesn't entitle you to plan my diary. I'm here tonight because I'm being paid. If that's all right by you," she snapped at him.

"Alright. Keep your shirt on. I don't want any trouble either," he said, forgetting why Andrew had invited them all here for a drink in the first place. "I'm going back to the table. We can talk about this another time."

"Fine." She leant over and pecked him gently on the cheek. "Don't forget to call me."

"Shit, shit and shit again," he swore, as he ambled back to the table.

"Hope you don't mind but your mobile rang while you were away so I answered it," said David.

"Thanks. Who was it?"

"Suzanne."

"Fuck no!"

"She said she'd be here in a minute."

"Where is she now?"

"Outside trying to get in presumably."

"You're kidding me?"

"He's not," said Symes, jabbing an index finger in the direction of the doorway.

Beside himself with grief, Calum's heart sank as she sashayed towards them. "I don't fucking believe it!"

"Surprise, surprise. Hope I'm not interrupting anything important."

"Not at all sweetie. Come and sit next to me," David insisted. "We can talk girlie talk."

Grateful for David's timely intervention, the singer kissed Suzanne full on the lips before ordering her a drink.

"Would you excuse us a moment," he said when her cocktail arrived, indicating to Jay they should leave the table.

"This is getting surreal," he said, as the pair relieved themselves in adjacent urinals. "What the fuck am I gonna do if the two of them meet?"

"Why are you asking me? You got yourself into this mess. Get yourself out of it."

"Gee, well, thanks a bunch, Mr Pure as the Driven Snow. Don't forget I know about that little Greek tart and her friend you bonked down in Brighton."

"Listen, you arsehole. This is getting us nowhere – you in particular."

Neither of them had noticed the stocky figure standing in front of the hot air dryer. "Are you Calum James?" he asked.

"What's it to you?" snapped the singer, irritated by this untimely interruption.

"Nuffink," replied the stranger. "Nuffink at all, panhead."

At that precise moment, with a single headbutt, he propelled Calum backwards straight into a vacant stall.

"Fuck!" he screamed in pain, lodged in the toilet bowl, his backside almost touching the water, nose beginning to bleed.

"Who the fuck are you?" demanded Jay, about to pile in until he spotted the two massive bodyguards he'd seen earlier emerging from adjacent stalls.

"Me? I'm Luke Charrington, that's who," sneered Collected Thoughts' guitarist, before taking his leave with the two gorillas who'd walked in with him.

Helped to his feet, staggering from the blow, Calum wiped the blood from his nose as he stared at the mirrored wall to assess the damage done to his previously flawless features.

"Who the fuck was that?" he grimaced, accidentally touching a second wound on his forehead.

"That," replied Jay, suddenly feeling a degree of sympathy for his friend, "was Luke Charrington."

CHAPTER FIFTEEN

"What do you mean you got the story in the News of the World? We didn't want to be in the fucking News of the World. Don't tell m-e to calm down," Symes screamed down the line. "One of the animals you represent tried to maim my singer. Who, in case you've forgotten, is going out on tour next week. I'm so angry I don't even want to be having this conversation with you, Seymour. Do I make myself clear? Good. And don't bother calling me. Good fucking bye to you, too," he added, slamming down the receiver in disgust.

At precisely the same time, Calum was making a call on the other side of town. Sporting a wound requiring six stitches to his forehead, ready for the biggest row of his life, thinking about the person he'd like to punch in the head, he punched in the number instead.

"Hi, it's Calu…"

"Hello. I'm afraid there's nobody here to take your call but if you'd like to leave your name and number I'll get back to you as soon as I return. Please speak clearly after the musical tone."

"Is that fucking Luke Charrington there with you?" he screamed at the machine. "You know who it is so call me. You've got my number. And if you've forgotten it, check inside your bra," he added, before tossing his mobile across the room.

"My, we are in a bit of a tizzy today," observed Jay, catching the phone in the nick of time before it landed on his guitar.

"I'm telling you if that ugly bastard Luke Charrington's bonking her I'll fucking kill him."

"Wake up, man. I imagine half of London's bonked Katrina. She's a slapper, and that's what slappers do. Stick with Suzanne. She's pretty, intelligent and, for all I know, gives great head. What more could a guy ask for?"

While the band spent the following two days putting the finishing touches to their live show in King's Cross, their album performed in spectacular fashion, leapfrogging Collected Thoughts to reach number five. In addition, Symes had secured the band back-to-back dates at Shepherd's Bush Empire and the Kentish Town Forum right at the end of what would now be a fifteen-date tour.

"Hands up those in favour of 'Walk on the Wild Side'," Brian directed, acknowledging the show of hands. "Now those in favour of 'Eve of Destruction'."

Canvassing each member of the band in turn to choose the song that would precede their entrance onstage each night on tour, Brian had whittled it down to just two songs. David's suggestion, 'Glad To Be Gay', was turned down out of hand. 'Yellow Submarine', Simon's choice, was also vetoed.

"'Walk on the Wild Side' it is, then," he announced, acknowledging Calum and David's hands and his own casting vote. "And Basil, don't forget to hand our 'Walk on the Wild Side' CD to the guy manning front-of-house mixing in Exeter."

"Anything else?"

"This time try not to erase anything before you leave the building."

Relaxing with the Sunday papers, supping a convivial lunchtime pint at one of their local haunts, Calum was scanning the News Of The World.

"Anything interesting in yours?" Jay asked, trying to appear absorbed in his Mail on Sunday.

"There's a great story in here about a couple caught having it off in a graveyard. They must have frozen their arses off. The headline's 'SPOOKY NOOKY'. Quality journalism at its finest. The caption they've printed underneath the photograph of the graveyard is even funnier."

"What does it say?"

"'HOW WAS IT FOR YOOO...OOOO?'"

"Quite frankly, I can't believe people get paid to write such crap. That said, any more scandalous titbits in there that might amuse?"

"Can't see anything for the moment."

"There must be something," Jay insisted, tired of the patronising crap pouring off the pages of his Mail.

"Fuck!" shouted the singer, immediately disturbing the other patrons who'd been quietly browsing their own newspapers.

"Keep your voice down."

"Cunts!"

"Tell me what it says but keep your fucking voice down and stop swearing."

"I don't believe it. I do not believe it," he repeated, before reading aloud the article.

"In a dispute over a girl earlier this week at London's trendy Steamer Bar, Collected Thoughts' guitarist Luke Charrington allegedly punched SSB vocalist Calum James in the venue's toilets. An anonymous eyewitness claimed it was in the mouth.

The girl at the centre of the argument is glamour model and former high-class prostitute, Katrina Terracciano, who drives a top-of-the-line Porsche and owns a luxurious £450,000 apartment in London's Maida Vale. Miss Terracciano, who exited the busy bar sometime after midnight in floods of tears, refused to comment on the incident.

*Emerging from the same bar hours later, a somewhat worse for wear Charrington denied the assault. As he pulled off at high speed in a chauffeur-driven Mercedes, the rock star attacked our NOW photographer, screaming, 'It's none of your ****ing business, panhead.'"*

"Wow! Did they use the picture of him leaving?"

"No," replied the singer, passing the newspaper to Jay. "The fucking bastards used one of me."

Chapter Sixteen

The following day, reading a letter that had been delivered to the apartment by hand, Calum discovered his troubles weren't over. It was from Suzanne.

Although I foolishly believed you to be a man of substance, I now realise you were duping me all along with your protestations of love and tales of tour buses. I, too, have access to newspapers. And trade journals. While the latter helped you in your deception, I find solace in the former, which has at least played some small part in your downfall. Long may the press hound you. Suzanne

"Hardly surprising in the circumstances," remarked Jay, having scrutinised the contents of the letter. "What did you think she was going to send you? Her thesis on sexual incontinence absolving you of all responsibility."

"No, but I thought she'd..."

"....Thank you for humiliating her? Do you know she found three reporters and a photographer lurking on her doorstep this morning?"

"God. What did they want?"

"I'll give you a clue. They didn't stop to ask for directions."

"Uh?"

"What do you think they wanted? They were all desperate to find out if you really are the fantastic shag you crack yourself up to be."

"Maybe I should consider celibacy."

"You? Calum James? Celibate? And when do you think we'll be able to obtain tickets for this unlikely event?"

"I could do it."

"Not in my lifetime."

"I could."

"Only if you had your dick surgically removed prior to taking a vow of chastity."

"I could do it. No problem."

"I'd say there's more chance of The Beatles reforming on the day Keith Richards renounces alcohol."

"You underestimate me."

"You think? Anyway, who are you phoning?"

"A couple of girls I met while we were doing the radio interviews. They perform this lewd double act free of charge for fellow members of the entertainment profession."

"You're incorrigible."

After their successful opening date in Exeter the previous evening, they were in ebullient mood on board the tour bus. Calum had left the after-show party early having persuaded Basil to drive him and two girls he'd met at the radio station back to the Holiday Inn. Attractive in that hard-faced Essex girl way, both boasted the type of breasts that don't come cheap.

Safely ensconced in the privacy of the singer's room with the *Do Not Disturb* sign dangling from the door, Donna and Denise disrobed. Armed with a selection of exotic fruits, cream and ice cream, these wenches with tongues for hire went about their business. Their routine, very much 'Häagen Dazs meets Tits and Arse', combined much writhing, munching, licking and slurping of these comestibles from each other's bodies.

It had all been going swimmingly until Donna impaled her pudenda on a chunk of pineapple someone had forgotten to remove the spiky bits from. There followed a high- pitched scream and Donna's frantic dash to the bathroom to find a pair of tweezers to remove the offending spikes, leaving in her wake a trail of fruits of the forest. These she trampled into the carpet on the return journey from the bathroom.

"Go on, tell us what happened again."

"Why? It's impossible to make it sound sexy."

"Go on," Simon goaded him.

"By the time that pair had finished the room looked like a bloody bomb site, there was cream on the bedspreads, fruit ground into the flooring, strawberry stains on the drapes, cream smeared all over the furniture and what looked like shite on the sheets."

"Errrr," said Simon. "Was it?"

"Nah. It was chocolate sauce. Place looked like a battlefield. Like something you'd imagine seeing in your wildest dreams. I'm sure the tour accountant won't be very happy when he sees the bill for the damage they did to the room."

"So which part did you enjoy best of all? The bit where she coated your wanger with chocolate sauce?"

"Definitely not."

"How come?"

"Well, after she'd plastered my John Thomas in chocolate sauce and I was about to shoot my wad, I looked down at this poor girl and it just completely finished me. Her hair, her face and her tits were all covered in this clart. Sauce, cream, fruit, ice cream, you name it. When I looked at her, all I could think of was Coco the clown."

"That's hilarious, man. What happened next?"

"You mean what didn't happen next. I got an attack of the giggles, she got shirty and bang went my boner. When I told her it was the first time I'd had oral sex with a clown that was the fucking end of that."

"You're a star, Calum. A true star."

"He's a dirty, sick fucking bastard. That's what he is," Jay offered his own unsolicited opinion.

Christened the Tarts & Tantrums Tour unofficially, its progress continued through Bristol, Cardiff, Birmingham, Manchester and Glasgow before it reached Edinburgh. They were staying at the Holiday Inn in the heart of the Royal Mile. What they found was a city that said as much about heroin as it did about heather.

"I'm going out with an old friend tonight," David volunteered after the gig, keen to take advantage of a city that hosted the largest active gay scene in the United Kingdom.

Joined by Symes, the rest of the band and Basil, eschewing the thrills of S&M, set off down the Royal Mile in search of something a little tamer.

"I still think it's perverted," said Basil, craning his neck to get a better view of the pole dancer. "All that S&M shit. It's sick," he said, knocking his glass off the table before it shattered on the floor. "Fucking disgusting," he shouted.

"Keep your voice down," said Jay. "Oh Christ. Here he comes again."

"Keep this up and you're out," threatened the bouncer, who'd already had to reprimand Basil twice. "You've already knocked over a tray of glasses and I know you goosed one of my girls because she told me you did. Now, I'm warning you: step out of line again and you're out. And you'll be taking your friends with you." He glared at them all.

Later that evening, having sampled the delights of several local hostelries, they floated on an alcoholic haze back to their hotel. On arrival, the band made a beeline for the bar.

Lagging behind, them still talking on his mobile, Symes was stopped dead in his tracks when he recognised the man seated on the opposite side of the lobby. The same man who'd bought him an expensive lunch was deep in conversation with none other than Katrina Terracciano.

Too drunk to recognise her or anybody else, Basil and the band were already sat at the bar facing away from the lobby. Unnoticed, Symes made his way over to the interlopers' table.

"What brings you here?"

Seymour Levy, coincidentally visiting Edinburgh on perfectly legitimate business, was as surprised to see Symes as he was to see him.

"Usual shit, Andrew. I assume you two have already met." He indicated his carcinogenic companion.

"We have indeed."

"Look, I'm really sorry about what happened."

"Me too."

"And the News of the World business."

"Likewise Seymour. But I do think we need to differentiate between publicity and the serious beating my singer endured at the hands of that out-of-control lout you represent."

"Andrew. I'd desperately like to make it up to you."

"There isn't time."

"Why? Are you going somewhere?"

"No, Seymour. You are. Allow me to explain. First of all, I'm going to shut my eyes and count to ten. When I open them, both of you will have disappeared."

"If we refuse?"

"Seymour, you know how easily refusal can offend. Young lady, in case you hadn't noticed, Calum and the rest of the band are sat just over there behind you." He pointed towards the bar.

Katrina's face registered shock. "Oh my God!"

"I think it would be fair to say he'd be more than a little upset if he saw you. Having said that, Seymour, he's hardly in love with you either."

"You win," Levy admitted grudgingly, as the pair rose to take their leave.

CHAPTER SEVENTEEN

Cocooned in comfort aboard their luxury coach, they were oblivious to the torrential rain lashing against the porthole windows as they thundered down the M1 towards Sheffield.

"I'd hate to live in Edinburgh," said Simon, unable to sleep. "All that grey stone and grey sky would drive me mad. Wouldn't it you?"

"Probably," yawned David.

"Never stops raining and if that isn't enough you've got the locals to contend with. The place is full of drunks who hate the English."

"True."

"So did you and your friend go cruising in Edinburgh after all?"

"Pardon?"

"Did you visit any of those bath houses?"

"What's it to you?" snapped David, nursing a bruiser of a hangover in his bunk bed above.

"Because that's where I heard most of the 'trade' is."

"Look, if it's all the same to you I'm trying to get some sleep."

"I only ask is because I've never been in one."

"That's not my problem, is it?"

"I know, but I've always wanted to know what goes on in them."

"Simon, I don't think…"

"What about felching? Have you done any of that?"

The band's gay icon was incredulous. "Have I what?"

"Or isn't that your sort of thing?" the tub-thumper pressed on regardless. "How about fisting?" he asked, wrinkling his nose.

"Simon!" screamed the exasperated keyboard player. "While I'd like to satisfy your curiosity, the job of furthering your sex education is your parents' responsibility. Not mine. And what's more, I am extremely tired right now. So if you don't mind, I'd like to get some sleep."

"I was only trying to bond."

"Well go and bond somewhere else with someone else and leave me in peace."

"Fine. I'll go, then, shall I?"

"Please."

"Err David…"

"Good God. What now?"

"I know it's none of my business, but are you active or passive? What I mean is, do you like taking it up the old Gary Glitter or the other way round? Shoving it up somebody else's," added the master of superfluous information.

"I don't believe I'm hearing this. What happened to all the good manners your parents taught you? Didn't they teach you to respect other people's privacy?"

"Sorry, but I couldn't think of a better way of putting it."

"Clearly. Then I suggest you take a dictionary to bed instead of that stream of foul groupies you all seem to pass around."

"David…"

"Simon. Just go away and leave me alone. Please."

By the time the tour reached Oxford, the single was sat at number two, the album at number nine. And although Collected Thoughts' single had dropped out of the charts altogether, what troubled Calum was CT's album. Currently occupying the number three slot, it was threatening to go all the way to number one.

In high spirits on the journey back to London for the penultimate gig at Shepherd's Bush Empire, they were all looking forward to the end-of-tour party after the final gig in Kentish Town.

"When will we know?" asked Jay, tucking into his motorway service-station egg and chips.

"Why is this shit dripping in grease?" David interrupted.

"It's called a fried breakfast," the guitarist reminded him. "What did you expect to find on the menu here? Lobster Thermidor? I'm sorry," he apologised, turning his attentions back to Calum. "What did Andrew say?"

"He was very excitable. Not like him at all, as you know. Said he was expecting a call later today to confirm our spot this week. A spot which, as he put it, is still tentative."

"Fantastic," enthused the guitarist, looking forward to his first appearance on *Top of the Pops*.

"There is a drawback."

"There always is with Andrew."

"If it's a 'yes', they'll want us in the studio tomorrow to record the programme."

"Bollocks!" moaned Brian. "I was looking forward to a day off."

"Well, that's tough shit isn't it?" returned the singer. In common with most of them, he'd never appeared onscreen and relished the thought of making his television debut.

"So what's it like standing in front of those cameras being scrutinised by millions of people, all waiting for you to screw up?" he asked Brian, who'd already appeared on the programme twice.

"Bloody hot under all those lights. Boiling hot if you're dressed up as a turkey, which I was," honked the bass player.

"No, you fucking prat! Without the turkey outfit."

"First, they'll ask us to rehearse the song we're going to play. Then much later there'll be a proper dress rehearsal with full cameras, lights and sound. Later, much later in my experience, we'll be live on air. I warn you: there's an awful lot of hanging around doing nothing waiting for things to happen."

"What are the people at the Beeb like to work with?"

"Dead stuffy. Chock full of Oxbridge types. People who think they know more about music than the musicians who fill their fucking programme schedules. You've got to laugh."

"So what did you do to kill time while you were at the BBC, Brian?"

"Drugs mostly."

CHAPTER EIGHTEEN

The gig at Shepherd's Bush Empire had been a resounding success. The following night they were playing in front of their home crowd at the Forum. It was notorious for its expensive, allegedly watered down beer, of which large amounts were regularly spilled all over the carpets, making the act of crossing the bar in this former art deco cinema akin to walking on Sellotape.

"Thank you, Kentish Town," Calum bellowed into the microphone. He waited for the applause to die down. "Let's cool it, now," he urged the whistling, stomping audience that was threatening to bring down the balcony at any moment. "I want to thank you all for coming out here to see us tonight and before we go I'd like to dedicate this last song to all of you."

On cue, as the band powered into their closing number, their singer walked off the front of the stage into the crowd. Supported by a sea of hands belonging to the faithful, it was as if he were walking on water. Sensing the messianic power he could wield over an audience made him feel invincible. And tonight, wild eyed with coke, his delusion was complete.

"How was the show tonight?" Calum shouted, his voice audibly shot through at the end-of-tour party.

Symes cupped his hands to the singer's ear to make himself heard above the din in the Forum's balcony bar.

"Phenomenal."

"Cool," the singer noted lethargically, while adjusting his shades. "Really cool. So how's it looking for us in America? Will we be touring there next month?"

"Without wishing to make promises, I'd say it looks extremely likely."

"How are record sales doing there?"

"Steady. Airplay for the single in the major and secondary markets is strong. MTV have taken a shine to the video and they're threatening to put it on heavy rotation, which would be very good news indeed for potential sales all across the US."

"Tremendous. I'm sure the rest of the band will be thrilled when you tell them." The singer grinned and raised his glass in a toast. "Cheers, Andrew. You're a star. You're doing a great job for us."

"Perhaps someone should tell Brian," he replied.

Holding court over at the bar with members of the road crew, the increasingly inebriated Basil hadn't been able to get his end away on this tour.

"Some girls think I'm an ugly, fat bastard," he complained to anyone who'd listen.

Acting increasingly strangely throughout the evening, he became much the worse for wear as the night wore on. After casually enquiring of the Australian barmaid whether she'd 'fancy a fuck', he'd begun to hit on the girl in alarming fashion. Emboldened by the booze and confusing his lecherous slurs with searing wit, Basil made matters worse by exposing himself and asking what she'd do in return for a backstage pass. He'd forgotten the tour had ended hours earlier.

"Piss off and put it away you dirty bastard!" the flustered goth swore through a mouthful of face furniture. "Give me any more trouble and I'll have the management call the police. Then we'll really find out how big you are."

"Aw come here," he beckoned.

Basil, mistaking her words for affection, took a lunge at the goth before landing up on the floor on the other side of the counter to absorb most of the beer spilled that evening.

"Fuck off you pervert," she screamed at him, before picking up the phone on the wall behind the bar, her attacker still laid out on the floor motionless, soaking up yet more beer.

Sensing trouble, Scrotty and Bender, the only two members of the road crew still sober enough to do so, picked their boss up from the floor.

"What seems to be the problem, young lady?" intervened Symes, who'd heard the commotion from the other side of the room.

"This animal attacked me. I'm calling the police."

"Will this take care of things?" he asked, waving a £50 note as she continued with her threats to call the police.

"You can do better than that," she said, determined to milk the situation for all it was worth.

"Does that solve the problem?" he asked, doubling the amount he'd already put in her hand.

"Try harder," she rasped. "And my cab fare home."

Symes pressed a further £50 note into her hand.

"We'll leave it there, shall we?" he asked. "Or do you live on Mars?"

"Fair enough," she said.

"What a beautiful day it is," noted Symes, hands thrust deep in pockets, standing by the window admiring the view of Regent's Park. "And how are we all feeling?" he asked the band, still recovering from the end-of- tour party.

"Knackered," volunteered Brian.

"Fine," muttered David.

"Empowered by a new life force," said the singer.

Symes blinked. Like the others in the room, he hadn't a clue what he was talking about.

"So tell me again why we're doing this German tour?" said David. "It's not a huge market for us there."

"It occurred to me that since you've got to fly out there for the European radio interviews Platinum has scheduled, why not get handsomely paid for three gigs while you're there. Killing two birds with one stone. Remember, it's your money we're spending – or conserving, as the case may be."

"What radio interviews?" Brian barked at his manager. "You didn't mention any radio interviews. Now I come to think of it, you didn't mention any gigs either. I'll bet you're not coming along for the ride are you?"

"I've other business of yours to attend to."

"You could have told me at the party."

"Brian, it's up to us to promote…"

"….The product?"

"The fucking record! The record. As I was about to say," he continued, fixing his gaze on Brian, "so far your radio interviews and promotional efforts here in the UK have paid off."

"Fair comment but the single's still stuck at number two."

"Stuck at number two!" snapped Symes. "Most bands would give their right arm to be stuck at number two, Brian."

"That bloke in Def Leppard did. Went flying through the windscreen and left his arm on the backseat. Check it out if you don't believe me."

The others all laughed, welcoming a little light relief from Brian's continued onslaught.

"Well, I'm grateful for that nugget of information, Simon. Perhaps we can move on to topics closer to home now," he suggested, holding a copy of Music Week. "Your album has moved up four places to number five. Collected Thoughts," he jabbed a forefinger at the latest set of charts in front of him, "have slipped down to number eight."

"Well, there's a relief. Who did you say we were supporting in Germany?" asked Calum.

"Supporting?" thundered Brian. "Why the fuck are we supporting anyone? We should be headlining, not supporting."

"As David mentioned earlier, had you been listening, we're not exactly shifting bucket loads of records in Germany at present. And if you don't believe me, pick up the phone and call your record label. They'll tell you. Call your agent while you're at it – ask him why you can't headline in Germany. I mean, why take my word for anything anymore?"

"Do we get to soundcheck?"

"Yes, David," he lied.

"I'll bet we fucking do," snorted Brian, speaking from bitter experience. "What's the name of this band w-e-r-e supposed to be supporting?"

"Das Kapital," revealed Symes, a name that was foreign to all of them including him.

"What's their unique selling point?" asked David.

"I'm told they sing in German."

Prior to the tour, Simon was shattered to receive a phone call from his mother bearing far worse news than his manager ever would. His father, a genuine cockney and former dance band drummer, had passed away in his sleep. A quiet, gentle man, he'd been a non-smoker and teetotal all his life. It was he, offering encouragement every step of the way, who'd taught the young Simon to play drums. Unlike most of his own generation, Johnny Harding had been fiercely proud of his son's chosen profession.

The funeral took place the day before the tour began. Johnny Harding had been much admired in the local community and could boast many friends. It was well attended.

Responsible for ordering the flower arrangement that would adorn his father's hearse, Simon had left the details of this personal tribute to his father to an old school friend and general jack the lad, Barry Jarvis. But what Simon had forgotten in his unswerving loyalty to his old chum who ran the florist in the high street was that Barry was dyslexic.

"I don't bloody well believe it," uttered one of Johnny's elderly friends when he saw the wreath featuring Johnny's favourite lilies. He watched in disbelief as the cortege took a right hand turn before sweeping down Walthamstow High Street on the final leg of its journey to the cemetery. "None of the buggers can spell these days!" he harrumphed.

From his vantage point on the pavement Johnny's former snooker partner rubbed his eyes in amazement as the funeral procession headed towards him. Straining his eyes to read Simon's tribute, he too spotted the spelling error on the wreath mounted on the front of the hearse.

The tribute to Simon's dearly departed dad spelled 'DED'.

CHAPTER NINETEEN

There were a number of reasons the record company chose Frankfurt as their base. The city was equidistant from the gigs they'd booked in Berlin, Hamburg and Stuttgart. In addition, excellent transport links from Frankfurt Airport meant journeys to and from the gigs and the interviews in Copenhagen, Oslo and Stockholm were far easier than anticipated.

Travelling to Frankfurt on Lufthansa, the musicians were disappointed when a stewardess directed them to economy having failed to grasp that coach class was a euphemism for the same.

"Bloody Germans!" Simon shouted, soon after the seat-belt sign had been switched off. "They killed my grandfather. Now my dad's dead, too. Bloody Germans!" he howled uncontrollably, oblivious to the fact he was travelling with the country's national carrier and attracting unsolicited glances from the other passengers sitting nearby, most of them Germans.

"Listen! We don't want to get chucked off this plane because of you," Jay reprimanded him, ignoring the fact they were cruising at an altitude of 15,000 feet rendering this option impossible. "So just shut the fuck up and stop dribbling."

"Leave him alone, you odious bully," David defended the distraught drummer.

Supporting Das Kapital in Hamburg, on the opening night of the tour SSB were denied a soundcheck. The headline act also refused to communicate with them, preferring instead to use one of their road crew as a go-between.

"Come in, it's not locked," Jay called out, an invitation to the person hammering away at the dressing room door.

Flinging open the door with all his might, the love child of a one-night stand with Attila the Hun stood before them blocking out the light.

"Be careful vot you are sayink tonight. Uzzervise, zer kut be trouble," the massive frame awash with swastikas and chains informed them before taking his leave.

"Don't like the sound of him," said Calum, looking nervous all of a sudden. Understandable since he'd be the one on the receiving end should any trouble befall them onstage.

Hours later, when the house lights went down, Basil spotted the same German roadie donning a tin helmet circa World War II, handing out packages to similarly attired groups of fans sitting in the front rows.

Basil ran over to him. "What the fuck do you think you're doing, you Bavarian bastard?"

"Relax und ve haf no problems," advised his charmless opponent, continuing to distribute the mysterious packages to Das Kapital's grateful followers.

They were, in fact, cherry bombs – extremely dangerous, industrial-strength fireworks. The first landed on the stage right in front of Calum as soon as Jay struck the opening chord, a prelude for what was to follow. Almost immediately, others seated in the first five rows followed suit launching a series of bottles, cans, coins and other assorted missiles at the band.

"Get off," Basil screamed from the side of the stage at the close of the song. "Get off before they kill you."

Ignoring this sound advice to his detriment, halfway through the second number Jay was hit full in the face by a plastic bottle filled to bursting point with warm piss.

"Cunt!" he screamed in pain.

He watched in disbelief as it rolled off the front of the stage for somebody else to take a pot shot at him. Pints of piss later, another bounced back off an onstage monitor before it exploded and discharged its putrid contents over a deserving group of Das Kapital fans seated right by the stage.

"Get off. Now!" Basil yelled again, watching the melodrama unfold from the side of the stage.

Disgusted by this display of cretinous behaviour they were being subjected to, the band followed his advice. Unplugging their instruments, with a swift "Auf wiedersehen" from Jay and a curt "Fuck off!" from Calum, they left the stage as missiles continued to rain down on it and them.

"Follow me, you fucking dickheads," Basil commanded the troops as they made a concerted dash to the relative safety of their dressing room and barricaded themselves in.

Calum shuddered, watching as Basil bolted the door and wedged a pair of four-by-twelve speaker cabinets against it. "What the fuck was that all about?"

When riot police eventually arrived, armed to the teeth, they hurled canisters of teargas into the hall and evacuated the building. Hours later they escorted the shaken band members back to their hotel.

Like it or not, Berlin was the venue for the second concert SSB were legally contracted to play.

While the level of audience participation turned out to be the equal of Hamburg, there was one concession: the Berlin crowd permitted the band to complete two songs before the assault began. Eschewing the use of explosives and piss, they opted instead for a variety of exotic timbers, sticks of furniture their parents no longer had use for which they hurled at the band. By the end of the gig, the audience had thrown enough wood at them to make a dining table, six chairs and a sideboard.

At the final gig in Stuttgart, Das Kapital fans showed remarkable restraint waiting until SSB struck up the opening chord of the final song before taking careful aim. The musicians, fearing for their lives in the highly charged atmosphere, were forced to flee for cover and the safety of their dressing room once more, leaving behind their precious instruments.

In the aftermath, after Basil had sifted through the wreckage, it would turn out to be a very expensive evening for the company that made the mistake of insuring them.

Trashed beyond all repair were three of Jay's electric guitars, the acoustic guitar he'd walked through customs, both of Brian's basses, an electric piano, two cymbals and a snare drum plus Calum's favourite microphone. Intriguingly, many of the objects responsible for this wanton damage were identical three-pointed stars. Fashioned from metal, in normal circumstances they could be seen adorning the bonnet of a luxury carmaker.

Less than twenty-four hours later, still reeling from the shock of their Teutonic tour, the five of them were sat in the relative tranquillity of Tangent's boardroom. Hundreds of miles from a country that seemed to have forgotten the war with England was over, they were eager to offer first-hand accounts of their experiences on the front line.

"I'm telling you, it was like World War III out there," Jay began to recount his tale of terror at the hands of the Hun. "They made British soccer hooligans look like care in the community workers. Lunatics. The lot of them."

"Nearly filled my bloody pants during the show in Berlin," Calum admitted.

"Me too," said Jay. "Almost choked a darkie."

"Bastards in Stuttgart left a couple of skiddies in my pants," David grimaced.

"And they killed my grandpa," Simon reminded them all over again.

"I was sorry to hear about your father," Symes consoled.

The drummer burst into tears again. "Thank you," he sniffled, before parting company with enough snot to fill a bucket.

"And how did you find the tour Brian?"

"Keep it up and you might just earn yourself a good kicking," he encouraged Symes, taking umbrage at this question that should have earned the latter a public flogging.

"Have I offended you?"

"Did Hitler offend half of Western Europe when he declared war on Poland?" Brian barked back in his face. "You've offended all of us, you arsehole!"

"Just a minute," countered Symes, struggling to get a grip on the situation, desperate to exonerate himself. "It wasn't me who booked the tour. It was your agent."

"Listen, you scumbag. If you'd actually been with us in Germany doing your job, half of this would never have happened. It's dereliction of duty – nothing more, nothing less, Andrew."

CHAPTER TWENTY

He surveyed the wreckage that had in a previous incarnation comprised three electric guitars, two electric basses and an acoustic guitar.

"Jeez," exclaimed Brad. "I thought Pete Townshend overdid it, but you guys... And you," he tutted, turning his attention to Basil.

"Me?"

"They would have listened to you," he berated the roadie. "You could have stopped them," he insisted, indicating the sixty or so pieces of splintered timber. "Most guitarists would have given a limb to own any one of these."

"Some of us nearly did," Jay replied huffily.

"Not only that," the young American continued to dribble on, "they'd have looked after the guitars much better than you did. They certainly wouldn't have trashed them."

"What are you talking about? We didn't trash the guitars."

"Who did then?"

"Fans."

"They did this to your equipment?"

"Maybe 'fans' is too strong a word," Basil conceded. "'Animals' would be a more accurate description."

"It was unbelievable, man. Riots everywhere we played."

"Wow!" said Brad.

"Complete and utter mayhem," affirmed the guitarist, somehow making his exploits sound heroic.

"Now I understand," nodded the salesman, wondering where the band would be spending the cheque from the insurers. "Isn't a riot meant to be a good sign on the Continent? Like they really appreciate you?"

"Not in my experience," Jay replied.

"It is in Italy."

"We weren't frigging well in Italy. Look, we didn't come in here to discuss with you how we nearly died onstage in full fucking Technicolor. We came in here to talk to your repairman. Is Dr. Rock here this afternoon or having lunch? Or is he out the back cracking one off?"

"He's down there," said Brad, ignoring this last comment, pointing to the stairs. "He's had his lunch."

Their reason for visiting Denmark Street was to ascertain the damage done to their instruments in Germany, to find out whether they could salvage anything from the tangled mess of wood and metal they were carrying. Leaving a baffled Brad scratching his head in wonderment, the pair of them descended the rickety stairs leading to the repair department.

"They don't look too happy, do they?" declared the repairman, catching his first glimpse of the sad specimens they'd brought along for inspection. "They don't look too good at all," he observed, adjusting his pince-nez, "or what's left of them."

Jay watched intently as the experienced wood surgeon laid out the crippled, twisted bodies on the countertop.

Maintaining complete silence punctuated by the odd gasp and occasional grimace, he began to sift through the remains as if searching for some sort of provenance, perhaps a small label bearing the inscription, 'Approved For Abuse – Pete Townshend'. He cleared his throat.

"What's the verdict?" asked Jay. "What can we expect to salvage?"

"A couple of pickups. Three at most."

"What else?"

"Possibly a couple of necks," motioned Dr. Rock, indicating the largely useless parts heaped up in front of them.

"Any machine heads?"

"Couple of sets."

"Is that it?"

"Pretty much, guys. Unless you want me to test all the components separately."

"How long will that take?"

"Hours and it could lead absolutely nowhere."

"I think we'll pass on that one," Jay decided.

"I know it's none of my business, but may I ask you a question?"

"Fire away, dude."

"Why do you all seem so cheerful all of a sudden when I tell you you're holding enough inventory to start your own guitar repair shop? Am I missing something here? Some vital piece of information?"

"Insurance job," confided Jay, tapping his nose.

"Oh, I get it," the repairman chuckled. "You trashed this stuff on purpose so you could make an insurance claim?"

"Not again," groaned the guitarist, exhausted by the prospect of having to repeat the whole story frame by frame, blow by blow. "Why don't you ask Brad how it happened? I'm sure he'll be happy to fill in all the details for you."

"Thanks guys, I'll be sure to. You take care now," he drawled, as they disappeared up the stairs, swag in hand, out of the shop and into the alleyway.

With a spring in his step that morning, the decidedly affable Symes was certainly acting like the cat who got the cream. The reason being he'd received a cheque from the insurance company that morning – funds that more than covered the cost of the instruments he'd had to replace. Not that he mentioned to the band the tidy profit his creative accounting division had reaped as a result.

"While I freely admit that on the surface things didn't exactly go according to our plans on the German tour…."

"On the surface? What are you bloody talking about?" Brian fumed. "On the surface, as you so blithely put it, is where most of the action took place. And they weren't o-u-r plans. We didn't make any. You did. They were y-o-u-r plans, Andrew."

"Brian, will you get off my case for just one minute?" Symes asked.

"Yeah, shut up!" complained the guitarist, tired of the bass player's carping and constant interruptions. "Why don't you stop needling Andrew for a minute and listen to what he has to say for a change?"

"Thank you, Jay. The single has now dropped out of the charts altogether, putting us on a par with Collected Thoughts' efforts in this department. That much said, divine intervention has also seen their album drop out of the Top 30, while providence appears to have intervened on your behalf."

"Could we have that in plain English please?"

"I beg your pardon, David. Your album has been sitting at number three for the past two weeks and could quite feasibly go to number two. Number one, even."

"If we include a miracle," Brian concluded.

Symes smiled. "Oh ye of little faith. Platinum also wants to release 'Part Of A Plan' as the follow-up single to *Hearts & Souls* here in the UK."

"Great choice," acknowledged Calum, who wrote the song and would wind up with the lion's share of the royalties.

"Once again I've been saving the best news till last."

"Why? To make yourself look shiny?"

"No, Brian. It's just that some days I'd do anything to bring the hint of a smile to your sad little face."

At this juncture, the bass player resisted the urge to punch his manager in the face.

"As I was about to say, the single and the album have both gone Top 30 in the United States. And on this basis," he concluded, "Platinum has agreed to underwrite your first US tour."

"Excellent," said Calum.

"Ace," declared the guitarist.

"What are the implications for us?"

"There'll be more gigs to complain about, Brian."

"Very funny."

"Let me see," mused Symes. "There'll be more aeroplanes to complain about and more hotels to complain about. And let's not forget the women."

"Women?"

"Yes, Brian. It's good to know there's something even you won't be complaining about."

CHAPTER TWENTY-ONE

Preliminaries taken care of, and with Andrew accompanying them this time, SSB touched down at New York Kennedy Airport in the middle of a scorching July. As the thermometer rose, the temperature on the ground that afternoon had reached a blistering 95 degrees with humidity at 96 per cent and rising.

Managing to stay cool but looking anything but, Symes was sporting a Panama hat and shorts that hadn't been on vacation for at least five years. The others, embarrassed by his choice of clothing apparel, which accentuated his knobbly knees, trailed twenty paces behind as he led the way. After waiting what seemed like an eternity, they presented themselves in turn at the immigration desk.

As they soon discovered, being grilled by a government official felt more akin to appearing on a TV quiz show: get all the answers correct and win a holiday in the USA; get 'em wrong and Lord knows what would happen. Being forced to break rocks on a chain gang down in Louisiana for getting your postcode wrong seemed mighty harsh. As did five years rotting away in Alcatraz accused of importing controlled substances after the authorities had confused the apple you'd bought for lunch with a gun.

"What is the purpose of your visit?" demanded the uniformed officer packing the loaded gun in his holster. "Business or pleasure?"

"Business."

"Do you have any previous convictions for drugs?"

"No," lied the guitarist, avoiding all eye contact.

"And how long do you propose to spend in the US?"

"Six weeks."

"And where will you be staying during your visit?"

"The Holiday Inn most of the time," replied Jay, as if one Holiday Inn served the entire country.

"I meant here in New York."

"The Chelsea Hotel on West 23rd Street."

"That's a mighty dangerous place you're planning to stay," the immigration officer informed him. "It's notorious for the high level of drug consumption rife amongst its residents, its guests and those who frequent the premises."

Thinking better of it, Jay omitted to inform him this was the very reason Symes had booked them into this legendary establishment in the first place.

The reason they'd come to America was simple: it's where the money was. It would have been easier to continue touring in Europe but until they'd cracked this massive market, all future earnings from the band would be absorbed by Platinum, eager to recoup its advance.

Almost an hour after leaving the airport, the occupants of the two yellow taxis were snarled up in traffic at the entrance to the Midtown Tunnel.

"Wow!" Simon marvelled. "Check out this little baby." He wound down his window and pointed towards the classic bright red, sixties Chevrolet Corvette Stingray sitting alongside. "One day I'm going to own one of those."

As they continued on their journey, the drummer breathed deeply to inhale the heady mixture of diesel and petrol, source of the intoxicating, perfumed smell that constantly permeates the air hanging over New York City.

"I do believe we've arrived," Calum remarked as he stepped out of the first taxi to arrive outside the Chelsea. "Take a look at this," he said, pointing at the commemorative plaque to Dylan Thomas adorning the wall by the entrance. "Here are the others Andrew," he signalled, as the second cab and the remaining musicians pulled up at the kerb.

"This place is so cool," said Jay, gazing around the lobby where junkies were allowed to crash on the floor at night whenever there was torrential rain.

Minutes later, he was stunned when he realised the man checking them in at the front desk was the hotel's legendary proprietor, Stanley Bard.

"A pleasure to meet you, Mr. Bard," acknowledged the guitarist. "Your reputation precedes you."

"Does it?" acknowledged the laconic Stanley.

The following morning, having breakfasted like kings on what was still the finest meal of the day in America, the band headed for the musical instrument stores off Times Square. These shops put those they'd visited on Denmark Street in the shade.

Symes, meanwhile, spent most of his time on the telephone hammering out last-minute details with Marcella Mingovitch, the no-nonsense PR that had been assigned by Platinum's West Coast office. Due to fly in that evening, she would chaperone the band for a series of interviews scheduled for the following day. As hard as nails, taking prisoners was not her style.

Later that evening, at her insistence, they all dined out together at a vegan restaurant in Greenwich Village where she outlined her vision of what Americans refer to as 'where it's at'.

"When I whisper," bawled the southern belle, "folk listen."

"What happens the rest of the time?" asked Calum.

"Shut up when I'm talking!" she attacked the singer in front of the others. "And when I shout," she continued, "people shake."

"Is this woman for real?" Jay whispered in his ear.

"And if I swear, someone's gonna eat shit. But when I scream, and believe me I can, people know I'm gonna tear somebody's fucking balls off," she spat.

"Imagine being married to her," returned the guitarist.

"And how long have you been with Platinum?" Symes enquired, wishing to appear friendly, desperate to locate her off switch.

"Don't patronise me!" she snarled. "Then we'll all get on just dandy."

And on it went.

"And don't forget," she reminded them as they all got up to leave some three and a half hours later. "There'll be no swearing when you're on air tomorrow. D'ya hear me? No fucking swearing!" she bellowed, as they strolled out of the restaurant into the muggy night air.

CHAPTER TWENTY-TWO

"Jesus effing Christ!" spluttered the drummer.

"Is everything all right, Sir?"

"What is this stuff?"

"Grits, Sir."

Simon frowned at the disgusting grey concoction the waitress had presented him with.

"I thought I should try it but I'm sorry, I can't eat this," he apologised, pointing at the gruel-like mixture on his plate that could have passed for elephant semen. "Can I see the menu again?"

"Sure," she replied, mindful of her tip. "Are you guys with a band?"

"We are," said Calum, affecting a fruity English accent. "Would you like tickets for our show later this week?"

"Gee thanks, I would."

"You can bring a friend if you like."

"Awesome!"

"I'll tell you what," Simon interrupted. "I'll have the Wild West Special."

"You do realise your breakfast will arrive on two plates?"

"I didn't, but that's fine by me," he grinned at the prospect.

"You got it. By the way," she said, fluttering long, dark eyelashes at the susceptible singer. "My name is Candice. Friends call me Candy. Call me whatever you like. Is there anything else I can get you?"

"Not at the moment thanks," said Jay, surveying the mounds of cooked breakfast taking up every available square inch of space on the table. Eggs over easy, sunny side up, eggs Benedict, hash browns, crispy bacon, sausage links, patties, waffles, pancakes, yogurt, rye toast, cinnamon toast, English muffins, butter, jam, water, orange juice, coffee. "I think we're there now."

"Well, you guys enjoy your breakfast. I'll be back with that new order," she said, pleased as punch at having met these English guys.

"I'll bet she's a lot of fun between the sheets," observed Calum.

"She's a little slapper like all the others you attract like flies," announced David. "Simon, does this mean we have to sit and watch while you trough a breakfast the size of Manhattan?"

"I suppose we could chat while I'm eating."

"About what?" asked the ivory tickler.

"What do you think of Marcella Mingowitch?" he asked, anticipating the biggest breakfast of his life.

"Marcella whingeing bitch," Jay said, using the nickname Andrew immediately assigned her. "I'd say she's deranged. Reminds me of the big sister I never had – and never wanted. Anyway, what's your take on her, Brian?"

"Maybe I'm being unfair, but did someone beat her senseless with the ugly stick? Or did she hit every branch as she fell out of the tree? The woman's hideous."

"How about you, David?"

"As I'm sure even you must be aware, Simon, I've never been a huge fan of vaginas and women's wobbly bits. I far prefer a nice hard stiff dick."

"Ssshh, keep your voice down!" he urged, always the first to show any sign of embarrassment when somebody else was being blunt.

"That said, Simon, I'd imagine any red-blooded hetero-sexual male possessing an ounce of sanity would shoot themselves rather than contemplate spending the rest of their lives in the company of a foul-mouthed trollop who dresses like a bag lady."

"I'd shoot the bitch first," Jay assured him.

The interviews were taking place in the Chelsea Hotel and were, for the most part, with the musical instrument press. They'd all been looking forward to talking about a subject they understood. They would sound knowledgeable for a change.

As she darted from room to room in the suite hired for the occasion, Marcella was already raising objections to some of the questions being asked, most of them innocuous.

"Hold it right there, buster," she intervened. "You can't ask him that."

"All I asked was why he prefers a .009 gauge top E string on his guitars in preference to a .011," protested the dumbfounded member of the fourth estate.

"I don't want every guitarist in North America stealing his ideas."

"It's not just the gauge of the string but the amount of pressure applied to it that determines how the same string will sound in the hands of another guitar player," pointed out the bemused hack.

"So why ask in the first place?"

As the morning wore on her demands grew ever loopier and by lunchtime had reached their nadir. Without prior warning she suddenly insisted on full copy approval. Not only that, she wanted picture approval, too.

Two journalists said no, one said maybe, and one said thank you but no thank you. Another called his editor. Three said no way. Two more told her to fuck off before walking out mid-interview.

Later that afternoon, still intent on stamping her authority on proceedings, Marcella marched into the MTV studios with SSB in tow, minutes before Basil arrived from the airport carrying a guitar case. This time nobody was going to screw up her meticulously laid plans.

As the cameras began to roll, the veejay asked the guitarist to demonstrate how he played the opening riff on 'The Devil Inside Of You'. Happy to oblige, he pulled out the new instrument Basil had handed him earlier. A split second later, seated in the green room transfixed by the monitor, Marcella caught her first glimpse of the new guitar live on screen.

"What the fuck is that?" she yelled at the screen.

Half guitar, half cartoon, 'The Flasher' had been custom-built for the US tour. The body of the guitar was cut into the shape of a human figure. Depicting a smiling, lecherous old man, 'The Flasher' was also holding his raincoat wide open to reveal a huge erection.

Deemed too risqué by those charged with controlling the nation's airwaves, this segment of the programme was duly axed, much to Marcella's subsequent relief, before the show went out 'live'.

CHAPTER TWENTY-THREE

When Andrew promised them he'd seen her off in a taxi bound for the airport, and Los Angeles three thousand miles away, the musicians heaved a collective sigh of relief.

"Hmmm," he mused, straining to conjure up a single decent word in defence of the indefensible. "I suppose you could say she was good at her job. Well meaning and all that. She's very efficient, Jay."

"So were the folk who ran Belsen."

Having exhausted the subject of Marcella, the other topic of conversation was the tour that would take them all over America, mostly by road and air. Today, however, they were travelling by rail. As the train bound for Poughkeepsie, a sleepy town in Upstate New York travelled on a track running parallel with the Hudson River, they were able to admire the ever-changing views.

The itinerary was arduous: New York City, Rochester, Buffalo, Boston, Philadelphia, Baltimore, Washington, Cleveland, Detroit, Chicago, Cincinnati, St. Louis, Kansas City, Nashville, Atlanta, Jacksonville, Miami, Tampa, New Orleans, Memphis, Baton Rouge, Houston, Dallas, El Paso, Tulsa, Oklahoma City, Tucson, Phoenix, Denver, Salt Lake City, Las Vegas, Seattle, Portland, Sacramento, Bakersfield, Oakland, San Francisco and San Diego, before the final show in Los Angeles.

Immediately after registering at the front desk of the Holiday Inn, they unpacked as quickly as possible before each musician conducted a swift examination of their respective mini-bar facilities. Nobody wanted the room with the smallest mini-bar or a room with no mini-bar, which became a major source of friction as the tour wore on.

Making his way back to the lobby, Calum caught sight of an obese figure lurking beside the elevator located at the far end of the corridor. Interestingly, he was dressed in a white rhinestone cape with matching white flared trousers. Minutes later, sitting in the hotel's coffee shop, the singer related what he'd seen.

"That's odd," Symes frowned. "So did I."

"Where?"

"In the lift."

"No kidding."

"The only difference was my Elvis was black."

"Black?"

"You'll never guess what I've just seen," enthused Jay, as the waitress set down two mugs of hot coffee.

"Bet I could," said Calum.

The guitarist was just about to say the words "Mexican Elvis" when Brian walked around the corner.

"Guess who I just saw in the lift?"

"Elvis," groaned the singer. "Now can we play something different?"

Seconds later, Simon hove into view. "You'll never guess who I just saw in the lobby."

"E-L-V-I-S!" they bellowed in unison.

"Actually it was Harvey Robertson."

"I'll be damned," declared Symes. "He'd better steer clear of the gig or I'll wring the scrawny little bastard's neck. I wonder what he's doing here?"

"You do pick some strange hotels," David admonished him as he was making his way over to the table. "Do you know what's going on here?"

"Right now if you told me we were about to witness the second coming of Jesus Christ I'd believe you. So you might as well tell me anyway."

"A convention."

"David, there are hundreds of conventions going on in America every day of the week."

"I know."

"So what's so special about this one?"

"It's an Elvis impersonators convention."

"Christ!" spluttered Symes. "I believe you. We've spotted four between us already."

"Reception told me they've booked ninety per cent of the rooms here for the event. Incidentally, Andrew, there's something else you ought to know."

"What's that, David?"

"They're all gay Elvis impersonators."

"Jesus wept," exclaimed Symes. "Congratulations, David. We're all delighted for you. Your lucky day."

"I'm told there's a sprinkling of transvestite Elvis impersonators here, too. I thought it might be an idea to invite one or two of them to the gig," he added with a sly grin. "I took the liberty of handing out a few tickets."

"How many, David?"

"Twenty, if you must know."

"Twenty?" repeated a nervous Symes

"Shouldn't be long now," tittered David, relaxing at the bar after a successful gig that evening.

"You'll never hear the end of this one."

"Don't worry, Calum. It's all going to be worth it."

As the others continued to chatter away in the bar, up on the fifth floor Basil swiped his keycard in the door.

"Bugger."

He watched it light up red, refusing him entry to his own room. After a second successful attempt, it lit up green and he flung open the door. Mouth agape, he wondered if he'd taken a wrong turn by the elevator. In twenty years on the road he'd never seen anything like it.

There were twenty gay Elvis impersonators in his room. Pants down, they were performing unspeakable acts on each other with a selection of microphones.

"H-E-L-L-O Basil," the Elvis with a huge willy greeted the astounded roadie. "What took you so long? We've been waiting for you. Haven't we boys and girls," he tittered, acknowledging the two transvestites lurking in the shadows. "Are you ready?" he asked the bamboozled Basil. "Press play."

In an instant the sound system began pumping out the tune to Jailhouse Rock. Lyric free, it swung like a bitch when they added their own.

Elvis Presley was a gay guy's dream
Always something tugging at his trouser seams
Tight crotch, tight arse, Presley he could wail
That's fine, suck mine, Elvis take me any time

Let's rock,
Baby suck my cock
Oh yes it's real,
Woncha come and feel.

Shagged in a Cadillac, his dick's out in the hall
Fucks his buddy up the butt – Priscilla's at the mall
Memphis Mafia man he's got some southern horn
Buy toys, rent boys, we can play till dawn

Let's rock,
Baby suck my cock
Oh yes it's a real,
Woncha come and feel.

Fell from his throne before he hit the bathroom floor
Too many drugs and then his body screamed no more
Had it up the arse and he'd had it up to here
Elvis wasn't feeling well 'cause he was feeling queer

Let's rock,
Baby suck my cock
Oh yes it's a real,
Woncha come and feel.

"Did you like it?" asked Captain Cock, when they'd finished a routine the likes of which Basil hoped and prayed he'd never have to witness again.

"I need to speak to somebody," he insisted, backing out of the room. "Urgently."

"Ungrateful bastard," pouted Captain Cock. "Didn't even have the manners to say thank you."

CHAPTER TWENTY-FOUR

Two weeks into the tour, Andrew returned to London to attend a meeting with Platinum before rejoining the band in Nashville. During his sojourn, he was disturbed by something he'd learned during this forty-eight-hour stopover. Harvey Robertson's visit to Poughkeepsie had been far from coincidental. Somebody seeking a novel way to show a tax loss had paid for his flight so he could embark on another savage mauling of the band. And the culprit was Seymour Levy.

Days later in the Renaissance Hotel in downtown Nashville, Symes explained what had happened.

"I hear you," nodded Calum, displaying traces of white powder that hadn't quite reached their intended destination. "Heavy shit," he added, before adjusting his white Stetson.

"The other bad news," snuffled the manager, displaying the first signs of a cold, "is that in our absence, and without a great deal of help from our label's promotional department I might add, the single has stiffed."

"Got any more fantastic news?"

"Unfortunately I have, Brian. Shall we get it over with while I still have the strength to deal with the petty objections you raise to everything I have to say?"

"I'm listening," mumbled the bass player.

"The album, I'm sorry to say," he sniffed, reaching for a handkerchief, "has dropped out of the UK Top 20. Which means," he blew his nose, "we have a real job on our hands making this US tour work."

"And if it doesn't?" Brian dug deeper, looking for the bottom line.

"Platinum has too much money invested to drop you so let's not get too depressed. As I mentioned earlier, the single and album are both in the lower reaches of the Top 20 here in the US, which is very encouraging news for me to come back to. Simon, you seem to be in some kind of pain. What's the problem?"

"My carpal tunnel syndrome problem is getting worse. It's causing me a lot of grief today."

"Will you be able to play the gig tonight?"

"I'm not sure."

"Simon, I'm going to call a doctor. He'll give you a cortisone shot and I'm sure you'll feel fine. Then hopefully you'll be looking forward to playing the gig tonight." He didn't want to be on the receiving end of a lawsuit resulting from a cancelled concert.

As they rose to leave, Calum made his move. "Can you ask the tour accountant to loosen up some cash for me? I'm running low again."

"What do you spend it on? Cowboy hats?"

Calum always appeared to be broke, always the first in line, hand outstretched, demanding money from the band's merchandising operation after sales began to generate more revenue than the gigs themselves. As Calum would admit, had he not been addicted, it was cash he readily needed to convert into cocaine.

In the weeks that followed, Simon didn't stop complaining about his carpal tunnel syndrome and spent much of his free time on the telephone explaining it to his mum in mind numbing detail.

On tour David missed his boyfriend and the material things in life people recognise themselves by. The vast wardrobe of clothes he'd left behind and the pictures adorning the walls of his apartment. Most of all he missed his two cats, Bubble and Squeak.

Although he hadn't discussed it with the other musicians, Brian considered quitting the band. He didn't like Andrew's style of management or agree with much of what he said, even if the others did. Nor did he approve of Calum's coke habit.

Jay was different. Like Keith Richards, he adored life on the road. So long as he could have room service to back it up, he would have been happy to spend the rest of his life on it.

By the time they arrived in Salt Lake City, burning the candle at both ends had begun to take its toll on the band.

Brian had begun to drink heavily. The previous week he'd become so inebriated before their gig in Tulsa the others had considered cancelling. At Symes' insistence they went ahead. The support band's bass player saved the day.

Largely due to the ongoing love affair he had with narcotics, Calum's health was also giving them cause for concern. He'd collapsed onstage in El Paso, although he recovered sufficiently to finish the gig. The singer then took a heavy tumble from the stage in Baton Rouge. Blinded by the lighting rig, he'd walked out into the arena after seeing the audience beckoning with outstretched palms. What had looked like a sea of hands from the stage turned out to be the audience fanning themselves with a sea of programmes.

CHAPTER TWENTY-FIVE

With the tour bus travelling a sedate fifty-five miles an hour, the journey through the Tennessee countryside seemed to go on forever. And it was during the long drive to Memphis that Jay in particular began to understand how Elvis Presley had arrived at the unique sound everybody described as rock 'n' roll.

"Calum, have you noticed how the music playing on the radio has gradually metamorphosed from country into blues the further south we travel?"

"I have. And it sounded almost effortless. Pretty astounding. It really does sound like the most natural progression when you truly hear it for the very first time."

"I swear it sent shivers down my spine when I made the connection and began to realise what was happening."

"How much fucking longer do we have to sit on this poxy thing?" Brian complained loudly from the back of the bus.

"Driver told me another hour."

"Good," said Brian, who found the long ride into Memphis tedious. "Incidentally, whereabouts are we playing tonight?"

"Mud Island," Jay reminded him.

"Is that what the building's made from?"

"No, you twat Simon! It's made of reinforced concrete like most of the other places we've played in. It's a natural amphi-theatre, seats about five thousand. Quite atmospheric from what I've heard. What with the stage being right by the Missis-sippi River and the Memphis skyline in the background."

"Isn't that where Jeff Buckley was swept to his death last year?"

"Yeah. Sadly," acknowledged Jay.

Rather than opting for another night at another Holiday Inn, Symes had booked the band into the best hotel the city had to offer. The Peabody had played host to Elvis and was the place Martin Luther King should have been staying the night he was assassinated outside a sleazy motel on the other side of town. Rather bizarrely, it was even better known for the live ducks it kept on the roof.

Every day of their lives the poor creatures took part in a staged ritual where they were herded into a lift and taken down to the ground floor. On arrival, they were paraded around a lobby dotted with statues of themselves and every other animal under the sun, as they performed on cue for the benefit of gawping guests. One of the hotel's bars had been named 'The Dux' in their honour.

Desperate to slake his thirst before they were bussed to Mud Island for a soundcheck, Calum strode over to the white liveried flunky on desk duty.

"Excuse me," he enquired. "Where is The Dux?"

"Up on the roof," responded the hotel employee, the tone of his voice suggesting he was asked the same question every hour, every day, every week.

"You misunderstand me," the singer corrected him. "What I meant was, 'Where i-s The Dux'? Not, 'Where a-r-e the ducks' if you catch my drift."

"Oh, I'm sorry!" the concierge laughed at his mistake. "What you do is take a left by those elephants you can see over there, and hang a right as soon as you get to the giraffes. Then, if you keep on going a little bit further, you take the third on the left by the monkeys and you'll see The Dux on the right by the snakes."

Calum looked totally baffled. "Is that right?"

"Trust me," implored the guy behind the desk. "Oh, and if you do come to the tigers, you've gone too far," he added for good measure.

"One of us has," remarked Calum, wishing he'd never asked.

Very late the following morning, over a huge cooked breakfast, the band had been discussing the previous night's gig – and the two Southern belles who'd entertained Calum until the early hours.

"Are we all set to go?" asked Jay. "The car's waiting outside with the engine running."

Minutes later, breakfast over, bill taken care of, they all piled into the limousine to set off in the direction of Sun Studios, where Elvis had made his earliest records in the fifties.

"Isn't this just fantastic?" Calum exclaimed on arrival, immediately admiring the tiny front office.

It had been left exactly the way it looked when Elvis walked through the door to cut his first demo all those years ago. The judiciously placed photograph on the desk showing the office as it was fifty-five years earlier offered conclusive proof. Quite eerily, nothing had changed. Lamentably, by far the most interesting part of the tour for anal-retentive folk like Calum and Jay was the studio's control room, which was closed to the public.

"These," revealed the tour guide, pointing towards the synthetic ceiling tiles, "are the same tiles Elvis stared up at for inspiration."

"I don't think I've ever heard so much crap in my life," said Calum, incredulous at the tripe this woman was spouting.

"And these," she blathered on, pointing to the floor this time, "are the same tiles Elvis walked on. But what is truly amazing," she continued to dribble, "is most of the instruments you see here also date from that period."

"Bullshit!" Jay exploded. "She's making all this up." He knew for a fact most of the instruments dated from the seventies or later. Hadn't she read any of the hundreds of books on the subject? This was a gigantic scam. "You should be ashamed of yourself," he chastised the girl, who was trying to make a few bucks for herself during the holidays.

Truly disappointed by the Sun Studios experience, they climbed into the limousine ready to fall on their knees and worship at the single biggest tourist attraction in Memphis.

"Graceland," Jay directed their chauffeur.

"It's eye-ronic," confided the driver, about to give them a local history lesson. "Since Elvis died, Elvis Presley Boulevard has become a predominantly black neighbourhood."

"Why is that ironic?" asked Jay.

"I'll tell you what's ironic my friend," he replied, revealing the meanest cackle this side of the Mason-Dixon line. "The black folk around here fucking hated him."

The first thing that struck them when the limousine stopped opposite Graceland was how low the surrounding walls were.

"Amazing to us, in this day and age of security-conscious stars," opined Jay. "I reckon virtually anybody below the age of fifty could vault over it at any point along the street. I'll bet even I could do it."

"Go on," Simon encouraged him.

"No wonder he was so fucking paranoid," sniggered Calum as he gazed at the famous wrought iron gates with musical stave motifs that Elvis had often been photographed beside. "These aren't very tall either," he commented, pointing towards them. "He must have been shorter than they said," concluded the singer. This was borne out later in the tour when they took a close look at some of the suits Presley wore onstage. "So which tours do you think we should take today? I'd like to see his planes myself."

"The platinum tour," Simon shot back. "That way we get to see the house, the planes, the bikes and his vast car collection."

In order to get Elvis Presley's personal jets all the way from the airport to the lot they now occupied opposite Graceland, it had been necessary to tow Hound Dog II and the Lisa Marie there, minus their wings. Then, after their final leg of the journey down Elvis Presley Boulevard, the wings were reattached.

"God, this is tacky," whined David, after taking a cursory look around the interiors. "I can only assume the designer responsible was given a ginormous pile of cash and the brief 'taste no object'."

Whereas it was fair to say The King's taste in interior design had been the subject of much derision, nobody could fault his choice in motorcycles and automobiles, least of all Simon.

"This is blowing my mind," he said, scrutinising the contents of the car museum.

Presley's unique collection included Harley Davidson, Triumph, Porsche, Rolls-Royce, Mercedes, Ferrari, Lamborghini, Cadillac and plenty of others.

"The lucky bastard had twenty-two cars and bikes," Simon bemoaned his lot. "I'd settle for just one of them."

"Which one would that be?" David asked, sensing the drummer was in his element.

"That one over there." He pointed towards a restored pink 1955 Cadillac.

After spending another half hour indulging the drummer, they boarded a courtesy coach that ferried them across the road to Graceland.

"This is all too much," admitted Calum, a lump forming in his throat as they made the short journey up Presley's driveway to the front door, a journey Elvis would have made thousands of times.

Alighting from the coach, he marched straight over to the huge Corinthian columns that supported the Palladian arch dominating the comparatively tiny entrance. Tapping on one of the columns with his bare knuckles, he was greeted by a hollow ring.

"Thing's a fake. What a fucking swizz!"

Bitterly disappointed by this discovery, he'd always assumed the columns were hewn from solid blocks of stone shipped over from Italy.

"First Sun Studios, now this."

Setting aside his initial disappointment, closely followed by the others, Calum took a deep breath before stepping through the front door of Graceland.

"I think I've just died and gone to heaven," he said, coming over all misty-eyed.

While they traipsed through the rooms located on the ground floor and the basement, rooms Elvis had used in his lifetime, visitors weren't allowed upstairs to look at the toilet he fell off the night he died. Though given access to his dining room and kitchen did offer some small compensation.

"This is interesting," opined David, gazing at a dinner table built to accommodate eight diners at the most. "He couldn't have done much entertaining around a table this size. The one I have at home is bigger than this."

The kitchen area too was far smaller than David had imagined.

"No wonder Elvis sent his boys out at all times of the day and night to fetch him peanut butter and crispy bacon sandwiches. There's no room to cook in here."

"Surely it would have been cheaper and made more sense to extend the kitchen?" argued Calum.

"Maybe he couldn't get planning permission."

"I think we can discount that theory, Simon," said the singer. "Do you know what I find the most baffling aspect of this entire visit? There hasn't been a single reference to drugs.

Not one," he said, an aspect he found dishonest, prudish, and so typically fucking American.

"Actually there was," said Jay. "Our courtesy coach had a tiny, 'SAY NO TO DRUGS!' sticker on one of the windows.

Pacing the lawn outside in the searing Tennessee heat, Jay sensed this may be the best opportunity he would ever get to commune with The King on such a personal level. With this in mind, he reached into his pocket to retrieve the joint he'd rolled specifically for the occasion.

"Elvis," he muttered, "this is for you, man."

As he made to light the joint poking out of his mouth, he could see a security guard heading towards him.

"Excuse me, Sir," the man in uniform began to rebuke him, gesticulating at the offending stogey firmly clenched between the guitarist's teeth. "This is a no smoking zone." He pointed towards another uniformed person in the distance. "Can you see the policeman standing over there?"

"Yes."

"If you light up your cigarette I'll have him come over here and arrest you… Sir," he added.

"Cigarette?" Jay repeated. He grinned awkwardly as he replaced the joint in his top pocket. "No problem."

Quite frankly, he found it hard to imagine Elvis would have given a toss one way or the other. But if he had been there, wouldn't he have flashed the police badge President Richard Nixon gave him and told the guy to fuck off? Looking more paranoid than usual, Calum, who had until now been observing from a distance, strode over.

"You were taking a bit of a risk there."

"You're right, I was," he agreed, before breathing a small sigh of relief. "I think it's time to pay our final respects," he said to the others, who'd gathered around to see what all the fuss was about. "Time to visit The King's grave," he added, still seeking value for his tourist dollar.

Gazing in awe at Presley's grave, Simon noticed something wrong with the tombstone. He couldn't quite put his finger on it. Then he remembered his dad's funeral and the dyslexic florist.

"This is monstrous," he pointed towards it. "Check how they've spelled his middle name. The stonemason who inscribed it has spelled Aaron with just the one 'a' instead of two. You think they'd have spotted it by now and changed it," he said, overcome by emotion. "If only out of respect."

"I ask you. Is nothing sacred?" proclaimed the singer, amazed at the Americans' lack of interest in their own rock history. "Imagine how the English would react if they spelled Paul McCartney's name the wrong way on his gravestone. There'd be a national outcry."

"Well, I'm not sure about that," Jay mused, ready to stick the boot in for a good cause. "I think either the English would be pissed off because we're such sticklers when it comes to spelling, or there'd be dancing in the streets."

"Why?" asked Simon.

"Because we'll never have to look at his thumb sticking up in the fucking air again or listen to those horrible fucking records he keeps making."

CHAPTER TWENTY-SIX

After slogging their way across the southern states, the band had earned the right to a weekend off in Malibu. It was imperative they recharge their batteries before embarking on the final leg of the tour. Tired of Holiday Inns, where the rooms looked identical, they'd taken it in turn to lobby Symes for an alternative this weekend. Sensing they wouldn't take 'no' for an answer, he'd booked them in at the renowned Casa Malibu. While it backed right on to the beach, it offered a number of suites facing directly on to the ocean, two of which the band had commandeered for the weekend.

Basking in the warm evening sun outside on the deck, Calum wished his mates could see him now. Lost in thought, he drained an ice-cold Bud, marvelling at the descending fireball on the horizon that signalled the end of another day in paradise. Too knackered to do anything but savour this magical moment, he surrendered to nature, listening as the waves crashed on to the majestic Pacific shoreline. Then, with one annoyingly deft squeeze of an empty beer can, Simon shattered this peaceful idyll.

"Don't suppose any of you fancy coming to Disneyland tomorrow? I spoke to Basil and he said we could use the tour bus."

"I'll come if I don't have to navigate," indicated the cartographically dyslexic member of the band.

"Me too," Brian volunteered. "I could use a little light entertainment."

"You can count me in," croaked David, on the verge of losing his voice. "Sounds like fun. Are you coming with us?"

"Am I fuck!" replied the singer, still gazing out at the horizon.

"Why not?" asked Simon.

"What you see over there is what it's all about," he motioned, pointing in the distance towards the setting sun. "By comparison, Disneyland is a total irrelevance."

"Maybe it is. But I still want to go."

"Why Simon?"

"So I can tell all my mates I've been there."

"Simon, in terms of entertainment it's nothing more than unsophisticated tosh for the masses. It's displacement activity for people with nowhere else to go and nothing better to do. It's bogus, Simon. So do me a favour and count me out."

"Can we bring you anything back then?" he persisted, unhappy at leaving Calum behind on his own.

"Not that I can think of."

"I know! I've got it."

"Got what?"

"Why don't I bring you one of those Mickey Mouse hats with sticky out ears on it? I'll buy you one as a present if you like."

"No thanks."

"What colour would you like? Blue or red?"

"Simon. Why don't you all fuck off there and leave me out of your plans?"

"Surely there must be some sort of souvenir we can bring you back."

"Now I come to think of it Simon, there is."

"Oh? And what might that be?"

"A photograph of some stupid bastard falling off one of the rides," replied the singer, suddenly brightening up at the prospect.

"It's a tall order," acknowledged Simon, still eager to please. "But I'll take my camera along and do my best."

Originally intended for children, Disneyland was built in the fifties on land in Anaheim previously utilised for fruit farming. Today it played host to a different type of customer. All of them large and over the age of twenty, many of them obese, not one would admit to acting like a child. A Mecca for people who refused to grow up, today Disneyland was one full of adults clutching ice creams the size of sombreros.

The band and Basil were in their element as they pulled off West Katella Avenue into the gigantic car park that sits behind the theme park.

For those who regard queuing as a life-enhancing experience, the morning was well spent. David could hardly wait for his own birthday to come round, let alone queue. Neither did he care for the overpowering, sickly aroma generated by the churro and doughnut stands that peppered the premises.

Taking a break over lunch that had more to do with calories than common sense, he made a swift calculation on the back of his napkin. It transpired that at least ninety per cent of their morning had been spent shuffling along in slow motion, standing in line in the burning heat.

Polishing off his third hot dog of the day, Basil turned to find a five and a half foot mouse standing beside him.

"I'll bet it gets fucking hot in there," he grinned at the mouse, its arms outstretched ready to pose for another shutter happy punter.

The mouse nodded dutifully, but said nothing.

Blatant curiosity getting the better of him, Basil began to probe at the mouse's rear, the other hand still clutching a hot dog.

"Don't your bollocks cop a serious toasting inside all that fake fur?" he speculated, as he began to stroke the furry creature's chest. Then, before Mickey Mouse had a cat in hell's chance to reply, Basil took a well-aimed lunge at its crotch.

"Pervert! You vile bastard!" the woman inside the costume yelled at the top of her voice. "Take that," she added. Slugging her assailant in the face, she felled poor Basil with a single blow.

"Jesus!" he complained to the security men dragging him to his feet. "What does she do in her spare time? Eat nails for breakfast?"

"She's a stuntwoman," grinned the older of the pair. "Piece of work, ain't she?"

"She's what?" winced Basil, touching the bruise on his forehead as they ejected him from the premises.

Back inside Disneyland, the others, taking pity on Basil, decided to take just two more rides before joining him in the car park and heading back to Malibu. Twenty minutes later, disaster struck.

Calum called him careless. Jay said he was jinxed. David insisted he was downright dopey. But it was Simon, who had no opinion on the subject whatsoever, who managed to capture it on his new video camera.

Brian had his own theory as to how he'd slipped as they disembarked from the water ride, insisting a combination of impatience and bad luck had been his undoing.

Though it would have been easy to sympathise with anyone who'd broken an arm in two places, Brian had in this instance been his own worst enemy. He'd been drinking steadily from the moment he set foot in Disneyland, swigging Jack Daniel's from a hip flask concealed carefully from the others in a brown paper bag. Drunk or unlucky, the outcome was the same. The remainder of the tour was cancelled and Brian's future with the band looked distinctly shaky. He had, in effect, signed his own death warrant.

CHAPTER TWENTY-SEVEN

Days after their premature return to England, Brian, his right arm in plaster supported by a sling, tendered his resignation. Interestingly, instead of quoting the usual 'musical differences', he came clean in the official press release by stating his heart was no longer in the project. While their parting had been a fairly amicable one, given their rocky relationship, Symes wasn't particularly sad to see Brian go.

Since Symes had promised US promoters they'd return before the end of the year to fulfil all outstanding contractual obligations, the need to find a new bass player was imperative. The search for his replacement began in earnest.

Two weeks after the first ad had appeared in the music press, they'd auditioned what seemed like every second bass player in north London, with no sign of a replacement in sight.

"How many are we due to see today?"

"Ten of the fuckers," complained the guitarist. "One's coming down from Scotland for the audition. I hope he doesn't expect us to pay his train fare."

"Any of them read music?"

"Calum, none of us can except for David. I doubt if this guy can read English, he's from Glasgow. Talk of the devil," he said, motioning towards the door.

"Am I in the right place?" asked the six and a half foot bass player dressed in a kilt.

"Certainly are."

"Ma name is James but you can call me Jamie."

"Why are you wearing a kilt?" asked the guitarist.

"I thought it would make me more memorable, if you get ma drift."

"What do you usually wear?" inquired David, thinking he looked frightful. "Jeans? Leather jacket maybe?"

"If I'm doing a gig it's usually striped leggings with a matching top and a headscarf with skulls and crossbones. Cool huh?"

"Very," lied the keyboard player.

"Anyway, shall we try a couple of numbers and see what's happening? Or not, as the case may be?"

"Ready when you are," replied the man in the kilt after Basil had plugged him into a spare amp.

"How about we kick off with 'Brown Sugar'," Jay suggested. "Do you know that one?"

"No."

"What about 'Walk on the Wild Side'?"

"Ah, don't know any of David Bowie's stuff," admitted the Scotsman, blowing his chances of landing the gig with those eight words.

"He was bloody useless," said Simon, after they'd shown him the door. "Couldn't keep time, couldn't lock in, all over the bloody place he was."

And on it went, one dud musician after the other. But when they'd almost given up hope of resolving the situation, Symes received a CD in the post. On it were four of the finest songs they'd ever heard supported by some stylish bass playing that put them in mind of McCartney at his very best. Not only that, this guy could sing, too.

Days later at their rehearsal studio, Grant Thomas stunned them all with his audition. Funk, soul, blues, metal, country, jazz, or hardcore – he had it all nailed. They'd never heard a player like him. Their search was over.

After giving his seal of approval, Symes put Grant on salary for a six-month probationary period prior to his being invited to join the band as an equal full member. Smart guy that he was, Grant joined the band that afternoon.

"So tell us something about yourself."

"I'm the son of Trinidadian immigrants who made a bomb running a highly successful pharmaceutical supplies company in the Home Counties."

"Yeah," Calum laughed. "But what about you? What have you been doing with your life?"

"Three US tours supporting different artists. Artists you've probably never heard of. It was all a bit of a drag but good practice for the real thing."

In the following weeks Simon, David and Jay spent time rehearsing Grant until he could play all their songs backwards. Apart from being note and word perfect, the diligent bassist had memorised amp settings and effects patches for every song he'd be required to perform live.

Across the river, getting his act together as best he could, Calum had checked himself into the Priory Clinic in Roehampton. Trying to come to terms with substance abuse, he was determined to clean up once and for all and kick the ferocious cocaine habit he'd picked up on the road.

"Can do it. Can do it," the singer intoned.

As the cold turkey took hold, sweat began to ooze from every pore in his body. Both he and the bedclothes were soon drenched. Then he started to shiver again. This process would repeat itself throughout the night.

"Can do it. Can do it."

Partaking of his third consecutive bottle of Merlot, Jay talked shop with Grant, oblivious to the presence of his girlfriend, Allanah. In addition to cancelling the newspapers while he and his chums had been gallivanting around America, she'd cancelled the milk, watered his marijuana plants, made sure the bills were paid and scored some dope for all of them. Nobody had even had the courtesy to thank her and she was furious.

"Self, self, bloody self!" she exploded, bringing the conversation to a grinding halt.

Jay frowned. He hadn't been shagging anybody while he was out on the road.

"Something I said? Just tell me what I've done to annoy you."

"You take me for granted." He looked bewildered. "You fucking well do." A study in provocation, her face was a mere six inches from his. "Why don't you shove it!" she yelled at him before storming out of the bar.

"What the fuck was that all about? Wrong time of the month? Must be the wrong fucking time of something."

"Perhaps," Grant suggested, "you just need to spend a little more time with her. I'm sure she loves you."

"Well, she's got a funny way of showing it."

With the stakes high and pressure building, Symes knew that if the album or single failed to go Top 10 in America, Platinum would pull the plug on the vital funding the band required to continue as a unit. This blunt message had been given to him after the abrupt cancellation of their US tour – one he had yet to communicate to the band.

There was another skeleton in his closet, too. As Brian had suspected for some time, his former manager was far from squeaky clean. And after unearthing evidence to prove his claims, which came from a friend at Scotland Yard, Brian decided to pay Calum a visit in Roehampton.

Positively glowing when they hugged, Calum looked fitter than Brian had seen him in a long while. He'd responded well to treatment and appeared to have rid himself of his dependency. It wasn't long before Brian imparted what he'd learned.

"What a con artist!" exclaimed Calum, when Brian revealed Symes was a discharged bankrupt who'd served time behind bars for fraud and embezzling a former employer. "That's incredible."

"That's not all," Brian continued, out for revenge. "Seymour Levy was serving time for exactly the same offence, at exactly the same time, in exactly the same prison."

"Is all of this true?"

"I'm afraid so. I also discovered the two of them shared a cell together for a short while. If you ask me, that's more than pure coincidence."

"I'm gob smacked. I really don't know what to say about all this. I need to talk to the others. Is there anything else I should know?"

"Yes. After inspecting the recording and management contracts we signed, a qualified barrister told me they weren't worth the paper they were written on. Basically, we've all been stitched up. Symes has us by the short and curlies."

"What do you think we should do about it?"

"If I were you I'd get the contracts checked independently. As soon as possible."

What idiots they'd been. How many times had they been advised to have their contracts read? How many other bands had been ripped off in this fashion over the years? The answer was hundreds. It hardly mattered. Studying the remains of his coffee, Calum recovered his composure.

"You didn't have to do this," he said, placing both arms around Brian's shoulders in a warm embrace. "I'm grateful to you. We all are."

A single tear rolled down his cheek.

CHAPTER TWENTY-EIGHT

The engraved brass plaque on the mahogany door read Hamilton, Michael, Davies & Partners. Located in Great Portland Street in London's West End, this legal practice had strong ties with the music business. It had also come highly recommended by a friend of Jay's, who'd called upon their services after a spectacular falling out with his own record label. And the person who'd solved his problems was the man they'd come to see today, Marcus Davies.

A flamboyant dresser with a penchant for one-of-a-kind, hand-painted silk bow ties, this modern day dandy adorned his buttonhole daily with a fresh carnation. The owner of impeccable manners and a self-deprecating sense of humour, he could have found work on the alternative comedy circuit. And if anybody doubted him on this score, his voice mail played 'The Sting'.

Seated in the lobby area, the band had all sworn off booze the previous night realising they would all need clear heads to have the remotest chance of understanding the intricacies of their management contract. Like their recording contract and every other contract they'd never read, it was peppered with the kind of language only lawyers understood.

"He's ready to see you now if you'd like to follow me," beckoned Davies' pretty secretary. All smiles and uplift brassiere, the girl sporting the little black Agnès B cardigan reserved her biggest smile of all for Calum.

Since his recovery, and with the help of a new hairstyle featuring judicious highlights and thick, angled sideburns, the singer had begun to look his devilishly handsome self again. David had already noticed how the new look amplified the singer's finely chiselled cheekbones.

"Good morning," Davies greeted them, as he shut the door behind her. "Do be seated and make yourselves comfortable. That's better. Now, is there anything I can get you?"

"A new manager perhaps?" suggested Jay.

"Is that all?" beamed the lawyer. "Nothing else?"

"How about your secretary's phone number?" said Calum.

"Very good, V-E-R-Y G-O-O-D," enthused Davies, recognising a fellow comedian when he was in the presence of one. "While I have been known to move mountains, there are certain aspects of life beyond even my control. Ha-ha."

The man with the florid complexion unfastened the middle button of his double-breasted suit to reveal a well-upholstered girth and settled back into his equally well-upholstered leather chair. He began to study the notes pencilled in the margins, punctuating the silence with only the occasional gasp. Davies cleared his throat.

"Whilst your manager has in the past been convicted of fraud, the wording of this contract would suggest to me he's still keeping his options open in that respect. I'd go even further than that and say this contract is so heavily biased, you'd need to be the most successful band in the history of rock 'n' roll before you'll see a penny from the fruits of your labours." There was deathly silence. "In addition to this, I've also examined your recording contract."

"And how does that look?" asked Jay.

"From the record company's point of view? Rather wonderful. From your standpoint? Horrendous. Though what truly baffles me is how Platinum managed to keep a straight face when you signed this odious document in their presence. It would be fair to say that between them, your manager and record company, you have been fleeced in the worst possible way imaginable."

"Forgive me if I'm slow on the uptake," David apologised, "but am I correct in saying we've all been well and truly shafted?"

"That is my view," replied the urbane Davies, fiddling with the garish turquoise silk handkerchief spilling out of his top pocket. "Your manager has you locked in tight. I would go even further than that: he owns you, body and soul. Hardly a desirable situation to be in," he continued unabashed, "but not irreversible. And I have seen worse, though for the life of me I can't remember when."

Jay shifted nervously in his seat. "So how do we get out of this mess?"

"First of all, I suggest you honour your outstanding American dates. We don't want your US promoters suing us when we already have all the litigation we need on our hands for the foreseeable future. Another recommendation I would like to make is this: take great care to extract as much cash as you possibly can from your merchandising sales."

"Why?"

"It may be the only money you'll see for some time to come. In the meantime, I'll make some discreet enquiries on your behalf in order that we can make some progress in changing what are, at the moment, legal and binding contracts. Now, have you any other questions?"

"What should I tell our new bass player?" asked Calum.

"Nothing."

"That's not fair."

"Simon, what is unfair to you and the others are these pieces of paper that you all signed. So far as I'm aware, Grant... is that his name?"

"Yes."

"Grant, unlike yourselves, has avoided the dubious privilege of signing his life away. Furthermore, he's on wages, which, to my mind, is a sounder proposition than either of these," he reiterated, waving the documents in front of him. "Meanwhile, in order that I may be effective on your behalf, it is of paramount importance that you discuss this matter with no one. Do I make myself clear?"

"Can I tell Brian we've discussed this? Because if it wasn't for him we wouldn't be here today."

"Since his name appears on both documents, you may."

"Can I tell my mum?"

"Certainly not," Davies groaned, wondering whether the drummer was deaf. "It is imperative we remain discreet at all times."

Feeling he might have a future in rock 'n' roll after all, Calum tested his luck with one more roll of the dice.

"Marcus, are you absolutely sure I can't have your secretary's phone number?"

With a burning desire to throttle his newest client, Davies shook his head, making it abundantly clear Calum wouldn't be winning the lottery that day.

The week after their meeting with the lawyer, SSB were back in America honouring the concert dates they'd cancelled. In their absence, their single 'My Day' had benefited from heavy airplay on FM radio stations on the West Coast. Identifying an opportunity to raise the band's profile further still, their manager capitalised on the buzz by adding a sprinkling of new dates, all in California.

On top this exposure was the series of radio spots lined up by Marcella, who lost no time in getting her message across. She laid into them from the moment they got into the limousine waiting at LAX.

"There's no margin for error, no room for fuck-ups!" she bellowed in the manner of a TV evangelist. "Screw up and you are five dead mother-fuckers… Simon!" she bellowed at the jet-lagged drummer. "Are you listening?"

Never letting up for a moment, her jaw on autopilot, she vented for the entire journey as they snaked their way through the rush-hour traffic down the San Diego Freeway bound for their hotel.

Throughout the remaining dates of the tour, the musicians did as the redoubtable Marcus Davies had advised them. At the end of every gig they demanded and got instant cash from the sales of T-shirts, sweatshirts, posters, baseball caps and other assorted memorabilia.

After handing over so many used dollar bills, Symes began to wonder how they could have developed such ferociously expensive drug habits in so short a space of time without any noticeable side effects.

While this tour had been nowhere near as punishing as the earlier one, by the time they boarded a plane for London, Simon was totally exhausted – only this time he couldn't blame the drugs and booze for his poor physical condition. His new lover was responsible for that. The same one he'd pleasured, served and obeyed during the band's stay in Los Angeles.

CHAPTER TWENTY-NINE

"Who's a dark horse now?" David taunted him. "Welcome to my sordid little world," he said to the drummer, as they began boarding the flight back to London.

"Was she wearing a Batwoman mask, shiny black PVC leggings, eight-inch spikes and a corset?" asked Jay.

"Did she crack her whip?" asked David, who'd been invited to make out in a bathtub filled with cold custard during the brief stopover in San Francisco.

"That dominatrix thing's not my cup of tea," claimed Calum, who entertained most forms of sexual deviancy.

"I find that hard to believe," commented the guitarist. "I'll bet you wouldn't say that if Ms Wonderbra offered to make you her sex slave for the day."

"On the contrary, dear boy. I'd be more than happy to lick any part of her scantily clad anatomy. Any part of it you care to mention. Including her boots."

"What about Marcella Mingovitch?" he said. "Would you lick hers?"

"Not in a million years. Woman's got feet like fucking boats. Must have taken Simon an hour and a half to lick them clean. Am I right, Simon?"

"What's your mum going to say when she finds out?" Grant asked. "What will she say when she sees you've had both of your nipples pierced?"

"I haven't had both nipples pierced," Simon protested. He was still pondering the merits of having the other one done.

"You're only jealous," he added, eyes smarting as he replayed in his mind those mad nights with Marcella.

Spiked black stiletto heels digging into the raw pink flesh of his flaccid stomach. Third-degree carpet burns on elbows and knees. Whip-induced welts across back and legs. Neck chafed by constant rubbing of the spiked dog collar he wore while she acted out her fantasies. He strapped to a rack. Her stretched to breaking point. Both suspended stark naked upside down from a cross.

"Actually, if you must know, she's quite shy."

"Shy?" they gasped, to a man.

"Next thing we know you'll be telling us how sensitive she is."

"She is, in private."

"You mean her privates are sensitive?"

"Just because you didn't get your end away while we were in California."

"Wrong again," corrected the singer. "I did shag one rather obliging, horny-as-my-dick-is-long beauty while we were staying in Los Angeles. Couldn't get enough of me."

"You dirty old sod," chortled Jay. "You were shagging that Mexican chambermaid, weren't you?"

"Have you been spying on me?"

"No need. I already know how your squalid little mind works. So you did shag her?"

"I did, and more than once, I might add. Had a two-up one night – her and an exceedingly obliging friend."

"*Two-up*," Jay whistled, impressed by his chum's energy levels since his stint at the Priory. "Hope you didn't leave the room splattered with fruit and ice cream this time around."

"Her friend was particularly accommodating," smiled the band's resident lothario, casually sniffing the fingers of his right hand. "I've no idea where they learn all this perverted stuff."

"From people like you," said his mate.

Within weeks of their return to the UK, 'My Day' had gone Top 10 in the US, while their debut album had been clinging on to the number 14 slot for the past three weeks.

Relieved their investment was finally showing signs of a return, Platinum had committed to releasing a second album. On the debit side, they'd insisted the band return to the US as soon as possible to capitalise on their chart success. But despite their status in America, the musicians were still pleading poverty. How on earth were they supposed to act like rock stars on £150 a week when their manager appeared to be rolling in the stuff?

Symes had bought a BMW Z4. Then he'd splashed out on a Harley Davidson. Soon he would put down a sizeable deposit on a large property in Notting Hill Gate. And while he was spending fifty-pound notes faster than the Bank of England could print them, the band was rehearsing new material underneath the railway arches in King's Cross.

Taking a break from laying down the backing tracks, they'd despatched Basil to buy a carton of milk, some king-size rolling papers and the latest issue of Q Magazine.

As soon as Basil returned, Jay snatched it from his hands. Scouring the pages, joint in mouth, he searched for mentions of the band, pictures of himself and anything else that might feed his ego. When he turned the page his eyes popped out on stalks. It was the headline that caught his attention: 'Q MAGAZINE JOURNALIST JOINS COLLECTED THOUGHTS'.

"Fuck me!" he coughed uncontrollably, before passing the joint back.

"Easy does it," Calum patted his back.

"Shut the fuck up. All of you, shut up and listen." He began to read.

'*Following in the footsteps of The Pretenders' Chrissie Hynde and the Pet Shop Boys' Neil Tennant, Q scribe Harvey*

Robertson has quit journalism to become the new drummer with Mancunian band Collected Thoughts, replacing former stixman Curt Levinson. Said Robertson: "Collected Thoughts have always been my favourite band and I'd like to think I can give them a shot in the arm." He went on to say, "We're giving notice to SSB, fronted by that mouthy Calum James. I predict by the end of the year they'll be consigned to the annals of history.'

"Well he should know all about mouthy twats, shouldn't he?" Calum fumed. "He wrote the fucking book, didn't he?"

"We've got to have a word with Andrew about all this bad press coverage we're receiving," David protested. "It's getting out of hand."

Calum's mobile rang. "Sshh," he directed, unable to hear what was being said. "Say again... Tell them what? I will... Bye." He turned to the others. "What's the most unimaginable gig you can think of us playing?"

"Madison Square Garden?"

"And how would we fill it, Simon?"

"With sand?" Jay speculated, much to the amusement of the others.

"How about Wembley?" said Calum.

"Wembley Arena!" whooped the drummer.

"Wembley Arena!" echoed Jay. "Unbelievable."

"Just bloody amazing," squealed David.

"What a fucking result," said Grant, who didn't normally swear.

"Guys," the singer interrupted, holding one hand aloft. "What Andrew actually said was Wembley Conference Centre."

CHAPTER THIRTY

"Let's not be naïve here, Andrew. People can get hold of police files. Are you sure your guys haven't twigged what's going on?"

"No. Everything's fine apart from the fact I heard they've hired the services of a lawyer."

Levy groaned. "What do you think they're up to?"

"They probably want someone to read the contracts. Whatever they're doing, we still have time to get things organised."

"And our other business? Are you sure they don't know anything about that?"

"Calm down, Seymour. I'm absolutely certain they know nothing of it. Anyway, how are things progressing with your mob, for want of a better word?"

"If bands' names were based on their intelligence, mine would be morally obliged to change theirs to Collected Noughts. They're as thick as pig shit, every last one of them."

"Well, there's a lucky break. Takes the pressure off you."

"They think I'm Mother Theresa, especially after I got Harvey Robertson to appear, as if by magic, saving their collective arses when that twat Curt Levison walked out on them. Don't you love it?"

"How long do you think it'll take before they tumble to what's going on?"

"Your lot or mine?"

"Both, you clown. While your boys may be thick, and one or two of mine may not be the sharpest tools in the box, we do know for a price they can hire people who do have brains. So for the time being, I think it would be wise if we both kept an eye on the ball. And remember one thing…"

"Yes?"

"We are not friends. We are sworn enemies. Don't forget that. It's important to maintain the illusion."

"You're absolutely right. Hazarding a guess, I'd say it would be two or three months before they get the faintest whiff of what's going on. By which time we'll be out of mind, out of sight and, with a bit of luck, out of the country, leaving behind ten brainless twats who'll have to learn how to fend for themselves."

"You did say ten?"

"Yes. Harvey Robertson thinks we should add a keyboard player as soon as possible."

"Next thing he'll be wanting your job," mused Symes. "Anyway, the money you paid him to stitch up my boys should help maintain his liquidity for some time to come. I have to go now."

"What's the hurry?"

"We're gigging."

"Where?"

"Wembley."

"When?"

"Tonight."

"I haven't seen any advertising for the gig around town and it's the kind of thing I would notice – after all, we are in the same business. Did you forget to pay the people who organise your flyposting? Or is this gig by sole invitation only?"

"No, I didn't. And no it isn't." Symes sounded peevish.

"Well, I didn't know you were playing the Arena. And if I don't know, I doubt if anybody else does. Did you advertise it on your website?"

"No, it hasn't been advertised on our website. For the simple reason we haven't got a fucking website, you snot-nosed bastard. And we're not playing at Wembley Arena either, you opinionated arsehole."

"So where are you playing?"

"Wembley Conference Centre. Not that it's any of your business."

"Wembley Conference Centre! You're a pisser, Andrew. That's easily the funniest thing I've heard all week. Wembley Conference Centre. Strapped for cash, are we?"

"Something like that. The new place in Notting Hill is eating up my reserves and carpeting the place cost far more than I'd originally budgeted for."

"You're beginning to sound like Michael Caine."

"What the hell has Michael Caine got to do with any of this?"

"Didn't you know? It's not as if Michael Caine ever stops banging on about it. Telling the world the reason he made so many lousy films was to pay his carpet bills. You, on the other hand, play lousy gigs to pay yours. I'm grateful you don't manage me."

"The feeling's mutual. Oh, and by the way, we're taking delivery of the new flight cases today."

"Excellent," chuckled Levy. "Progress at last."

"You played where last night?" asked the lawyer.

"I already told you. Wembley Conference Centre."

Having imbibed one too many brandies over lunch, the lawyer thought his mind was playing tricks on him. "I did hear correctly, didn't I? You did say Wembley Conference Centre?"

"I did," replied Calum, failing to share Davies' amusement on this occasion.

Calum was ashamed they'd agreed to play the gig in the first place. Who the hell played at Wembley Conference Centre? 'Nobody' was the answer. As far as he was concerned, the Conference Centre was a malignant tumour attached to the body proper. While Wembley Arena said you were hot and getting hotter, Wembley Stadium said you'd arrived at the very pinnacle of your chosen profession. But what the fuck did Wembley Conference Centre say about a band? Calum consoled himself knowing they hadn't invited anybody to witness their collective embarrassment first-hand.

"My, my, we have been industrious," Davies enthused, acknowledging the bagful of dollar bills. "I see you managed to make the acquaintance of the folk running your merchandising." Transfixed, he watched Calum tip the contents of the brown paper bag on to his desk as if it were confetti.

"I'm sorry it's all in ones, but that's the way most fans pay for the stuff. Count it if you want. There should be ten-thousand dollars."

"If it's all the same to you," Davies demurred, thinking better of soiling his hands on untaxed income, "I'll have my secretary do that for us.

"Jocasta," he called into the intercom, "could you possibly spare us a minute or two? I need you to count some money. It will stand you in good stead when you meet your rich, handsome young knight on a white charger." The old roué grunted lasciviously as he released the red button he'd been holding down. "Daresay I wouldn't mind boffing the young filly meself," he chuckled, much to the surprise of the others.

Breezing into the room, the fragrant Jocasta Templeton had it all – and she knew it. Aware of this effect she had on men, she'd inherited an exquisite bone structure and inhabited a body most women would be happy to rent. She'd also benefited from an expensive education that had developed an already pin-sharp mind. Added to all this, she was kind, keen, eager to please, quick to learn and a pleasure to be around. Men just wanted to fuck her senseless.

"Did you make any progress with the contracts while we were out of the country?" asked the singer, watching Jocasta's rear cross the room as he searched for any traces of a visible panty line.

"Just a little," blinked Davies.

Similarly distracted, his gaze was riveted to her cleavage, the latter swelling before his eyes as she leant over the desk to scoop up the mound of dollar bills.

"Progress in these matters tends to be slow," he added, half-heartedly, dreaming of the day he would drown in her perfumed crevice.

"Really?" said Calum, unable to wrench his eyes from her pert arse, mere inches from his face now.

"I'm afraid so," averred Davies, staring blatantly at her protruding nipples as she picked up the last of the cash.

"I see," said Calum, temporarily blinded by her bodacious buns.

"Oh! I'm so sorry," she blushed after reversing bottom first into the singer's surprised but welcoming face.

"No problem," he assured her, a cross-eyed grin spreading across the bit that came closest.

"I hear you're quite big," she said, twirling her hair.

"Jocasta!" Davies scolded her. "What would your father say?"

"I meant in America," she insisted, her salacious smile suggesting otherwise.

CHAPTER THIRTY-ONE

"And where the fuck am I supposed to put all this shit?" Basil swore, taking a well-aimed kick at the large silver box on wheels standing beside him.

"How would I know?" replied the driver, his fat, white, hairy arse hanging out of greasy, over-sized jeans.

"Where do you want these?" the guy who was helping him asked. Someone else who worked for cash in hand, he wheeled two more flight cases into the already overcrowded rehearsal space.

"Do you think Andrew bloody Symes told me they were coming?"

"Dunno mate. Dunno who he is, do I?"

"Of course he fucking didn't."

"If you say so."

"Do you think he made arrangements to get rid of the old ones?"

"How the hell would I know?" said the bewildered driver. "Like I was saying, I've never met this bloke Andrew whatever-his-name-is."

"Well, he fucking didn't."

"Listen, mate," declared the man who was merely following orders. "Early this morning I left Manchester with instructions to deliver this lot..." He indicated the valuable but apparently unwanted cargo. "Which I'm doing."

"You want to know what my boss is?"

"Tell me."

"A fucking cocksucker!"

"He might well be, but then I'm not clairvoyant. So, if you could sign and print your name right here to say you've taken delivery of thirty-two boxes on wheels, I'll be on my way."

"Thirty-two flight cases we don't need," Basil continued to complain, glaring at the gleaming new deliveries cluttering up the room's every available inch of floor space. "Where do I sign?" he asked, admitting defeat at last.

"Right here, mate," indicated the driver. He winked. "Gratuities are, ahem, at your discretion."

"You must be joking."

"Wot! No tip?"

"My tip to you is get your fat fucking arse and irritating northern accent out of here and fuck off back to Manchester, or wherever it is you came from." And with that sterling piece of advice he slammed the door shut in the driver's uncomprehending face.

"You were a bit rough on him there," Jay laughed, keeping out of harm's way on the other side of the rehearsal room, effectively cut off from Basil by a gigantic wall of flight cases. "He was only doing his job, mate," he shouted over the top.

As Jay clambered over to reach Basil on the other side, he glanced at these new acquisitions, which came in all shapes and sizes.

"They're beautifully put together," he observed, stepping into view before disappearing inside one of the larger flight cases for a closer look. "I wonder why they made the interior walls so deep?" he said, his voice deadened by the thick foam padding. "I don't think I've ever seen so much padding in a flight case."

"They're bloody heavy, I don't know about anything else," moaned Basil, whose job it was to manhandle them. "Not that you give a toss. You won't be lifting them."

Sleek, shiny, silver. All of them were stamped with SSB's unmistakeable logo featuring the three letters intertwined.

Flight cases were a key element in any band's armoury, designed to withstand the punishment of being hauled in and out of venues and rolled on and off trucks and planes.

"Why do you think Andrew ordered them?"

"Search me."

"It's not as though the old ones are falling apart."

"No, they're not. There's absolutely nothing wrong with them, as far as I can see. Why don't you ask?"

"What do you think of them?"

"Me? I couldn't give a shit," said Basil, a restorative cup of tea in his hand but nowhere to drink it.

Days before the band returned to America, Calum developed an inexplicable fear of flying. The more he flew, the more scared he'd become of taking off, landing, clear air turbulence and black holes in the atmosphere. But what had begun to bother him of late were the Kapton wiring assemblies he'd been reading about in the newspapers. Despite the plethora of warnings about this potentially lethal fire hazard lurking in the tail of some jets, most of those fitted with these systems were still flying. Which ones, he had no idea.

"Why don't you take a sleeping pill before you get on the plane?"

"Why? Because if the flight's delayed by two hours, Andrew, he'll be lying comatose outside duty free and nobody will be able to wake him when they call for us all to board," Jay explained. "Our singer will be more Rip Van Winkle than rock star."

"I hadn't thought about that aspect," admitted Symes, whose job it was to think about the important details everybody else missed. "Then why not take a sleeping pill right after you board, as soon as you're seated? Why are you frowning at me like that?"

"I don't do drugs anymore."

"Of course, it completely slipped my mind. Silly me," Symes sympathised, though for the life of him he couldn't see the connection between taking a sleeping pill and shovelling untold quantities of cocaine up one's nostrils.

"What's the story behind these new flight cases, Andrew?"

"Huh?"

"We were all wondering why you bought them."

"Isn't it obvious, Jay?"

"Not to simple souls like us."

"I ordered them because the old ones were looking rather tired and sad."

"They look fine to me. And they look fine to Basil."

"You mean you bought thirty-two new flight cases because you thought our old ones looked grubby?" said Calum, another who didn't consider they needed replacing.

"Precisely," argued Symes, about to play the vanity card. "After all, a band of your stature must manage its image. Wouldn't you agree?"

"Who's paying for them?"

"Since they'll be your property I presume you will. Is there a problem with that?"

"No," replied Jay. "Not at the moment. But can I use this opportunity to broach another subject that's been bothering us for some time?"

"Go ahead."

"Calum, David, Simon and myself have a number of significant reservations regarding the management contract we signed with you. And, to a slightly lesser degree, the way you've handled certain other issues on our behalf such as our recording contract with Platinum – one we signed in your presence, I might add."

"And what do you propose to do about it?" he inquired politely.

Symes, visibly stiffening, didn't like what he was hearing. Threatening people with lawyers was his territory and third-party warfare didn't come cheap. He knew litigation had drained the coffers of men mightier than he.

"We've hired a lawyer to study both contracts and we're taking it from there."

"Haven't you left it a little late in the day for all that?"

"Not according to our lawyer."

"What's the name of this firm you've hired to attack me?" He fidgeted nervously, beads of sweat beginning to form on his brow.

"Hamilton, Michael, Davies & Partners in Great Portland Street."

Symes took a deep breath. He'd heard about this firm and knew they were highly rated, a factor that was hardly likely to help him.

"Surely we can sort things out amicably, without resorting to law?"

"Not at this late stage," said Calum, speaking on behalf of the entire band.

The US tour began in earnest the following Friday when they boarded a jet bound for Dallas. Scheduled to open in Texas, it would wend its way through dozens of minor markets in states they hadn't played on previous visits. Calum, still coming to terms with his fear of flying, hadn't proved to be the liability the others had imagined, though the flight had its moments.

Halfway across the Atlantic the singer awoke with a jolt when he thought he smelled burning. More worrying, the accompanying message on the overhead Tannoy sounded like '*This is your Kapton calling*' to his ears, if nobody else's. After Jay had calmed him down and Calum fell asleep again, the latter was woken a second time by the Tannoy and a message that sounded like '*Die last, torched earth*'. It was, in fact, the captain announcing their imminent arrival at Dallas-Fort Worth.

Still disorientated by the time difference, Symes was awoken early the following morning by his bedside telephone.

"Andrew," he acknowledged, in his bleary state of consciousness. "I hope whatever you have to tell me is important. *Extremely* important."

"Andrew, I have some great news for you." It was Jack Weisberg, Platinum's US head of A&R. "Are you sitting down?"

"No, Jack – lying down, since you ask. I believe it's called a bed," he yawned. "Do you have any idea what time it is here? Because according to my watch, which I have already adjusted to local time, it's four fucking thirty in the morning."

"I'm sorry but it's only two-thirty in the a-m here in Los Angeles and I'm so excited I couldn't sleep."

"Jack, what is it that's so urgent you couldn't have called me later when both of us would be awake? You better make it good."

"Are you listening?"

"Of course I'm bloody listening. You woke me up, remember?"

"The single has just gone to number one on the Billboard charts."

"You don't say."

"'My Day' has just gone to number fucking one, Andrew. Are you still listening to me?"

"Do I have any choice?"

"How does it feel to be number one in the USA?"

"Jack, stop!" Symes admonished him, his free hand disappearing beneath the crisp white cotton sheets for a furtive tug at his stiffy. "Is this some kind of game? Because if it is," he continued, transferring his affections to his balls to give them their first scratch of the day, "I'm way behind you on this one."

"Game?" returned the A&R man. "I'm not playing any fucking games here, pal. This is serious. This is business."

"You did say 'My Day' has gone right to the top of the Billboard singles chart?"

"I did," confirmed the native New Yorker, somewhat taken aback by Symes' apparent lack of enthusiasm.

Sprawled out on the bed with the sheet thrown back, the Englishman didn't make for edifying viewing nursing his burgeoning boner.

"Why don't I call you back later when the message has sunk in?" suggested the breathless Symes, tugging at his penis for all he was worth.

"Jeez!" spluttered the American through clenched teeth. "You Brits are so anal. Didn't you ever get excited just once in your life? On your birthday? Christmas? Halloween? Ever? Andrew? Hello?"

"I apologise if we English act a little too reserved for the likes of you Americans," Symes responded haughtily, ready to come any second. "But I suspect," he offered, eyes narrowing as he reached the final approach to the supreme moment of ejaculation, "it has a lot to do with upbringing."

"You don't say."

"In the end," he explained, groaning involuntarily, face contorted in ecstasy. "It's all about manners."

Suddenly reaching the vinegar stroke, conversation ground to a halt as he shot his load over the side of the bed to score a direct hit on a stray Gideon Bible lying on the floor.

"Is that so? Well, you can tell those stuff-shirt Brit clients of yours the only way they'll need to act from now on is famous."

"Why?" demanded Symes.

"Because they fucking well are now and this is fucking America not fucking Blighty, you fucking asshole."

"Well, thank you for that sound piece of advice."

"Don't mention it."

"I won't."

"I'll talk to you later, old buddy."

"I look forward to it, Jack."

A look of contentment on his face, a load off his mind and a second one over the side of the bed, Symes lay back on the pillow and went back to sleep.

"Does this city actually have a centre?" David asked, somewhat mystified.

"Los Angeles does during the day. But at night, the place empties out."

"Why is that?" he asked the limousine driver.

"The folk who work in the downtown area where the major businesses are located return to their homes in the suburbs in the evenings. They're scattered all around here off the freeways, so downtown is safe during the day. But I wouldn't advise wandering around the area at night, especially if you're alone and don't know your way around. It's easy to get lost and there are some people hanging around out there you most definitely don't want to be having a conversation with. Drug dealers and the like."

The City of Angels being a haven for rock 'n' roll musicians, the band were all in ebullient mood as they negotiated the busy downtown traffic on their way to collect their first gold record in America in recognition of one million sales of 'My Day'.

During the ceremony each member of the band was presented with a gold record in turn. Highly prized by the industry, it was a well-known fact that these gold records were produced from 'cutouts', another artist's records the label couldn't sell. Sprayed gold after the original name had been covered up with the recipient's, they were then handed out to bands like SSB in recognition of chart success. When the hand shaking and backslapping was over with, Jack Weisberg approached Symes.

"How are you doing, you old bugger?" he said, adopting the American affectation of pretending to be British when clearly you're not.

"Hello Jack. Managed to calm down?"

"I have, what about you? Last time we spoke you sounded like you were jerking off. Then again, given my impression of the British with their hidden depths of reserve and reservoirs of charm, I imagine you wouldn't stoop so low. Would you?"

"Never," replied Symes, his cheeks taking on a pinkish hue.

"How's the tour going, buddy?"

"Very well, all things considered.

As you know we've been breaking in Grant Thomas, our new bass player. To his credit, he's really pulled out all the stops, hasn't let us down yet. He's delivering the goods onstage every night and you can't ask for more than that."

"Pleased to hear it, Andrew."

"Anyway," said Symes, "I'm not feeling too good – upset stomach I think. So I'm heading back to the hotel to rest for a while. I'm sure if I take something I'll be feeling far bouncier for the show tonight. Will you be coming?"

"I'll be there waiting for you."

Lost deep in thought for the entire drive back to the hotel, Symes inadvertently jumped a set of red lights at a major intersection. Fortunate there were no police present to record his misdemeanour, he narrowly escaped totalling the rental car.

Still shaking from his ordeal behind the wheel when he arrived back at the Holiday Inn, he took the elevator up to his room on the twelfth floor before double-locking the door behind him. With the *Do Not Disturb* sign in place, he proceeded to make a series of protracted calls on his mobile phone.

The last call he made to Miami that afternoon was odd in the sense that neither he nor the other person revealed their identities. Instead, they resorted to a code that rendered parts of their conversation unintelligible.

Meanwhile, back at the record company presentation, Simon, sporting a silly grin, was wearing a T-shirt bearing the legend 'WHIP ME, BEAT ME, MAKE ME FEEL CHEAP, BUY THE RECORD AND GIVE ME A WANK'. Hovering on the sidelines, Jack Weisberg approached him.

"What's a wank, Simon?"

CHAPTER THIRTY-TWO

Although SSB had been acting like rock stars for as long as any of them could remember, coping with fame wasn't something any of them had been trained to deal with. They were besieged day and night wherever they went, whatever they were doing, by either autograph hunters wanting to share in their fame or hangers-on desperate to bathe in the reflected glory.

During the earlier part of the tour none of them had raised any objections to being the focus of attention. They loved it or were too busy getting high to notice. But midway through the tour, this erosion of privacy was beginning to take its toll, with hotels in particular presenting a major problem if the band wanted to maintain any kind of anonymity.

This led to the adoption of pseudonyms. So throughout the tour David checked in as P. Soles. Competitive by nature, Calum went a step further, adopting the name R. Slicker. Meanwhile, Grant would become Richard Head, while Jay, posing as Terence Watt, now signed the register as T.Watt. The new, obedient Simon simply did as Marcella instructed him.

While there were distinct disadvantages to being famous, there were certain advantages to consider. The companies who constantly plied them with free musical equipment and the clothing manufacturers doing the same. The preferential treatment they got in restaurants. And how else would they have amassed such an impressive homemade porno collection?

One of the more ridiculous aspects of life on the road, though, was room service. What had started out as a simple request for a BLT or a club sandwich had degenerated rapidly into demands for moveable feasts of a different nature. Who could blame the band when hotel employees were vying for the chance to meet them, willing to do their bidding?

The truth, quite sadly, was that somewhere along the line these impressionable young women had confused fame with infamy. For them, balling a British rock star would enrich their lives. For them, the allure of reflected glory was sufficient reason to cast caution to the wind for an experience they might not treasure for the rest of their lives. What these women shared in common was the inability to resist the magnetic attraction of fame.

Relaxing by another pool after another sell-out concert in Scottsdale, Arizona, Jay and Grant were looking forward to visiting the Fender factory that afternoon after the legendary guitar company had offered them an endorsement deal. Under the terms of the agreement, Grant would play Fender basses exclusively and, in return, be allowed to select two instruments from the catalogue.

Jay had negotiated a signature-model deal for a guitar that would satisfy his exacting requirements, however ludicrous they may be. Guaranteed to assuage the vanity of the artist concerned, artist 'signature' models were also designed to whet the appetite of fans. The guitar companies prayed they would show up in droves at their local music stores to buy exactly the same model their hero played. The Fender Musical Instrument Corporation delivered another collective massage for the band's rampant egos when it chose Jay and Grant to front their new international marketing campaign.

They certainly had plenty to be happy about as they lingered over a late breakfast by the pool. Jay had his head buried in Ben Elton's latest book, while David scanned the showbiz section of USA Today. Grant, meanwhile, was admiring his own likeness in the tour programme. Symes smiled when he saw Simon's lips move as he leafed through a Superman comic.

"What are you reading?" he asked Calum.

"*Mr. Nice.*"

"Don't know it. Who wrote it?"

"Howard Marks."

"Never heard of him either."

"Everybody else has."

"What's it about?"

"This and that but his career mostly. He used to be in the import/export business."

"How could anyone make an interesting book out of something as banal as that?" asked Symes, shovelling another forkful of breakfast into the slot marked hungry, failing to realise it was already on the best-seller list. "Who'd be remotely interested in buying a book about something so prosaic? What did this Howard Marks fellow trade in?"

"Something highly desirable."

"You mean like precious gemstones or expensive automobiles?"

"No, Andrew. Howard Marks was the biggest dope smuggler on the planet bar none. I think it would be fair to say he was the grand pooh-bah of pot. Before he was caught and locked up."

"Christ! How long did he get?"

"Twenty years, fifteen on appeal. Which is a bit harsh if you ask me, he was only smuggling hash."

"What do you mean O-N-L-Y?"

"Imagine how long he'd have been banged up if he'd been smuggling coke."

"Imagine," Symes winced. "Can I borrow the book when you've finished with it?"

"Why? Are you planning to go into business?" the singer teased.

With the tour about to reach its climax in Florida that weekend, the band had assembled in New York City having spent the morning cruising the musical instrument stores on West 48 Street. Symes, who'd elected to stay back at the hotel, was perched on the end of a bed the size of a football field, talking into his mobile.

He called the local airport to check if the band's equipment had left, bound for Miami. During a second call, this time to Miami Airport, he chose once again to communicate in a coded language throughout his conversation with the other person.

"What colour are the lights?" he asked.

"We have orange," replied the Latin-American voice at the other end of the line.

"Today we have green," revealed Symes, this information finding immediate favour with whoever he was talking to.

"Eez eet een the air?"

"Today is my day, and tomorrow," Symes added cryptically, "will be yours."

Nobody said goodbye.

It was around midnight the following day when twenty people assembled in a virtually empty warehouse in downtown Miami. Acting like the professionals they undoubtedly were, they set about restoring the power, without which they couldn't work. Dressed in identical orange overalls and matching surgical gloves, they went about their business in total silence. Two of them started to unload the silver boxes from the truck backed up at the loading bay, others wheeled the recently arrived consignment into the warehouse.

They set to work immediately, systematically taking the boxes apart with power tools. Carefully, they removed the hundreds of rivets that had been holding them together. After achieving their goal in under three hours, the twenty workers, still dressed in their matching fatigues, proceeded to remove the white polythene packages secreted in the cavity wall linings. These appeared to contain some kind of powder. When the job was done, the hollow spaces in the boxes were painstakingly refilled with identical-sized white packages.

As the new day was dawning, the men, paid well for their time, began reassembling the final box utilising brand new rivets as they had with all the others. Satisfied at last with their night's work, the men began to reload the cargo on to the same truck that had delivered it to the warehouse the previous evening.

Before the door was closed and sealed, one of the younger men stepped forward, to break the code of silence they'd observed for six hours solid.

"Hey Domingo," he hissed, pointing towards the logo adorning the last box they'd loaded. It was the same logo stencilled on to all the silver boxes they'd loaded on the truck. "What does eet mean?"

The older man shrugged his shoulders. Either he didn't know or he didn't care. To him it was just another job. Still curious, the younger one examined it again. It comprised three letters, interlinked.

"SSB," he muttered to himself. "SSB."

CHAPTER THIRTY-THREE

By the time they arrived in Miami for their final concert, the band had been touring relentlessly for four months solid. While some were elated and others exhausted, they all agreed they were receiving the type of acclaim they'd been hankering after for years. The charts reflected this, too. While *Hearts & Souls* had dropped out of the US Top 20, 'My Day' was occupying the number one slot on the Billboard singles chart, a position it had held for six weeks now.

After storming into the band's dressing room minutes before they were due onstage, Symes failed to see the partially clad girls wedged behind the door, languishing on the floor. Tripping over the youngest, who was rolling a joint, he inadvertently fell arse over tit before joining them.

"Out, out, out!" he barked, dragging himself to his feet. "Go on, get out," he shouted at the tacky twosome. Shooing the semi-clad space cadets and their missing garments out into the corridor, he closed the door behind them.

"You might have let her finish rolling up before you booted them out."

"If I'd known you cared so much, I would have let her," said Symes sarcastically.

"I just fancied a smoke, that's all."

"Can we be serious for a moment? I have something important to say," he began in earnest. "First of all, let me start by saying I think we owe a huge debt of gratitude to Platinum."

"Fuck you!" Jay tore into him, still seething over the contract they'd signed with the label. "We don't need you to remind us of our obligations to Platinum."

"Andrew," said David. "I thought we had an unwritten rule? We don't discuss business before we go onstage. Well, go on, then," he urged him, his curiosity getting the better of him. "What is it?"

"Platinum," Symes continued, "have been able to work miracles on your behalf during your absence from the UK."

"Does that mean they're prepared to renegotiate our contract?"

"Erm, no, not exactly. But what they have been able to do is help secure your first number one there."

"Hang on a minute, did you say 'My Day' has gone to number one in England?"

"Jay," Symes squeezed his shoulder tightly. "Yes, you have achieved the nigh on impossible. Not only are you number one in the USA, you're now number one in the UK, too. It is something every band dreams of, yet so few achieve. I salute you."

At these words the room exploded around him.

"There's going to be one hell of a party tonight," beamed the singer.

"And this time the drinks are on me," his manager grinned, before turning serious again. "I do have another piece of news."

"Oh, here it comes, here it comes. I knew it, there had to be a catch. It wouldn't be the same otherwise," he berated Symes. "Well, go on, let's get it over with. Give us the bad news."

"What I have to tell you isn't bad news, Calum – at least, not for you it isn't. While you've been touring America these past months, things haven't been going so well for your favourite band. And if my information is correct, and it usually is, you'll be thrilled to hear that Collected Thoughts are on the verge of losing their recording contract. But then they do say revenge is best served cold."

"Christ!" exclaimed Calum. "You can say that again."

Not helped by the constant infighting, Collected Thoughts had, even with help from the repugnant Harvey Robertson, failed to make sufficient impact on the American charts to appease their paymasters at Sony. Unimpressed by its investment, the label was about to pull the plug.

"When did you find out about this?"

"When I called England earlier today," lied Symes, who'd received the call. He also omitted to tell them he'd learned about their fall from grace from Seymour Levy after they'd been discussing matters of a more pressing nature.

"There's a turn up for the books," Calum sneered. "I can just imagine that tosspot Robertson shouting out 'Big Issue'."

Cheered by news of Collected Thoughts' troubles, and with their own fortunes riding high, SSB threw caution to the wind as they hit the stage in Miami. With the pressure finally off, they delivered a storming set and what turned out to be the best gig of the entire tour. Basil, riding high on the party atmosphere, had his own plans for the show that night. Strapped into a safety harness, his bulky frame was winched down from the roof during the band's first encore.

"Check that out," said a guy watching the proceedings with his girlfriend ten rows from the front. "What a fucking jerk!"

Basil drifted down gently towards the stage. Dressed as a fairy, he was clutching a wand and wore a tutu, his beard covered in silver glitter. "Shitheads!" he mocked the people below who'd given him a hard time for the last four months.

"What a fucking prick," said the guy in the tenth row when Basil hit the stage with a resounding thud.

Hanging on to his wand, he continued to shake the maracas he was holding, all the while maintaining perfect time with the band. A truly credible performance for someone trained as neither a dancer nor a musician.

David, out for revenge after Basil had sabotaged their first encore, seized his moment during the second one. He'd also had the good sense to bribe the road crew, so when he gave the signal, two of them dragged the now handcuffed Basil onstage.

The guy in the tenth row with the twisted sense of humour was grinning like a madman. "Now that fat fuck's gonna get it."

With handcuffs firmly in place, egged on by twenty-thousand cheering fans, members of the road crew began to tar Basil from head to foot with strawberry jam, before they feathered him with the contents of three pillows. When they'd finished, they tied him to the lighting rig.

"Right on, motherfuckers! Kill the fat arsehole!" the excitable young man in the tenth row hollered at the top of his voice, as Basil was untied and unceremoniously bundled offstage.

With the sell-out crowd baying for more after the second encore, the band gathered in the wings ready for the finale. It was then Simon made his move – he reached out and grabbed Marcella. Gazing into the eyes of the woman who'd watched him drum up a storm, he spoke to her softly.

"Will you marry me?" he asked, trying to make himself heard in the noisy, crowded arena. Thinking she'd misheard him say the four words most girls want to hear, she asked him to repeat what he'd said. "WILL YOU MARRY ME?" he yelled in her ear.

"Yes, I will," she nodded, tears filling her eyes.

As the band filed back onstage to deafening applause from a full house, Simon held Marcella's hand and strode purposefully to the apron of the stage. After snatching the microphone from the bemused singer's hand, he got down on bended knee.

"Will you marry me?" he said, proposing to the girl of his dreams a third time in front of twenty-thousand cheering witnesses.

"Yes, I will," she replied, accepting this spontaneous proposal of marriage to roars of approval from the baying crowd.

"Well, you don't do things by halves, do you?" Symes joshed him back in the dressing room.

"I'll never find anyone like her," declared the drummer, mooning over his wife-to-be while the champagne corks popped all around them. "Never."

While the idea of marrying a woman like Marcella seemed repugnant to the more refined Symes, he had to admit, in the end, there was somebody for everybody.

"You're right," he concurred.

He was just grateful it wasn't him who'd be waking up to her face on the pillow next to his every morning, for the rest of his life.

CHAPTER THIRTY-FOUR

With the resounding success of their final US concert still ringing in their ears, and the excesses of the previous night rendering the musicians fragile to a man, SSB were nursing monster hangovers for the flight home. When they boarded the plane in Miami, all of them were wearing dark glasses to hide eyes resembling piss-holes in the snow. Even Symes had managed to get completely blotto at the end-of-tour party.

Too weak to make their usual tedious demands on the trolley dollies, and too ill to do anything other than dream of a better afterlife, the band slept like the little angels they patently weren't for the entire journey back to England.

"I still don't know why Andrew splashed out on these fucking things," Basil moaned, arms folded, as he watched the driver loaded the last of the flight cases on to the red Dodge truck with huge chrome bumpers.

"What eez een them, señor?" asked the driver, the son of Cuban immigrants. Proud of his origins and the inquisitive nature he'd inherited from his mother's side of the family, he also had his father's sense of humour. "Eez cocaine?"

"I'll tell you what it is," growled Basil, his anger now directed at the trucker. "None of your fucking business!"

Sensibly acknowledging that Basil was twice his size and fearing his nosiness might get him into more trouble, he backed off.

"If you're so damn clever, tell me why every other truck driver I meet in America thinks he's a comedian?"

"I don't know," shrugged the Cuban. "Maybe eez the boredom factor keeking een, señor. All we do eez drive here, drive there. Still, eez a job, right?" He pointed towards the SSB logo on the nearest flight case. "Are dese guys famous?"

"You could say that," Basil smiled, after slipping him ten dollars.

"Thank you, señor," he beamed, his faith in mankind restored. "Now I remember. You're the guys with the number one record this week."

"For the last six weeks," Basil corrected him.

"What's eet called? 'My Day'?"

"Correct," confirmed the roadie, who couldn't resist bathing in a little reflected glory himself when it suited.

Curiosity satisfied, clutching his ten dollars and the relevant documents and associated paperwork he'd need to present to the authorities, the happy Cuban climbed back into his truck and sped off in the direction of Miami International Airport.

On arrival, the driver immediately headed for the customs house, where he lodged the matching carnet to reconcile with his precious cargo. In normal circumstances this would have involved someone vetting the paperwork to reveal any discrepancies. You would also normally have seen a customs officer accompanied by a trained dog checking the flight cases rigorously prior to clearing them for loading on to the Boeing freight plane. All mandatory procedures, none of which were adhered to during the handling of this particular consignment.

Over in another corner of the vast hangar, a forklift truck driver dressed in regulation orange overalls permitted himself a smile when he saw the silver boxes. He recognised them from another job he'd done the previous week, one he'd undertaken with other members of staff he was in regular contact with during normal working hours. After summoning a work mate, he pointed towards the logo adorning the nearest one.

"Numero uno."

"Beeg in America," his friend confirmed.

Due to clear US soil later that day, this precious cargo was scheduled to touch down in England forty-eight hours after the band arrived back in the UK.

"So what are you planning to spend yours on?" asked Jay, already dreaming of a better life in some far-flung paradise.

"I dunno," said Simon, deep in thought for once. "But it's nice thinking about it, isn't it? Might buy myself one of those big fuck-off solid gold Rolexes the rappers all wear."

"Doesn't sound too extravagant," opined David.

"Then again, I was considering buying Marcella a Ferrari as a wedding present. She'd like that."

"But Marcella doesn't drive."

"True," he mused, blinded by love. His love of fancy automobiles.

"If you decided to buy a Ferrari," Calum pressed him, "which colour would you choose?"

"Red. Is there any other colour for a Ferrari? Nobody wants a blue one."

David, more financially astute than the other members of the band, was shocked by the drummer's fecklessness.

"Considering the woman doesn't drive, I'd call that a bit rich."

"But I will be," countered Simon. "We all will. Won't we?"

"What are you going to spend yours on?" he asked.

"Something dull I would imagine. I was actually thinking about putting down a deposit on a small apartment in town. How about you, Jay?"

"I'm still thinking about it."

"Another guitar? One studded with diamonds, perhaps?"

"I was thinking about taking a Caribbean cruise. Then again, I had been considering drinking myself to death, but I think we can safely discount that idea now. What about you, Calum? Planning any treats?"

"Oh, I don't know," he replied nonchalantly. "A new microphone stand, or if the money's rolling in, a down payment on the first shag in outer space. The possibilities are endless, aren't they?"

Having exchanged all the dollar bills they'd amassed from their merchandising sales for one-hundred dollar denomination bills, their master plan was to avoid paying punishing amounts of income tax. After collecting around a thousand dollars apiece in cash after each concert, they'd all been able to hang on to a considerable sum of money. The final amount they had to split between them amounted to a little over three-hundred thousand dollars.

Symes gazed glutinously at the two large bowls of sticky toffee pudding and homemade vanilla ice cream the waiter had set down in front of them.

"Glass of Sauternes with that?" he chivvied his dining partner.

"Thank you, Andrew. Always a fabulous way to finish off a spectacular lunch."

"In that case," he addressed the waiter, "we'll have two glasses of your very finest Sauternes, if we may."

"Certainly, Sir."

"Tell me again, Andrew. What time does the plane arrive?"

"It's scheduled to touch down at Heathrow around nine-thirty this evening."

"Just as I thought. Excellent. Perhaps we should drink a toast to the future."

Raising a glass that contained the remains of a decidedly fleshy red burgundy, it fell upon Symes to propose the toast.

"To rock 'n' roll," he declared, to the luxurious soundtrack of crystal clinking against crystal.

"And the riches to come," proposed Levy.

"And the riches to come," acknowledged his partner in crime.

Chapter Thirty-Five

Calum turned on the TV before grabbing another beer from the kitchen. "You guys want one?" he called out through the open door.

"Please," Simon shouted, eyes already glued to the screen.

"Me too," said Jay, looking up after slotting a roach into the joint he'd assembled.

"I hope you guys haven't forgotten we've got an appointment with our lawyer tomorrow," Calum reminded them as he passed the beers around.

"Marcus Davies," mouthed the drummer, as *The Flintstones* flickered on the screen.

"Christ, I'd almost forgotten. Thanks for bringing it to my attention, Simon."

"No problem, Jay."

"You know how I'd hate to miss anything Marcus has to say."

"I wonder if he made any progress with our contracts while we were in America?" said Calum, his own eyes glued to the TV now.

"Who knows?" Jay took a long, hard pull on the joint. "Why are we watching this shit?"

He snatched the remote from Simon and began to surf. Plumping up the cushions in preparation for the ten o'clock news, he wasn't sure why he bothered. There was nothing on it that would make any great impact on his life. Did he really want to see the self-satisfied Tony Blair coming on like everybody's newest best friend when none of them would have invited the guy to share the same toilet seat, let alone a cold beer?

"I need another beer," he declared, one eye on the television as he drained the last dregs from the current one. "Anybody else?"

"Yep," said the other two, eyes still riveted to the TV screen.

Over in Notting Hill, Andrew Symes waited for the ten o'clock news to appear on his screen.

"Urgh," he cursed, nostrils flaring, the result of a particularly poor line he'd snorted earlier that evening – cocaine that had been stepped on more times than a London bus. Not that he would ever do it in front of the band, of course.

Sipping a large glass of Taylor's port of the wonderfully complex 1970 vintage, he shuddered as a poor black child's fly-strewn face hove into view on the gigantic plasma screen. It didn't seem fair somehow when he could afford the luxuries in life. Minutes later, the self-righteous Blair was extolling the virtues of the health and education systems he was actively trying to dismantle.

"Hypocrite!" Symes shouted at the screen.

The next news item focussed on yet another politician accused of lining his own pockets, accepting backhanders for what he euphemistically termed "consultancy work". The Labour MP insisted, "I have done absolutely nothing wrong."

"Hypocrite!" Symes exploded again, before raising the volume slightly.

"Earlier today," reported the newsreader, *"a freight plane crashed into the Atlantic Ocean hours after take-off from Miami International Airport in Florida."*

Ears pricking up, his body snapped forward to crank up the volume.

"Coastguards who launched air and sea rescue services to search for the missing pilot and co-pilot were forced to call off the hunt for the men when the operation was hampered by poor weather conditions. No other passengers are believed to have been onboard the aircraft, which crashed into the sea after disappearing from air-traffic control radar screens shortly after sending out a distress call. Meanwhile, the search for the missing pair and the black box recorder will be resumed as soon as weather conditions permit. We will, of course, bring you the latest developments on the situation as we receive more information."

"Shit!"

Paralysed by fear, Symes tried desperately to take onboard what he'd just heard. Surely it couldn't be the plane carrying the band's equipment. Suddenly unnerved, he reached for his Filofax. Feverishly, as if his very life depended upon some nugget of information contained within, he began to scan the hundreds of entries that filled its bulging pages.

"Ba-be, ci-co, fe-fi, la-lo," he mumbled, as if reading a nursery rhyme. "Ma-mu, na-ni, pe-po, ra-re, ri-ro, rock, rocket. Got it!"

He punched the air in triumph after locating the telephone number of Rocket Air Freight Services. Then he scribbled down the number as fast as he could before heading towards the office he'd set up at the far end of the hallway.

"Where is it? Where is it?" he intoned, scrutinising the pile of documents littering his desk. "Got it!" he said at last when he'd located the Post-it note.

On it, he'd scribbled the air waybill number that matched the consignment he'd entrusted to the freight company.

He glanced at the telephone then examined his watch. It was almost ten-thirty. He began to dial. The wait was interminable.

"Get on with it, you useless bastards!" he bellowed into the handset, pounding his clenched fist on a stack of telephone directories. "Fuck no!" he swore when he heard a pre-recorded message. Consumed by panic now, he dialled Seymour Levy's home telephone number. "Fuck!" Once again, nobody answered. "Shit! Shit! Shit!" Gripped by fear, Symes had nobody at the other end of the telephone line to assuage it.

When he finally turned out the bedside light, he tossed and turned for eight hours solid. A troubled man, he didn't sleep a wink that night.

Calum and the others had also watched the news. While most of it washed over them, all three sat bolt upright staring at the screen in silence as news of the crash unfolded. Now minutes later, rendered speechless, they stared at one another open-mouthed.

"Do you reckon it could have been ours?"

"Fuck, I hope not!" Jay groaned, before it suddenly dawned on him what might be lying in store.

"Whatever. We'll just have to wait until the morning to find out," concluded a decidedly uneasy Calum.

CHAPTER THIRTY-SIX

As he listened to the rain beating against the windowpanes, Symes peeked over the top of his duvet. He wondered whether it was worth getting out of bed this morning. He certainly knew it wouldn't be one of the best days of his life, but he would have to sooner or later. Bleary-eyed, he staggered from the bedroom down the hallway into the blue-carpeted bathroom. He stared hard into the mirror. Should he be examining his reflection or his conscience? Frowning his displeasure at whatever it was he saw, he moved on to the kitchen.

After turning on the ludicrously expensive espresso machine that took pride of place, he tried to make sense of what had happened the night before. Lost in thought, he sipped at the tiny cup of life-giving liquid before asking himself a series of questions.

Was he any greedier than the politicians who were supposed to be setting an example to people like him? Not according to the media. Was he greedier than the record companies he dealt with? He didn't think so. Hadn't he always paid his taxes on time? He even stopped to buy a copy of the Big Issue once in a while.

Going nowhere with this train of thought, he switched on the radio. Flicking randomly between stations, he listened for any updates on the plane crash that might throw more light on the situation. He didn't have long to wait.

"Coastguards who launched air and sea rescue services have located the missing pilot and co-pilot from the plane that was

lost at sea off the coast of Miami last night. Both were found close by to their inflatable dinghy but appear to have been too weak to reach it. Both families have been informed."

"Poor bastards," said Symes aloud.

There was still no sign of the plane. Presumably it had sunk without trace to the bottom of the ocean and, for reasons better known to himself, he certainly hoped so. Unwilling to prolong the agony a second longer, he reached for the phone and called Rocket Air Freight Services.

"Good morning. I'm calling to check on a consignment I was expecting delivery of today from Miami."

"Can you give me the airway bill number please?"

Symes spoke slowly and clearly, taking care to enunciate every single number and letter as he read out the reference number in front of him. A number that would, one way or another, seal his fate. He'd never bought a lottery ticket in his life. Today it seemed he had no choice.

When he'd noted the relevant information, the freight agent put Symes on hold before scuttling off to deliberate with a senior colleague. Barely a minute later, during which time Symes saw his life flash before him, the agent came back to the telephone.

"Regrettably, it's my duty to inform you that your consignment was on a flight that crashed into the Atlantic Ocean off the Florida coastline last night. You may have seen it on the news."

"Are you sure?" asked Symes, his throat dry as a bone.

"Yes, Sir. I'm certain. But then perhaps you should look on the bright side."

"Bright side? What fucking bright side? I don't see any bright side," said Symes, unsure whether to laugh, cry or throw up.

"What I meant, Sir, was that nobody was killed in the crash."

"I think the pilot's widow may beg to differ on that score. The co-pilot's, too."

"I'm truly sorry, Sir. What I meant to say was that apart from both pilots, nobody else was killed. As I'm sure you're already aware," he added, about to dig another hole for himself, "you are fully insured for all losses in transit and thereby able to claim compensation accordingly under the terms of the Warsaw Treaty."

"Tell that to the wives and kids those poor bastards left behind!" Symes castigated him. "Some things you can't insure, you uncaring arsehole!" He slammed down the receiver in disgust and took a deep breath before dialling again. "Come on!" he coaxed. "Pick up. Hello? Is that you Seymour?"

"Hello Andrew."

"We've lost the lot," Symes revealed at last. "Everything."

"What do you mean?" asked his less-informed partner.

"The whole fucking shooting match. We've lost the lot, I tell you."

"Andrew, Andrew, slow down."

"Listen to me carefully. The plane, our plane, the one carrying the band's flight cases, crashed into the Atlantic Ocean last night. It's been on the radio and TV news. Surely you must have seen it?"

"No, I didn't. Crashed into the Atlantic you say?"

"That's right Seymour. Your money, mine, everybody else's. All gone."

"Christ Almighty! And the pilot?"

"Dead. The pilot and the co-pilot. Both dead."

Calum and Jay both rose early. After breakfast comprising little more than a pot of tea and one of the Calum's bespoke spliffs, Jay telephoned Basil. Telling the latter no more than he needed to know, Basil soon returned the call along with the freight company's phone number, relevant air waybill and carnet numbers. Coincidentally, when Jay eventually got through he was talking to the same person at Rocket Air Freight Services that Symes had spoken with just half an hour earlier.

"If I'm not mistaken, I had a similar conversation with somebody else about the same shipment earlier this morning," confirmed the agent. "A rather strange fellow, if you don't mind my saying so. As I said to him, you are fully insured for all losses in transit and thereby entitled to claim compensation accordingly under the Warsaw Treaty."

"You may think so," Jay spat at the man down the line, "but there are certain things you can't insure." He, too, slammed the phone down on the hapless agent.

"I just don't get it," the man confided in his colleagues. "Neither had lost any relatives in the crash. And I told both parties they could claim compensation. I tried to help."

"What did they both say?"

"Oddly enough, the same thing."

"Which was?"

"There are some things you can't insure for."

CHAPTER THIRTY-SEVEN

None of those involved in the fallout from this disaster had been in possession of all the facts. Like the freight agent, the pilots had no inkling of the nature of the illicit cargo they were carrying when they took off from Miami for London.

For reasons not too difficult to assimilate, Andrew Symes hadn't felt compelled to inform the band what he was attempting to smuggle into the UK inside their flight cases. Nor had the band let on to Symes what they'd put inside the flight cases designed to carry musical equipment. Freight agents apart, they were all losers.

Seymour Levy lost three-quarters of a million pounds. Andrew Symes lost a quarter of a million. Both were small fry compared to the three-million pounds other wealthy friends and investors had lost. By comparison, the band had seen a mere three-hundred-thousand pounds trickle through their fingers without reaching their pockets. Both plans had backfired and a staggering four and a quarter million pounds of their money was sitting at the bottom of the ocean.

Following Jay's recommendations, they'd wrapped their merchandise cash in polythene bags before secreting them inside a variety of musical instruments. Much of the money had been hidden inside Simon's drum kit, with thin packets each containing three-thousand dollars apiece taped inside the drum shells. With Basil's help, Jay had taped more bundles of cash inside two acoustic guitars. Some of it was hidden inside effects units, yet more deposited inside recording equipment.

The rest found homes inside amplifiers, speaker cabinets, cable chests and microphone cases.

Unlike Symes, the band members could have salvaged one hundred-thousand dollars in cash between them, had they realised it was legal to carry twenty-thousand dollars apiece between the USA and the UK.

Symes, by contrast, had far bigger fish to fry. He'd hired a team of bent baggage handlers working in tandem with aircraft maintenance crew. The men in orange overalls had been paid handsomely for their night's work. They'd concealed six-million dollars' worth of cocaine inside the false walls he commissioned to be built into the new flight cases that he'd ordered. It had a London street value of sixty-million pounds.

In order to further facilitate the success of the operation, he'd also given backhanders and made additional payments to ensure the consignment would pass through both airports with the minimum of fuss. This money wound up in the hands of corrupt officials and officers employed at Miami International and London Heathrow.

Although neither Symes nor Levy were bankrupted by the spectacular failure of their first venture into the world of international drug smuggling, the former was forced to sell the home he'd purchased months earlier in Notting Hill.

Surprisingly, Symes also agreed to tear up SSB's contract and renegotiate a fairer one. For the band, this was far easier to expedite than they'd imagined. Marcus Davies had drawn Symes' attention to the kind of legal bills he might expect to incur should he attempt to draw out the litigation process – bills he could no longer afford to pay. Subsequently, Symes had settled for a more reasonable fifteen per cent of their earnings after previously helping himself to a predatory forty.

Having sorted out this contractual problem and renegotiated a more favourable deal for the band's second album with Platinum, Davies was called upon to intervene once again when Calum was served with a paternity suit on his return from America.

The suit, much to the band's amusement, was served on behalf of Jocasta Templeton after she left the employment of Marcus Davies. Calum, the devious bastard, hadn't told any of them he'd been slipping one to Ms. Templeton on the sly. Taking advice, he settled out of court after she agreed not to drag his name through the gutter and sell her story to the tabloid press, who would have been fighting each other to publish it.

On a happier note, after his betrothed had put together a lucrative deal with *Hello* magazine, who paid a very welcome £50,000 for exclusive photographic rights to their wedding, Simon finally married Marcella. And he bought the Ferrari he'd promised her, along with some driving lessons. While readers of *Hello* may have thought the S&M in red icing adorning the top of the wedding cake stood for Simon and Marcella, the band and all those attending the reception held at the London Dungeon knew otherwise.

Two other notable events occurred.

Their former bass player, Brian, had used part of the severance pay and royalties he was owed to start a lawsuit of his own. On the recommendation of Marcus Davies and working on a no win/no fee basis, he'd hired the services of a hotshot lawyer in Los Angeles.

The silver-tongued attorney, who could persuade a jury his client was acting in self-defence when he'd shot a man in the back, sued Disneyland for his client's mishap on their water ride. When the verdict went against Disneyland, Brian found himself considerably richer after the judge awarded him half a million dollars – a tidy sum he shared with his new hero, the silver-tongued attorney.

Down on his luck since Sony cancelled their contract and Collected Thoughts disbanded, Harvey Robertson had not been so fortunate. He died in tragic circumstances after the car he'd been travelling in was involved in a fatal collision. Ironically, Robertson had been on his way to his mother's funeral at the time.

Almost a year to the day after the plane had gone down, following exhaustive examinations of the black box and tail section of the plane, crash investigators released their damning report, extracts of which appeared in the Press.

The report offered conclusive proof as to why the freight plane had fallen out of the skies and explained what previously had been described as "mysterious circumstances". Every single shred of evidence pointed to one thing and one thing only: a faulty wiring system. This alone had been responsible for creating the sparks that ignited stray vapours from the fuel tank, causing an almighty mid-air explosion, seconds before the aircraft plummeted into the Atlantic Ocean.

Although SSB's debut recording had done respectable business in America, the units they'd shifted were insufficient for any of the four original members of the band to make their fortune from the subsequent royalties. Nevertheless, they took it in their stride. Every one of them was convinced things would change with the release of the follow-up album and they'd finally see the kind of money they dreamed of.

Jay, meanwhile, stretched out on one of the rehearsal-room sofas, appreciating his first joint of the day after reading a newspaper report of the plane-crash verdict.

"At least we're all still alive," he said, folding up the newspaper.

"What caused it?" asked Calum.

"A faulty Kapton wiring system."

Side

B

CHAPTER THIRTY-EIGHT

"Is this going to go on all bloody afternoon?" demanded Andrew Symes.

SSB gathered for a meeting with their manager at his office in Primrose Hill. Regarded as one of the hottest live acts in the UK, they now had the chart success on both sides of the Atlantic to back it up. Every available inch of office wall space was adorned with gold records, glinting in the sunlight that poured in through the tall sash windows, testimony to the vast quantities of units the band had already shifted around the globe.

This particular meeting had been convened to iron out the small print in the contract drawn up for their forthcoming UK tour. Still arguing the toss after two hours at the table, Symes and the band had failed to reach an agreement on the riders contained within.

Originally intended to protect artists' rights, over time the rider had metamorphosed into the ultimate tool, offering unlimited scope to terrorise and abuse promoters. Symes, casting a practised eye over a thick sheaf of paperwork peppered with any number of ridiculous requests, while ever mindful of his need to balance the books, was eager to press on with what looked like turning into a protracted meeting.

"Perhaps we can move on to the food now," he urged. "Now that we're in the lower reaches of the Premier League I've decided to engage the services of Eat to the Beat to handle the tour catering." The first choice of calibre artists such as

Eric Clapton, Eat to the Beat was noted for its culinary excellence throughout the rock industry.

"Could they fly in fresh lobster, scallops, Dublin Bay prawns and fresh oysters to every gig? I only mention the fresh part in passing because you don't want me going down with any bugs, do you?" mused the increasingly neurotic singer.

Demonstrating an uncanny ability to combine breathtaking speed with pinpoint accuracy when dealing with numbers, Symes regained control of the meeting after consigning yet another rider to the trash.

"Forget it, Calum." He braced himself in readiness for the next topic on the agenda. "Is there anything we've forgotten to add to the list of fermented beverages? Options that aren't in the realms of the ridiculous."

"Could you ask the promoter to chuck in a case of Bollinger Grand Année 1990 at every other gig?" enquired the guitarist, his face a picture of innocence. "For the band," he reasoned, as if naming the end-user somehow legitimised the request.

"No, Jay, I will not ask the promoter to throw in two cases of Bollinger for the band," his manager exploded, face contorted in rage. Tired of being arsed around, all thought of co-operation was now on hold. "If you haven't cottoned on, and not one of you has given me any indication to believe otherwise, as a band you've got some way to go before we can make demands of that nature. Bollinger Grand Année 1990 my arse!"

Well-groomed, clean-shaven, fit, tanned, alert and fastidious – none of these adjectives described the figure sat at the desk. Dishevelled in the extreme, the pot-bellied owner of ill-fitting clothes and mismatching socks was already sprouting a seven o'clock shadow long before the lunch hour.

"You must be joking," he muttered to himself, astounded by SSB's demands. Scraping his free hand and filthy fingernails through matted, greasy hair that hadn't seen shampoo or been near a comb in a week, the less than meticulous Danny Gosling yawned, his halitosis-ridden mouth agape. "Saucy scumbags," he cursed, revealing a revolting set of crooked, rotting molars. Some were yellow, some green, some black, the others mostly missing. "Cheeky fuckers!" he bellowed, voice hitting a crescendo as he tossed aside the offending paperwork.

Unlike fellow promoter Harvey Goldsmith, he'd never rubbed shoulders with royalty – and it was easy to see why. After easing one cheek of his massive backside from a chair it was threatening to demolish, he let rip an almighty fart. Part of his daily routine, this ritual signalled that the master was ready to start his day.

Eager to confront the perpetrator of this mischief, Gosling picked up the phone. He stroked his unshaven chin before emitting a serious of groans, indicating his displeasure with the contract now spread out in front of him.

"Andrew, is this some kind of practical joke? Is this something you dreamt up with the sole aim of pissing me off?"

"What are you driving at?" countered Symes, knowing full well the source of the man's irritation.

"I'm talking about the contract you biked over to me earlier this morning."

"I certainly didn't set out to annoy you."

"Well, you've succeeded. Tell me, where the fuck am I going to find sushi food in Bradford?"

"I think you'll find there's a host of shops and wholesalers, not to mention restaurants, all specialising in...."

"Shut up, you upper class, privately educated, silver-spooned, stuck-up arsehole," he yelled. "According to my information, Bradford is chock full of Pakistanis, not slitty-eyed fuckers who make cars," he growled, confusing Geordies who churn out Nissans in the North East with their oriental paymasters in the Far East.

"I share your concern," concurred Symes, a man who certainly didn't share the bigot with bad breath's far-from-politically-correct views on any number of subjects. "But no need to panic. I'm pretty certain Eat to the Beat will be able to find whatever we need in Marks & Spencer."

"Is that right?" retorted somebody who'd never heard of Delia Smith. "And would I be correct in assuming every branch of Marks & Spencer keeps unlimited quantities of sushi parked right next to the groupie fish, or whatever the fuck it is your band wants to shove down their throats?"

"Groupie?"

"You heard me," admonished Gosling, not in the habit of repeating himself or the names of exotic fish.

"I've no idea what you're talking about."

"Well, someone must have added it to the list."

"I can assure you, I didn't," insisted Symes, having no recollection of the species, let alone adding it to a list that already ran the length of a football pitch.

"What the fuck are groupie fish? I've been in the rock business a fucking long time, my son, and I've never heard of the bastards."

"Danny, I think we're talking at cross-purposes here and what you're referring to is the grouper fish."

"Grouper fish, Groper fish, groupie fish. I don't give a toss what they're called and I'm certain Eat to the Beat have got far better things to do with their time than trawl around fishmongers in the middle of fucking Scunthorpe tracking them down."

"We're not playing Scunthorpe. We're playing Sheffield."

"Sheffield, Scunthorpe. It's all the fucking same, isn't it? And another thing…"

"Y-e-s," drawled Symes, aware his troubles were far from over.

"What the fuck is all this nonsense about redesigning tour buses?"

"Ah, I knew we'd get there in the end." Symes grimaced knowing Gosling was referring to the page marked 'Excess' – in particular, the clause headed, 'Additional Transport Requirements'. "Could that be the bit about the bus?" Uncomfortable with the silence, he was grateful to be sitting a good ten miles away from the sometime violent Gosling.

"You can't expect me to provide a luxury tour bus with these fucking specifications."

"I think you'll find we can." Symes realised if he could tough it out with this mean-minded son of a bitch that he had shared an umbilical cord with and promise him a favour at a later date, he might, just might, get away with plan B. "Basically, I owe you fuck all."

"Absolute bollocks… And you know it."

"Fuck all, Danny… And you know it."

"Is there a point to this conversation?"

"I'm getting there."

"Not soon enough for my liking."

"Tell you what, I'll make a deal with you."

"What kind of deal?"

"If you provide the bus we've specified at no extra cost, I'll return the favour. How does that sound?"

"I'll tell you how it fucking sounds: airy bloody fairy. More to the point, do I get to promote the Wembley Arena dates at the end of the year?"

"Sure. If that's what it would take to butter your muffin."

"It's a deal then," agreed Gosling, who recognised a good one when he'd negotiated it. "Speak to you later. Be lucky," he signed off, resorting to the lexicon of cockney crap.

After replacing the filthy telephone on the grimy handset, he began to muse on what he might do to Symes should he fail to deliver on this particular deal. Or, more precisely, what he might have done to Symes.

CHAPTER THIRTY-NINE

The specifications of the double-decker tour bus Gosling eventually located were impressive. For a start, there was an eight-seat lounge, one of three on a bus bristling with the latest technology. In addition, this vehicle, which would be the band's mobile home from home for most of the tour, had one other very important feature. Originally installed for the gratification of Robbie Williams, this modification had required the addition of a hydraulic ramp fitted to the side of the bus, allowing the item in question to be loaded onboard and, if necessary, taken out for fixing.

Measuring a massive twelve feet by six feet, this bizarre request from a man who could have asked for anything he wanted was a full-size snooker table. The cues, rather cute ones, were six inches shorter than standard due to the restrictions placed on players' movements by the bus width. Also supplied was a tray of dust-free chalk – 'dust-free' so it wouldn't play havoc with the onboard air-conditioning system.

If satisfying their ludicrous tour bus demands had been relatively easy to achieve, locating the type of fish that would satisfy the members of SSB was beginning to prove more difficult than catching them. After rifling through his address book, Gosling at last placed a call to an old-school chum. One of his few friends who made their living by legitimate means, the Billingsgate buddy arranged to have a constant supply of fresh molluscs and tropical fish delivered to every town on the band's itinerary. Another problem solved.

Although he'd complied with most of the band's wackier demands, Gosling refused point blank to entertain certain other riders. So there would be no feng-shui master for Calum and no martial arts instructor for Simon. Similarly, Jay had to go without a personal oenologist while David didn't get the make-up artist he wanted. Grant, the newest member of the band, had made no such demands.

While the last album and several singles from it had charted around the world, it was also true the band hadn't shipped anywhere near the quantities Platinum had been expecting. Fortunately for Calum and Jay, they could expect to fare somewhat better than the others. Under the terms of their joint publishing deal, the band's songwriting team would be the major benefactors when the record royalties started rolling in.

Not exactly chump change, it was still a long way off the riches they could all expect to reap if they shifted greater quantities of the next album. And according to employees who'd heard the demos, the chances of this happening had never been greater.

Another sure-fire way to improve cashflow had nothing to do with music. The name of that game was sponsorship. Seen by many as legitimised prostitution, endorsing products was a lucrative source of income for any band.

"The money is certainly good," beamed Symes. "The only trouble with sponsorship," he pondered, still scrutinising the numerous offers laid out in front of him, "is that some of these products could be detrimental to the kind of image we've been trying to create for you. Some of these deals are, for want of a better word, tacky," he explained, though he couldn't imagine anything too tacky for Simon's taste. "Inappropriate, if you like."

"Cut to the chase: what's your definition of tacky?"

"Well, David, I can't see KY Jelly as a product we'd want to endorse."

"Oh, I might," he cackled, when nobody else in the room did.

"While the money would be welcome," Symes admitted, "we could all live without the amusing publicity that's bound to come with it."

"So what are the alternatives?" asked Jay, who would endorse anything he couldn't eat, drink or snort given the opportunity.

"We've had approaches from double-glazing firms and supermarket chains. Neither offering any meaningful sort of tie-up."

"Any more approaches that might fit the bill?"

"We did get another offer from an insurance company who'd like to enlist your services to help sell their increasingly worthless endowment policies to your fans."

"Really?"

"Now, correct me if I'm wrong in saying this, but I'm sure not one of you, not a single one of you, would consider stooping that low. Am I right?"

"How much are they offering?" asked Jay, rapid eye movements betraying his own personal interest.

"An impressive sum, I'm sure you'll agree – in the region of a quarter of a million pounds." Five pairs of eyes swivelled in the direction of Symes. "We also have interest from a bank that thinks you could attract a new generation of savers for them in the coming financial year."

"Screw that for a game of soldiers," sneered Calum, dismissing the high-street banks who'd harassed him most of his adult life.

"At the risk of parodying an image you have at great pains carefully cultivated and projected over the years, the best offer to land on my desk thus far is a third of a million pounds from a major player in fermented beverages." The room fell silent.

"That would be the one then," beamed the guitarist. "Can we all go now?"

"We do have one other offer on the table."

"From who?"

"IKEA."

"IKEA? You can screw flat-pack furniture," complained Simon, missing the irony.

"Fermented beverages it is then," sighed the manager. "Meeting adjourned."

Weeks later, after countless meetings and phone calls, Symes' prayers were finally answered when his search for a sponsor bore fruit, resulting in a cheque for just under three-hundred-thousand pounds now tucked safely in the band's account.

After receiving this welcome boost to ailing finances, the manager was busy working on ideas for incorporating their new benefactor's logo into the advertising and merchandising materials that would promote the forthcoming, second-album tour.

Conceived and recorded in six months, most of the songs that eventually made it on to *Crimson to Blue* were penned by Calum and Jay, while the band was on tour promoting their Platinum debut, *Hearts & Souls*. The new release, designed to show two different sides to the songwriters' talents, was split neatly into two distinctive parts. Side one saw the band in 'up' or 'Crimson' mood. Meanwhile, side two, the 'Blue' side of their new opus, offered a contrast with a far more melodic approach demonstrated on their ballads.

Having turned down the entreaties of furniture makers and insurance companies, Symes had eventually agreed with SSB it would best serve their interests to tie-up with a major player in the brewing sector. In this, the band's first ever venture into the murky world of sponsorship, the brewer had agreed to underwrite the entire cost of their forthcoming tour.

To fulfil their side of the bargain, SSB were expected to promote the brewing giant's new alcopops drink in a series of print and TV ads. Yet another marketing scam designed to hook young people on their parents' drug of choice, this curious-looking concoction went by the name of FrothFace.

A less appealing liquid, mused Symes, would be hard to find. There was no other drink like FrothFace, which deposited a sticky red stain on the lips of those unfortunate enough to indulge in this dubious new development in underage drinking. Equally perturbing, failure to wipe away the offending stains resulted in a crimson moustache, which then metamorphosed into an inky blue tattoo on the upper lip where it would remain for the rest of the evening.

Although none of SSB would develop a craving for this new-fangled potion, the tie-in, bearing in mind the name of their new record, was entirely appropriate. In addition, FrothFace, they discovered to their collective delight, would work a charm in aiding the seduction of the same under-aged youngsters the product had been aimed at. Crass, cynical and exploitative though it may have been, this dangerous potation – guaranteed to loosen inhibitions and copious amounts of knicker elastic with it – was, in its own, unique way, bloody effective.

CHAPTER FORTY

Symes, striding around his office sporting a telephone headset in the middle of fighting another fire, was beginning to feel as though his entire life revolved around telephone calls.

"What I propose is this," he told the editor of the fanzine, who'd been directed to speak to him by the Platinum press office. "The lucky winners of the competition will be invited to dinner with the whole band and chaperoned by our fan-club secretary, Sandra Barnes."

A bit dopey, the gushing Sandra was the kind of girl anybody could introduce to their mother. Flat chested and plain with it, the acne-ridden Berkshire girl idolised the band and would have done anything for them – especially Calum.

"In addition, we'll arrange for the runners-up to meet SSB, who'll be happy to pose for photographs. On top of that, the band will autograph twenty copies of their forthcoming release, *Crimson to Blue*, which you can give away as you wish – perhaps in a separate competition."

No longer the rookies they once were, SSB tended to dislike these opportunities to press the flesh with their fans. On the other hand, knowing where their bread was buttered, and coerced heavily by their record company and manager, they could usually be relied upon to co-operate. Well, they could if the winners happened to be female and unspeakably pretty.

Symes, having outlined his plans for this 'meet the band' competition, was ready to name his price. "And I want the front cover. After all, I'm offering you an exclusive, which, as we both know, will help your ailing cover sales no end."

"I've always wanted to come here ever since I was a kid," revealed the prettier of the two schoolgirls. Seated with members of the band by a window at the Oxo Tower restaurant, she was admiring the night-time view of the river and St. Paul's Cathedral opposite, its roof bathed in a magnesium glow.

Perched beside her, and edging ever closer, Calum was under strict instructions from Symes to keep his lecherous paws off both of them. Looking like jailbait on the rampage, Mandy and Yasmin were the lucky winners of the competition Symes had arranged with the editor of Fan E, yet another magazine feeding off the fears and insecurities of impressionable young women.

Calum couldn't tear his eyes from Mandy, a redhead who, at sixteen, was the eldest of the two. Radiating innocence, she wore a tight bottle-green velvet dress set off by the paste emerald necklace borrowed from her sister, enhancing the luminous quality of her matching eyes.

Yasmin, at fifteen already a statuesque brunette, was the shiest of the pair. Blessed by classic rather than outright good looks, any shortcomings she might have admitted to were balanced by her other assets – and they were very much on show that night. Revealed and supported by a saucy red satin bustier, her fulsome breasts were trimmed with black lace.

Calum, a flirt by nature, but not particularly a breast man himself, was captivated by Mandy's presence. "So tell me, young lady," he exhorted her, in his never-ending quest for compliments, "which of our songs do you like best?"

"Wow," gushed copper locks, blushing at all the attention she was receiving, momentarily lost for words. "All of them really."

"Hmmm. But what if?" Calum persisted, locking piercing blue eyes with her dazzling green eyes, "what if you could choose only one?"

"Just the one?"

"Yup."

Well and truly stumped, she deliberated a second or two. "If I had to choose just one song, the song I like best of all, I'd have to say 'That Crazy Feeling'."

"He didn't write that song," the keyboard player reminded them all. "I did." Calum's face hit the deck.

"Ooh, sorry," she cooed, realising she'd said the wrong thing and hurt his feelings. "I didn't mean to insult you." Ready to appease him, oblivious to the fact he wanted to screw her senseless, she placed a slim hand inside his own.

"Don't mention it, I wrote most of the others," he consoled himself.

"That he did," nodded Jay, edging closer to Yasmin.

"Wow!" gurgled Mandy.

"And most of the songs on that album were written with me," announced the guitarist, staring at the biggest pair of breasts he'd clapped eyes on in some time.

Eager to attract more attention than she was already receiving, Yasmin tugged at Jay's sleeve, pulling his willing elbow towards her heaving bosom. "What's an album?" she whispered.

"It's one of those old-fashioned vinyl recordings your parents used to play."

"Ooh," she trilled, none the wiser.

Clearly delighted to be there, besotted fan-club secretary Sandra Barnes was becoming a bit tipsy from the champagne that was now flowing like water. Keeping a beady eye on proceedings, she was also growing increasingly anxious about the behaviour of certain members of the band – her blonde Adonis in particular. Obliged to be pleasant to these young girls, she was nevertheless jealous of the attention being heaped upon them.

Rising from her chair, Mandy squeezed past the singer on her way to the loo, careful to brush his outstretched arm with her pert backside.

"You," Calum drooled, addressing her tits, forgetting everything Symes had told him, "have the most delightful arse."

"So sweet," she squirmed, grinding her crotch against a warm, welcoming shoulder simultaneously.

Simon and Grant, tired of playing gooseberry and having had enough fun with their fans for one evening, decided to head for home. Still at the table, Sandra, who rarely touched alcohol, had also had enough – enough to drink and more than enough of the shenanigans Calum and Mandy had been getting up to underneath the tablecloth all evening.

Seeing that the writing was on the wall, David, who'd shown no interest in women of any description from a very early age, departed shortly afterwards, taking the still inebriated fan-club secretary with him.

"God, it's huge!" shrieked Mandy. Drunk and unable to see in the dark, she groped at the long, hard, sticky object that had until a moment ago been poking at the base of her stomach. "Feels so tight," she panted, breathlessly, as he straddled her across the drive shaft of the white stretch limousine requisitioned for the evening.

Seated opposite them, Yasmin ignored the chauffeur sat on the other side of the smoked glass window. Jay, for his part, was oblivious to the law-forbidding sex with underage minors.

"More," pleaded Yasmin. "More! Your cock's the biggest I've ever had." Now on all fours, her face pressed up against the window, she began to yell at its owner, wishful thinking overtaking logic. "Fuck me harder!" she begged.

Stretched out on the massive seat having gone at it hammer and tongs, too smashed to perform one of his own songs let alone a sexual act, Jay was comatose.

CHAPTER FORTY-ONE

"It's hard to deny the reviews for *Crimson to Blue* have been truly exceptional," raved the NME journalist. "Certainly so far," he added cryptically.

Still pretending it was a cosy fireside chat, this member of the Fourth Estate failed to mention the trashing their latest opus was about to receive in the forthcoming issue at the hands of a colleague.

Unaware of this, but cautious nevertheless, Calum was understandably wary of the UK rock press, notorious for their build 'em up, knock 'em down style of journalism – or in the case of the NME, knock 'em down and kick the fuckers so hard they won't want to get up again. Whether journalists asked impertinent questions to justify the cover price or their own existence, he wasn't sure.

"Do you believe this tour will establish you as an international force to be reckoned with?" asked the thin-lipped hack at his most disingenuous. "The one that will rank you forever alongside the all-time rock 'n' roll greats?"

"We certainly hope so."

"Because I have heard," the NME continued, "that Platinum intends to drop you."

Unnerved by this information, Calum shifted uneasily in his seat. "News to me, mate."

"I mean, if the band fails to deliver the numbers with *Crimson to Blue*."

"There's a possibility of that happening to any act. Anyway, where do you get your information from?"

"Here and there. Gossip on the grapevine and all that."

Taking time out from the soundcheck to talk to the press, Calum was soon realising that he had drawn the short straw. Already wary of the person pointing the tape recorder at him, he steeled himself for the next question – the nosey sort that magazines feel bound to ask on behalf of their readers, half of whom don't give a shit.

"Are you clean these days?"

"Am I what?"

"Are you clean right now?" persisted the bloke from the NME, relentless in his pursuit of the truth.

"I've had a bath today, if that's what you mean."

"I was talking about coke."

"Never touch the stuff."

"That's not what I hear."

"More of a Pepsi man myself."

"I was referring to cocaine."

"I know damn well what you were fucking referring to!" exploded the singer, welcoming this intrusion as he might a freshly laid turd floating in his jacuzzi. "We could even have a conversation about it if you switch off your tape recorder."

"We could?"

"Aha."

"Ready when you are," offered the man from the NME, before theatrically switching off his machine.

"Now, should I make what I say sound deep, so that when you write it up you can make me sound shallow?"

"I wouldn't do that sort of thing."

"Wouldn't you? How about if I come on all shallow? Then you can read between the lines and turn whatever I say into even more meaningless drivel."

"But…"

"Alternatively, we could do a couple of lines, head off to the pub and scrap this interview altogether."

"Are you winding me up?"

"Unlike you, Barry, I have done my homework. And what I've discovered is that you're rather partial to a drop of the old devil's dandruff yourself, aren't you, Barry?"

"Am I?"

"I even know your dealer."

"You seem very sure of yourself. How could that be?"

"Because I used to use him myself."

"He didn't tell me."

"Why the fuck would he?" Reputation and a severe dose of apoplexy on hold, the reporter opted to button his lip and listen for a change. "Though there is one potential snag to my earlier suggestion: you'll be on your own."

"Is that a fact?"

"Pure fact, Barry. But unlike most of the stuff you've managed to shovel up what's left of your septum, this is one-hundred per cent pure."

"Are you trying to tell me you checked into the Priory Clinic to take up religious orders? That you visited this shrine to the terminally rich in the hope of being converted rather than cured?"

"I'm implying nothing of the sort, you pathetic excuse for an arse wipe. Listen and I'll tell you exactly what I was trying to say. But this time, watch my fucking lips." The man from the NME didn't have any choice. "I, as in me, no longer touch cocaine, which you would know if you'd done your homework. I do not, and have not, snorted cocaine for some considerable time. One other thing…"

"Uh huh?"

"This interview is over."

CHAPTER FORTY-TWO

Barry Morton had been right about the reviews. Apart from the severe tongue-lashing the NME had dished up, they were spectacular. Fortified by this and a sold-out tour, and all pumped up by sales of their new album, which had entered the charts at number eight, the band were in high spirits when the tour opened in Sheffield.

About to indulge in a spot of grazing backstage before they were due to go on, the band were positively spoiled for choice. Hot dishes, cold dishes, meat, fish, poultry, seafood, soups, salads of all varieties, vegetarian, vegan, hot puddings, cold puddings, all begging to be eaten.

"What's this strange looking stuff?"

"Today's special." answered Eat to the Beat's helpful catering assistant.

David, eyeing dinner as though it had committed a crime, wasn't convinced. "It doesn't look very special to me. What is it?"

"Today," she repeated by rote, "chef has utilised whole honey-roasted quail as the basis for this unique recipe, which consists of a melange of sweetbreads, shallots, minute slivers of black pudding, puréed pumpkin and pigs' trotters in the traditional style, marinated in their own urine."

"I presume you were joking about the pig's pee?"

"No," she replied, managing to keep a straight face. "The dish also benefits from the merest drizzle of the chef's own tarragon, lavender and nettle vinegar, complemented by a light sprinkling of truffles."

"What a horrible thing to do with truffles."

Stood behind David, taking it all in, was Basil. Weighing in at around seventeen stone and built like a brick shithouse, their tour manager and former roadie loved his food.

"Got any poached panda on the menu tonight, my love?"

"'Excuse me?" said the startled young assistant.

"Poached panda bear," repeated Basil. "Served up on a bed of couscous accompanied by a mosaic of ceps, artichoke hearts and juniper berries, drenched in a jus of pulped scrotum. And if you could throw in an arctic pilchard in aspic with a sprig of parsley stuffed up its arse, I'd be very much obliged."

"I'm afraid I can't help you there," she sniggered, wondering what it might taste like nevertheless.

"Now far be it from me to be difficult. It's not as if the food here is up its own arse. So how about some kippers then, darling?"

"Fresh out of that, too," she shrugged, finally getting the hang of this game.

"What? No kippers and custard?" guffawed the man who ate nothing but curry. "On second thoughts," mused Basil, growing serious for a moment, "give me the chicken tikka. Lots of it."

"My pleasure," rock 'n' roll's answer to Delia Smith smiled back at him.

On the second night of the tour, with little under an hour to go before showtime, SSB were relaxing the only way they knew how. Interrupted mid-spliff by the sound of loud voices and knocking at the dressing room door, the band were greeted by the unwelcome sight of their manager along with twelve others, none of whom they recognised.

"These gentlemen," beamed Symes, proffering an outstretched hand in the direction of people who looked nothing of the sort, "are your new sponsors."

Along with the others, David in particular, Calum loathed being introduced to unannounced strangers in their dressing room before the show. Staring blankly at the less than hip assortment of characters in their midst, he saw they were all wearing similar cheap, off-the peg double-breasted suits, all filled to bursting point by a succession of beer guts, each one larger than the last.

"Break a leg," grinned the owner of the biggest. Calum scowled. "Just joking!" chortled the former to a chorus of deferential sniggers from his lackeys and assorted plus ones.

The MD was certainly proud of his achievements, his greatest to date, discounting a balance sheet showing continuous heavy losses for the last two years, having been the introduction of twist caps to the drinks industry. Now there was FrothFace, the alcopops drink the beleaguered suit was banking on to turn the fortunes of his ailing company around.

"And, lest I forget, their exceedingly beautiful better halves," Symes chipped in, ingratiating himself.

Beautiful? Calum stared at them, then stared harder. Which planet was Symes on? All he could see were hard-faced trophy wives who could halt the rush-hour traffic on Oxford Street. That, and backsides that would have looked enormous in anything significantly smaller than a circus tent.

"Hello," he muttered grudgingly, acknowledging their unwelcome presence at last.

Attempting to suppress a fart in front of people he'd never met, people he didn't want or ask to meet, he clenched his own, very slim buttocks. What gave them the right to barge in when all he wanted to do was smoke a bowel-moving joint?

Ever the diplomat in these situations, Grant reacted with split-second timing. "So pleased to meet you all," he said, waving in their direction, his words drowning out Calum's plaintive fart. "Fantastic new product you've come up with."

"A pleasure to meet you," Jay pretended, wishing the lot of them would piss off. All he wanted to do was share a joint with his mate, stuff a pair of socks down his underwear and change into his stage gear. "Enjoy the show."

"Tonight's show's going to be the dog's bollocks, the full donkey's dick," the drummer assured them all in the mistaken belief he was offering his sponsors added value for their money. Sponsors who'd paid in the region of three-hundred-thousand pounds for the privilege of listening to this foul-mouthed tirade in the presence of their wives.

"Erm, thank you, Simon, perhaps a little more information than we need," Symes interrupted. "And this," he continued airily, making a mental note to exclude the drummer from all future sponsorship activity, "is our keyboard player, David."

"H-e-l-l-o!" he snarled, in no mood for pleasantries with strangers, however important they were. Illuminated by the heavily lit mirror, he continued to apply his makeup in silence. Under the harsh lighting, his half made-up features and down-turned mouth glared back at his unwelcome, uninvited guests.

"Call me a party pooper," he said, directing his anger at the mirror, "but you'll have to excuse me…" Pausing long enough to gather up precious pan sticks as he reached the door, he delivered his final stinging rebuke to the suits. "Some of us have jobs to do." As the door slammed shut behind him an embarrassed silence engulfed the room.

"May I offer you a drink?" chivvied a nervous Symes, motioning their sponsors out of the room in the direction of the bar.

"We don't drink," deadpanned the incredible bulk and owner of an ill-fitting toupée.

"But you chaps run a brewery?" gasped Symes, failing to grasp the intended irony.

"Just kidding," giggled the brewer, the sound of his hollow laugh echoing in the hallway outside.

"Christ!" exclaimed the singer. "How much FrothFace do you have to swill down your gullet to wind up with a gut the size of his?"

CHAPTER FORTY-THREE

By the mid point of the tour, *Crimson to Blue* had risen to number two in the album charts. Intended to capitalise on this success, the first single to be culled from the album, 'It Had to Happen', patently hadn't and was languishing at the wrong end of the singles chart. Keen to maximise sales while SSB were still on tour, Symes was insisting they release a second single from the album, whereas Platinum favoured a more dance-friendly remix of the first cut. They both acknowledged, though, that this latter option wasn't one that appealed to the band.

The combined stress of concert appearances and the small matter of a follow-up to their first single were just two of the many issues SSB had to contend with. Other daily impositions included radio interviews, despite the fact they'd pre-recorded any number of slots to aid promotion, and enforced chinwags with the Press in ever town on their itinerary. Wedged in between these and the soundchecks that seemed to go on forever, they were also contractually obliged to attend in-store record signings and the regulation 'grip and grin' photo opportunities for the fans.

Yet all these minor irritants paled into insignificance when it was time to make the FrothFace commercial.

"Action!" bawled the director through the hand-held megaphone. It was the seventeenth time he'd done so.

Akin to being asked to control the storming of Sarajevo with a only a trumpet for support, he'd been struggling all afternoon to control the shoot. David refused point blank to wear clothes supplied by the costume department, while Simon didn't fancy forgoing his lunch hour. Calum couldn't lip-sync to *Crimson to Blue* and Jay wouldn't mime the guitar parts or let somebody he'd never met tamper with his sound at a later date. Unsurprisingly, neither was Grant willing to deliver his lines off-camera with a West Indian accent.

"Cut!" the director yelled into the megaphone again, sensing someone else was not a happy bunny.

"If you so much as go near the controls, if you dare so much as touch my amplifier," Jay railed at the sound engineer, "I'll kick your teeth right down your fucking throat."

Slight of build, timid by nature, the sound guy who'd been taking liberties tampering with his amp without seeking prior permission took a full two steps backwards.

"I won't warn you again, keep your hands off my equipment or you'll get it," the guitarist snarled through gritted teeth at the cowering engineer, who quite wisely had decided to take temporary refuge behind the mixing console. "Do you hear me?"

"Mmmm," he mumbled.

After altering Jay's sound levels, the misguided knob twiddler had succeeded in removing the kind of natural distortion Jay had spent years striving to achieve and even more learning how to control. Those warm, round, rich, fat tones produced when air interacts with speaker cone and red-hot valves to produce the very essence of rock 'n' roll. A point entirely lost on the engineer.

"Could you turn it down just a tad?"

"Can I fucking what," bellowed the guitarist, standing mere inches away from the terrified engineer. "Do what?" he taunted, undecided whether to clock this idiot with his fist or deal a glancing blow courtesy of the Stratocaster slung around his neck.

"Surely you could turn down the volume just a little bit?"

"No I fucking well couldn't. Turn it down on the desk," Jay ordered, indicating the pathetic excuse for a mixing console. "Isn't that what you're paid to do?"

"Take five," the megaphone ordered, eager for some respite before the next round of sparring began in earnest.

Taking a breather in the trailer provided and a well-earned toke on a heavily loaded spliff, Jay inhaled deeply before addressing the others. "What the fuck does any of this have to do with the music?"

"Aren't you forgetting something?" prompted Calum, memory less blunted by cannabis than the guitarist's. "Why did any of us agree to do this? Apart from the money," he reminded all the others. "Excuse me a moment Jay... Is that someone at the door? Come in, come in," he urged the three models the agency had sent to decorate the set. "Come and join our miserable little party," he urged them again, patting the sofa beside him.

Adding a dash of light relief to the proceedings that afternoon, one of them had provided the only comic interlude thus far. This occurred when a cameraman attempted to chat up Ruby, the tallest and arguably fittest of the girls. Not one to mince his words, Andy had gone straight for the jugular.

"Where's the dirtiest place you've had sex?" he asked.

Ruby, the owner of a rapier-like wit, immediately responded, "Up the butt, Andy." She'd then asked him, "How about you?" A real piece of work.

"Are we going to get a hit on that spliff?" she demanded, "or is it just for boys?"

As she settled back into the sofa next to him, Calum took an instant shine to her, mesmerised as she wrapped full red lips around the end of the joint she was holding between long, slender fingers.

"So," she began to probe, passing the joint to Simon. "Where's the dirtiest place you boys have had sex?"

"The last train to Brighton with another man," volunteered David.

"Ooh," cooed the three models, all the open-minded sort.

"I once did it in a pigsty," revealed Simon, incongruously licking his lips as he did so.

"Err," groaned Ruby, visibly revolted by the notion of any coupling between a pig and the percussionist.

"I didn't fuck the pig if that's what you were thinking."

"I was thinking nothing of the sort," Ruby assured him. "How about you, Calum?"

"Why me?"

"Speaking from personal experience, it's the singer who's always the kinkiest member of any band."

"I suppose there have been one or two notable highlights," he smiled, more eager to flaunt his credentials than he let on.

"Go on."

"Disgusting though it may sound, and ashamed as I am, I do recall one particularly reckless adventure involving a rabbit, a top hat…"

"And your wand, perhaps?"

"Correct."

"Ooh, now that's what I call magic," sniggered the shameless Ruby.

"Could we have you all back on set, we're going for one final take," said the clapperboard man, head appearing and disappearing around the door.

CHAPTER FORTY-FOUR

Faced with the moral dilemma of just how far they were willing to stoop in order to capitalise on their success, Symes, like most managers faced with the same predicament, had favoured taking a hard-nosed financial position. The tour subsidy and massive accompanying cash injection they received for the commercial ensured the band wouldn't be up to its neck in debt at the end of their travels. Taking the FrothFace dollar may have dented their credibility, he'd reasoned, but they wouldn't be going hungry while fans decided whether to laugh at them or with them.

Backstage, after the band had soundchecked at Leicester's De Montfort Hall, he had another problem to contend with. Their record label was anxious to resolve the situation regarding the release of a second single and he had until five o'clock that afternoon to come up with a compromise.

As expected, Grant and Jay wanted to put out another track from the album, a move he'd initially approved of. In common with their label's hopes of improving their chances of breaking into the singles chart, the others favoured releasing a dance-friendly remix of 'It Had to Happen'.

"Ultimately, Platinum would rather we put out a remix," said Symes.

As someone who disliked handing over artistic control of their work to anybody outside the band, Jay had more misgivings than most about taking this particular route. "Who would remix it?"

"Jonathan Storey," revealed Symes, the producer who'd previously mixed *Hearts & Souls* for them.

"No way am I working with that fucking prick again," Jay exploded, still blaming the producer's over-layered mixes on their first album for its failure to sell in double digits. "I could do a better job myself."

"I'm sure you could – and when you've sold as many albums as Radiohead, Platinum might be willing to grant your wish. All of them, I would imagine. Until then it would be more helpful if we stick to the realities."

"How low do we go? Where does all this end?"

"I think," reflected Symes, about to indulge in a spot of waffling, "it's important to keep an open mind, Jay. To retain, if you like, a flexible approach. Would you agree?"

"Yes, Boss. Whatever you say, Boss. Soon it'll be cabaret, then pantomime. After that we'll be opening supermarkets. Before you know it, we'll be doing commercials flogging carpets or flat-pack furniture or whatever other dodgy deal you can dream up on our behalf. In case you'd forgotten, we're musicians, not performing seals."

"I'm well aware what you are," conceded Symes, knowing him to be as greedy as the rest of the band, if unwilling to admit it in front of his peers. "Before you decide to use me as target practice, I think you should ask yourself a few meaningful questions. Are you a survivor? Do you have what it takes for the long haul?"

"What's all that supposed to fucking mean?"

"What I'm driving at is this, Jay: if you're not careful, the next time you see your face, the next time any of you see your faces in the music press again, might be when you appear in one of those 'Where Are They Now?' features. As you know, there's no shortage of acts available to fill those cruel little columns. There are plenty of has-beens out there. If you want to join them, just keep up the good work, Jay."

"Okay, you've made your point. But if you're wrong about the remix…"

"If I'm wrong about the remix what?" repeated Symes as he texted Platinum to confirm their next single release.

"Forget it."

With tickets for the tour completely sold out, Symes had, with the approval of an eager sponsor and even more eager record label, added further dates. Although SSB weren't deliriously happy about the new arrangement, they all knew these additional gigs playing to live audiences could secure their album the number one spot. Another reason they were happy to oblige was their remix of 'It Had to Happen' would be on sale in record stores.

"I heard on the grapevine you blagged a spot on *Top of the Pops* for your band with that new rap record of theirs," chuckled Gosling. "What's the damn thing called?" he asked, scratching his balls and belching into the mouthpiece simultaneously.

"It's N-O-T a rap song," boomed Symes, appalled by this display of bad manners. "It's called 'It Had to Happen'."

"Well, I've heard it twice and it sounds like fucking rap to me, whatever it's called."

"Well, it isn't," denied Symes, aware it wasn't the kind of comment the band would appreciate. "But you're right about *Top of the Pops*. We'll be recording our slot later this week."

"Didn't know you were in the charts."

"We're not."

"Still, you're on *Top of the Pops* this week, which must be good."

"Only if our new record dents the charts, otherwise our pre-recorded segment will be consigned to the musical graveyard at BBC HQ, never to see the light of day. So in answer to your question: no, it's not good. Not yet, anyway."

"By the way, did that lad of yours enjoy his fish?" enquired Gosling. Squinting all the while, he was comparing the T-shirt in front of him with an almost identical one, both bearing the band's logo.

"What fish?"

"You mean I went to all that trouble and you can't even remember? There's gratitude for you."

"I've no idea what you're talking about," insisted Symes, who had a lot on his mind that morning.

"The groupie fish I went to a great deal of fucking time and expense to find for that poxy singer of yours."

"Huh?"

"Do you always go blank when people mention fish in your presence or are you trying to wind me up again?"

"No, Danny, I'm not trying to wind you up," Symes assured him, suddenly realising the promotor had been referring to grouper fish. "Be certain, I'll ask Calum when I see him."

"You do that. Ask the ungrateful little twat," he admonished the man who's business he relied on before hanging up.

"Now," he addressed the person standing in front of his desk, "I want ten thousand of these with the band's logo reproduced just here." He pointed to where it appeared in the correct place on the band's official merchandise. "And I want them all by Friday." Owned by Gosling, this garment factory situated in Bethnal Green produced his lucrative sideline.

Days later, in the confines of the television studio, SSB were warming up in front of the *Top of the Pops* cameras and the deceptively small audience. An anachronism, *TOTP* still remunerated artists appearing on the programme with a flat rate of £200. Calum, in particular, was tickled to learn he'd be collecting the same as Rod Stewart.

"Can I have your autograph?" asked the girl standing by the side of the stage as soon as they'd finished their run through. Sixteen at most and clutching her autograph book, she'd managed to blag her way into a show that stipulated all guests be aged at least eighteen. "I love your playing," she said, passing the book to Jay. It was certainly true, but what she liked most of all was to masturbate while gazing longingly at the large glossy photograph of Jay pinned to her bedroom wall.

"How about your boyfriend?" he asked, nodding at the lanky nineteen-year-old standing beside her.

"He likes Kylie Minogue," she giggled, embarrassing the acne-ridden youth.

"No I don't!" he protested.

"He's not a fan of ours like you, then?"

"Him?" she volunteered, retrieving her autograph book. "He thinks you're complete shite."

"So who are you here to see?" demanded the slightly baffled guitarist. "Kylie's not on the show."

"We both wanted to be on the telly innit," she blurted out the truth. "Our own fifteen minutes of fame."

Boyfriend still in tow, she was herded back on to the dance floor, ready to wave and stick out her tongue for the benefit of the cameras. It was the first time her mum and dad would see the new piercings that now adorned it.

CHAPTER FORTY-FIVE

"So, young lady, what's it to be today?" Basil was ravenous.

Into her stride after a month on the road, the game catering assistant he'd fancied since the tour began had adapted rapidly to her new environment and one of her customers' increasingly bizarre requests. All she had to do was humour him during this pre-dinner ritual, which he enjoyed and she looked forward to.

"This evening," she began, looking Basil right in the eye, "chef has excelled himself in his never-ending quest to tantalise your taste buds. On this occasion, he has melded the humble crumpet with heaps of horseradish before adding a crunchy coating of crisp, crushed caraway seeds."

"And what culinary conquest, may I ask, has chef prepared for dessert?"

'Where to begin?" she confided in the seventeen-stone teddy bear she'd developed a crush on.

"I'm all ears," grinned the randy road warrior.

"Tonight, we have meringues and marshmallows accompanied by a mousse of mandarin and mangoes soaked in a vat of sherry, topped with a tickle of the stickiest of treacles. Or maybe," she added seductively, "I could tempt you to a taste of this old tart."

"Christ!" he groaned. "What's for main course?"

"You are."

Wondering what to say next, but mostly wondering if he'd heard correctly, he decided to play it cool. "So what are you going to have?"

"Basil."

"In everything?"

"Everything," she purred provocatively. "Everything, my darling."

Jay held the Gibson Les Paul Standard up to the light to take a closer look. Slowly, turning the instrument, he inspected each part in turn, searching for clues. Telltale signs that would determine whether the axe in front of him, this Stradivarius of electric guitars, was in fact a real one – that, or as many others had discovered to their cost, a fake.

"Are you sure it's all original?"

"As the day it was made," nodded Larry Symonds, sitting in the band's dressing room after the soundcheck in Brighton. While the rich and famous, Jay included, clamoured for his services, others had cast doubt on some of Symonds' less ethical practices.

Cradling the Holy Grail of electric guitars in his lap, with the large publishing royalty cheque he'd received earlier that week threatening to burn a hole in his pocket, he weighed up the pros and cons.

"How much did you say?"

"A hundred and thirty thousand pounds."

"The serial number suggests it's a 1959 model so I guess it's worth what you're asking."

"I think you're bloody mad to pay that kind of money for a guitar," snorted Symes, someone whose extensive knowledge on the subject could be accommodated on one side of a cigarette packet.

"Not for Eric's old guitar," argued the dealer.

"Eric's?" echoed Symes.

"That's right," insisted Symonds. "This instrument is an investment. Guitars like these sell for twenty times what they fetched at the end of the seventies and they're still going up in value. Anyway, ask Jimmy Page how much he wants for his flame tops. He wouldn't flog 'em for all the drugs in China, I'll bet."

"Drugs?"

"I meant tea."

"That's not what you said."

"Excuse me," Symes interrupted, as impressionable as the next man. "Are you saying this guitar was Eric's?"

"I did."

"This guitar in front of us belonged to Eric Clapton?"

"Not him," said Symonds.

"Who then?"

"Eric Baker."

"Who the hell's he when he's at home?"

"The guy used to front a blues band in the North of England back in the sixties. Bloody legend he was. Dead now."

"May I ask how it fell into your hands?"

"His widow asked me to sell it for her, since you ask. Said I'd get her as much as I could for her."

"Well, I think it's an insane amount of money to pay for a guitar," argued Symes again. "Whoever owned it, whoever's selling it."

"I've got to have it."

"Why have you got to have it?"

"Page has one. In fact, I think you'll find Jimmy has two of them," he corrected himself. "I want one, too, it's as simple as that. And I want this one."

Symonds, sensing it was his lucky day, moved in for the kill. "Christie's recently sold a similar Les Paul Standard… One that did actually belong to Eric Clapton," he added emphatically.

"And how much did that go for?" Symes asked, voice dripping in sarcasm. "Two-hundred thousand dollars?"

"Pounds actually," replied Symonds.

"Two hundred thousand pounds for a plank of wood!?"

"Will you shut up and quit interfering," the guitarist scolded him before turning his attention back to Symonds and the guitar sat on his lap that he was cradling like a baby. "You were saying?"

"Based on that price you'd have to say that mine, at a hundred and thirty thousand quid, is cheap."

"Cheap!?" spluttered Symes, allergic to paying the full price for anything. "I still think you're making a huge mistake." Jay was having none of it.

"What's the lowest you'll go?"

"Jay, I've got a queue of artists a mile long searching for pieces like this one."

"Won't take less then?"

"Can't budge on the price. Got to be the full hundred and thirty thousand."

"I'll take it."

CHAPTER FORTY-SIX

"Can I have your attention please for a minute," pleaded Symes, fearing he was about to lose his voice. "Calum! Shut up! And you, Jay. You too, David."

"All right, no need to get your knickers in a twist."

"Grant, would you please put down that book you're reading? And Simon, please tell whoever you're talking to you'll call them back."

"What is this? The army?"

"I can't see you in uniform," snapped the manager. "Can you?"

"No, Sergeant!" hollered the percussionist.

Sensing he finally had their complete attention, Symes lowered his voice to address the band he hoped would make him his first million.

"I've just spent half an hour on the phone with Platinum. You'll be pleased to learn the single has gone straight into the charts at number five."

"Well, I'll be blowed," said Calum.

"You have been every night of the tour so far," his bitchiness on keyboards reminded the singer.

"And that," added Symes, congratulating himself on securing the prized spot on the programme in the first place, "is unarguable evidence. Concrete proof of the power *Top of the Pops* still wields over the record-buying public. I think you'll agree, it's a great result."

Not entirely convinced, Jay shrugged. "I suppose so. What about the album?"

"The bad news…"

"Oh, here we go."

"Is that *Crimson to Blue* has dropped two places in the charts. However, our label thinks we'll recover our position."

"*Thinks*," sneered the guitarist.

"Possibly going all the way to number one."

"*Possibly*."

"If the single continues to rise up the charts."

"There you go again. So far, and correct me if I'm wrong, I make that one 'think', a 'possibly' and did you just say 'if'? Surely you can do better than that."

"Better?"

"Yeah, better," Jay continued his tirade, pointing an accusing finger at his manager. "You told us the album would go to number one. 'No doubt about it,' you said. 'Mark my words,' you said."

Somewhat drained by the guitarist's emotional outburst, his manager deemed it wiser to defuse the situation by resorting to flattery with them all.

"*Crimson to Blue* will go to number one, that I guarantee you," he beamed, sticking with flattery for the moment. "And do you know why your album is destined for the number one spot? Because SSB is T-H-E best, T-H-E hottest rock band this planet has ever fucking seen."

"Aaa… men," sang the singer.

"And remember… your fans love you."

Like the others, Jay was hypnotised by Symes' words. "They love us?"

"As much as you do. Now get out there and give them hell!" he exhorted the troops.

"What a piece of crap."

"Fucking rip-off, more like it" complained the disgruntled fan holding aloft the offending T-shirt.

"Rip-off! Rip-off!" the others chanted in unison.

Leant on the other side of the counter, the bald-headed guy in his early thirties was ten years older than his tormentors. His face was covered with tattoos, piercings and, where there was any space, dreadful acne scars – a reminder of his own youth.

"What do you mean?" challenged the tattoo parlour's dream client.

"You can buy better quality in the local market here," claimed the mouthiest of the bunch, who'd elected to articulate on behalf of his friends, all ardent followers of the band.

"Not with our logo on it," insisted the vendor, who earned his living running one of SSB's thriving merchandise concessions.

"You wouldn't want to bet on that," the young smart arse piped up to the approval of his not-so-ballsy mates. "So, are you gonna tell me why your stuff's so expensive?"

"Maybe it's just expensive to you."

"Errr, maybe it's expensive to a lot of people."

"Look, do you wanna buy this shirt or not?"

Leaving no room for doubt, the fan who'd already forked out a king's ransom for a ticket to the concert threw the offending item back on the pile marked '£16.99'.

"Have you ever wondered why people bootleg bands' overpriced merchandise?" he demanded, supplying the kind of clue rarely heard on *Who Wants to be a Millionaire*.

"Enlighten me," instructed the salesman, suddenly noticing Symes out of the corner of his eye.

"I know people in town who can silk-screen your logo on T-shirts twice this quality at half the fucking price."

"In which case, it's bootlegged merchandise – and what's more," he said, towing the company line before he repeated the company mantra, "it's illegal."

"So fucking what!" barked the increasingly huffy fan, revealing the T-shirt he'd been hiding under his jacket – one sporting the band's logo. "Look! Check out the quality.

If bootleggers can turn out stuff like this at fair prices, bands deserve what they get. Stands to reason dunnit?"

"Mmmm," muttered the salesman, humming and hawing, keenly aware of Symes' presence. "You've got a point but I'm sure the band wouldn't see it that way."

The fan, a university philosophy undergraduate who would, if he could find a job, one day understand what it's like to make a living in the real world, was having none of it.

"I'm sure the band wouldn't. But if they're going to put their name on garbage like this," he indicated the selection of shirts on offer, "what do they expect? My sympathy? In my opinion, if they rip off their fans, they deserve everything they get."

At this point, despite knowing he'd agree with anything this intelligent young man said, including the answer to his next question, he decided to ask anyway. "What exactly is it you think they so richly deserve?"

"Fuck-all out of my pocket," his unwanted customer announced to loud guffaws from the others, who were also fed up with the antics of greedy, grasping rock stars.

Proud of his command of the language when using insulting behaviour, the undergraduate selected another gem from his burgeoning repertoire.

"See you in hell, baldy," he jeered at the hapless salesman before blending back into the crowds thronging around the merchandising stands, all of them massive profit centres for the band.

"Thanks a bunch," the vendor shouted back, though he didn't bear any grudge.

Far from it, in fact. He'd grown tired of defending avaricious employers, even if they did pay his wages. He'd found himself nodding along to every single word the kid said. He'd worked for tonnes of bands and, while every one of them couldn't take enough care over their sound quality and production values, when it came to merchandising, not one of them gave a toss about the issue of quality control.

The message was clear: paying peanuts for the privilege, rich rock stars and their managers were happy employing children in the Third World to make their T-shirts. T-shirts they had the temerity to sell at their concerts for seven times the price they'd paid before emblazoning the band's logo across them. T-shirts they'd paid a paltry two pounds for.

Symes, standing in the background quietly observing this altercation with Danny Gosling, was taken aback. "Cheeky little sod."

"Kid's got a point," rasped the promotor, emitting his throaty chuckle. "You could strain curd cheese through one of these. But when did your lot give a monkey's about quality?" he bated Symes, a veiled dig at the new record. "Why bother with quality when you can mint it with garbage like this? Sixteen fucking smackers for a piece of shit like this." He marvelled at the nerve of it all.

"Seventeen," Symes corrected him. "And it's not shit."

"I take my hat off to you."

"Don't bother, you haven't in the past," said Symes as Gosling chuckled to himself. "Quite clearly you're unimpressed by our endeavours in the garment industry."

"Andrew, it's blatantly obvious why the bootlegging industry exists, why it continues to thrive and, if my information serves me correctly, why it's destined to experience record growth – if you'll excuse the pun."

"And just how do you suggest we combat the situation?"

"We? It's not my fucking problem, is it?" grunted Gosling, eyeing the washed-out merchandise. "You might want to start by improving the quality."

"Quality, as you know, costs money, Danny."

"Tell me about it," whistled the promoter.

Unbeknown to Symes, Gosling ran a profitable sideline, albeit on a 'need to know' basis, outside his regular promotional activities. Who did Symes think had organised the illicit street vendors standing outside their gig tonight flogging a variety of merchandise – all of it bootlegged, all bearing the band's logo – Jeffrey fucking Archer?

"Got any more bright ideas, Danny?"

"You could try reducing your prices," he advised, though for the life of him he didn't know why.

"Reduce prices?"

Fully intent on topping up his pension fund with some of the tax-free proceeds of their lucrative merchandising activities, Symes was disappointed by Gosling's recommendations. It certainly wasn't the kind of advice he was looking for, nor was it the kind of advice he'd expected from an East End penny-pinching spiv.

What Gosling had forgotten was that, like himself, Symes lived in perpetual fear of paying full retail price for anything, while taking enormous pleasure deriving the maximum profit for minimal effort wherever possible, whenever possible.

"Well?" demanded the bootlegger to the stars. "Are you going to reduce them?"

Symes deliberated a second or two before delivering the answer the bootlegger had been praying for.

"I'd rather rub sand in my eyes."

Unthinkable though it may have seemed to a certain member of the band, with the end of the tour in sight, what Symes predicted actually happened. Fuelled by a feeding frenzy at record stores, the band had, with assistance from management, relatives and girlfriends, shifted vast quantities of the new single in a matter of days.

But it was a second appearance on *Top of the Pops* they had to thank for nailing them the coveted number one spot. Piggybacking the success of 'It Had to Happen', *Crimson to Blue* had started creeping back up the charts and by the following week both single and album were sat at the top.

"What did I tell you?" Symes crowed to the guitarist backstage. "What did I tell you?"

CHAPTER FORTY-SEVEN

It was one of the most difficult career decisions any band had to make. Very few were given the chance. One option was to take the path of least resistance, stay put and reap the rewards in their home country during an important crossroad in their career. The alternative, and less palatable, option was taking a serious crack at the American market.

The latter meant cutting all ties at home, upping sticks and going to live there for a period of six months. While opinion in the band remained divided on how they could best achieve their goals, Symes was adamant on the subject. In his eyes there was no alternative: they were going to do it.

In the weeks following this significant decision, Symes, liaising with their new US agent, began planning the itinerary for the first leg of this make or break tour with military precision.

Another problem had been accommodation and where to establish a base. Manhattan had far too many distractions, while Upstate New York offered little in the way to amuse oneself on days off – although, as Symes was quick to point out, there weren't many of those pencilled in.

Somebody who'd watched too many episodes of *The Sopranos* had suggested they relocate to New York's fifth borough, Staten Island. Sure, it lacked the razzmatazz of its more glamorous neighbour, but then Manhattan was only twenty-five minutes away by ferry.

"Did you pack these bags yourself?" demanded the ticket agent.

"Yes."

"And since then has anybody else given you anything to pack or take onboard?"

"No," said Symes.

"Have the bags been with you at all times?"

"They have," he lied, throwing a cursory glance in the direction of Basil, the person he'd delegated this relatively minor task to.

"Your flight departs at 1400 hours. Boarding," droned the new recruit, who could already speak in a monotone when conveying important information, "begins one hour prior to departure, at 1300 hours. Please make sure you're in the departure lounge at least twenty minutes before boarding."

"I don't suppose there's any chance of an upgrade?" Symes enquired, about to wave his Frequent Flyer card in her face.

"I'm afraid not," she apologised, before adding the four words that strike fear into the hearts of all frequent flyers. "Your flight is overbooked."

"Damn!" he cursed, dreading the prospect of this trip to New Jersey before he'd even set foot on the plane.

Simon hadn't heard a single word of this exchange while he'd been tapping frantically on the countertop. "What time does our plane leave?"

"Fourteen-hundred hours!" snapped the ticketing agent. "Boarding is at 1300 hours."

"And what would that be in earth minutes?" queried the man who made his living keeping time.

Symes settled back in his seat as the plane levelled out at 35,000 feet. Musing on the perils of flying economy, he knew that, eating garbage apart, the single biggest challenge facing air travellers was keeping boredom at bay. He could only read, write, watch, play, compute, eat, drink, daydream, doze and sleep so much. The Mile High Club seemed a splendid idea to him.

Further towards the back of the plane, keeping each other company, were Simon and his wife, Marcella. There in her capacity as the band's international publicist, she was the sole female allowed on this tour. To keep herself busy while the trolley dollies plied her husband with a constant flow of booze, she was putting the finishing touches to an updated biography of the band – one Americans would understand. Competing for the drummer's attention with a tumbler full of Baileys, she thrust a sheet of paper under his nose. "Read it," she commanded.

"Be careful, Marcella! You nearly spilled my drink."

"You drink too much."

"And you talk too much."

"Read it!" she yelled at him.

Scanning the page, Simon struggled with the text. Peppered with words that were vaguely familiar, the beginnings he recognised – but the endings?

'*Featuring the humungous talents of five individualistic musicians all rolled into one, synergistic melting pot, the bi-coastal SSB combine the virtuosic vocals of Calum James and the guitaristic exploits of foil Jay Jackson. Further highlighting the musicality and functionality of this conceptual unit is the diva of all keyboardists, David Edwards. Last but not least, providing guts and glue to bind together the commonalities that make this band a totally and utterly bodacious unit, are the bombastic playing of bassist Grant Thomas and the monumentally mesmeric percussion and demon drumology of Simon Harding.*'

"Whaddya think?"

While tact had never been one of Simon's strong suits, he felt entitled to an opinion. "Complete and utter drivel."

"Skip the beginning and read the last bit I wrote about you, Honey."

"I already did."

"And?"

"That's rubbish, too."

Seated directly across the aisle from them, Basil played contentedly with the selection of video games provided. David was snoozing in the row behind. Not an entirely happy camper, Basil had begun to experience trouble with his guts.

Like any number of passengers on the flight he was suffering from a change in cabin air pressure. Trying his best to suppress a series of involuntary stomach contractions, Basil suddenly let rip with the deadliest of farts. David, who'd been dozing peacefully downwind, suddenly shot bolt upright in his seat. "You filthy bastard," he hissed between the seat backs.

"Wipe your arse and call it a shit!" called out Jay, sat further afield but also subjected to the blast. Shame-faced, the out of control Basil buried another series of silent farts deep into the upholstery.

Seated right at the back of the plane while this execrable business had been taking place, Calum was beginning to make serious headway with the young American who was sharing her life story with him. Within minutes of meeting she'd already given the singer her name, telephone number, e-mail address and cup size.

"I give great head," revealed the star-struck youngster who didn't look a day over seventeen. "I'm the best," she boasted, tugging at his todger, her handiwork hidden from prying eyes in the adjacent rows courtesy of the blanket she'd spread out across their laps. "I could suck cock for Colorado," she volunteered, giving away her final destination and another statistic he was far too well brought up to ask for.

"Worrrr..." groaned the singer, eyes welling up, the vinegar stroke approaching faster than he would have liked.

"Would you care for a demonstration?" she purred, nuzzling up to his ear, her tugging becoming more frantic.

"Would I?" he replied too late, her head disappearing under the blanket. "Not here," he said, yanking it backwards.

"What are you waiting for? Halloween?"

"I don't think I can wait that long."

"Me neither," she reassured him before wiping her lips on the sleeve of his jacket.

The old lady who'd been observing these shenanigans from the seat opposite frowned her disapproval. They didn't do that sort of thing in her day.

"Why don't we go in here?" suggested Calum, a backwards nod indicating the only free toilet on the plane, which was situated directly behind them. Choosing a moment when the elderly lady turned away, they wandered into the vacant stall after checking the coast was clear.

"Make sure the door's bolted," she said.

The lady with the wrinkled face turned to the recently vacated seats and raised a quizzical eyebrow before rubbing her rheumy eyes in disbelief. "Dis-gusting."

"May I get you another drink, madam?" enquired the flight attendant, who'd hoved into view.

"You can get me the captain," she replied, without a moment's hesitation.

"What seems to be the trouble?"

She pointed to the vacant seats occupied previously by Calum and his rock chick girlfriend.

"I'm sorry," apologised the steward, "I don't follow. But then I've been having one of those days myself," he confided, dabbing his forehead theatrically with the voluminous white cotton handkerchief he'd produced with a flourish.

"Never mind that, young man. Follow me," she scolded, rising to her feet. "They're both in there…" She pointed accusingly to the cubicle where they were ensconced. "Doing something they shouldn't be."

"Come out!" demanded a voice that displayed little in the way of authority.

Calum and Rhiannon froze, mid-fuck, locked in suspended animation, her pert arse perched on the sink, his dick jammed between her thighs.

"At once!" shrieked the steward at his petulant best, tiny fists pummelling the door. "We all know what you're doing," he insisted, to the delight of the old lady, who was taking a very keen interest in proceedings.

"Tell me this ain't happening," moaned Calum from the other side of the door, the only thing protecting their modesty.

Interrupted by the commotion outside, the couple disentangled their semi-naked bodies and rearranged their underwear rapidly before checking the mirror to repair ravaged appearances. Heart in his mouth, fair ready to shit his pants, Calum hesitated a moment before shooting back the bolt. With the wild child following behind, fearing the worst, he stepped outside to meet his fate.

"You two," the flight attendant accused the pair, "have been smoking." This came as a shock to the old lady.

"No they haven't!" she protested. "That's not what I said at all."

Calum looked shell-shocked. "Errr... smoking?"

Complete novices, the pair had failed to grasp that, like any other institution, the Mile High Club had its own set of rules – rule number one being that if you are overcome by the uncontrollable urge to make out in a cubicle at thirty-five thousand feet, remember to ascertain first whether the previous occupant had been smoking in it.

"Oh yes you have," another steward butted in, offering her two-penneth. "I can still smell cigarette smoke in here."

"Me too," a third member of the cabin crew chipped in.

Calum, detecting the faintest whiff of tobacco himself, spotted a neat way out of this, and his other worse predicament.

"I haven't been smoking at all," he said, brimming with new-found confidence.

"You certainly have," argued the first flight attendant, his face mere inches from the singer's.

"If you're so sure about that, can you explain to your associates why you can't smell tobacco on my breath?" he smiled triumphantly.

Exhaling in his face, the singer could see the steward's look of astonishment at the absence of any clear evidence to support his theory – and the gravity of his error when Rhiannon did the same.

"As I was saying," continued Calum, savouring the moment, "somebody might have been smoking in there, but it certainly wasn't me."

"He's right, they haven't," the ashen-faced steward declared for the benefit of his co-conspirators. "I'm so sorry. I can't apologise enough, Sir."

"Apologise?" fumed the old woman. "Apologise for what, may I ask? They were up to something in there. Weren't you?" she glowered at the luckiest two people on the plane.

Choosing wisely to ignore this latest entreaty from the crabby old trout who'd caused him enough trouble for one day, the steward decided to steer clear from becoming embroiled in any further confrontations with anybody else for the rest of the flight.

"Perhaps you'd like to follow me," he gestured, removing his sleeve from the senior citizen's grasp. "It would be my privilege to offer you superior accommodation in the nose of the plane."

"That would be fantastic," said Calum, thrilled with this turnaround.

"F-a-b-u-l-o-u-s," drawled his companion.

Panic attack averted, the flight attendant turned to lead the way to First Class. Rhiannon, bidding her farewell as she swept past the cause of all this kerfuffle, took great pleasure in trampling on the old woman's toes.

"Have an arse day," she taunted, giving her a backwards glance and the first outing to an expression Calum had taught her in the departure lounge.

Chapter Forty-Eight

"Magnificent, isn't it?" grinned Symes, waving an outstretched hand at the building.

"I suppose it'll do," David grumbled, half jokingly.

Situated at the very top of the hill on Staten Island's Bard Avenue, their new home looked fairly impressive. A mansion in miniature, built entirely of brick, it was highly unusual for the area with a compelling green tiled roof. Stood regally atop a grassy knoll, the house looked down on the rest of the neighbourhood – literally – the steeply raked steps leading up to the front door adding to the illusion.

The band's sleek black limousine swept around the building, before depositing the party of eight in the parking lot at the rear of the house.

"It was built for a former senator of Staten Island," revealed Symes, showing he'd done his homework. "Rumour has it he lived here – until the Mob took him out," he added, unable to resist embroidering his conversations.

While a genuine US senator had indeed been a previous occupant of the building, the line about the Mob had been a fib, but Symes was aware of the area's strong links with the Mafia. Infamous for grassing up his associates, Sammy 'The Bull' Gravano had until recently lived up the road.

After arguing the toss over who had which room, dumping their bags on beds to signal they were reserved, they all piled back into the limo to set off in search of something to eat.

As they slid down Bard and took a sharp left on to Forest Avenue, Jay gesticulated through the blacked-out window.

"Hey guys, look over there. Mandolin Brothers."

"Who are the Mandolin Brothers?" Simon asked, quite innocently.

"There are no Mandolin Brothers as such."

"But you just said you saw them."

"No, I did not," snapped the guitarist, his eyes glazed after the rigours of an eight-hour flight, his frayed nerves beginning to jangle. "I said I saw Mandolin Brothers. There are no brothers involved. It's the name of a shop, a famous store."

"Fair enough. But why call it Mandolin Brothers?"

"Good question. No answer. Bloody good question, though."

"Do you have to be able to play mandolin to get a job there?"

"How the fuck would I know? Apply for a job there and find out," he advised the luckless percussionist,

"Anyway," Basil interjected, determined to break this deadlock. "Who the hell plays mandolin these days?"

"Taking a wild guess, half of America," Jay declared, regretting he ever mentioned the subject, determined to drop it.

Mandolin Bros, to give its correct spelling, was, in fact, the most famous musical instrument store on the island. Paul McCartney's Hofner 'Beatle' Bass had been lovingly restored there, while Joni Mitchell mentioned it by name in one of her songs. Owned and run by Stanley Jay, guitar stores didn't come much sharper.

CHAPTER FORTY-NINE

Doffing a peaked cap as he held open the door, the chauffeur watched attentively as his passengers climbed out of the limousine. He liked English rock stars, they had better manners than their American counterparts – better educated, too, he thought. His work done for the day, driver Ben was himself ready to turn in. "Enjoy the rest of your evening," he called out.

"You too," returned Symes, admiring the skill he employed manoeuvring this enormous vehicle in so limited a space.

With one last wave Ben pointed the stretch limo in the direction of home and his own more modest accommodation on the south shore of the island.

"Lovely man," declared Symes, joining the others who were waiting by the back door. "I know the keys are here somewhere," he frowned, rummaging through his pockets. "Ah, here they are. Now, can anybody remember how this alarm system works?"

"We assumed you must know."

"Odd as it may seem, David, these instructions tell me how to switch it on. But they don't say anything here about switching it off."

"What use are you as a manager?" Jay sneered, as if the man's only task in life was to let him in and out of buildings.

After Symes had wrestled with the intricacies of the alarm system for a full twenty minutes before gaining entry to the house, Marcella made a beeline for the bathroom, where she barricaded herself in for the next hour. Worn out by his travels and the trials and tribulations of sorting out the alarm, Symes rather sensibly headed straight for bed. Calum and Jay, meanwhile, had other plans.

"Where did you put it?"

"I didn't put it anywhere."

"So who the fuck's got it?"

"I don't know – maybe Grant does," returned the equally puzzled Calum. "Grant!" he shouted towards the kitchen.

Seated at the table with Simon, Grant was enjoying one last drink before turning in for the night. He looked up from his beer. "What's up, man?"

"I don't suppose you'd know what's happened to our stash?"

"I wasn't aware we had one."

"Are you kidding me?" sniggered Calum. "We always bring something. Don't we?"

"Yup," acknowledged Simon.

Jay, taking in all this new information from the lounge, strolled into the kitchen to confront the drummer.

"Do you know where it is?"

"I do, I do," he confided, sounding rather like Yogi Bear.

"So why the fuck didn't you say so?"

"No one bothered to ask me."

"Well, I'm fucking well asking you now," Jay fumed, his craving for a smoke beginning to get the better of him. "Who the fuck's got it?"

"Andrew has."

"Andrew is holding our stash?"

"So far as I'm aware."

"And why would he be holding it?"

"Maybe you should ask Basil. He's the one who hid the stuff in Andrew's case in the first place."

Amused by this revelation, Jay liked the idea of his manager being arrested in possession of the band's drugs. "You mean to say Basil hid the stuff in Andrew's case?"

"Aha."

"You actually saw him put it in there?"

"Yes," nodded Simon, beginning to see the funny side himself.

"Well, fuck a duck's arse!"

"Too funny for words, man," Calum laughed. "Priceless."

"So tell me," beamed Jay, grateful to Simon and his manager, "where is the case right now?"

"In his room, I would guess."

"I think we need to have a word with Basil."

Under strict instructions from the pair, Basil waited until he heard Andrew snoring before attempting his audacious break-in. Crawling into the room on hands and knees to avoid waking the sleeping beauty, he rifled through the plethora of zip pockets that festooned suitcase before locating the pouch containing their stash.

Egged on by the other two standing in the doorway, Basil was approaching the final hurdle when it happened. Still on all fours, aiming for the door, stash clenched firmly between his teeth, objective achieved, he collided with a table to send a Styrofoam cup and its contents flying.

"Shit!" he hissed. "Shit, shit and more shit!" he cursed under his breath, before reaching the door and being accorded a hero's welcome.

"Okey-dokey!" Marcella cried, about to put the band through their paces. "This is the part where I talk and you listen – and I'm not gonna say this twice. On no account is Dave to be fucked with," she reminded them all, in reference to their forthcoming appearance on *The David Stampman Show*. Her fears, bearing in mind the band's last appearance on American television, were not unfounded.

"We wouldn't do that," Jay assured her.

"They may not," acknowledged the angry press officer, nodding towards the others. "But you," she said, pointing an accusing finger.

"Me?"

"It was you who sabotaged the band's appearance on MTV," she spat at him. "Not them."

Simon bit his lip. He knew the drill. Went there three times a day.

The source of Marcella's discontent had occurred live on air when Jay was treating viewers to a peek of his new custom-made guitar, shaped to resemble a human figure. Christened 'The Flasher' by its owner, the unique instrument was airbrushed to depict a lecherous, dirty old man holding his raincoat wide open, revealing a huge cock forming the neck of the guitar. Marcella was outraged, while MTV dealt with this unwanted departure from schedule in the editing suite.

"Just remember," she reiterated, praying no one would embarrass her, "this show's built around Dave."

"Why?" asked her husband.

"How many more frigging times?" she moaned, ready to rip his head off. "To make Dave look good. And woe betide anybody who doesn't," she barked at all of them.

A groggy-looking Symes appeared at the doorway, rubbing his eyes.

"Good morning," he said, greeting them with a degree of suspicion.

"Morning Andrew," they all chorused.

Symes stifled a yawn as he helped himself to a fresh pot of coffee. "I hate to interrupt your meeting…"

"I think we're all done here now, so you can fire away," Marcella invited.

"Now far be it from me to go around making petty accusations, but I was wondering whether you can throw any light on a small matter that's bothering me."

"And what might that be?" asked Jay, as if he didn't already know.

"Could anyone explain how, during the night, a cup of coffee emptied itself all over my clothes, all over my suitcase and," he raised his voice, "all over my room?"

"That's terrible," sympathised the guitarist, tutting at Symes while avoiding Basil's gaze. "But to answer your question: no, I've no idea how it could have happened."

"How about the rest of you?" All five shrugged their shoulders and stared blankly at him. "Well, I appreciate all your help," he thanked them sarcastically.

Enquiries having led nowhere, a puzzled Symes returned to his room. Thoroughly pissed off by this lack of co-operation, he was now faced with the unenviable prospect of clearing up the sticky mess.

"That was a close one," the singer whispered to Basil with Symes out of earshot.

"Too fucking right," agreed the hero of the day.

Eschewing the use of the limousine on what had turned out to be a fine day, Basil accompanied Calum and Jay on the relatively short walk to Mandolin Bros. Jay, toting his Les Paul Standard, was taking the opportunity to have the authenticity of his valuable instrument vetted by the store.

Upon entering, they sailed right past Stanley, who was seated behind a desk with a telephone glued to his ear. Dubious Hawaiian shirt apart, it was hard to fault the man. A wheeler dealer at heart, he had an inability to say no when offered vast amounts of money for a guitar – and a complete inability to say yes when asked to pay similar sums.

"You're asking way too much for the piece," Stanley informed the caller, "even if Roy Rogers did own it for a weekend. And stapling a picture of Trigger to the back of the guitar won't improve its value, not in my lifetime. I'm sorry,

I can't pay the kind of money you're asking. No, I'm sorry. You too. Goodbye." Stanley removed the telephone headset and smiled. "What's in the case?" he asked, never one to miss a beat.

"It's my '59 Les Paul Standard. I'd like you to take a look at it."

"Delighted to. Mind if I ask who or where you got it from?"

"Bought it in England earlier this year. Guy called Larry Symonds."

"Surely not T-H-E Larry Symonds?" exclaimed a surprised Stanley, who was already examining the instrument.

"You've heard of him?"

"Certainly have. Bit of a rough diamond," recalled the man whose wardrobe contained only variations on the garish shirt he was wearing. Today's tasteless offering was emblazoned with parrots in fluorescent red, offset nattily by flashes of yellow. "He's a one-off alright," insisted Stanley, "and so," he concluded, glancing up from the instrument, "is this. It's a fake."

Mouth bone dry, gasping for breath, Jay froze.

"Fake?" he murmured, as if repeating the word would reverse the process.

"I'm afraid so. Can I ask how much you paid for it?"

"No, you can't," returned the guitarist, suddenly overcome by nausea. "How much is a fake worth?"

Stanley shrugged. "Eight-thousand dollars. Ten thousand tops."

"That's $190,000 less than you paid for it," Calum reminded his gobsmacked guitarist.

"That's right," acknowledged Basil, pointing to the spot where Jay had been standing. Traumatised in an instant, Jay had fainted and lay motionless on the floor.

While he had been economical with the truth, Symonds had a reason for failing to divulge the real provenance of this particular instrument. The genuine articles – and only 643 of them were made in the halcyon year of 1959 – were produced at the Gibson plant in Kalamazoo, Michigan. This one, however, was manufactured on somebody's kitchen table in Kensal Rise at some unspecified time in the new millennium.

CHAPTER FIFTY

"How many fingers am I holding up?"

After landing heavily and gashing his head against the counter on the way down, Jay's mishap had necessitated a visit to the local quack. Following normal procedure, the doctor shone a light in the eyes of the addled guitar player. Jay, suffering from blurred vision, could see only two fingers. Still disorientated and mistaking the doctor for Larry Symonds, he took a wild swing at him.

"Hey fella, calm down! I'm here to help," the quack reminded Jay as his punch missed its intended target.

After assuring the patient he was no such person, the doctor began stitching up the gaping wound still visible on Jay's forehead before wrapping a wide bandage around his head.

"If you can take this kind of punishment," joked the medicine man, pointing to the injury he'd sustained, "dealing with Dave should be no trouble at all." Then, much to everyone's surprise, he pronounced Jay fit enough to take part in the television recording.

"He's only a talk-show host," Calum reminded him.

"You may think so," grinned the doctor. A big fan of Stampman himself, he handed the guitarist a laminated pack of painkillers the size of golf balls. "Take two of these every four hours," he advised. "They'll help ease the pain and reduce the swelling."

Rehearsals the day preceding their television appearance had presented few real problems. Certainly nothing to compare with their adventures in guitar stores and doctors' surgeries, at least. With a string of European TV shows under their belts, the band already understood the importance of spots and camera angles. What they struggled with, however, was the concept of making Dave look good.

This took many forms: Dave making Dave look good; his guests making Dave look good; the audience making Dave look good; and spotlight-hugging, house-band musical director Paul Parker making Dave look good. It was something he achieved with alarming monotony.

While Stampman was a complex character like most human beings, others questioned whether he was human at all. After all, why did he need the studio air-conditioning system set at maximum during rehearsals and recording?

The answer was that the chat-show host suffered from hyperhidrosis, a condition that produces unwanted bouts of sweating in sufferers, brought on by heat, exercise or anxiety. Put all three together and it's a recipe for disaster. In normal studio conditions sweat would pour from Dave like water from a tap he couldn't turn off – something he sought to avoid it at all costs.

Luckily for Dave, with the show built around him, he called all the shots. So while his guests, the technicians and audience were left to freeze in this permafrost environment, Stampman kept his cool. There was no way the great American public would see him sweating live on air.

Another source of power was the army of researchers Stampman fielded to unearth information for him, valuable ammunition to embarrass his guests.

Master of the snide aside and smugness personified, the owlish Stampman lorded it from the other side of his familiar desk, waiting for the credits to roll, ready to wow America again. He took a sip from his ever-present mug of coffee, his lanky frame parked behind a Shure microphone that wasn't even plugged in. Like almost everything on the show, it was only there to make Dave look good.

Sat upstairs in the green room, Marcella waited for the applause to die down, ready for the action to unfold. A Stampman fan herself, she gazed up in awe at the large video monitor suspended from the wall. On top form today, Dave wasn't about to disappoint.

"Tonight, folks," Stampman beamed, "we have a great show lined up for you. First off a new band from England by the name of SSB, which I'm led to believe is some kinda shorthand for Soft Southern Bast... Let's put it this way," he leered into the camera, repeatedly tapping the desktop with his cue cards. "It has something to do with illegitimacy."

"Illegitimacy?" mocked foil Paul Parker, off-camera.

'And maybe we should leave it at that," teased Dave, before the house band struck up. The studio audience, obliging in the extreme, rocked with laughter.

Calum, viewing this act of treachery from the green room, was having none of it. "You tosser!" he shouted at the screen.

"Later on the show," grinned Dave, acknowledging the applause, "they're going to be playing a couple of tracks from their new album. The album... erm," he deliberated, searching for the correct answer and the cue card holding the pertinent information, "is called *Crimson to Blue*, which currently stands at number one in the UK charts. Hey guys," he mugged for the camera again, "well done. A big round of applause, if you please," he directed, for anyone who'd failed to see the flashing signs directing them to do just that.

"Say," cut in the ubiquitous Paul Parker, this time on-camera.

"What's that?" interjected Stampman, pretending to throw caution instead of cue cards to the wind.

"Weren't these guys called The Crack Heads?"

"I don't allow crack heads on my show. You know the rules, Paul," he said, tapping the cue card he'd been reading from before, then tossing it over his shoulder.

"Rules?" queried Parker, a man who wouldn't have recognised an ad lib if it had landed in his lap gift-wrapped with a ten-foot bow tied around it. "What rules?"

"No dope."

"Too bad," sympathised the balding keyboard player, who liked a toke himself.

"Too bad," concurred the host.

"How about dopes then?" Parker persisted.

"Dopes?"

"Dopes," he repeated, as if half of America had suddenly developed Alzheimer's. "When I saw the guitar player at rehearsal this afternoon he was sporting T-H-E most enormous bandage."

"Bandage?"

"Yeah. A bandage wrapped round his head like a towel."

"Imagine that," exclaimed Stampman, getting into his stride. "And he's been in the city how long?"

"Three days," prompted the sycophantic MD.

"Can you believe that? Three days and mugged already."

Much to the disgust of the band, the entire audience erupted in laughter bang on cue. Stampman, grinning insanely at the camera, pounced on the punchline.

"Fellas," he intoned, feigning humility as only Dave knew how. "On behalf of New York City, we owe you an apology. Hit it maestro…"

Right on cue, the house band led by the irrepressible Parker began to hammer out one of Queen's most popular stadium anthems.

"You bunch of cunts!" Jay shouted back from the green room. "I'd like to piss on your graves, too," he swore at the wall monitor, watching helplessly as the audience pulled off the audio equivalent of the Mexican Wave clapping in time to

'Another One Bites the Dust'. Musical interlude over, the chat-show host had a final message to deliver.

"Jay," he glowered from the monitor. "Get well soon."

"Go fuck yourself you talentless twat!" he screamed back, raising a middle finger to the monitor.

"Shut up! boomed Marcella, glaring at the guitarist.

"You scumbag!" shouted Simon.

"And you behave, too" she bawled back at him.

"Are we all agreed?"

"Let's do it."

"It'll be a laugh," sniggered Basil.

"Not for him it won't," promised the guitarist.

"He fucking deserves it," Calum piped in.

"And a serious kicking, too," rasped Jay, adding it to the mental check list of things he intended to do to Dave once he'd finished with Larry Symonds.

"Do I have to join in?"

"Afraid so, Simon. All for one and one for all and all that nonsense."

"Whatever," he sighed, not entirely happy with the outcome and unsure whether to act like a rock star or pliant husband.

"Then let's break out the FrothFace."

"Coming up, Jay."

After extracting five bottles from a flight case in the far corner of the dressing room, Grant distributed them to the rest of the band. When they'd downed five more bottles of the unctuous red alcopop, making sure their lips were moist, they all felt ready to do battle with Dave.

"They're calling for you now," Symes informed them, appearing at the doorway.

Jay signalled for the others to follow him. "Time to go."

"It's showtime," Symes chivied them.

"Or time to show the world Dave doesn't control it," declared the guitarist.

In less time than it takes to roll a joint, SSB had cranked out a blistering version of 'It Had to Happen'.

Stampman, meanwhile, squinted at the action on his monitor and blinked hard. As they launched into the album's title track, 'Crimson to Blue', he couldn't tear his eyes from their lips.

"What's that?" he asked the aide talking to him through his earpiece.

"It's what happens when you drink FrothFace," replied the aide.

"And what is FrothFace?"

"The alcopop drink the band endorses."

"But that's free product placement for their sponsors, not ours!" he shouted at the luckless aide. "Our advertisers will be fucking furious."

During the first number he'd just assumed they'd been a little heavy-handed in makeup. Now, as the band launched into the chorus, he stared in disbelief as five sets of crimson lips metamorphosed into inky blue ones.

Clearly enjoying themselves, Jay and Calum were treating Stampman to a new chorus line they'd just crafted in the green room to honour him.

The chat-show host pretending he's the news
Claims to care about your different views
Then one day he sees his ratings fall
Now he's drinking FrothFace in your mall

"Bastards, bastards, bastards!" fumed Stampman, furious at being upstaged by a guest on his own show.

With the show over, its host, still insulted by the words of a chorus he couldn't get out of his head, was pacing the corridors of CBS TV Studios looking for answers. Rattled by the band's 'tribute', he took little consolation from the fact they'd never be invited to appear on his show again.

"OK, I just wanna know one thing," Stampman challenged a recent addition to his team, watching the audience filtering out of the building into the streets below. "Who booked those assholes?"

"You did," came the reply.

CHAPTER FIFTY-ONE

Having failed spectacularly in charming the pants off America's most famous chat-show host, SSB accepted it would be asking too much to expect a Christmas card from the man that year – or the one after.

They were far from despondent, though, as they'd benefited from the appearance more than they could have imagined. Their date with Dave had generated more column inches in the press than a scissor-wielding army of record company PRs could handle.

Rewarded for the avalanche of media coverage they'd generated, the band received an unexpected bonus: a six-figure sum from their very grateful sponsor. Sales of a certain alcopop shot off the graph within days of the show being aired.

Media coverage aside, SSB's performance as the FrothFace Five had guaranteed them a place in the hearts and minds of the record-buying American public. Viewers had admired them for getting one over on Dave, a man many had believed was bullet-proof. More importantly, they'd rattled Stampman in his own cage – and on his own territory.

To top it all, contrary to record company predictions and the band's own modest expectations, sales of *Crimson to Blue* had skyrocketed in the States. After entering the Billboard chart with a bullet, the album was currently sitting at number 29 in the charts, and set to rise.

With large pockets of the community won over by their zany antics on TV, the band was now recognised and fêted wherever they went in New York. In mood for celebration after their toast-of-the-town Stampman showing, SSB dined out in style the following evening. Symes was able to reserve a table at one of Manhattan's most prestigious but conveniently star-struck eating establishments, EastWest, situated roughly halfway along Central Park South.

On arrival, with the maximum of fuss, both band and entourage were spirited towards a section at the back of the vast restaurant. Once safely on the other side of the red silk rope, in an area cordoned off for visiting VIPs, they found their every wish catered for, with fawning staff falling over themselves to serve them.

"My name is Alfonso," the sycophantic maître d' greeted their table, radiating slime. "First of all," he wheedled, bowing to each of them in turn, "on behalf of EastWest I'd like to welcome you all to New York City. And perhaps," he continued to ingratiate himself, "you'd be kind enough to allow me the honour of offering you a bottle of champagne on the house? French, of course."

"Perfect," grinned Symes, who loathed the Californian version the Americans always served up.

"Jay doesn't drink house champagne," Simon interrupted.

"I had no intention of offering you house champagne," hissed the maître d', underneath slicked-back, brilliantined hair you could see your face in. Used to customers challenging his authority, he knew his bluff had been called. But with professional instinct taking over, he turned on the charm that had got him this far. "And what would Sir like to drink?" he asked, adopting a weasel-like tone.

"I don't suppose you have any Bollinger Grand Année kicking around the building?" The maître d' was affronted. "The 1990 would go down a treat," Jay informed him.

"Would it now?" queried his ruffled host, trying to memorise the wine list as he continued with his charm offensive.

"Or some Perrier-Jouët Brut? You might even have a bottle of that lurking in your cellar."

"Perrier-Jouët Brut?" This conversation was growing more expensive for the house by the minute.

"Perhaps a magnum of the '92?" proposed Jay, instead of quitting while he was ahead.

"I'll do my best," returned the maître d', a little huffily. "I'll have somebody check our current inventory for you right now. Meanwhile, on behalf of EastWest, I hope you all enjoy yourselves this evening," he added, superfluously.

"Thanks to you I'm sure we will," replied Symes, watching as the maître d' passed a slip of paper he'd scribbled on to another flunky.

Pleasantries over with, Alfonso marched back to his post by the dimly lit front-of-house lectern, ready to be insulted by the next high roller gliding through the restaurant's revolving doors.

It wasn't long before an out-of-work actor posing as a waiter arrived at the table bearing a magnum of Bollinger Grand Année 1990. He was joined immediately by a second waiter carrying a magnum of Perrier-Jouët Brut 1992. With a flourish, each in turn passed Jay the precious cargo they were cradling for further inspection.

"These will do just fine, dude," said Jay, slipping into the local lingo.

"If this is the down side of crossing swords with Dave, give me more," said Symes, congratulating Jay on his choice of bubbly.

There was, of course, another knock-on effect from appearing on America's most popular chat show: namely, every single ticket for their two concerts at New York's prestigious Radio City Music Hall had sold out within hours. All it had taken was a single appearance on *The Stampman Show* and word of mouth had taken care of the rest. And like Dave, the one commodity New Yorkers had in abundance was mouth.

The band signed autographs for guests and staff alike before they ate, even posing for photographs with the manager of EastWest. Then they chowed down as if told it was their last day on earth. With caviar and foie gras accompanying the champagne, the meal started with lobster before rolling into a selection of shrimp, smoked salmon, sole and sea bass, all washed down with quantities of the finest Premier Cru white burgundies that would have filled a small aquarium. If it was on the menu, they ordered it – and if it wasn't, they asked anyway.

Following the fish and seafood extravaganza was a bovine blow-out of epic proportions comprising beef, lamb, duckling and quail accompanied by the finest first-growth clarets and burgundy money could buy. By comparison, dessert was a complete non-event, which was a shame. Unlike the other courses, it had experienced no pain on its way to the plate.

By the time the debris of dining had been cleared away, a slightly worse for wear Simon and Marcella were deep in conversation with two love-torn ice sculptures adorning their table. Also plastered, Jay and Basil were communicating in a language that made Klingon sound comprehensible. The pair's exchange, eschewing the use of all consonants, consisted of little more than a series of grunts linked by cascading vowels.

Ignoring them all, Symes and Jack Weisberg, Platinum's A&R man in the USA, were enjoying large cognacs. The well-brought-up Symes, leaning across the table puffing on a cigar the size of the Chrysler Building, felt bound to congratulate the man who was paying the bill.

"You're the man, Jack," he declared, landing a hearty slap on his supposed benefactor's shoulder. "That was truly exquisite. Thank you."

"A pleasure," returned Weisberg, eyes narrowing through a haze of curling blue smoke, omitting the word 'my'. What he should have said, if he'd had an ounce of honesty, was: 'Why thank me?' After all, it wouldn't be him or the label footing the bill for this evening's lavish entertainment. And if Symes had any doubts on that score, he'd only have to check the next royalty statement when it landed on his desk.

"David, where's Calum?" enquired Grant, one of the only people sat at the table still remotely sober.

"Shagging, I shouldn't wonder."

"Again?"

"Never stops, does he? I presume you saw him sloping off in the direction of the bathrooms with that over-enthusiastic waitress?"

"I didn't. Hang on, do you mean the one with huge jugs?"

"That's the one. He's been flirting with her practically all evening. Still, he's getting more exercise than we are."

"Excuse me for butting in, Sir," the sommelier interrupted Symes' conversation, beckoning to a flunky holding a magnum of champagne. "The gentlemen standing over by the lectern have sent over this with their compliments, Sir. The people you see talking to Alfonso, our maître d'," he indicated.

"Really? How kind of them."

As curious as Symes regarding the identity of their mystery benefactors, Weisberg clipped on a pair of wire-rimmed spectacles.

"They asked me to congratulate you on your performance on *The Stampman Show*. They also said they looked forward to seeing you at the concert. Tomorrow..." the sommelier trailed off.

Symes frowned. "At Radio City Music Hall?"

"I believe so."

"Do they have tickets?"

"Oh, they won't have trouble getting in," he confided, his voice sounding distinctly nervous.

"Well, it is sold out. Anyway, you be sure to thank them from me," said Symes, nodding in the direction of three sharp-suited gentlemen he guessed to be of Sicilian or Italian extraction. "How extraordinary," he mused, as they recipro-cated with a curt bow. "Looks like we're still winning them over in this town, Jack."

The A&R man, resisting the urge to speak until the bearer of this news was out of sight and earshot, chewed anxiously on the cigar lodged in his mouth. He removed his spectacles and threw them on to the table before turning to face Symes.

"Andrew, do you have any fucking idea who you're getting getting into bed with?"

"By the looks of them, businessmen of some sort, I would guess."

"They're businessmen all right."

"Why? Are they friends of yours?"

"Friends of mine? I hardly think so," Weisberg harrumphed.

"So who were they?"

"Andrew, this is no time for naïvety," the native New Yorker exhorted him.

"I'm sorry, Jack. You've got the better of me on this one. Who are we talking about?"

"The Mob, Andrew. I'm talking about the Mob."

"Are you absolutely sure, Jack?"

"Well, I wasn't talking about the three fucking bears."

CHAPTER FIFTY-TWO

Dominating 6th Avenue between 50th and 51st St, Radio City Music Hall was nothing short of an architectural masterpiece. An American institution erected in the early thirties by John D. Rockefeller Jr., it boasted a marquee that took up an entire city-block, justly earning its reputation as 'the largest indoor theatre in the world'. From the time it opened its doors in 1932, this former home to the Rockettes had played host to the cream of Hollywood's movie actors, while in the ensuing years went on to present the 'new' talents of the day such as Frank Sinatra, Count Basie and Ella Fitzgerald. Now, musical pedigree still in tact, Radio City Music Hall would showcase rock acts.

Symes stepped outside to examine the queue that was forming already for the first concerts and was flushed with pride when he saw the line of concert-goers stretching back along Broadway and around the corner before disappearing from sight altogether. He cast his eye up and down it, sensing this audience was the next major hurdle to overcome if they were to take the album to the top of the Billboard charts. And with *Crimson to Blue* currently sat at number fifteen, Symes knew the live shows scheduled over the coming weeks could only help it on its way. What the manager also understood was that, with an extremely successful TV appearance to their credit, SSB were in a stronger position to crack the big time than most bands would ever be. It was something he was patently aware of when he strolled back inside the building.

Radio City Music Hall, in common with most venues, operated a strict ban on the consumption of alcohol in the auditorium. Implementing this code of conduct was another matter, though, and tonight the venue was packed to the rafters with SSB fans hell-bent on having a good time. As the house lights dimmed, a solitary voice rang out of the massive PA system.

"Ladies and gentleman, would you please give a loud, warm welcome to the band that rattled David Stampman. All the way from Engerrlund. May I present ESS! ESS! BEE!!"

As the curtains rose, Jay struck the opening power chord of 'Crimson to Blue' while flash pots placed around the stage exploded in sequence, lighting up the band to announce their arrival. The fans, reciprocating in a demonstration of unswerving loyalty, greeted their heroes with an almighty roar. From the stage, blinded by the lights, all the band could make out was a sea of faces, every other one sporting crimson or inky blue lips. Captured on video for future broadcast, this 'look' would soon become the norm amongst hardcore followers as the band criss-crossed America.

Lurking in the shadows, watching the band from a vantage point in the wings, the sharply dressed man with the sleek black vicuna coat draped around his shoulders smiled benignly. Giving the impression of being deeply engrossed in the music, he was suddenly alerted to the presence of someone who'd taken up residence behind him. He turned slowly to acknowledge the figure.

"Your guys sure are hot tonight," acknowledged the silhouette, an Access All Areas laminated pass dangling from his neck.

"These guys," insisted the second silhouette, "are hot every night."

"Is that so?" drawled the thickset man, tapping the stage with the ebony cane he'd been leaning on. "Then I would say that makes you a very lucky man."

Eager to learn his identity, the second silhouette stepped from the shadows. Standing directly in a pool of light, he proffered his hand to the larger man still bathed in darkness.

"I'm sorry, but I don't believe we've met. I'm Andrew Symes and, at risk of sounding rude, you are?"

"Mario Volante," returned the first silhouette, now emerging from the shadows to reveal himself.

Grateful though Symes was for this information, he was as yet none the wiser, although he vaguely recollected seeing him earlier, skulking around the backstage area during the soundcheck.

"Should I know you?" he asked, unable to oblige his inquisitor, though he'd noticed the man's face was heavily scarred. The right side had been slit from ear to mouth, while the left side bore evidence of a skin graft.

"You, my friend, have exceedingly poor recall."

"It's true, sometimes I do. Actually, on reflection, I do remember you now. It was you and your two associates who kindly sent over a magnum of champagne to our table in the restaurant last night. I can't thank you enough, it was fabulous." Then he remembered the advice Jack Weisberg had given him – and the profession of his benefactors. "I apologise profusely for not recognising you."

"Think nothing of it, Andrew," insisted the mobster.

Symes, feeling the beads of sweat gathering on his fore-head, was desperate not to appear anxious. "And to what do we owe the honour of your company this evening?"

The mobster looming over him narrowed his eyes, penetrated Symes'. "I suppose you could say it's business. A friendly business call."

"How friendly?"

"Well, Andrew, that would depend on how friendly you want it to be."

Unsure why he'd asked the question, and wishing he hadn't but remembering his mother always telling him 'In for a penny, in for a pound', he took it upon himself to ask another he might also come to regret.

"Exactly what kind of business is it that you're involved in, Mr. Volante?"

"Union business, my friend."

'Union business? Hmmm," hummed Symes, eyebrows raising of their own accord.

"That's correct. You got it in one."

"And what exactly is it you do for them?" Symes continued, digging his own grave.

"What do I do for them?" snapped the the Mob representative, tired of being treated like a quiz-show contestant.

"Yes, what function do you perform on their behalf, Mr. Volante?"

Deliberating whether the man in front of him was having a laugh at his expense, or just plain stupid, the mobster began explaining the facts of life.

"You seem like a nice guy to me, Andrew. So I'm gonna level with you."

Symes, still wondering whether his less than reluctant line of questioning would lead to premature death – his own, in particular – took a deep breath. "Go ahead, level away," he urged playfully, unwise given the gravity of his situation.

"We..."

"We?" Symes said, his buttocks clenching. He could only be referring to the Mob.

"I'm sorry, Andrew," the thug corrected himself, before mopping his brow with a freshly laundered handkerchief. "What I actually meant to say was this. I'm here to make sure our brothers, by which I mean the members of my union, are not being sidelined by your people. People," he frowned, "who might be of an illegitimate nature. People not in possession of the correct paperwork, so to speak. People without yellow cards. Do we understand each other?"

"We do," confirmed Symes, offering immediate reassurance. "I think you'll find us bulletproof on that score," he added, before regretting his choice of words.

"Then I'm happy for you," confirmed the resident of New Jersey.

"And why is that?"

"Why? Today I'm feeling loquacious, Andrew. So I'm gonna tell you." Moving closer, he placed an arm menacingly around Symes' shoulder. Then he began to squeeze, harder and harder. "Andrew," he reduced his voice to a baritone whisper, designed to instil terror in the listener, all the while increasing the pressure exerted on Symes' shoulder. "There are some not very polite bands out there. Bands who live in cloud cuckoo land. Bands who think they can do it all on their own."

"Huh! They all think they can do that."

"Bands," he continued, ignoring the interruption, "who would dearly like to avoid dealing with us," he added threateningly, veins beginning to bulge in his forehead. "You know what I'm saying?" Diatribe over, he loosened his vice-like grip.

"Us?" repeated Symes, rubbing his sore limb, trying to to ascertain any damage.

"The union. Same thing," snapped the odious character, who just seconds ago had seemed rather taken with shoulder dislocation.

Feckless beyond the call of duty, Symes had one more question.

"Which union might that be?"

"Does the name 'Teamsters' mean anything to you, Andrew?"

CHAPTER FIFTY-THREE

Symes breathed a huge sigh of relief, feeling eternally grateful as the audience began to signal its appreciation at the close of the first number. The fans, showing their unbridled enthusiasm for rock 'n' roll, cranked up the volume in the auditorium to fill the air with solid sheets of sound. Piling decibel upon decibel, between them they built up the sound pressure level to an ear-splitting crescendo.

Conveniently for Symes, if not his interrogator, the fans had eliminated all forms of conversation. Engulfed by the mighty roar and still standing shoulder to shoulder with his uninvited guest, Symes took three, slow steps forward. Cast adrift, he revelled in the sheer spontaneity of the spectacle, welcoming the noise drowning out the dying chords as the audience continued to show its appreciation.

Symes bided his time before turning, reluctantly, to face his aggressor. Volante was nowhere to be seen. Antenna on alert, he scanned the backstage area before spying him heading towards the exit. Tempted to follow, he instead observed as the mobster was joined by two other men he thought he recognised his accomplices. Eager to be relieved of his burden, he watched as his three unwelcome guests left the backstage area, heading towards the stage door.

Ordeal over for the time being, Symes turned back towards the crowd, ready to be battered into submission by the deafening applause surging in waves towards the stage. Imagining they were baying for his blood, it sent shivers of a different kind down his spine.

"Need more bad company?" chuckled Weisberg, who'd joined Symes in one of the quieter area backstage areas. "I saw you making conversation with one of those goons who bought us champagne in the restaurant last night. Remember? Andrew, do I detect a note of reticence here? Don't tell me: they've forbidden you to discuss sensitive family business with outsiders," he mocked the Englishman. "I presume you recognised him."

"Of course I bloody recognised him," snapped the man who hadn't.

"Did he have anything interesting to say, Andrew? Anything I should know about?"

Traumatised by the indignity of being physically manhandled, Symes declined the opportunity to offer a blow-by-blow account. "Something about yellow cards."

"Now there's a surprise."

"Very funny. Have you ever considered making a living in stand-up?"

"Listen up, and listen hard, Andrew. If you don't play ball with these guys, if you don't make sure your people have legitimate work permits, T-H-E-Y are gonna come down on you."

"You don't say."

"Very hard."

"I think I get the message."

"Don't mess with them."

"Don't worry, I wasn't about to," the increasingly riled Symes bristled. "Do I look like somebody who wants to end up at the bottom of the Hudson River?"

"No but…"

"Do I look like the kind of person who has a burning desire to spend the rest of time propping up a freeway?"

"No, but…"

"Then just shut the fuck up!"

"Whatever."

"I've already issued Basil with strict instructions. I've made it quite clear to him we're not hiring temporary labour at any point on this tour unless people can show us the correct paperwork. No yellow card, no gig – satisfied now, you bullying shithead?"

"Whoa, get a grip, buddy."

"I've got a fucking grip – and, before you ask, I intend retaining it for the rest of this tour."

"Fine, Andrew. Then I won't have to worry."

"What have you got to worry about?"

"Insignificant though it may sound to you, Andrew, my main concern is what head office might say. Because I know damn well they don't want to hear that their precious investment has been put out of action for the rest of the tour after being physically attacked by some loony psychopath due to your negligence."

Symes had heard enough about 'accidents' of this nature, they happened with alarming regularity in their industry. And like Jack, he knew that musicians with broken fingers didn't fulfil contractual obligations, they cancelled tours.

"You don't fuck around with these people, Andrew. You deal with the Teamsters, or you deal with the Mob – it all adds up to the same thing."

"So I was informed."

"Shit happens."

"I hear you."

"And shit will happen if you don't play ball with them."

"I said I fucking hear you, Jack. Now can we drop the subject?"

"Sure. I hear the band's been nominated for some kind of award in Blighty. Is that true?"

"Yes."

"Damn awards ceremonies. Who's handing out the gongs this time?"

"CRAFT."

"Never heard of them."

"It's an acronym."

Due to the fact that he and his generation had largely emailed or text-messaged their way to the top, Weisberg was rarely called upon to exhibit any serious grasp of the English language. "Acronym?"

"A word formed from the first letters of a series of other words."

"Is that so?"

"According to my dictionary."

"Sounds like some kiss-ass disease to me."

"That's because you're American."

"Is that right?" returned the New Yorker, desperate to score a point for his country. "So what does CRAFT stand for?"

"It's an abbreviation…"

"Abbreviation?"

"You know, Jack, some days you render me speechless," he admonished him. "Days like today, days when I find my patience stretched to breaking point."

"You Brits are legendary for your lack of sensitivity."

"Beg your pardon?"

"I was being ironic."

"I wasn't aware anybody in this country knew the meaning of the word."

Weisberg was having none of it. "So are you going to tell me what CRAFT stands for, you son of a bitch?"

"Centre for the Recording Arts, Film & TV."

"That's a mighty fancy title for an organisation that has any connection with the grubby industry we earn our living from."

"That I'll grant you."

"Where do they get these names? Do they pay some dumb-ass Brit to come up with these acronyns or whatever you call them?"

"I've no idea, Jack."

"Is it any wonder England's in deep doo-doo when you Brits have nothing better to do with your time than sit around making up stupid names? In fact, I'm willing to go out on a limb here and say that ranks as a fuckin' crime when there's a whole universe out there waiting to be explored."

CHAPTER FIFTY-FOUR

Despite the atrocious weather conditions hampering progress soon after take-off, the musicians stepped off the chartered jet in the dead of night after touching down safely at Newark Airport. Almost blown towards their transport parked on the rainswept tarmac, the band walked in complete silence with Symes, Basil and Marcella in tow. Operating on autopilot with yards to stagger, they climbed into the back of the black stretch limousine.

With thirty-five concerts under their belts by the time they'd completed the first leg of the tour, SSB had made serious inroads on the East Coast. Their fans had rushed out to buy the new record, effectively pushing sales still higher until *Crimson To Blue* sat at number nine on the Billboard album chart. But while they may have been elated by the impact they were having and thrilled by the raucous receptions they'd received, the band members were far too exhausted to congratulate themselves.

His lanky frame stretched out in the rear of the limo, Jay yawned. Taking their cue, the others began to yawn, too.

"Ben," he mumbled, summoning up what little strength he had left. "What time is our plane tomorrow?"

"Pick-up is six am," the driver announced over the intercom. "Your flight is at nine."

"Spare me," groaned Calum.

"Five minutes past nine, if I'm not mistaken."

After easing the limo down the off-ramp and stepping on the gas, Ben shifted up a gear as they connected with the freeway leading to Bard Avenue, home and bed.

While the others were preparing to take a break from touring, Jay and Calum, the band's songwriters, would be otherwise engaged over the weekend.

"Surely we could make it a bit later?"

"Only if you want to miss the plane."

Wasted by the exertions of the preceding weeks, Calum was ready to sell his own mother for a decent night's sleep.

"You know, Ben, being a rock star isn't all it's cracked up to be."

"The likes of me will never find out."

Essentially a good person at heart, Ben too would have sold his mother if it meant trading places with one of these guys. Stepping inside their shoes, being exposed to the same financial pressures, the same physical temptations... wouldn't he just?

"Sometimes it sucks, man. It can get really tough out there."

Hardly sharing his viewpoint, the driver and former Marine knew the meaning of the word 'tough'. And 'out there' was where he lived.

"Tough? Depends what you mean by tough. I ain't got nobody out there buying shitloads of my records. Nobody out there queuing up to buy tickets for my concerts. Nobody offering to suck my dick. How tough can all that shit be? You know what I'm saying? Hell, I'd swap with any of you guys in a heartbeat. Then you could do my job," Ben laughed.

"I bet I could."

"I bet you couldn't. Because if we swapped gigs you'd be the one getting up earlier still to drive M-E to the goddamn airport."

"You think we're pampered," David interrupted, "don't you?"

"I do," nodded the driver.

"And you think he's ungrateful, don't you?"

"Yes, I do," acknowledged Ben, risking his job.

"Well, we are, and he is. End of argument. Satisfied, Ben?"

"Oh, I'm satisfied," he grinned, happy to set the record straight.

Jay, feeling decidedly delicate after polishing off serious quantities of champagne the previous evening at Ronnie Scott's, had been dreading this meeting. Decent bloke though he was, the band's lawyer Marcus Davies operated in a rarefied atmosphere far removed from the rock 'n' roll world he inhabited.

"Did you pay cash for the instrument?" enquired the rubicund faced senior partner at Hamilton, Michael, Davies & Partners.

Along with Calum, the jet-lagged guitarist was due to attend the CRAFT Awards later that afternoon after being nominated for 'Best Songwriter'.

"Did you pay cash?" repeated Davies. "Fah, folding stuff," stuttered the lawyer, sporting one of his trademark, hand-painted silk bow-ties.

"Yes, much to my disgust."

"And how much did you pay this rogue Larry Symonds?"

"One hundred and thirty thousand pounds." Jay gulped.

Davies gulped, too. "I'd no idea it was possible to spend that amount of money on an electric guitar," he grimaced, trying to compute how many cases of Château Latour first growths he could have purchased with the sum. "And not even for a real one."

"It's possible," squirmed the guitarist. "Otherwise I wouldn't be here, would I?"

"Quite," responded the lawyer, fiddling with his cuffs. "Best leave me all the details then and I'll see what I can do."

Clad from head to foot in black leather, crotch-tight pants leaving little to the imagination, Calum swaggered into the Dorchester Hotel. Testosterone on legs, dressed to kill, he hoped to pick up an award, get pissed and, if the gods were smiling down on him, get laid. Indeed, as soon as he and his fellow nominee were ushered to their allotted places in the noisy ballroom, the latter option turned into a distinct possibility. From the moment the sexually incontinent singer set eyes upon her, it was lust at first sight.

"You owe me twenty quid," mouthed Jay, trying to attract his attention.

"For what?" Calum queried, when he could tear his eyes from this angel the organisers had been foolish enough to sit beside him.

"You owe me twenty smackers if you don't bonk the girl sitting next to you before the afternoon is up."

"What kind of a person do you think I am?"

"I already know. I was merely trying to establish the price."

"You're on," said the randy singer.

She was Jade McLoughlin, the red-headed beauty who fronted The Duds, a four-piece Irish band recently signed to their record label.

"Twenty pounds it is then," decreed the man who would be pimp. Ready to savour this Kodak moment, he watched the cocky singer launch into his chat-up line.

"If I told you your beauty outshone the legendary Venus de Milo," Calum said, eyes caressing the elfin-faced colleen. "If I said your skin possessed the lustrous sheen of polished marble…" He examined her lily-white cleavage at close quarters. "If I told you the goddess of love, Aphrodite, wafted you here from a faraway place," he continued to flatter, while mentally stripping her naked. "If I told you all of these things, my dear, what would you say?"

"Feck off," she retorted. "I know what you said when you were talking with your man there." Gifted with the ability to lip-read since childhood, the Belfast-born singer pointed an accusing finger at Jay.

"Heard what?" Calum protested.

"You durty bastard!" she seethed in her Irish brogue. "Your attitude sucks and so does his," she added, pointing to the shrinking violet sat next to him.

"I've got nothing to hide," volunteered the man, who only minutes earlier was willing to wager twenty coins of the realm on what now appeared to be a lost cause.

"That I would doubt."

"Is there anything else that sucks?" asked Calum.

"Yes, you, you poxy bastard!" the red head snapped at him, ready to deliver her final rebuke. "Your fecking band sucks, too!"

Nobody had ever spoken to him like this before. He was lost, momentarily, in admiration for this feisty young woman who'd rendered him speechless.

"Well, I know you may find this hard to believe," he began, searching for the right words, "but I do have a sensitive side, too." He smiled sweetly, captivated.

"Boy, did she read you the riot act," declared Jay over breakfast the following morning. "That's the first time I've ever heard any woman trash you. That Jade McLoughlin's quite a handful – the way she busted your chops last night was superb. I'd no idea you had a sensitive side, too. You never cease to amaze me. You had us fooled all this time Calum."

Unperturbed by these wild allegations, Calim shrugged as another forkful of bacon and eggs headed south. "It's not as though we came away empty-handed. We got the award didn't we? The Duds didn't get one."

"True enough," he conceded. Like Calum, Jay had been thrilled to pick up the prestigious 'Best Songwriter' award. "But did..." he hesitated for a moment, "did you, erm..." Ready to collect his pound of flesh, or twenty pound notes in this instance, he opted for the blunt approach he knew so well. "Did you shag her?"

The singer looked like the cat who got the cream. "Yes."

"Really?" chortled Jay, thrilled at the prospect of earning twenty pounds for being evil.

"Got this, too," he grinned, waving a piece of paper in the air. "Gave me her mobile number, said she'd call me."

"Blimey! Serious already and you've only shagged her the once. Are The Duds going out on the road, then?"

"Yeah, the poor buggers are starting their first US tour next week. Supporting," he sneered, thankful his own days as a support act were over.

"Who are they going out with?"

"Marilyn Manson," said Calum, passing his friend a twenty pound note.

"Thanks," said Jay. "Rather them than us."

CHAPTER FIFTY-FIVE

Thirty-five thousand feet above the Atlantic, the tedium of long-distance travel was taking its toll. Bored trying to guess which stewardess was screwing the captain, they'd arrived at the conclusion they all were. To kill more time, Calum and Jay were catching up with reading some of their American press coverage.

"Calum, do you remember that really cute journalist from Music Market Magazine?"

"Her," he purred, seat reclined at a pitch guaranteed to yield maximum comfort for him and maximum discomfort for the person seated behind.

"She's described you here as a 'tortured genius'."

"What else did she say?" he asked, desperate to have his ego stroked.

"She says you gave the 'spunkiest performance of the millennium'."

"She's right there."

"I heard you were the one who got it right there," observed the guitarist, tapping his crotch. "You did shag her, didn't you?"

"Whatever gave you that idea?"

"Well," he began, armed with a list of clues. "We all know she had huge tits."

"Foolish to deny."

"And even from a distance I'd say it was safe to assume she had a pulse."

"Once again, hard to deny."

"So if we take into account the skirt she was barely wearing when she dragged you into the interview room and add a little encouragement from your permanently priapic pecker, I'd say that within minutes of the interview kicking off you either fucked her senseless or she blew you and your balls into oblivion."

"I did," conceded Calum. "And she did," he remembered.

It all started innocently enough when he'd asked, "Do you like 'Bend Over'?" a reference to a song the band had recently worked into its stage act. "Sure do," she responded before removing her panties and prostrating herself across the nearest photocopier. Towards the end of the interview she produced two tampons from her handbag and demanded the singer autograph them. In her fertile imagination it would be the next best thing to having him inside her when they were thousands of miles apart.

"This one's a real blinder," Jay enthused loudly for the benefit of other passengers in business class. "*Singer Sucks For His Supper*."

"Jumped-up twat."

Realising it was his cue to get in on the act, relishing revenge for having his kneecaps compressed, the obese businessman wedged into the seat behind Calum stepped up to the plate. "He's right. You are."

"That slimy little toe-rag. The first time he met me he couldn't tell me enough how much he loved me. Then when I bumped into him weeks later, he virtually accused me of banging his girlfriend."

"Which you did, as I recall."

"Not this time," revealed Calum, voice tinged with regret. "Anyway, let me take a look at that magazine. I bet you don't come out of this smelling of roses either." He cast a practised eye over the copy before alighting on Jay's mention. "Are you ready?"

"Fire away."

"Soloing with the sparsity of Eric Clapton but delivering with the precision of a sledgehammer, guitarist Jay Jackson plays with balls but lacks conviction."

"Cocksucker!" snapped the guitarist.

"That you are," guffawed the fat businessman, chipping in again with his ten-penneth.

"At other times Jackson seemed devoid of feeling altogether, particularly when stringing together power chords in the fashion of the great Pete Townshend. The difference is Townshend sounds like he means it, whereas Jackson struggles to even fake it."

"Well, fuck him."

Calum smiled, happy to have levelled the playing field. "Finally we agree on something."

"Purpose of your visit?"

"I'm touring with my band."

"O-U-R band," Jay corrected him, carelessly stepping over the 'STOP' sign etched into the floor to make his point.

"Stay back behind the line," the immigration official at Newark Airport barked at him. "Is he with you?"

"Yeah," muttered the singer

"I beg your pardon?"

"Yeah," repeated Calum, his voice conveying boredom and disrespect.

"Tell your friend to come over here."

"What?"

"I said," growled the officer, "to tell your friend to come over here. Are you aware of the stance we take on drugs in the US?" he asked when the pair were standing in front of him. "Well?" He looked up for the first time.

"We know you're not wild about them."

"We've seen all the posters."

"JUST SAY NO," they announced in unison, sniggering like schoolboys.

"This is no laughing matter." He signalled another official standing at a distance to join them.

"What seems to be the problem?" asked the man from the DEA, America's drug enforcement agency.

"These two gentlemen from England seem to think drugs are a laughing matter."

"No we don't," Calum protested too late.

"Perhaps you can escort them to our 'hospitality suite' and convince them otherwise."

"My pleasure, Don," he beamed back at his colleague behind the desk. "Now, if you gentlemen would follow me..."

After being taken to a more secure part of the building, Calum was petrified to hear the snap of surgical rubber – and the words 'bend over' for the second time that day.

"Look," he pleaded, his lips puckered up in competition with his arse. "If I was a junkie I'd have track marks on my arms, wouldn't I?"

"Believe me, buddy," promised the official pulling tightly on a surgical glove, "if you don't co-operate you're gonna have track marks all the way up your asshole."

Jay was faring little better at the other end of the corridor.

"Just because we're in a rock band doesn't mean we take drugs," he reasoned.

"Is that so?" challenged his interrogator. "We had Keith Richards through here a few weeks ago. Have you heard of him?"

"Who does he play with?"

"You really don't know when you're telling the truth, do you?"

"Of course I do. I tell it all the time."

"Well, you'd better start telling it now. I'll ask again: do you take drugs? And do you know who Keith Richards is?"

"Of course I do, I was kidding."

"About the drugs?" demanded the man from the DEA.

"No, Keith Richards."

"So now you admit you were lying?"

"About Keith, yes. But not about the drugs. I wouldn't do that."

"How can I be sure when half the time you don't even know if you're telling the truth yourself?" He reached into a drawer marked 'surgical apparatus' that contained nothing but tubes of KY Jelly, pulling out a single tube before placing it on the countertop between them. "Now, run that story past me one more time…"

CHAPTER FIFTY-SIX

The pair had been ill prepared for the New York winter weather that greeted them when they stepped off the plane. Neither had they been expecting the humiliating body search they were subjected to on arrival. Homosexuality, they decided, was not their cup of tea.

"Poxy taxis," Jay cursed as the tenth yellow cab in a row sped past.

Stranded in the middle of New York's garment district with the mercury falling, he and Calum were stood at the intersection of Broadway and 38th Street, a wind chill factor of ten already freezing their ears off and promising to bestow the same favour on their balls. They tried desperately to hail a taxi before their heads imploded from the whistling wind.

"Cunts," hollered Calum. At this precise moment a yellow taxi swerved across three lanes of traffic before grinding to a halt beside them. "Times Square," he directed, dispensing with politeness now he was back in New York City.

"You guys from England?" asked the Eastern European driver.

"Yeah," said Calum, lacking the enthusiasm for a grilling courtesy of someone he'd never met and, in all likelihood, would never meet again.

"What do you guys make of New York?" asked their quizmaster, clearly already acquainted with the nosiness associated with his job.

"Colder than a polar bear's chuff, if you must know."

"That's really funny man."

"Not for us it isn't."

"So have you guys ever met the Queen?"

"Met the guitar player once."

"Huh?"

"Jolly nice bloke he was, too," revealed Jay, attempting to curtail the conversation.

"So how do people in the UK feel about drugs?" he continued to probe.

"Listen," said the exasperated guitarist. "Why don't you just shut the fuck up and drive?"

A stone's throw from Times Square and home to most of the city's guitar stores, West 48th Street had become a favourite hang for the band. Today, their first port of call was Manny's, possibly the most famous musical instrument store in the world. The entrance lobby was plastered from floor to ceiling with signed photographs of clientele past and present: The Beatles, The Rolling Stones, Bob Dylan, Jimi Hendrix, Buddy Holly, The Who, The Doors, Eric Clapton, Ella Fitzgerald, Benny Goodman, Frank Sinatra, Charlie Parker. An endless gallery of greats.

"Can I help you?" drawled the assistant with the long, frizzy hair.

Jay was admiring a bright orange Gretsch 6120 reissue, the type Eddie Cochran had played with a big letter 'G' branded on to the front. He'd always wanted to own one, even if it was just to hang on the wall. Why not? He was a professional musician and it was tax deductible. Not only that, if he smuggled the instrument back to England, he wouldn't have to pay VAT or import duty either.

"Who's the most famous rock star you've ever served in here?"

"I suppose that would have to be Eric Clapton," said the assistant.

"Was he friendly?" asked Jay.

"Was he funny?" asked Calum.

"He was a miserable bastard. Always looks to me like he's carrying the world's problems on his shoulders. With the kind of money he's got you'd think he'd lighten up a bit."

"I'm sure he's not always miserable," said Calum. Jay's eyes were still glued to the Gretsch on the wall.

"Put it this way, man. Whenever I've seen him in here, he's always got a face way down to the ground."

"Hey, some days white guitar players have the blues, too, you know."

"Well, if Eric's got the blues, I'd say it's terminal," mused the assistant, before he realised he was employed to sell guitars, not offer psychological insights into the store's more famous clients.

"Is this a playing guitar?" Jay drooled, pointing towards the Gretsch 6120, "or is it a looking guitar?"

"I know exactly what you mean, dude. But unlike the originals, these suckers play great and stay in tune."

"You're kidding me."

"Nope. And they're better-made."

"How much is this instrument?"

"List price is $2,000. But since we offer a 40 per cent discount, we can get it to you for $1,200 plus sales tax."

"Wrap it up," said Jay, without bothering to try the instrument first. "By the way, I don't suppose you know of a decent Italian place to eat not too far away from here, do you?"

"I can recommend somewhere in the Village," offered the salesman. "I'll write the address on the back of one of our business cards."

Celebrated for its pastrami on rye, Il Cavaliere was one of a host of small Italian restaurants that flourished on Carmine Street in Greenwich Village. It was also notorious for the hoods that could be found lurking in the shadows provided conveniently by the booths at the very back of the establishment.

"Isn't that Ashley Page?" observed the singer, pointing discreetly at the booth opposite.

"You know I think you're right," affirmed the guitarist, who also recognised the formerly handsome rock star.

During the early eighties, before fate had intervened, Page ruled the charts on both sides of the Atlantic. By the end of the decade he was resigned to working with independent labels. At one time he could have filled Madison Square Garden four nights running, but today he took any gig offered. Viewing the man sat opposite, the pair felt a degree of sympathy.

"Let's buy him a drink... Excuse me!" Jay called across to his table. "We're huge fans of yours and we wondered if we could buy you a drink?"

"That's very generous of you. And to whom do I owe this pleasure?"

"Jay Jackson."

"And I'm Calum James. We're in a band."

"Might I have heard of you?"

"Does the name SSB mean anything to you?"

"I remember you guys. I saw you on that prick David Stampman's TV show. You were wonderful. I like the new record, too. Why don't you come and sit over here with me," insisted Page, motioning for the starstruck pair to join him.

"Delighted to," declared Calum, shuffling across the aisle to shake hands before sitting down with the man. "I know you must have been asked this a million times and I really hope you don't mind me asking, too," Calum began in earnest. "But if you could wind the clock back, would you have done things differently?"

"Easy questions first, then?" chuckled their hero. "I'd be lying if I said I didn't miss the limousines and the attention of the ladies. Coke, on the other hand," he revealed, referring to the start of all his troubles, "I don't miss at all."

"Wish I could say the same," Calum admitted.

"If I had my time all over again I certainly wouldn't have sold my soul to the record company," he said, helping himself to the last of the red wine. "Neither would I have walked through their door backwards pointing to my arse before handing them the publishing rights to my songs on a plate. They're parasites."

"Too bad man."

"Then, of course, there's 'change a word'."

"How does that work?"

"It's an old con trick that unscrupulous song publishers foist on naïve young songwriters. The publisher will bring in some loser he owes a favour who's supposed to help out with the lyrics. In my experience, nine times out of ten that person winds up changing a couple of words, three at most."

"What does that entitle them to?"

"Just a third of your fucking publishing royalties," fumed Page. "Happens all the time. Happened to me. The same goes for remixes, I hear."

"Fucking hell!" Jay made a mental note to check the royalty split for the remix of 'It Had to Happen'. "Is there anything else we should look out for?"

"Let me see… There's managers, agents, promoters, journalists, record producers, bootleggers, merchandisers, hangers-on and coke dealers. And lest I forget, people who want to invest money on your behalf. Avoid them like the plague. Vintage guitar dealers, too, for that matter."

"Quite a list," marvelled Jay, though stung by the mention of the latter category. "Anybody you've missed out?"

"Only the lawyers you'll need to clear up the mess afterwards. And they're the worst of the lot."

"Really?" Jay gulped, wondering if the bill from Marcus Davies would double the loss he'd already incurred on the guitar he bought from Larry Symonds.

"All lawyers are trained to do is bleed you dry while they smile at you and shake your hand. They, my friends, are a shower of shit. The kiss of death."

"Anyone in particular?"

"Didn't you hear what I said? All of them. I should know because at one time or another I've done business with most of them. And they all made more money out of the situation than I did. They're a bunch of thieves and petty crooks, believe me," confided Page, pleased with his denouncement of everybody working in the industry apart from himself. "It's a vicious world out there."

Throwing back the last of the red wine, he replenished his empty glass from the full bottle the waitress had just set down on the table.

"Of course I've made mistakes, we all know I have. But then so will you," he warned.

CHAPTER FIFTY-SEVEN

Soon after the chance meeting with Ashley Page, the band's TV appearance and constant touring had begun to pay dividends. 'It Had To Happen' shot up the Billboard charts to number one while *Crimson to Blue* did the same on the album charts a week later. Buoyed by their triumphs, SSB were elated at the prospect of becoming the most successful British band in America for over a decade as they started the final leg of the tour, taking in most of the West Coast.

"This is truly insane." Jay was scanning the itinerary his manager had handed him. "Couldn't you have squeezed a few more dates in?"

Calum wasn't too happy either.

"San Diego, Long Beach, Pasadena, San Bernadino, Bakersfield, Santa Monica," he began to reel off the list of dates. "Fresno, Santa Barbara, San Jose, Sacramento, Oakland, Berkeley, San Francisco. That's thirteen concerts in the first two weeks of the tour alone," he calculated before flipping the page. "Reno, Bellingham, Vancouver B.C., Salem, Portland, Tacoma... Andrew! This is fucking ridiculous! We'll all be fucking dead before we get to San Francisco."

Ridiculous or not, Andrew Symes had waited a long time for this moment – and like the record company, he knew nothing lasted forever. To recoup their investment he needed to work SSB to a frazzle while they were still hot and in demand. Wouldn't any sane manager be doing the same in his position? He knew the band were beginning to feel the pressures of touring, but like him they were just going to have to put up with it.

"The good news," Symes pressed on, "is that towards the end of the tour, mid-January to be precise, I've arranged passes for you all to visit the NAMM show."

"Are you winding us up?"

"No, Jay."

An annual event held at the Anaheim Convention Centre, NAMM was the biggest musical instrument trade show in America. It was also a magnet for musicians, rock stars and groupies. This being California, it was also the land of silicone, spandex and sex.

"Do we have a date?"

"You're playing Arrowhead Pond in Anaheim, January 18th – a seventeen-thousand seater." When the tour began, they'd been playing to three-, four-thousand people maximum. "The NAMM show starts the following day, which, incidentally, happens to coincide with your first weekend off."

"Hallelujah! So you're not the sadistic, evil motherfucker we had you down for after all."

"I hope not, Jay. We'll be staying at the Anaheim Hilton. I hear Lemmy from Mötorhead is a fixture in the bar."

"Then it must be crawling with groupies," surmised the guitarist.

"What does NAMM stand for?" asked Simon, calling a halt to all his tapping.

"Bearing in mind the seedy nature of this business, I'd say it's an acronym for Narcotics And Music Making," suggested David.

"Actually," Grant waded in, "it stands for the National Association of Music Merchants."

While Simon resumed tapping on the nearest filing cabinet, Jay was already fantasising about the free guitars he would blag from the guitar companies exhibiting at NAMM.

"You may be interested to hear I've already been in touch with a number of your equipment suppliers," continued Symes. "And judging by their response I'd say there's a strong possibility we could tie up a number of endorsement deals. Right now you're hot."

"How hot?"

"Let's put it like this," their manager enthused, back to laying it on with a trowel. "If Leo Fender were here today, he'd want to meet you."

"Will he be at the show?"

"He's dead, Simon," corrected Jay.

Calum, standing in the wings of the Santa Monica Civic Auditorium moments before he was due onstage, was determined to make his point once and for all. He grabbed Symes by the lapels of his jacket and pushed him abruptly against the wall.

"I've asked you on countless occasions, Andrew, now I'm fucking telling you," he seethed, before loosening his grip. "This is the last time I intend to share a dressing room with Jay – and that goes for the rest of this tour. Do you hear me?"

"Loud and clear," replied Symes, who could hear every word despite the band's introductory music blaring out of the vast PA system. "Can we talk about this later perhaps?"

At this juncture Basil, torch in hand, strode into view, ready to lead the band the last few steps of the way up to the performance area. Foregoing the traditional band huddle, Calum and Jay made their entrances to rapturous applause from opposite sides of the stage.

"Good evening, Santa Monica! I said, 'Good Evening, Santa Monica!'" Calum yelled into the microphone. Scowling at Jay, he swung the microphone stand in the air, clipping the guitarist's head just as hit the opening chord.

"Cocksucker," mouthed Jay.

Calum, legging it to the other side of the stage, took refuge in a cloud of dry ice. Still beside himself with rage, he seemed to have forgotten that Jay was using a wireless belt-pack that allowed him to roam the stage at will. Until the guitarist appeared from behind the drum riser, that was.

"Take that you fucker!" With one deft swing of the guitar Jay caught him a glancing blow, causing Calum to lose his balance and topple over on to the keyboards.

Oblivious to the arguments that had been fermenting in the dressing room, the audience merely thought it part of the act.

Under no such illusions, Symes watched from the sidelines, knowing some of this trouble could have been avoided. He'd failed to acknowledge who got the biggest hotel room or who had the best seat on the plane. Trivial shit to deal with but easier than fighting fires on what was becoming a daily basis. Bracing himself for the worst, he waited for the singer to retaliate as Basil replaced the toppled keyboards.

As the tumultuous applause died down, Calum walked over to the backline and calmly began to pour his cola drink into the top of Jay's prized vintage Marshall amp. This, as he knew, was the worst punishment you could inflict on a valve amplifier. Sensing a sudden change in temperature, the red hot valves began to fizz.

As Simon counted them in for the next number, plumes of smoke began to billow out of the amp. Oblivious to the drama unfolding behind him, Jay turned to Calum.

"We're even now, you fucking arsehole!" he shrieked over the top of a power chord, failing to notice the first ten rows gesticulating wildly towards his treasured Marshall.

The amplifier, now in flames, was clearly visible from the back of the small hall. Jay, wheeling round to locate the ironically named hot spot for his solo, looked on astonished as two roadies wielding fire extinguishers rushed past him. Watching helplessly, he stared in disbelief as they tried to douse the rising flames with foam.

"You fucking savage," he bellowed at Calum, who was now hiding behind the drum riser. "You cunt!" he yelled in the direction of the drummer.

Simon, unaware the singer was crouched below him, naturally thought the abuse was being directed at him.

"You sack of fucking shit," the guitarist yelled in his direction again.

Simon, thinking he was being persecuted through no fault of his own, leant back on his drum stool. After taking careful aim, he sent the crash cymbal and stand hurtling over Calum's head and off the front of the drum riser. Finding its intended mark, it sliced into the side of Jay's head – the side that hadn't already been injured.

With blood beginning to pour from his wound, it was Jay's turn to seek revenge. "And fuck you too, Simon!" Lunging at the bass drum, he pierced the outer head with the tuning end of his guitar. To Symes' dismay and the crowd's delight, as an encore Jay then sent his guitar sailing across to the other side of the stage. The audience roared its approval.

"Bring the bloody house lights up!" Symes shouted to the nearest crew member.

"Bring the bloody house lights up!" the crew member barked into his headset.

CHAPTER FIFTY-EIGHT

All Calum remembered was a flying guitar – a bright red one. He grunted at the sight of his bloodied reflection in the dressing room mirror, nursing a bump the size of an egg after the blow to his head had knocked him out cold.

The audience had howled its displeasure, demanding an immediate resumption of the show. Given the enormous amounts of claret that had already been spilled and with no guarantee of a ceasefire that evening, Symes had deemed it unwise for the gig to continue.

After finding himself fighting fires in the truest sense of the word, it had fallen on Symes' shoulders to pacify the Santa Monica crowd with the offer of a refund or tickets for a new date that he'd have to reschedule.

When the doctor had attended to Calum's wound and the last members of the audience had filed out of the building, the inquest began.

"He started it," snarled Jay.

"He stole my fucking coke."

"So what," seethed Jay. "You're not averse to helping yourself to mine."

"I wouldn't take your last fucking gram, man. That's beyond the pale."

"Beyond the pale? Trashing my treasured vintage Marshall is beyond the fucking pale. Wanton vandalism. I hope you're gonna buy me a new one."

"You said it was old."

"You know very well what I'm fucking talking about."

"Gentlemen, please," Symes intervened, determined to put an end to the bickering. "This is going nowhere. What you and Jay seem to have forgotten is there are three other members of this band. A band that's top of the US singles chart. A band that's top of the US album charts. And yet, for all your good fortune, all you can do is sabotage everything the rest of us have worked for. Simon! Will you stop that infernal tapping?"

"Sorry."

"As you're all aware, cancelling the gig could cause us severe problems. If we can't reschedule it, and I don't know whether we can, two things could happen. Your American promoter may sue you. And since he's responsible for a number of other tour dates, he could pull them, too, if he can find another act to replace you."

Calum and Jay locked eyes.

"In addition, should he decide to take this route, other promoters throughout the country are likely to follow suit. Do I make myself clear?"

"Since you put it like that," nodded the shame-faced guitarist.

"You too, Calum," barked Symes, taking control.

"I hear you," he mumbled.

"Now, shake hands and let's finish with this nonsense."

The Anaheim gig went without any hitches. easily one of the finest of the tour so far. Better still, they were all looking forward to visiting the NAMM show taking place right across the road from their hotel.

When they arrived around midday, as VIP guests they were fast-tracked through security via a side-door at the convention centre. Once inside, what confronted them was the biggest musical toy shop they'd ever seen. The sheer scale of a show comprising four gigantic interconnecting halls was impossible to take in.

"Welcome to the show," NAMM president Joe Lamond greeted them as soon as they were inside the massive complex. "I get the blame for everything that goes wrong here."

"You have my sympathies," said Symes. "Pleasure to meet you."

"Shit! It's huge," gasped the guitarist.

"And it's gotten bigger," continued Lamond. "Each successive year we attract more visitors from all over the world and here in the US. Now, while it would give me great pleasure to take you around the show myself, today as you know is the first day of the show and everybody seems to have a problem they're convinced I can solve. So right now it's 24/7. But if you do have any problems…" He flipped each of them a business card. "If there's anything at all I can do to help, call me on my cellphone. Have a great show." He beamed briefly, before disappearing in the direction of the adjacent hall.

"Nice guy," opined Symes. "Can I suggest we split up into groups and reconvene here in a couple of hours for lunch?"

"Fine by me," volunteered Jay, anxious to investigate the value of his name.

"Just don't sign any bits of paper," Symes instructed them all.

"Can I have your autographs?" asked the youth holding out a pen who was standing beside them.

"I spoke too soon," Symes acknowledged, staring at the man whose clothing was painstakingly ripped and rearranged for the benefit of those less cool than himself.

"Sure," smiled the singer, as always pleased to be recognised.

"I'm in a band, too," the young guy said, trying to ingratiate himself while his book was being signed. "Actually, if you're interested…" He dug into the shoulder bag that carried his future. "I've got a copy of our new demo."

"Perhaps some other time," frowned Symes, checking his watch.

"Maybe you'd like to see the press release. I wrote it myself, so it's not that…"

"I'm sorry to rain on your parade. We've only just arrived and we'd like to take a look around, if that's OK by you."

"Hey, sorry for taking up so much of your valuable time," the youth drawled sarcastically before putting the CD back in his bag. "Enjoy the show," he bid them, ready to trudge the aisles in search of someone else who might be interested.

When they parted company, Simon and David headed for the drum and keyboard halls respectively while Calum and Jay went off in the direction of the guitars. Grant, hoping to learn more about the art of negotiation, decided to tag along with Symes.

"It's not as if you're offering anything out of the ordinary," argued Symes, dismissing the proposal in front of him. "Why you'd expect us to sign a three-year exclusive contract based on this is beyond me."

"It's one of our standard contracts."

"So was the last contract we signed with you. We weren't happy with that one either."

"I wasn't here then, so I've no idea what the deal was," claimed the executive who collected rock stars' signatures for the sole purpose of commercial exploitation.

"Do you read Billboard?"

"Of course."

"Well, check out the charts next time you read it and rewrite your poxy contract," said the furious Symes.

"You seem unhappy."

"I wouldn't let one of my support acts sign this, let alone a band I manage. This, to me," he indicated, holding aloft the contract, "says one thing and one thing only: you're taking the piss."

"Why don't you think about it?"

"No, buddy, why don't you think about it? And while you're at it, we'll take a look around the show to see if anybody is prepared to offer us a better deal. Shouldn't be too difficult to find one, should it?"

"Think about all the exposure," pleaded the Fender executive.

"And you think about the contract," advised Symes before the pair marched out of the room and straight off the booth.

"Think about the full-colour page ads!" he called after them, wondering what he'd tell his superiors after bungling what would have been a major signing.

"Why did you turn him down out of hand?" asked Grant, trying to make sense of his manager's strategy.

"They'll get back to us," winked the man who got pleasure from negotiating the price of a cheese sandwich.

Meeting at the appointed hour in one of the convention centre's food franchises, the band began to compare all the freebies they'd netted.

"Blag anything interesting?" asked Calum, chomping on a hotdog smeared liberally with ketchup.

"A couple of T-shirts and some strings," said Grant.

"How about you, Simon?"

"These," he grinned, tapping away with a pair of drumsticks that changed colour constantly, "and a pair of drum gloves," he added, pleased with his haul so far.

"Somebody gave me this," said David, holding up a rubberised keyboard that rolled up and could be carried in a shoulder bag.

"What did you get?"

"Nothing," said Calum. Which was true if one omitted the quickie he had in the trailer park outside with a groupie he found rolling a joint behind a stack on the Marshall stand.

"And what have you got, Jay?" asked Symes, marvelling at how much pleasure his charges derived from so little.

"Five T-shirts, a guitar tuner, three leads, four sets of strings, and a capo. Oh, and by the way…"

"Yes?"

"I've just cut a deal with that new artist relations guy over on the Fender booth."

"You've done what?" spluttered Symes.

"All we need is Grant's signature on the contract next to mine and it's a done deal," he congratulated himself. "Surprised?"

"Horrified, more like. Has it ever occurred to you that these bastards want as much as they can screw out of you in return for as little as possible?"

"Isn't that the way you operate?"

"That's hardly the point. It's my job to get you the best deal I can. That's why you hired me, isn't it?"

"I suppose so."

"Anyway," he calmed down, "the contract you've described is invalid unless both of you have signed it. And since Grant was with me the whole time you were on the Fender booth, this is not the case."

"Where does that leave us?" asked Grant, as keen as Jay to sign along the dotted line.

"You refuse to sign the contract."

Jay glared at him. "Refuse!"

"Refuse?" echoed the bassist.

"Unless they put a better offer on the table, the mighty Fender Corporation can go fuck itself."

CHAPTER FIFTY-NINE

With both single and album still topping the US charts, Symes added yet more dates to an already heavy tour schedule to ride the crest of the wave. But with pressure mounting by the day, when the band discovered at the Beckman Auditorium in Pasadena that their contractually specified riders had not been met, tempers flared backstage.

"I can't eat this."

"Why not?"

"It's got holes in it."

"Swiss Lace cheese does have holes in it."

"That's my point. So I'm not fucking eating it."

"And what would you like me to do?"

"Tell the promoter we won't go on."

"Calum, are you pulling my leg? We're talking about a piece of cheese here. You are pulling my leg, aren't you?"

"No, I'm not. And I'm not eating this shite either," he insisted, flinging both cheese and plate at the freshly painted dressing room wall behind him.

"Don't worry, don't you worry about a thing," Symes mocked him in soothing tones. "I'll deal with it."

"So what appears to be the problem?" he asked at his next port of call, further along the corridor. "A lack of drugs?"

"No, it's cheese this time," complained Jay. "It hasn't got any holes in it. I distinctly remember asking for cheese with them."

"Hold it."

"It hasn't got any…"

"I said, hold it!" screamed Symes. "Your cheese doesn't have any holes when you requested 'with'. Calum's has got holes when he requested 'without'. Surely even a pair of idiots like you two can see the orders got mixed up. Perhaps if you'd talked to the man in the dressing room further along the corridor, you could have cut a deal with him. That was before he threw his supper, or what now appears to have been yours, up against a bloody wall. That way you could have solved two problems at a stroke and saved my time, too."

"Talk to the twat and ask him yourself," said Jay.

Brassed off by the band's shenanigans, Symes delegated a crew member to sort out the cheese dilemma before attending to the next crisis.

"But I remember you stipulating dark chocolate," argued Symes, as mystified by this complaint as he was the previous one.

"I did," acknowledged the keyboard player.

"So what's wrong with this stuff?"

"It's too bitter."

"What do you expect me to do about it?"

"You tell me."

"Would you like me to contact the Brazilian Embassy on your behalf?" asked Symes. "Perhaps they'll airlift in some lighter cocoa beans and knock up a new batch of chocolate for you."

"Do whatever you like. Whatever it takes, Andrew."

"I'll tell you what it fucking takes," shrieked Symes. "A walk to the dressing room next door, where you'll find Simon complaining his chocolate is too sweet. Then all you've got to do is ask him to exchange it. Can you fucking imagine that?"

"There's no need to swear at me and I'm not talking to Simon until he apologises for stealing my eye shadow."

"I don't know how much more of this I can take," muttered Symes, retrieving the offending chocolate to exchange with an equally unhappy Simon sat on the other side of the wall.

Symes eventually struck a deal with Fender they could all live with. Now, as well as seeing his face on the front cover of every music paper in America, Jay was beginning to see it in glossy full-page colour advertisements in musical instrument magazines, too. No product seemed too menial for him to put his name to. Apart from electric guitars, he was promoting strings, effects pedals, capos, electronic tuners, flight cases and banjos for any number of other companies. Symes, knowing when it was time to draw the line, cornered Jay backstage before they performed in Portland that night.

"We're talking over-exposure here," Symes warned. "Some people might say we're beginning to devalue the band name."

"You're entitled to your opinion."

"Jay, you've lent your name and the band's name to all these products, some of which will never see the light of day on stage or in the studio."

"Name one."

"The banjo, for a start. You're not playing one in this band."

"I might be tempted."

"You didn't hear me. I said you're N-O-T going to be playing a banjo in this band."

"Why not? None of the others had to pose for pictures, did they?"

"Precisely my point. They didn't, and that's just the trouble. It's starting to bother other members of the band. Frankly, they're sick of seeing your mug in the musical instrument magazines morning, noon and night. Do you see what I'm driving at?"

"No, I don't, and you can all fuck off! I've worked for years to put myself in this position."

"That I understand, but you've got to take into account the others' feelings."

"Don't fucking lecture me," he yelled at Symes. "I've worked my arse off to get to the point where manufacturers give me this stuff. When I was a kid, when I needed it, they'd give me fuck all. Now I don't, they virtually throw the gear at me, irrespective of whether I express any great interest. Now do you see my point?"

"Get out of MY car!" screamed David.

"What's the difference?" said Calum, telltale traces of white powder visible around his nostrils, fine trails of drool trickling from the corners of his mouth.

"I'll tell you what the difference is, you doped out dickhead. I don't ride in white limousines and this one's black. Your white monstrosity is parked out front."

"Come on, mate. They're all limousines at the end of the day, aren't they?"

"White limousines," David brushed the singer's arm away, "are for Essex girls. That, pikey weddings, gangster funerals and hairdressers on hen-night parties. So get out of my car before I kick you out."

David's driver, taking in the drama unfolding behind him, had seen it all before. Get a hit record, tour, tour some more and some more, then begin to argue about anything and everything. Personally, he blamed the managers who squeezed their charges dry to top up pension funds and bolster bank accounts. Them and record companies who operated on the same flimsy principles. Neither cared about the musicians. As far as they were concerned, the bands were performing monkeys.

What the limo driver had also noticed was that at the beginning of a tour people actually behaved like well-balanced human beings. But as a tour progressed, problems would inevitably arise and coke-fuelled, self-destructive behaviour kicked in with a vengeance. Separate dressing rooms, separate hotels, separate limousines. The list was endless, and the arguments were pointless.

Her own schedule increasingly busy, Marcella Mingovitch had flown in from New York to supervise a series of press and radio-station interviews she'd lined up for SSB in Los Angeles. Adept at cracking the whip, her efforts on this occasion were failing to elicit the response she'd wanted.

"I don't really care who we field for the radio interviews – or the press interviews, for that matter."

"Neither do I," agreed Symes, "so long as it's not your husband." He headed her off at the pass. "Press and radio interviews are still off limits to him. I'm not having Simon fuck up again, or piss off our sponsors."

"He wouldn't dare," she countered. "Would you darling?" she glared at Simon.

"Since there's not the remotest chance he's going to get another chance, it's all rather academic, isn't it?"

"Well, somebody's got to do them," reasoned Marcella, knowing she could coerce her husband into doing a few. "Nobody else wants to do them. The rest of them are all telling me they're too tired – that or too fucking lazy," she muttered. "Anyway, the choice is yours. Me? I'm just doing my job. Creating profile, promoting the band, selling tickets, selling records, selling merchandise. Selling…"

"All right, Marcella, I think we get the point. But unless you accompany Simon on all interviews, the answer is still no. That or no deal. Now it's your turn to choose."

"Please withhold all but the most important calls," Symes instructed the switchboard operator.

To pacify the various factions in the band, he'd organised separate hotels for all of them apart from Grant, who'd taken up residence on the floor below. Both rooms offered spectacular views of the Pacific.

Sipping from a crystal flute filled with chilled champagne, he discarded the glossy magazine he was flipping through to pick up the TV remote. Try as he might, he found it impossible to locate a single channel not airing a commercial when he suddenly recognised the face of the person telling him that there'd never been a better time to buy a new sink. It belonged to Calum, although the name of the sink manufacturer escaped him.

"You stupid cunt!" he yelled at the gigantic screen. He picked up the phone feverishly and called down to the front desk. "I need to speak with a Mr. Calum James, he's staying at the Hyatt Regency Hotel. Yes, that is correct. Call me right back as soon as you get hold of him," he directed the operator. He took another quaff of champagne. The phone rang almost immediately. "Put him on the line."

"This is some fantastic hotel you've got me booked into," breezed the singer. "How's yours?"

"Fine, just fine."

"I went down to the gym and booked a sauna and massage for later. Then it's off to have a dip in the pool, followed by dinner with a couple of drinks before I turn in for the night. Anyway, you haven't mentioned why you're calling."

"I'll give you a clue."

"A clue?"

"Two words."

"And what might they be?"

"Think 'sinks'."

"Oh, that."

"Why did you do it without telling anybody? Why on earth did you do it at all?"

"To tell you the truth, it was a way of getting back at Jay." Symes groaned. "The band's sick of seeing his bloody face plastered everywhere. It's become a standing joke with the rest of us."

"To a degree I understand. To a degree. But why sinks? What have sinks got to do with the big picture?"

"Obvious isn't it?" chuckled Calum.

"Not to me it isn't."

"Jay's endorsed just about everything apart from the kitchen sink."

"I don't believe it."

"I thought I'd beat him to it."

CHAPTER SIXTY

From pomp to pimp, sluts to slots, all in the bat of an eyelid, Las Vegas appeared to have it all. None of them had ever visited this gambler's paradise and playground for Middle America. A byword for overkill, Vegas was Mecca for those with less discerning taste. For David it was anathema.

"Ugly! Ugly! Ugly!"

"They sure are," agreed the driver, jumping a set of red lights and taking his eyes off the road a second for a furtive look at three ageing hookers plying their trade at the busy intersection.

"Not them," said David. "I meant the buildings, for Chrissakes!"

"You ain't seen nothing yet, brother," chortled the Afro-American.

"I've seen quite enough appalling architecture for one day. And do me a favour."

"Sir?"

"I am not your brother."

"My apologies."

"Accepted."

"Sir, did you know there's a hotel here incorporating exact replicas of all the famous historic Pareeshun landmarks?"

"No, I did not," David replied, wincing at the man's mangled pronunciation of a language they reputedly shared.

"Not only that," declared this self-taught expert on local landmarks, "another hotel, the Bellagio, is designed in the Tuscan style."

"So I've heard."

"It has the finest art collection in Las Vegas."

"Had," David corrected him.

"Had?"

"The previous owner kept the lion's share of all the decent pictures when he sold the place. So far as I'm aware, the Bellagio is currently down to its last twelve Picassos," he announced with an air of authority, in that annoying way people do when they've read the brochure.

"Here on the Strip," the driver continued unabated, "you can enter the kingdom of Camelot in the Excalibur Hotel. Fantastic place. It even has an authentic drawbridge and a moat. You can't get any classier than that now, can you?"

"I suppose not," his passenger agreed reluctantly, rueing that he'd ever engaged him in this increasingly ludicrous conversation.

"If that's not your bag, there's always the Luxor."

"And what's so special about that?"

"What's so special?" exclaimed the driver, puzzled how members of the civilised world could be so ignorant of such wonders. "Not only does it have an accurate reproduction of King Tut's Tomb, the people I know who've seen it say it's superior to the original."

"I don't see how that can be."

"None of the bits are missing, dude. Why bother going all the way to Europe when you can experience the Egyptian Pyramids first hand without leaving America?"

"Just for the record," David intervened, tired of this fakery interlaced with ignorance, "Egypt isn't in Europe. It's in the Middle East."

"Is it?" exclaimed the driver. "Well, I'll be damned."

"Anyway, even if it was in Europe, it's unlikely you'd go there."

"Based on what information, may I ask?"

Dropping his voice to a conspiratorial whisper, David confided in him. "Did you know there are more people in America with herpes than passports?"

Outraged by his candour, the limo driver raised the glass panel to separate them for the remainder of the ride.

"All the sixes, gimme those sixes!" the punter pleaded, blowing gently on the dice before sending them hurtling down the baize. "Idiot!" he cursed, as two threes landed face up at the far end of the table.

The croupier agreed. Still, you had to admire her for always managing to look disappointed on behalf of the punters who lost money at her table. Not that it deterred any of them from coming back.

"I'm sorry," she sympathised. The guy has just dumped five-thousand dollars in the space of four seconds.

"Maybe I should call it a night," he deliberated, owning up to his distinct lack of winning streak. "What's your name?" he asked, flipping the croupier fifty dollars worth of chips that he'd separated from the rapidly diminishing stack in front of him.

"Lucky, and thank you for the tip," she smiled gracefully, granting him another glimpse of her superb décolletage, a useful accessory in her line of work.

"Is that your real name?" asked Symes, wondering why on earth anybody would name their daughter after a packet of cigarettes.

"Yes, I swear it," insisted the stunning, twenty-something brunette holding down the craps table.

Once owned by the legendary Chicago Mobster Bugsy Siegel, the eponymous Bugsy's Bar at the Flamingo Hotel offered every conceivable card game in town.

"Shall we raise the stakes?"

Apart from craps there was blackjack, poker, stud poker, three-card poker, let-it-ride poker, roulette, mini-baccarat and a game Symes had never heard of: pai gow poker.

"What would you like to play for, Sir?"

With a minimum five-dollar bet on all table games and row upon row of cheap slots winking and blinking twenty-four hours a day, Symes needed little encouragement.

"How about twenty thousand dollars a roll? Three rolls of the dice?"

"Twenty thousand a roll?"

"Aha."

"Let me see if the house will accept that, Sir."

She checked with the inspector stood behind her, who in turn spoke to his pit boss via his headset to OK the bet.

"Just a formality," Lucky assured him.

"Twenty thousand dollars a roll it is," the inspector nodded to Symes. "Three rolls of the dice," he added, leaving no margin for error. This was strictly business, after all.

"Well, what are we waiting for? Let's get it on," Symes urged, hell-bent on winning back every cent he'd lost.

As the stakes had risen, so the small crowd that had gathered to watch had grown. A mixture of gawpers, ambulance chasers and the plain curious had their eyes pinned on Symes. Would he weep if he lost? Or would he be laughing all the way to the bank?

His first throw was greeted with a collective gasp. His second drew a more raucous response from the assembled throng. After throwing the dice a third successive time he groaned quietly to himself.

"It's only money," he muttered to astonished onlookers as Lucky raked away the last of his brightly coloured chips.

The chips that, a moment ago, had felt like a security blanket now left him feeling naked. The chips he'd bought with his and the band's share of the tour merchandising profits.

"Goodnight," he whispered in a barely audible croak.

"Thank you, Sir," replied the croupier, utterly convinced that gambling was a sickness.

After the curtain came down the following night, Calum invited Symes and the band plus some of the road crew to join him for a late alcohol-fuelled supper at the Bellagio.

"Superb champagne," remarked Jay, ploughing contentedly through his second bottle of Bollinger Grand Année of the evening.

"Tastes like a great drop of bubbly to me," acknowledged Calum, chewing the velvety nectar before he swallowed. "Why don't you endorse it, Jay?"

"Now you're being provocative," said David.

"Nineteen ninety was such a beezer year," opined the band's resident wine connoisseur.

"At $500 a bottle, I should think it ought to be," argued Symes.

"It's cheaper than gambling," said the guitarist. "I heard some English twat dropped a hundred and twenty thousand dollars in the casino over at the Flamingo last night."

Symes' ears pricked up. "Where did you hear that?"

"One of our road crew was over at Bugsy's Bar last night. Said this guy was a complete fucking wazzock, didn't know when to fold. By the way, how did Simon cope with the interviews?"

"As I predicted," said Symes, welcoming a change of subject. "He struggled through most of them. His biggest problem is contrariness. He doesn't even seem aware of it half the time."

"To the point of exasperation," David chipped in.

"If he's asked a nonsensical question, he tries to give a meaningful answer. Faced with a meaningful question, you can virtually guarantee he'll wind up dribbling off at the mouth. It's infuriating."

"Give me an example," urged Calum, who'd missed the broadcast interviews Simon had given. He couldn't give a toss what he'd said as, like Simon, when he wasn't in the mood he'd make it up, too. "Go on, Andrew."

"The first radio interview went OK. But at the second one, the station's DJ, not realising we hadn't sent him the sharpest tool in the box, decided to ask Simon his thoughts on global warming. Which, of course, Marcella hadn't primed him for."

"What did he say?"

"He said he didn't know what all the fuss was about."

"Is that it?" demanded David, feeling short-changed.

"Allow me to carry on."

"Don't let me stop you."

"He then, live on air, proceeded to read out a list – and God knows how he remembered them all – of all the ozone-busting vehicles he's bought, crashed and continues to pollute the planet with."

"How sweet. How refreshingly honest. How marvellously politically incorrect," howled David. "And yet his capacity for being so green about almost any subject you care to mention is bordering on legendary."

"Isn't it just?" agreed Symes, who would have cheerfully throttled the drummer.

When the majority of the party had sloped off to go clubbing or take advantage of the rock 'n' roll version of an early night, Symes returned to Bugsy's Bar. Half hoping, half expecting to make up the losses he'd incurred the previous evening, he was laden down with chips.

Attracted by the dissolute image of a game he'd seen portrayed a hundred times on the silver screen, Symes decided to try his hand at roulette this evening. How, he reasoned, could he lose again on such a massive scale if he played a different game?

Within the space of an hour, his twisted sense of logic had begun to fail him. Whereas the previous night he'd dumped one hundred and twenty thousand dollars at the craps table, tonight he'd already dropped eighty thousand at the roulette wheel. Now he was in hoc to the band to the tune of a fifth of a million dollars, and still counting.

"Place your bets, ladies and gentlemen, please."

Although it had let him down all evening, Symes parked twenty thousand dollars worth of chips on number eight. Like all gamblers he harboured a blind conviction that his number would eventually come up trumps, bite the house on its arse and give his severely depleted finances a huge boost in the process. That's how a gambler's mind works when he's losing: no down, only up.

"Final bets please," commanded the croupier, before placing the ball that held the key to Symes' future on to the spinning wheel.

Tracking the shiny silver ball as it span around the polished mahogany wheel, he bit his lip when it landed on five, then harder when the croupier raked away his chips. He was now down a staggering two hundred and twenty thousand dollars.

"Place your bets please," the croupier continued to tantalise.

Two of the assembled high rollers who knew when to quit walked away. Symes, who didn't know the meaning of the word, placed his last thirty thousand dollars worth of chips on number eight again. This was it, he said to himself. The big one he'd been waiting for all night.

"Your final bets please."

His pulse racing, eyes riveted to the wheel, the cash-strapped Symes knew it was make or break. He watched intently while the silver ball skipped and jumped for what seemed like an eternity.

"Ah shit," he groaned, when it eventually came to rest on number twelve. He'd squandered a quarter of a million dollars – and most of it wasn't his. "Now I really am fucked."

CHAPTER SIXTY-ONE

"How come you're so sure it's mine?" Calum remonstrated, not quite taking the news in the spirit it was intended.

Back on Staten Island, during a short break from the tour, Calum had been keen to renew contact with Jade McLoughlin, the flame-haired Irish chanteuse he'd met at the CRAFT Awards. And she was equally eager to speak to him after she discovered she was pregnant.

"Because we're both singers," she barked back at him, incensed at his lack of compassion.

"That's hardly a good reason to insinuate it's mine," he protested.

"I can hear the little feller singing his feckin' tonsils off somewhere deep inside," she babbled, as if the whole world could hear.

"Maybe it's someone else's."

"Someone else's?" shrieked the lady who hadn't copulated with a soul since.

"I don't know, you tell me. I've no idea who you were balling while I was out on the road."

"You cheeky, callous bastard," she hollered down the line from a hotel room in Chicago. "You wouldn't dare say that if I was standing right next to you." She was right, he wouldn't. "What I'd like to know is who you were shagging while you partied your little ass around California?"

"Me, shagging?"

"You, shagging. How many girls have you slept with since you fucked me? Tell me that, you filthy fornicating little fop," she screamed, demonstrating her gift for alliteration. "I bet you can't even feckin' remember."

"Erm…"

She was right, he couldn't.

"What if I told you I'd been celibate?"

"What if I told you the moon was made of cheese?"

"Well, I could have been," he insisted, with no inkling of what it must be like to endure such deprivation.

"You could," she snapped, "and you could tell me until you were blue in the face, I still wouldn't believe a word. Soon," she continued her onslaught, about to use up the next excuse he was going to fob her off with, "you'll be telling me you shared your affections with the Playboy Channel and a box of tissues. The ones they put at the side of the bed to save that long, agonising walk to the bathroom to wipe your dribbling dick. Not that such niceties would ever have occurred to you. You'd have just wiped your cock on the feckin' curtains."

"You've got a very low opinion of me."

"Is it any feckin' surprise?"

"Look, I'm sure we can sort this out," he reasoned, as if dealing with some minor insurance claim.

"You really don't give a tinker's toss, do you?"

"What about a termination?" he suggested, as if it were possible to roll a dice to see which one of them went to the hospital.

"And I could insist you go for a DNA test, then we'll know who the feckin' father is."

"Whatever. Fine by me," he responded, thinking his magnanimous gesture had consoled her.

"Feck orf!" she yelled down the line and rang off.

"Blimey, that sounded a bit strong," said Jay, having just returned with groceries consisting of little more than vodka and nice things to go with it. "What's the problem, mate?"

"I… am about to become a father."

"Christ! How did that happen?"

"How do you think it happened? Fucking, that's how it happens," one of England's leading experts on the subject assured him.

"Who's the mother?"

"Jade McLoughlin."

"Her with The Duds?"

"The very same. She called me from Chicago to break the good news."

"What are you going to do?"

"Flee the country."

"Sounds a bit drastic."

"Maybe I should have her kidnapped," he mused. "That or pay child support to the bitch for the rest of my life."

"Seems more likely."

"I need a drink – a very large one."

"What'll it be then? I have vodka and orange, vodka tonic or vodka and cranberry."

"Don't mention the cranberries," he groaned, suddenly developing an aversion to Irish bands.

Hours later after consuming a litre and a half of vodka between them, it was Jay who received a call that was unexpected, unsolicited and unwanted.

"Hello Jay, Marcus Davies here. I'm sorry to be calling you so late."

"Have you tracked down that cunt?"

"Pardon me?"

"Larry Symonds. Have you tracked him down yet?"

"Sort of."

"Did you get my one hundred and thirty thousand quid back?"

"Not exactly."

"Well either you did or you didn't."

"I didn't. I did not."

"So why the call?"

Unaware Jay was just one more drink from falling down, Davies asked, "Are you sitting down?"

"Yes."

"They've found a body."

"Whose?"

"Earlier today, Larry Symonds was found dead in his apartment in Notting Hill. The police are treating the case as murder."

"Jesus Christ!"

"It would appear our Mr. Symonds had been making an extremely lucrative living selling fakes. So much so, the police have yet to rule out that one of his disgruntled customers may have hired a hitman to kill him."

"Where does this leave me?"

"I was getting to that."

"So what do we do now then?"

"There isn't much we can do. The trail's gone cold. For all we know Symonds may have died intestate. In which case, this could drag on forever and a day until his estate is sorted out, which means you may never be reunited with your money."

"Somehow, I knew you were going to tell me that."

"I'm sorry. There is one other thing I think it's fair I should warn you about. The police have told me you are one of the prime suspects."

"Are you joking?"

"Sadly, no. There's a warrant out for your arrest."

"Jesus fucking Christ!"

"Which means you'll be arrested as soon as you land on English soil and set foot back inside this country."

CHAPTER SIXTY-TWO

Given the fact that it had always been their ambition to play there, Madison Square Garden should have been the highlight of the tour. Their three consecutive nights at the legendary venue all sold out within a matter of hours, the ticket queue stretching around the block and bringing traffic outside to a halt.

Tracks from the album blared out of taxi windows with some New York radio stations running them back to back. MTV declared day one of their midtown Manhattan residency 'SSB Day'. Sales of magazines and newspapers carrying their image on the front page soared. They were the darlings of a besotted media, the city was obsessed. They could do no wrong.

Applying his makeup backstage in preparation for their second appearance, David stared at Symes' reflection in the dressing room mirror.

"How many more products can that little prick endorse? What's he going to surprise us all with next? Stannah stairlifts?"

"Nothing would surprise me anymore, David."

"More to the point, what are you going to do about it?"

"As you know, I've spoken to Jay about his scattershot approach to endorsements on so many occasions I've actually got to the point where I feel physically sick just thinking about broaching the subject."

"His reaction to your latest ministrations?"

"He just won't listen. He simply refuses to listen. Whatever I say falls on deaf ears."

"Andrew, you're his manager. If he isn't willing to listen to you, what hope have we got of getting through to him?"

"David, it's virtually impossible to manage people who have no wish to be managed," he observed. "And patently Jay has no wish to be managed – certainly not by me." His control over the band was being eroded, his power diminished by each new internal squabble.

"Hmm, before you know it he'll be launching his own fragrance."

"Well, if he did, I'd be the last to know. Look, I've got a lot of calls to make. I'll catch up with you after the show. Have a good one. And by the way…"

"Aha?"

"Last night's show was pure magic."

"Gee, Andrew, I appreciate you saying so."

"I'm glad somebody appreciates what I say."

His mind preoccupied by the continued lack of co-operation from certain quarters of the band, Symes arched his way through the circular pre-cast concrete catacomb. Dimly lit, this far from welcoming setting housed Madison Square Garden's dressing rooms.

On nights such as this, its vast, grey corridors were jammed with row after row of flight cases in a bewildering variety of shapes and sizes. Designed to protect the equipment in transit, some were big enough to sleep in and many a foolish young band had used the cavities within them for a little light smuggling. Experienced bands, meanwhile, just had their dealers follow them around the country, delivering all the drugs they needed to their next destination, hassle-free.

Arriving outside Calum's dressing room door at last, Symes flashed his Access All Areas pass to the security man standing guard. Almost willing the next catastrophe to happen, he knocked before he stepped inside.

"I believe you wanted to see me."

"I want top billing," barked Calum.

"You want what?"

"I want top billing from now on. I also want my name to appear above the band's."

"Well, that's guaranteed to go down like a bucket of shit in a perfumery. At risk of sounding like John McEnroe, you cannot be serious?"

"I've never been more serious in my life."

"Mick Jagger doesn't even get top billing over The Rolling Stones."

"Jay's no Keith Richards."

"And you're no Mick Jagger."

"You don't say."

"Tell me what right you have to expect top billing over the rest of the band?"

"Rod Stewart gets it."

"You're not fucking Rod Stewart," Symes exploded. "You're not even Rod fucking Stewart," he corrected himself. "Neither do you have a solo career."

"I could if I wasn't surrounded by halfwits," he fired back, pointing towards the dressing rooms occupied by the others.

"What makes you so sure?"

"One word?"

"Give it to me."

"Talent. Pure and simple. I am an artist. They," he sneered, pointing towards the dressing rooms again, "are not."

While their second performance had fed off the energy of the first, the final night at Madison Square Garden eclipsed both shows. An elated Symes had even managed to broker a deal between the warring factions of the band to bring about a temporary truce. When Jay agreed to stop engineering endorsement deals, Calum dropped his demand for top billing. David was thrilled by these turn of events, although still had plans to launch his own fragrance. He even had a name for it: Bordello.

"And if my new venture does come to fruition," he explained to one of the crew during the end of tour party, "I'd like the bottle to be penis shaped."

"In a perfect world everything would be penis shaped," howled the gay lighting director. "There'd be dick-shaped food – sweet and savoury just like the real thing." He rolled his eyes at the prospect. "There'd be dick-shaped flowers, dick-shaped wine bottles, dick-shaped chandeliers to swing on, dick-shaped ice cubes and dick-shaped beds to fuck in."

"How about a dick-shaped lighting console?" David suggested to the technician he'd had the hots for since the tour began.

"That would be heaven," he replied. "Full of knobs to twiddle with."

CHAPTER SIXTY-THREE

Four of the returning band members received a hero's welcome when they landed at Heathrow Airport. Jay, however, was less fortunate. After surrendering himself to the two policemen who awaited him as he stepped off the plane, he was interrogated thoroughly before they released and eliminated him from all further enquiries.

Why he was treated as a suspect in the first place, he couldn't understand. He'd been in another country when the alleged crime was committed – the evidence was there for all to see in his passport. Were policemen stupid, he asked himself?

With healthy bank balances already swollen by the proceeds of the US tour and lucrative merchandising revenues, the band received a further boost within months of returning. Royalties from record sales had began to pour in.

"I would be cautious in terms of how you spend your newfound wealth," Symes advised. Most of his advice, including buying gold bullion, investing in the stock market and acquiring fine art, fell on deaf ears.

Stinky rich but not affluent enough to afford the Belgravia townhouse he craved, Calum settled for a mansion in Berkshire. Fit to accommodate his most grandiose plans, he'd stuffed the twenty-three bedroom gothic pile to the gills with antiques. As well as an indoor swimming pool, billiards room and a library, the mansion boasted a vast ballroom where he intended to throw endless debauched parties.

The property also came with two old retainers, a husband and wife in their early seventies. Fred, who tended the gardens, was a good egg, but Bella less so. She strongly objected to Calum actually living in his house all of the time as the previous occupants had only spent weekends there.

Not to be outdone, Jay bought a mansion, too. Set in thirty prime acres of Surrey countryside, it boasted eighteen bedrooms and a stable block he'd had converted into a 24-track recording studio. The mansion also included a number of paddocks and a wine cellar – it was actually the latter that had convinced him to buy the property.

Jay, wasting no time, had already attended a number of wine auctions to replenish the previously empty racks with five thousand bottles of the finest clarets and Burgundies. Understandably, he was thrilled to bits with these new arrangements.

Simon had also decided to remain in England, where he was now comfortably ensconced in a brand new Barratt home on the outskirts of Essex that looked like a carbon copy of Graceland. With flamboyance the keynote, Simon had lit the house with chandeliers that wouldn't have looked out of place in the lobby of a seven-star hotel in Dubai. To further punish the eyes, an assortment of zebra-striped couches, rugs and leopard skin-print cushions vied for attention with gigantic plasma TV screens that dominated the walls of every room in the house bar the toilets.

In the garage, taking a lead from *Pimp My Ride*, the drummer had spent a great deal of money turning a perfectly good Bentley GT Continental into the type of low rider more regularly found in the ghettoes of East Los Angeles. Now, at the flick of a switch, the vehicle could be raised on hydraulics to the accompaniment of flashing violet fluorescent lights built into the underside. Simon's neighbours may have sneered at his lapse in taste, but he had plenty more in the garage to offend them.

His Hummer H1 was originally capable of twelve miles to the gallon. After the addition of a twenty-speaker surround sound system and all the other assorted paraphernalia he could cram into it, the fuel-hungry street tank now delivered a paltry nine.

A man of more discerning taste, David had looked further afield. After thinking he might become a resident of Monaco, he soon discovered that a small apartment in the Principality would cost him more than he would have to pay for a rundown villa further along the coast on the Côte d'Azur.

Nestling in the foothills behind Cannes, David's newly refurbished villa in Mougins offered panoramic views of the bay that could be enjoyed from any point while he floated aimlessly in the recently installed infinity swimming pool. Surrounded by scents of the Mediterranean, his heavily planted gardens were awash with cacti, palms and succulents. In between were fragrant, reddish-brown Bougainvillea and the hugely impressive birds-of-paradise. To David, this *was* paradise. This sunny place for shady people would be to most people.

Although Grant had initially welcomed his new wealth, he struggled with the notion of it when others in the world appeared to have so little. Coming from a privileged background, he was already aware of the connection between money and the responsibility it brings. Finally, after struggling with his conscience for some time, he purchased a modest apartment in London's Marble Arch and set up a charitable trust for the homeless, simultaneously.

Indeed, at the meeting to discuss their finances, Symes had tried to impress upon the band the need to remain solvent. "I cannot emphasise enough how important it is to hang on to a large percentage of your earnings in cash," he'd insisted. "Because one day the Inland Revenue will come knocking at your door – and they don't take IOUs."

CHAPTER SIXTY-FOUR

Thriving on his new elevated status as country squire, Calum found himself frequently hanging out with the A list – these days, it included him. At ease in the company of other major stars from the world of rock 'n' roll, his relationship with royalty was also far from uneasy. After all, he considered himself rock royalty. But politicians were altogether different, wanting to use him for their own ends with nothing else on their minds than screwing a handsome young rock star.

"Excuse me, Mr. James," Bella interrupted. She'd elected to address Calum this way from the moment he'd set foot in the house. "Can I have a word about next weekend's party? In private." She beckoned him towards her.

"Of course," he replied, breaking off his conversation. "What is it, Bella?"

"I'm not sure I'm up to it," she whispered.

"What do you mean?"

"Having all these guests stay the night."

"Really?" he exclaimed, still getting to grips with her odd ways.

"I've never had this many people staying at my house before."

"Your house?" interjected the man who held the deeds to the property.

"It's not as though I know any of them," she continued, ignoring the challenge to her self-appointed position as mistress of the house. "Except for that politician who stayed here a few years ago. And what a disgusting man he is, leaving his wife and kids to go off with that young Thai boy. I wouldn't mind, but he's a Tory. If you can't rely on them," she tutted, "who can you rely on?"

"Bella…"

"Today it's all about sex. It's all young people ever think about – that and pornography," she frowned, knowing at this very moment her husband was thumbing through a porno magazine in the potting shed. "Far too much of it about, if you ask me."

"I'll tell you what, I'll make a deal with you."

"What kind of deal? Because if it involves any kind of sex, I'm not interested. Not at my time of life. I'm nearly seventy-four, you know?"

"Bella…"

"I had a friend. Mary Hammerton was her name, lived in Shepherd's Bush. Wild for it, she was – 'friction' she called it. Couldn't get enough of it, even when she was seventy. Insatiable that woman was, where she got her stamina from I'll never know. She and her toyboy were at it like bleeding rabbits morning, noon and night until the day she dropped down dead."

"I actually had something a little less racy in mind, Bella."

"Well, there's a relief."

"If you don't mind us holding the party here, I'll make sure that politician you mentioned isn't invited. I don't know who put him on the guest list in the first place."

"You did," the party organiser he'd been talking to reminded him. "You can't disinvite him now."

"Yes, he can," crowed Bella, redrawing the line in the sand.

The mansion's driveway was jam-packed with limousines the following weekend as its ballroom burst at the seams. With the party in full swing, Calum was enjoying himself as much as his guests

"And whereabouts were you staying in the Seychelles during your photo shoot for Vogue?" he asked the model he'd lined up as his conquest du jour. He felt a familiar tug at his sleeve.

"Excuse me, Mr. James. May I have a word in private?"

"What is it now? Spit it out, woman, for God's sake," he urged her, eager to continue his pursuit of such an elegant example of deliciously groomed totty.

"I thought you ought to know that I just came across two naked men in one of the guest rooms."

"What the hell were you doing in there?"

"I was turning down the beds as I usually do for guests staying at my house."

"M-Y house," boomed Calum, correcting her for the umpteenth time that week. "What on earth does it have to do with us?"

"One of them was that young royal from Gloucester. Prince Wotsit."

"Christ Almighty!"

"Don't mind me asking. Did you buy the tangerines?"

"Bella, I haven't a clue what you're prattling on about."

"I caught that Prince Wotsit hanging off the wardrobe with one in his mouth."

"I still don't see what any of this has to do with us."

"You will if the press gets a sniff of what's going on here."

"But there are no members of the press here tonight for the simple reason I didn't invite any."

"That's what you said about that politician and I've already seen him here. Twice, to be precise."

"Where?"

"Going in and out of the same room you put Prince Wotsit in. Haven't you listened to a word I've been saying?"

Beginning to tire of the cranky retainer, he realised his mistake. The sensible option would have been to pension the old bugger off to the cottage at the bottom of the garden with her husband. Not that he had anything against Fred, of course – he felt sympathy for the man.

Bella had been right. It was all over the tabloids. Two reporters had managed to infiltrate the far-from-rigorous security at the country house to get their scoops.

Desperate to steal a march on the competition, the News Of The World splashed with 'Bugger Me!' and 'The Future Really Is Orange'. Refusing to be outdone, the Mail On Sunday headlined with 'You've Been Tangoed'. One of the broadsheets, well acquainted with the antics of the MP in question, added a little more jus to the story with the headline 'Fruit To Flagellation'.

"Jesus, this is depressing," said Calum, as he discussed these potentially damaging stories with Jay on the telephone.

Jay, who'd also attended the party, had snorted a line of coke off a hooker's arse but somehow managed to keep his name out of the papers. "Have you seen The Independent?" he asked.

"No, I haven't," admitted the singer, promising himself that next time he'd have proper security, not Basil and his mates manning all the exits. "Do I have to?"

"The sooner the better," advised Jay, leaving his friend to read what amounted to an obituary – his own.

Hovering over the page headlined 'Singer Names Father', Calum groaned. A scathing piece of journalism announced the birth of his child by Jade McLoughlin, which came as news to him. Citing him as a lousy parent and a bad example to his fans, the backlash Ashley Page predicted had already begun. Suddenly feeling a familiar, insistent tug at his sleeve, he turned to confront Bella.

"Fuck off!" he screamed. "Just fuck off and leave me alone!"

CHAPTER SIXTY-FIVE

"Michael row the boat ashore
   Allelujah
   Michael row the S-I-N-G you fucker *boat ashore*
   Allelujah
   Sister help to trim the sail
   Allelujah
   Sister help to S-I-N-G you spastic *trim the sail*
   Alleluj…"

"I am singing."

"Sing louder then."

"You asked me to row."

"Row faster then," Jay barked.

"I'm already rowing as fast as I can," the oarsman groaned, his bulky frame suggesting he wasn't cut out for this line of work.

"Well, splash your oars in time."

"If you don't wind your neck in I'll splash one of these oars over your fucking head," promised Basil, as the pair floated aimlessly on the water beneath the mansion.

The guitarist, completely oblivious to the suffering of his fellow men, was justly proud of this stunning example of one-upmanship. In tribute to one of his greatest heroes, he'd flooded the wine cellar beneath the mansion, a costly modification that allowed him to row instead of walk around his vast collection of vintages.

Perhaps Jay was unaware but George Harrison didn't actually flood the cellar of Friar Park, his former residence in Henley-on-Thames. This piece of aquatic nonsense was dreamt up by a previous occupant, Sir Frank Crisp, the building's eccentric architect. A firm believer of 'more is more', he'd added an Alpine rock garden and miniature mountains to the underground lakes before he considered his life's work complete.

Harrison, an ardent Monty Python fan and a man with an eye for detail, was not to be outshone and soon realised there was something vitally important missing from this monument to bad taste. Which is why he added a built-to-scale yellow submarine to the already bizarre Friar Park landscape.

Similarly not wanting to be outdone, Jay discovered a seaside waxworks museum that had fallen on hard times and was auctioning off its contents. After the auctioneer had refused to eliminate Ringo from the lot, he went on to outbid all opposition and paid well over the odds for a life-size, if not lifelike, set of waxen images of the Fab Four.

On delivery, Jay had John, Paul, George and Ringo all erected on the tiny island that formed the core of the cellar, where they stood floodlit and forlorn in the middle of all this madness.

Steadying the boat as they floated alongside, with torch in hand, Basil leant over the side to grab the nearest bottle. After scrutinising the information on the label, he replaced the bottle. It meant nothing to him.

"What are we looking for? Anything special?"

"Something to drink with dinner tonight that's guaranteed to lift our flagging spirits."

"Would that be more or less than a hundred quid a bottle?"

"I think a hundred should do it nicely."

"What a despicable fucking waste of money. I wouldn't even spend that on a lap dancer. But you rock stars, you've got money to burn."

"I do," agreed the guitarist, poring over the contents of the rack. "And if I don't, I soon will have," he insisted, selecting two bottles that had got his palate twitching in anticipation.

"What are we drinking tonight?" asked the man who couldn't give a toss which side of the vineyard his grapes were grown on.

Jay shone the torch on it as he read the label. "Tonight, old buddy, we'll be savouring the noble rot of Burgundy courtesy of a 1961 La Tâche Grand Cru."

"Is it any good?"

"Of course it is. I wouldn't serve you swill, even if I had any. It should taste wicked with the wild duck we shot at the weekend."

"What's in the other bottle?"

"Château Palmer Margaux, also of the 1961 vintage. We'll slurp that one with the cheeseboard," beamed the guitarist, looking forward to gulping down a thousand pounds worth of wine. "What do you say, Basil?"

"Got any beer?"

"Basil, have you ever heard the expression 'pearls before swine'? A plain thank you would have sufficed."

Spliff in hand, sipping a Bellini though a straw as he watched the sun go down from his perch in the hills above, David gazed out over the infinity pool to the Bay of Cannes below. It was a far cry from the old days. Never having enough to eat, not being able to pay the rent, borrowing money with no hope of ever paying it back. Things were different now he was an established member of one of the most successful bands in the world. He was determined to savour every single second of it.

"Can Aziz get you anything else?"

"I'm fine," said the old friend from London who'd joined him for an evening aperitif.

"Would you be a little treasure and roll us another joint?" he asked Aziz, while his guest ran his eyes over the olive-skinned Moroccan he'd heard gave superb blow jobs.

"Haven't you smoked enough hashish for one day?" hissed the usually placid houseboy, pointing at the joint David was still clutching.

"Please don't speak to me like that when we have guests here."

Aziz, muttering to himself in a mixture of French and Arabic, turned on his heel and stamped off back to the kitchen.

"Is he always like that?"

"Not usually. I'm sorry," he apologised, embarrassed by his houseboy's bad behaviour. "He shows off when I have visitors. Frankly, I'm not quite sure what to do with him."

"Send him back where he came from?"

"Now there's a thought," mused David.

Returning his gaze to the azure horizon that was now his to enjoy every day, he wondered whether he could reverse the exchange he made while holidaying in Tangier, where he'd 'rescued' Aziz for the price of three camels.

"It doesn't look right there." Simon frowned, shaking his head as he motioned for Marcella to move the object a fraction to the left. "Doesn't look right there either," he grumbled, equally unhappy with its new position on the wall above a garish Wurlitzer jukebox dominating one side of the games room.

"Why don't we try it on another wall?" she suggested.

She pointed to the empty space above the huge, ugly, stone fireplace that plainly didn't belong in this room – or any other in the house, if Marcella was being honest. Simon had paid an old mate from Walthamstow double bubble to crowbar it off the wall of an empty property situated a stone's throw from his own, then fit it.

"That doesn't work either," he said, beginning to wish he hadn't bought either the fireplace or the bloody piece Marcella was still holding aloft. "I suppose we could always hang it in the toilet."

"Sweetheart, the toilet's already chock full of gold records. We put them in there last week," she reminded him, as the blood began to drain from her arm.

"I forgot. Hmm," he sighed, scratching his head, baffled. "Where do you suggest we put it?"

"Can I be brutally honest?"

"Just tell me where to put it."

"Out with the trash."

Simon winced. "Surely we can put it somewhere else, can't we?"

Still at a loss to understand why he'd bought the damn trophy in the first place, Marcella began to shake the moth-bitten, stuffed zebra's head with the glass-eyed manic stare.

"In my opinion this piece of shit isn't gonna look good over here, over there, or anywhere else unless we buy a fucking hunting lodge."

CHAPTER SIXTY-SIX

Having spent six months away from the world's stages, taking a break from living in each other's pockets, the band had managed to paper over the cracks and patched up their relationships by the time the European/Far East leg of their world tour began. With the album still selling strongly throughout the Continent and all concerts sold out months in advance, these final dates could only further enhance their already impressive sales figures, adding millions more to their collective bank balances.

Symes was winding down backstage with the band, who'd been given a rousing reception by their Hamburg audience. The manager was particularly relieved there'd been no repeat of the problems they'd encountered on their previous visit to Germany.

"Do you remember the last time we toured here?" he began to reminisce.

"Yeah," marvelled Simon. "Right from day one, all the way through to the end of the tour, they couldn't stop chucking shit at the stage."

"They weren't chucking it at the stage," said Calum. "I know, I was on the front line."

"Yes they were," the drummer chuckled.

"Simon, they were throwing the shit at M-E. Not the fucking stage, you moron."

"Well, none of it came my way."

"That's because you were always sat out of range at the back of the stage," argued the man who'd born the brunt of the attacks. "The rest of us got it by the barrow-load."

"Whatever," shrugged Simon, eager to avoid any confrontation. "Anybody want to join me and Basil down the Reeperbahn tonight?"

"I'll come," said David, already acquainted with Hamburg's notorious red light district.

"Count me in," said Jay.

"Me too," Calum nodded.

"And me," echoed Symes.

"Are you up for it, Grant?" Basil asked.

"I think I'll take a rain check. Feels like I'm coming down with a sore throat," he croaked. "You guys enjoy yourselves. I need an early night."

"So does Simon," said Marcella. "He won't be going to the Reeperbahn with you all."

"Why not? The Reeperbahn's famous."

"Yes, Simon. And we know what for…"

"M-a-r-c-e-l-l-a!"

"N-O, No, Simon."

"That's a shame because I know a particularly naughty place on the Reeperbahn that has live sex shows," sniggered Basil.

"There are plenty of places like that," said David.

"Maybe so, but this one has an act going by the name of Samson and Delilah."

"The high point of the show features a seriously well-hung black geezer."

"Samson?"

"A seriously well-hung black geezer," Basil continued, "who appears to be in a trance the entire time he's fucking…"

"Delilah?"

"….This white bird who's also in a trance."

"M-a-r-c-e-l-l-a!"

"No, Simon. And T-H-A-T is final."

Sequestered at the Carlton Hotel on the Croisette on Cannes seafront, the band were taking advantage of the private beach situated conveniently across the road. Stretched out on sun loungers, people-watching from underneath parasols, they took a breather before their gig in Nice that evening.

"Would you look at the mazoomas on that?" said Calum.

No more than twelve feet in front of him, a nubile young girl parading topless appeared unaware of the attention she was attracting.

"Should be illegal," he said, admiring the fullness of her ripe, rounded breasts safely from behind mirrored shades

"Jailbait is. Besides, you're already in enough trouble with that Jade McLoughlin."

"How old do you think she is?"

"Fifteen."

"She may be eighteen for all you know. I reckon she just looks young for her age."

"I wouldn't get too carried away. When I was over by the bar, ten minutes ago, she told me she was fifteen."

"Blimey! What else did she tell you?"

"She's nuts about the band."

"Anyone in particular?"

"I suppose it could be you," Jay teased him.

"Fantastic," gushed the singer, barely able to contain his glee after assuming she'd been referring to him. "I don't suppose you had the presence of mind to put her on the guest list?"

"Her and a friend."

"Merci beaucoup," beamed Calum. "Did you organise backstage passes, too?"

"Oh yes."

"Excellent. Most excellent. I don't suppose she told you how old her friend was?"

"Seventeen."

"Seventeen?"

"Fifteen and seventeen," Jay said, reminding him of all the options.

Seated apart from the others, David was keeping Simon and Marcella company after Grant and Symes decided to go sightseeing in Monaco. Feet away, occupying matching striped sun loungers, Simon was reading a British newspaper while Marcella's eyes strobed the beach continually. Mystified by a strange ritual she'd noticed as soon as she set foot on it, her curiosity was aroused.

"David…"

Pausing to remove his sunglasses, he looked up from the novel he'd been engrossed in. "Yes my dear."

"Why do all the women wear so much jewellery on the beach here when they know they're going swimming? I've never seen anybody do that on any of the other beaches I've visited around the world, and I must have sat on hundreds of them."

"'More is more is more' is the dress code here, sweetie. Most of the women here can't hang enough jewellery around their turtle necks to match the designer label clothes they all wear. Then the stupid old trollops smother themselves in so much slap before adding heels so high they fall off them."

"Do these women have no dignity?"

"They don't know the meaning of the word. The majority wind up looking like caricatures or worn-out, old prostitutes. Having said that, their garish dress sense is probably how these sun-ravaged, dried-up old trouts attracted their phenomenally wealthy, recently departed husbands in the first place. The very sight of them makes my flesh crawl."

"Have you ever considered anger management counselling, David?"

"Why?"

"It would help rid you of all the negative stuff."

"Isn't that what I was doing, Marcella?"

If Germany had been a success story in terms of audience reaction, France had offered bonuses of a different nature. During a night of sexually charged madness he would never forget, Calum had enjoyed an après-gig threesome at the Carlton Hotel with the two girls Jay put on the guest list. Discovering they were sisters only added to his pleasure.

Symes had also spent an extremely rewarding evening in Cannes – at the Casino. There, in the space of an hour, he'd won a quarter of a million dollars. It was the same amount he'd embezzled from the band's petty cash during his disastrous stint at the tables in Vegas.

"I can't seem to wake Calum."

With the Far Eastern leg of the tour almost over and the end of the world tour in sight, storm clouds were gathering.

"Throw cold water over the bastard," said Symes, tired of the singer's attention-seeking behaviour.

"I can't do that."

"You did in Melbourne. And Sydney."

"This time he's locked and bolted the door. Nobody can get in."

"Have you called the room?"

"And his mobile. So what do you want me to do then?"

"Call hotel security. Have them break down the door. That should wake him up."

It did.

"Get off, you bastard! You're choking me!" he protested, fighting back when his head was submerged in freezing cold water a second time.

"Awake now?" Basil chuckled, gently releasing his grip.

"I'm fine," lied the singer, looking anything but in his bedraggled state, still wearing the clothes he'd passed out in.

"You are this time."

"I was last time."

"And the time before that, but only because I was there to help. Next time I may not be."

Basil was sick of bringing Calum around whenever he overdosed. It was beginning to happen with alarming regularity.

The venue for their performance that night was Tokyo's Budokan Hall. Built to house 1964 Olympic events, it was regarded throughout Japan as the country's most sacred venue.

"Didn't the Beatles play here?"

"That's what I heard," said Calum.

Unusually, the singer had spent two hours readying himself for the performance. Since this was the final date of the tour he'd decided to honour the Japanese by wearing full traditional Kabuki makeup.

After poring over books and surfing the internet, he was astounded by the choices on offer. Watôna, Namazubôzu, Sukeroku, Benkei, Momotarô, Kagekiya or Dannosuke? Narukami, Yanone, Sanbasô, Kitsune, Tadanobu or Bannai? He settled for Benkei, one of the more striking white Kabuki masks.

"You look phenomenal," squealed David as Calum walked through the dressing-room door. "In a spooky sort of way."

"Looks creepy to me," Jay frowned. "Well creepy."

"Doesn't it?" concurred the singer, who'd practised applying his Kabuki makeup in France with the two Cannois sisters who'd taken him to heaven and back. Gazing intently into the dressing room mirror, he stared at the figure he'd transformed himself into.

Dressed in a vintage kimono and wearing full stage makeup, which had started to melt mid-concert courtesy of the heat of the onstage lighting rig, Calum must have cut a strange sight to his fellow diners. That evening the entire band was in celebratory mood, dining out in the Ginza in the company of their Japanese promoter, Mr. Suzuku.

A chic, overpriced shopping area by day, the Ginza district was transformed into a vibrant, neon-lit entertainment wonderland at night. Frequented by badly behaved Japanese businessmen, it offered a dazzling array of overpriced restaurants and bars.

"This evening Japanese fans most impressed by Kabuki makeup," the promoter complimented Calum. "People remember for long time to come. I will also remember. People here now think SSB Japanese too."

"Very kind of you to say so, Mr. Suzuki," returned Symes. "Let's hope our record sales here bear you out on that one. And thank you for this wonderful dinner. Absolutely delicious."

"Some people say this best sushi in Tokyo," said the equally happy promoter.

At this precise moment there was a dull thud. Calum had collapsed head first, face down, into his sushi.

"Singer very tired after long tour," Mr. Suzuki grinned, allowing both to save face.

"Ye...es," observed Symes, knowing this was only half of it.

CHAPTER SIXTY-SEVEN

With the world tour finally over, SSB decided to take a year out. While it would allow Calum and Jay to write tracks for their next album, the rest of their time was free – and there was plenty of it. Calum, social butterfly that he was, merely enjoyed putting himself about more than usual, turning up to the opening of anything apart from a cigarette packet. He got to eat and drink for free and it ensured his face was rarely out of the gossip columns.

Another new interest most of them found absorbing was frequenting London's many auction houses. Jay had taken out annual subscriptions for the wine and fine art catalogues, while Calum opted for those crammed with antique furniture – much of it not quite what it seemed. David, an avid fan of porcelain and Bauhaus furniture, and Simon also received brochures, the latter's subscriptions reflecting his interest in sporting and rock memorabilia.

Sat in front of a crackling log fire, idling away another long afternoon, Simon examined the catalogue that dropped through his letterbox that morning. It contained details of the lots on offer in the forthcoming rock memorabilia sale he planned to visit.

His eye alighted on Lot 104, the microphone that almost electrocuted Mick Jagger at Altamont. But it was the final lot in the sale that piqued his interest: a vest and underpants formerly belonging to Eddie Cochran. Presumably stolen by a long deceased mortuary attendant, they were the ones he was purported to have been wearing all those years ago when the car he was travelling in crashed outside Cheltenham, killing him outright. The auction house, to its credit, had insisted the vendor have them cleaned after declaring itself happy with their provenance and before accepting the previously soiled garments for inclusion in the sale.

Jay, poring over his own copy of the same catalogue, swirled and sniffed before taking another generous glug of red wine. Turning the page, Lot 376 suddenly caught his attention. It was the original Stonehenge set Black Sabbath had requisitioned for a tour, later to be lampooned in *This Is Spinal Tap*. Still in two minds about whether to bid, he called Simon to canvas his opinion.

"Hmm, I begin to see your problem," said the drummer, responding to the call. "Where exactly would you put it? You can't stick it in the garden, can you?"

"Guess not," acknowledged the man still vying with George Harrison for the Theme Park of the Year Award. "The neighbours are bound to complain. Maybe I should just plonk it in one of the paddocks where none of them will be able to see it. Hey, I've got an idea! Why don't you buy it?"

"And where the hell am I going to put it? You're the one with the mansion and all the space."

"Maybe I should see if Calum's interested in buying it."

"Call him and ask."

"Good idea, I'll do that, Simon. By the way, are you going to be bidding for Keith Moon's old Rolls-Royce? The one they fished out of his pool? Says here they've had it re-sprayed and re-upholstered."

"I must have missed that one. Moonie's old roller? Imagine…" mused the drummer. "What's the lot number?"

"Four hundred and twenty eight."

"Thanks pal. I'll check it out."

"Found anything else you want to bid on?"

"A couple of things. The microphone Jagger used at Altamont."

"I saw that. I bet Calum would like to own Jagger's gob iron. Anything else?"

"Eddie Cochran's underpants."

"Are you serious, Jay? Am I missing something here?"

"Yeah. His vest."

"What are you talking about?"

"The vest and underpants Eddie Cochran was wearing the night he was killed. They're the very last lot in the sale."

"Who the fuck is going to bid for crap like that?"

"I am. And they have been cleaned up, Jay."

Already seated in a packed room, waiting for the auction to begin, Jay and Simon were flanked by a dozen members of staff manning the lines to deal with telephone bids. Overhead, a giant digital screen lit up to show the price of bids increasing in sterling, dollars, yen and euros.

"Exciting, isn't it?"

"Be careful, Simon. Some folk get so carried away that they end up paying way over the odds. Don't go there, my friend."

"Do you think auctioneers can spot punters who don't know what they're doing?"

"Oh yeah. I was here once when this brainless soap star and his mate were bidding. At one point in the proceedings the auctioneer asked whether they were with each other. When they said yes he told them they'd been bidding against each other from the moment they sat down. So, my dear friend," Jay reassured his pal, "the likes of you and me have nothing to fear."

"Sure about that, are you?"

"Do we look like a pair of wallies?"

While others fared rather well at the auction, Simon and Jay were not so fortunate. Outbid on Keith Moon's Rolls-Royce,

Simon dropped out of the bidding a second time when Jagger's microphone reached twenty thousand pounds. Desperate to make up for these disappointments, determined not to go away empty handed, he soon forgot Jay's words of warning.

Swept up by auction-house fever, he wound up paying twenty-five thousand pounds at hammer price for the privilege of owning Eddie Cochran's underwear. It was a figure that extrapolated, after the auction house's commission charge and value added tax, into £35,250.

With absolutely no idea where he was going to put it and ignoring his own good advice, Jay fared little better after paying a staggering forty thousand pounds for Black Sabbath's folly. Delivery not included, of course.

CHAPTER SIXTY-EIGHT

"What do you think?" enquired Jay, chest puffed out with pride, pointing to the catalogue where he'd marked Lot 376 with an asterisk in red felt-tip pen. "Impressed?"

Symes began to read the catalogue description. Still finding it hard to comprehend, he re-read the entry just to be sure. "Where is it now?"

"Sat over in my barn," Jay said, nodding towards the window. "You still haven't told me what you think yet."

Delivered the previous day, Black Sabbath's Stonehenge stage set was already proving to be a liability, rather than the asset Jay had originally imagined.

"To be frank, I think you're out of your mind. Only a lunatic would splash out forty thousand pounds on this tut," he lambasted the guitarist, stabbing his finger at the catalogue entry.

"It's small beer compared to the hundred and thirty grand I ended up squandering with Larry Symonds. At least I've got something to show for my money this time, wouldn't you agree?"

"When you put it like that, it's almost impossible not to agree with your crazy brand of logic. But I still think this is more bloody foolishness, just on a grander scale."

"Gee, nice of you to say so!"

"What on earth would anybody want to own a bloody useless collection of cruddy canvas-covered edifices for?"

"I'm still thinking about it."

"Well, keep thinking."

"I suppose if the worst comes to the worst I could always resell – at a profit, of course."

"What planet are you living on?"

"There's no need to be so rude," snapped the guitarist. "I'm sure I could sell it. If not for a profit," he conceded.

"Who could possibly be stupid enough to buy it?" He looked at Jay. "Apart from you and Iron Maiden. Time to get real. Here's the deal," Symes continued, about to explain the difference between an investment and a gigantic leap of faith. "One day, and perhaps very soon, the taxman will come knocking on your door looking for Jay Jackson."

"What for?"

"Presumably to collect whatever it is they think you owe them. My point is, the Inland Revenue won't accept 300 metres of dilapidated hessian stapled to 200 metres of four by two. They'll want cash unless they've changed the rules while we were out of the country. Think about it and draw your own conclusions."

"I already have."

"And?"

"At the end of the day, it's only money."

"Jay, it may have been money once upon a time, but you've just turned a large amount of it into a pile of meaningless crap. So it's not money anymore. You spent it, and you keep spending it, at a rapid rate of knots."

"Well, I did better than Simon at the auction."

"Oh really? And what could Simon have possibly bought that would make your faux pas look like deal of the century?"

"Eddie Cochran's underpants."

"You what?"

"Eddie Cochran's vest and underpants. Simon paid £35,250 for them. Thought they were some kind of bargain, which I find hard to believe. Mind you, coming from me that probably sounds a bit rich."

"Has the world gone stark raving mad?" groaned Symes, wringing his head in his hands. "So what does he intend to do with them? Wear them?"

"Frame them, I think."

It was hardly surprising in the circumstances, with no college courses dedicated to helping rich, famous rock stars better themselves and lead a more balanced, less dissolute lifestyle, but Jay and Simon weren't the only ones struggling with how to spend their recently acquired wealth.

Calum, having frittered away half his money throwing parties when he wasn't freeloading at other people's, had amassed a stack of unpaid bills from disgruntled party organisers, caterers and a legion of florists, all of whom wanted paying.

Apart from any number of actions already filed against him in the small claims courts, another more serious unpaid bill had been put in the hands of his solicitors: a writ from Jade McLoughlin, demanding maintenance payments and child support. Currently playing ping-pong with her lawyer, Marcus Davies, his own lawyer, had called an urgent meeting.

"Please take a seat."

"Where are we today with this?" asked Calum, who'd noticed that the figure Jade was demanding had been rising by the week as he delayed the process, trying to negotiate what he deemed a fairer settlement.

Davies, brandishing the latest letter from McLoughlin's solicitor, peered over the top of tortoiseshell, half-moon spectacles. "According to today's postbag, the plaintiff is willing to settle for two-thousand pounds a week."

"Doesn't want much, does she?"

"With an additional one-off lump sum of one hundred thousand pounds."

"Jesus, that's an eye-watering amount."

"In my experience, 'a woman scorned' is inevitably demanding in such situations, especially where there's a child involved."

"And is that her best offer?"

"Not necessarily. The plaintiff is also willing to accept fifteen hundred pounds a week to bring this matter to a close."

"Great."

"I haven't finished. Along with this Miss McLoughlin is also asking for a one-off lump sum payment of two-hundred and fifty thousand pounds."

"Who does she think I am? Andrew fucking Lloyd Webber?"

"No," chuckled the legal eagle, "but a very rich person, nevertheless – or so the press would have us all believe."

Calum groaned. "It's not exactly like she's broke herself. I reckon she must have at least a million stashed away on deposit. She writes most of her band's songs, you know?"

"I completely understand, and that may well be. But I'm afraid it has no bearing on this case."

"So what do you suggest I do?"

"Two questions: how good is your cashflow at present?"

"Could be a lot better."

"Secondly, and I do apologise for asking what must sound like an impertinent question, but how long do you expect to live?"

"How the fuck am I supposed to know? I'm not clairvoyant," returned the startled singer.

"The reason I ask is because if you plan to live for more than five years, fiscally speaking I think you'll find the plaintiff's second offer would be far more beneficial to you. Provided, of course, your cashflow can cope with the initial higher lump-sum payment."

"You make it all sound so simple."

"You could say that's what I'm paid to do," said Davies, grinning, adjusting the red silk handkerchief in his top pocket meticulously.

With the season of bad will in full swing, SSB's fortunes took another turn for the worse with news that Simon had been involved in a road accident.

Out strolling around his neighbourhood, he'd been struck by a moving vehicle seconds after stepping into its path. The slightly bemused policeman who was first to arrive at the scene of the accident insisted Simon was the luckiest man alive having got away with just a broken arm. In a sworn statement, the officer also reported the accident could almost certainly have been avoided had the drummer not been listening to his iPod at the time.

To compound the band's woes, one of the more sinister aspects of fame had returned to haunt Calum.

CHAPTER SIXTY-NINE

With his arm still in a sling, Simon had been using his convalescence wisely. Foolish though he may have appeared to some of the others, he was the one who hadn't blown a huge chunk of his earnings on real estate. Simon deemed the mansions Calum and Jay lived in a bit on the grand side for the likes of him.

So he still had a fair amount of cash to play with and, being an East London boy, plenty of flash to go with it. It certainly looked that way when he began collecting classic cars and, after studying form, he'd put together a breathtaking stable of vehicles.

Other than his Bentley GT Continental and Hummer H1, now both restored to their original specifications, he'd added the marques of Ferrari, Lamborghini, Maserati, Cadillac, Corvette and Studebaker to his expanding portfolio.

All housed in a vast hanger not too far from his home, they sat beside models from McLaren, Austin Healey, Bristol, Aston Martin, AC Cobra, Jaguar and, of course, Rolls-Royce. Simon had also managed to pick up a fine example of the little-known and incredibly rare Facel Vega, the nearest the French would ever come to producing a Rolls of their own.

Eddie Cochran's underwear, which he'd somehow managed to offload on an American collector, had paid for that one. The only glaring omissions from this list were Porsche and Mercedes, although given the drummer's feelings on the folk responsible for shooting his grandpa in World War I, it was hardly surprising.

Calum's clothes were drenched, sweat oozing from every pore in his body. With the heavy drapes shut tight, he lay sprawled out on the bed in the darkened room, all natural light denied, his faithful retainers Bella and Fred long gone.

With only a flickering candle for company, he reached for the opium pipe and relit it, inhaling deeply. Savouring the pungent aroma, desperate to leave this prison, he dreamt of liberation before taking another hit. Surrounded by discarded pizza boxes and half empty plates caked in congealed food, Calum hadn't left his room for days. But now breathing more slowly, he failed to register the overpowering stench of fetid air filling the room. The appalling fumes, a vile cocktail of sweat, excrement and intoxicants, would have overwhelmed your average person, but not a junkie.

After raising himself on one elbow, he glanced into the silver framed mirror on the bedside table. His once proud mane of hair had been replaced by a greasy, matted bird's nest, his prominent cheekbones now only serving to highlight the translucent, parchment-like quality of his skin. His pallor had turned a ghostly shade of grey, but saddest of all were the eyes – once a dazzling shade of blue, reduced to support act for increasingly dilated pupils.

Hours later, as the light outside began to fade, Calum was roused by a ringtone playing 'Sister Morphine'. Still bleary eyed, he retrieved the mobile he'd dropped by the side of the bed and breathed a sigh of relief when he recognised the caller.

"Calum?"

"Hi Jay."

"How are you keeping?"

"Bitdisorientated. Been doing too much Charlie, you know how it is. One line… then another… and another. But I've been thinking…"

"Really? About what exactly?"

"Lotofthings. Giving up coke, maybe."

"Stop lying to me, Calum, and listen. Y-O-U are fucked up, and you're not fucked up on cocaine. So stop all this self-deception. You're fucked up on heroin, and very fucked up at that."

"I was fucked up, man, but I'm off it now. Clean as a whistle. Poor as the driven snow," he slurred again.

"I wish you were. But you're not, and this time it's got to be tough love. We can't sort this thing out together, you've got to sort it out yourself. Do you hear me?"

"Don't worry. I'll be fine."

"Not if you continue to deny you have a problem. If you do, you'll still have this monkey on your back next year. And the year after. Calum, the day of reckoning has arrived. It's time to own up."

"To what? Own up to what, man?"

"That you are Calum James."

"Of course I fucking am. I know that."

"And Calum James is currently a fully blown junkie. That's junkie spelt 'j-u-n-k-i-e'. You know, it's very hard for me to be telling you this, but unless somebody confronts you with your problem, you're going to die. Come on, Calum, we both know that. You've been a very good friend, still are, and I don't want to lose you. I don't want you to die. So let's stop kidding ourselves, shall we? Am I making myself clear?"

"I think so."

"In the meantime," Jay added, hoping his message had got through, "if you need me I'm just a call away. You have my number. You've got to seek help," he remonstrated with his friend one final time before hanging up.

Calum averted his gaze from the bedroom ceiling, the sweat glistening on his brow, his eyes locked on the box sat on the dressing table at the far end of the room.

The green leather bound case that held his precious works and a supply of heroin that would almost see him through a few more days. Desperate for one last rush before he cleaned up his act, biting his lip, fighting his craving, Calum began to crawl across the room on all fours.

"One more rush. One more hit," he intoned, making the painfully slow journey across the Persian carpet running the length of the room. "It can't hurt me, can't hurt me," he repeated, as if to convince himself. "I'm Calum James, rock star. That's me, that's who I am."

Out of breath but smiling serenely when he reached the other side of the room, his bony hand outstretched, Calum reached towards the box to unlock the clasp. Once inside, he removed his tools of the trade. After examining the syringe he'd loaded before he'd nodded off earlier, he tied-off his arm with a length of rubber hosing, gripping the loose end in his mouth.

"This one's for you, Keith," he croaked, jamming the filthy syringe into the only artery in his arm that hadn't already been damaged. At that precise moment in time, Keith Richards had a lot to answer for.

Although he was genuinely worried about Calum's health, Jay hadn't been taking very good care of his own either. What started out as a hobby had quickly escalated into an obsession. The previous 'bottle of wine with lunch' had turned into two, while the two with dinner had become three, sometimes four. And when he was suffering from writer's block, he'd down another bottle between lunch and dinner. He was on the brink of permanent, irreversible liver damage.

CHAPTER SEVENTY

Symes had been mentioning the subject to them all for years. Grant and David had listened, as had Simon to a lesser extent, but the people his advice was likely to affect most of all certainly hadn't.

The Inland Revenue, hardly renowned for its benign attitude when dealing with those under its all-encompassing jurisdiction, had compiled a dossier on the band examining their liabilities under a microscope.

Scrupulously fair, the tax authorities had come up with a figure, doubled it and, in a moment of leniency, admitted they would be prepared to settle for approximately half the sum originally quoted. The figures in question would look jaw dropping to the average taxpayer, but were simply astronomical to the people being asked to pay them. And with Calum checking back into the Priory of his own volition, it was left to Jay and their manager to sort out the financial mess the pair had put themselves in.

As was his wont, Symes paced the carpet in his office while he talked on the telephone. "Jay, I have a question to ask before we get started on this tax business. I hear you narrowly escaped disaster in your cellar last week. Is that true?"

"Unfortunately it is. All I remember, and it probably isn't a lot, is taking it upon myself to go down to the cellar to fetch a couple of bottles of wine."

"Were you rowing that boat of yours?"

"No, Basil was trying to. At some point I must have leant over the side a bit too far. Next thing I knew, I was flailing about in the water."

"I didn't know you could swim."

"I can't," confirmed the guitarist.

"But Calum told me the water down in your cellar is twenty feet deep in places."

"That's right. Lucky for me Basil was visiting that day. He dived into the water, fully clothed, grabbed me and dragged me back up into the boat."

"Extremely auspicious timing there, if I may say so."

"Anyway, no sooner had he dragged me back on board, I fell out a second time. Fortunately he was there to fish me out again. Bless him."

"In which case, I'm lucky to be talking to you."

"Dunno where I'd be without Basil."

"Dead, I imagine. How did you feel afterwards?"

"Bleeding obvious, isn't it? Drenched to the bone."

"Quite," acknowledged Symes. "It must have been a harrowing experience for you."

"It would have been if I could remember most of it."

"Have you ever considered the 12 Step programme?" he asked, broaching the subject of Jay's increasing alcohol dependence.

"Have you?"

"Enough of this merry banter. Let's move on to more doom and gloom, shall we?"

"If you insist."

"Personally, I'd rather talk about golf."

"Personally, I'd rather you didn't."

"Fine. Instead, let's talk about the type of discussion your accountant will be having with the Inland Revenue."

"As the major joint songwriters in the band, the taxman is claiming both you and Calum owe them in the region of one and a half million pounds apiece. For a swift settlement, it's a figure they've agreed to reduce to around seven-hundred and fifty thousand."

"Between us?"

"Each, Jay. Each. Do you have anything approaching that kind of cash currently available to you?"

"In a word? No."

"Then my next question is this: what do you have available in terms of liquid assets?"

"Four-hundred thousand pounds worth," replied the guitarist, without the slightest hesitation.

"Excellent."

"Four-hundred thousand pounds' worth of wine," he qualified, still misunderstanding the question. "And another fifty thousand in vintage port."

"Well, it's good to know you're not going thirsty. What I actually meant by liquid assets are those that can be turned into cash fairly rapidly."

"Funny you should mention that."

"Oh, why?"

"I was thinking of putting my Stonehenge stage set back on the market."

"I think we may be deluding ourselves there. I can't see you getting more than two-hundred quid for it."

"It's worth a lot more than that."

"In my opinion you'll be lucky to see your delivery charge back on that impulse purchase. And that's only if some loony out there suddenly takes it into his head to open a heavy metal theme park."

"Could happen."

"I think there's more likelihood of Muhammad Ali regaining the world heavyweight title for a record fourth time. A more realistic approach to solving your problem could well lay in selling off the majority of your wine cellar."

"Sell my wine!"

"That and lease out the paddocks. Let's face it, you've never used them since the day you moved in."

"All sounds a bit harsh to me."

"Jay, you wouldn't be in this position if you'd listened to my advice in the first place. You may also want to consider taking out a larger mortgage for the time being, then you can pay off half of what you owe relatively quickly. Maybe the taxman will allow us to make regular stage payments, or alternatively accept a series of post-dated cheques for the balance. Could you do that?"

"Do I have any choice?"

"In your current predicament, I'd say no. It's time to foot the bill."

"Do you think Calum will be able to sort out his back taxes?"

"Well, it's a matter for him and the Inland Revenue to resolve. But I'd say, with the paternity suit he's involved in at the moment, he'll be forced to sell the mansion and move into somewhere smaller, barring a minor miracle. Perhaps when he leaves the Priory he could move in with you? Temporarily, of course."

"What a fantastic suggestion. Let me ask you something, Andrew: would you be willing to share your house with a registered junkie?"

"Perhaps I'll forego that pleasure."

A name synonymous with guns and trouble, the Armageddon in Brixton was not the kind of club he normally frequented. One reason he was there was to see rising young gangster rap star GanjaMan. The other reason was to get out of the house and away from the bottle. Wisely, he'd taken Basil along for support.

"Jackson plus one. We're on the guest list."

Barring his way, door security and Lambeth's answer to the Incredible Hulk studied his clipboard. "You're not on mine."

"I think you'll find Eddie, GanjaMan's guitar player, has us both down on your list. It should say Jay Jackson plus one there," he reiterated.

"According to you it should. According to my list, it doesn't. Tell me," demanded the colossus towering over him, "why would the brothers put a pair of honkies on the guest list?"

Basil clenched his fists behind his back. He didn't care for racism and he didn't take kindly to people taking the piss out of him or his friends.

"I'll give you two good reasons why," replied Jay, security failing to recognise him. "First of all, we're really nice guys. And apart from being a pair of fully paid-up, card-carrying honkies, I'd respectfully point out to you my album is still in the charts after twenty-eight weeks. GanjaMan's has failed to put a dent in them so far. So, my good man, a little respect if you please, it would make such a refreshing change. Remember, I started out with nothing so I know what it's like in the ghetto."

The security man looked askance at the rock star who lived in a mansion. "And which ghetto might that be?"

"Pardon me?"

"This ghetto you mentioned. Was it north of the river? Or south?"

"North."

"Oh, you must mean Hampstead," the doorman mocked.

"You don't believe me, do you?"

"No, I don't" he replied, suddenly recognising the man he'd been addressing. "And neither would you if you heard half the stories I get told night after night."

"Does that mean you're not going to let us in?"

"No, it doesn't," the doorman said, smiling benignly for the first time. "I recognise you now, even if you're not on my list. Look, somebody must have fucked up," he protested, showing Jay the guest list he'd been given. "I apologise, man, this shit happens all the time."

"It does at our gigs, too. But thanks for your help, man."

"Welcome to the Armageddon," he smiled, revealing a mouthful of gold. "Enjoy," he winked, unhooking the red velvet rope and ushering the pair past his bulky frame.

Once inside the club they could see they were in the minority. Very soon they realised they *were* the minority – a minority surrounded by some of the shadiest looking characters Jay had ever seen outside a police identity parade.

Though he assumed they weren't, most of the girls were dressed like prostitutes. The guys looked and acted like pimps and the air was thick with the pungent aroma of ganja and hostility. Which party the bad vibes were coming from, and whom they were being directed towards, was impossible to say, but they were tangible nevertheless.

"Let's get a drink in," urged the guitarist, pointing towards the bar. "I'm fucking parched."

"Dehydrated," suggested Basil, long acquainted with the truth.

"Hey man," drawled the youth with dreadlocks standing next to them at the bar. "D'ya wanna score?" he grinned, recognising the guitarist. "Skunk mon." He flashed a wrap of high-grade marijuana.

"Actually, I'm trying to give it up," said Jay, telling the man a porky pie. "But thanks for the offer anyway."

"No problem, mon. Have a great concert, mon."

"You too mate."

Several hours later, after the clock had struck eleven, GanjaMan finally took to the stage. His presence drew an almighty roar from the stoned crowd who'd been obliged to wait an additional hour after the star decided the karma wasn't positive enough for him to commence the show.

Performing in front of a backdrop featuring a green, red and gold flag, he bonded with his audience immediately. Overhead, synchronised lighting rotated across the stage, throwing beams of light that turned from green to red to gold throughout the performance.

"Bit fucking corny if you ask me," Jay shouted in Basil's ear.

Neither did he care for the threatening presence of the security guards standing at the front of the stage. Part of the act, the brothers faced out towards the crowd clad in militia-style uniforms, black shades and matching black berets.

Despite Basil's continued remonstrations, Jay's condition gradually worsened as the night wore on. He'd been tipping a constant stream of Red Bull and vodka down his throat from the moment he'd walked into the building. Now a little unsteady on his feet, beginning to experience double vision, he leant against a pillar in the converted church for support.

"That sounded cool," he grinned, thinking he'd just heard the staccato report of gunshot emanating from the band's PA system.

Immediately, Basil grabbed the guitarist by the arm and wrestled him to the ground. "We've got to get the fuck out of here."

"What the fuck are you doing?" asked Jay, unaware what was happening.

"Somebody's got a loaded gun," Basil screamed in his ear. "Look!" He pointed to where they'd been standing seconds earlier. There was a bullet firmly lodged in the concrete pillar. "And they're not firing fucking blanks either. Time to go, Jay."

At that moment, as they rose from the ground, a second shot rang out, then a third, then another. After that, it was silent.

Turning to face him, Basil looked on in horror as Jay keeled over in front of him, blood gushing from the gaping wound in his head.

The following day's edition of the Evening Standard carried a grim report of the incident with the headline 'BRIXTON CLUB SHOOTING – ROCK STAR FIGHTS FOR LIFE' splashed across the front page.

'*In the early hours of this morning SSB guitarist Jay Jackson was critically wounded when rival gangs opened fire on each other in Brixton's notorious Armageddon club. The twenty-nine-year-old multi-millionaire, who was caught in the crossfire, is reported to be in a coma and currently on life support after being rushed to St Mary's Hospital, in Paddington. Two other members of the audience are reported to have been wounded, though not fatally, and the identity of the gunmen is still unknown. "We believe another drug-related gang turf war lies behind this series of shootings," said a police spokesman. "It would appear that Mr. Jackson's only mistake was to be in the wrong place at the wrong time."*'

"Why do they always fucking say that?" screamed Symes, hurling the newspaper across the room.

CHAPTER SEVENTY-ONE

As breaking news of the incident was relayed around the world, more camera crews eager to supply their hungry networks jockeyed for position outside Brixton's Armageddon club the day after the shootings.

Keeping them in their respective places was the lumbering giant who'd been manning the door the previous night. Soon, the Hulk's face and massive frame would be beamed around the globe, too, making him an instant celebrity in places as far apart as America and Australia, neither of which he'd visited.

Still lying in a coma, Jay could have had no idea of the massive outpouring of love and the thousands of messages he'd received from grief-stricken fans, many of whom were already keeping a twenty-four-hour candlelight vigil outside the hospital.

Close members of Jay's family took it in turn to watch over him, cloistered within a private room inside St. Mary's Hospital. Simon and Basil prayed he would make a full recovery. But given Jay's low resistance due to his prodigious consumption of alcohol over the years, this wasn't thought the most likely outcome.

Jay's story seemed to touched the raw nerve of the nation and dominated the news bulletins, continuing to make front-page headlines around the country for the next forty-eight hours.

In the Commons, the Leader Of The House expressed his sympathy and concern for Jay's plight during Prime Minister's

Questions. A member of the Opposition questioned the wisdom and sanity of a nation revering a pot-smoking alcoholic.

Mindful of losing young voters, the Prime Minister was on his feet immediately, reminding the former pot smoker of his own misspent youth while at Cambridge to peals of laughter from his backbenchers – and the Opposition's. It was something the Honourable Member in question had so far tried, and clearly failed, to have erased from the records.

Symes, still coming to terms with the unforeseen tragedy, had stayed away from the hospital. Dealing with the situation as best he could, he attempted to capitalise on the media attention whenever a microphone was waved in front of him, mentioning all of the band's records by name. Predictably, these were then all edited out prior to transmission by broadcasters who preferred selling advertising airtime to giving it away.

Able to recognise the rancid smell of rotting flesh from the other side of the solar system, the gutter press had picked up the Calum trail after hearing of the singer's stay at the Priory. This, in itself, was not particularly newsworthy, but it was known that his treatment had hardly been an unqualified success. These low-lifes exhausted door-stepping distant relatives and moved on to whipping out their chequebooks for the band's disgruntled former employees, eliciting the quotes they needed to file their stories.

The Sunday tabloids, painting Calum as a fugitive from the Inland Revenue, had been able to bribe some of the Priory's poorer clients into spilling the beans. One former patient described the singer as "self-obsessed, frivolous and friendless", something the clinic's staff had also noted. Another who wished to remain anonymous described him as "beyond all reasonable help".

These damning epithets were further emboldened by equally damaging photographs depicting the beleaguered star trying to score. Others taken soon afterwards pictured him in the act of shooting up, while the worst showed him spark out on the floor as a result.

With his eye on damage limitation, Symes realised it was probably better to ride out the storm as Marcella had suggested. Besides, he said, record sales were still rising, as were downloads. The money continued to roll in – for how much longer, he didn't know.

David, still living in self-imposed exile on the Côte d'Azur, had taken the news of Jay's situation hard. Months ago his future looked secure, but today it looked far from that. He still had serious domestic problems to contend with, although paying his tax bill wasn't one of them.

Simon had been obliged to dispose of three of his prized automobiles to settle his outstanding debt. The financially astute David had kept enough liquid funds in reserve to pay the Inland Revenue in full.

"Aziz," he screamed at the boy who stood naked as the day he was born on the opposite side of the swimming pool. "I will not tell you again. You cannot and you will not be rude to my guests. Do you understand me?"

The houseboy, demonstrating complete indifference, began to play provocatively with his penis, hoping he could persuade his employer to change his mind.

"Now listen to me," fumed David, taking another look at the most beautiful, slender, smooth, olive-skinned dick he had ever seen. It was certainly the one that had given him most pleasure.

"What's the matter now?" asked Aziz, crossing over from the other side of the pool to confront him.

"You might be good in bed," David said, glaring at him, "and you know damn well you give great head. But that's still no excuse for the way you've been behaving."

Staring at him nonchalantly, the houseboy let his penis rub against David's bare shoulder before he resumed tugging it.

"Please stop doing that while I'm talking to you, there's absolutely no excuse. I will not stand for your bad behaviour anymore, do you hear me?"

"Piss off," his houseboy swore at him.

"I've had it. That's it, that's enough!" shrieked the keyboard player. "Pack your bags this instant."

"Don't worry. I'll go," he replied, turning towards the villa, his penis still semi-erect.

In London, the vigil at Jay's bedside continued with little or no sign of an imminent recovery in sight. Symes, worried about the cash cow he'd helped engineer and was determined to keep alive, had been attempting to contact Calum with no success.

Basil, who'd been despatched to the troubled singer's Berkshire mansion, found the building unoccupied and came away empty handed – unlike the small claims courts, three firms of solicitors and the Inland Revenue. Jointly appointing bailiffs to act on their behalves, hounding the singer's estate for their money, they'd completely stripped the imposing mansion bare of its contents.

Andrew and Basil's next port of call was phoning shelters for the homeless – again, to no avail. It was Marcella who suggested putting out a news release asking members of the public if they'd seen him. The only tabloid that hadn't run damning coverage on Calum was eager to set up a phone helpline offering a reward to the person who found him. What did Symes have to lose? The newspaper merely saw it as an opportunity to get one up on its rivals. It seemed a just reward for not regurgitating the same tired old story the others had all printed.

The results interesting, if patchy. Sightings were reported in Glasgow, Birmingham, Carlisle, Bradford and a remote village in Berkshire, the tiny parish of Bucklebury.

But where he was eventually tracked down to was the West Country.

Torquay had a long-standing junkie population that many living there would happily ship over the border to neighbouring Cornwall if they could. In the summer months, it doubled.

Strolling along the seafront today, Calum in his current dishevelled state, was recognised by nobody – apart from the man approaching, clutching a copy of the newspaper article with the singer's photograph printed below it. The photo of him had a large red arrow pointing towards his head and the caption: 'HAVE YOU SEEN THIS MAN?'

"Can oi 'ave my reward then?"

"Again?"

"Oi'd like to collect my reward," said the local, his speech largely unfathomable due to his rich West Country burr.

"Reward for what?"

"Finding you," replied the Devonian.

"But I'm not lost."

"Bloody well says you are 'ere," he insisted, brandishing the article in front of him.

"Don't believe everything you read, my friend. I've been to Torquay before, you know. As a matter of fact, my band once played at the Town Hall just up the road."

"Oi know that."

"You do?"

"Yeah. Oi was fucking there, wasn't oi? Never forget it long as oi live."

"Well, thank you," said Calum, touched by the compliment. "It means so much to me. Especially at the moment. Thank you again. Really, I mean it I…"

"Oi 'ate to burst your bubble, but it was the night oi met my wife."

"What a coincidence. My word, how romantic is that?"

"Might look that way to some, I suppose."

"Oh?"

"To me it was the night oi met the bitch oi had to marry – and have two more fucking kids by," he stated baldly. "But hey ho, we've all got our cross to bear, haven't we?"

"It would seem that way," frowned the singer, burdened by an even heavier cross, but envious of this man's domestic situation nevertheless.

"Anyway," the fan pressed on regardless, holding aloft his newspaper. "Who do oi collect this reward from?" he asked, failing to spot the telephone number printed at the bottom of the page in twenty-four point type.

Pained at just how awful he looked in the picture, the singer pointed to the paper. "It says call this number. Why don't you give it a try?"

"Oi would, but oi left the house without my mobile," he replied, as if his world had suddenly stopped turning.

"Pity."

"Didn't want the missus bothering me," confided the Devonian, clearly unconcerned by the fact he was bothering other people.

"Why don't you call from the phone box down the road. It's right over there, where you can see that ice-cream van parked. I'll wait here if you like."

"Great idea, back in a trice. Might even buy us both a nice cup of tea. Oh, by the way, how will they know oi've actually found you and oi'm not lying and oi'm telling the truth?"

"Be sure to ask for Andrew Symes."

"Andrew Soymes?" the Devonian repeated.

"And if you speak to him, let him know you're with me. Maybe you could ask him if Basil would be willing to drive down here to collect me."

"Who's Basil when he's all at home?"

"Never mind that now. Just ask to speak to Andrew Symes."

Calum's stalker, suddenly noticing his shabby appearance, wondered whether he'd been sleeping rough in one of the county's infamous hedgerows.

"If they ask me, where shall oi tell them you're staying?"

"The YMCA."

"Righto," enthused his would be saviour. "Oi'll be back in a jiffy. Tell you what," he added as an afterthought. "Why don't oi get us both an ice cream instead?"

"You do that."

CHAPTER SEVENTY-TWO

Police who arrived at the scene of the accident reported it as one of the most gruesome they'd ever attended.

The man had been on his way to visit friends when tragedy struck on Monaco's Lower Corniche in the place where it hugs the Mediterranean coastline below it. Tens of metres from where his open-top Mercedes had come to rest with its wheels still spinning, they located the armless, decapitated corpse.

Ironically, the vehicle he'd been driving before it plunged over the edge of a ravine had also been a Mercedes – only this time it didn't belong to former screen idol Grace Kelly. It was David's.

Nice-matin, drawing parallels between his death and that of Monaco's beloved Princess Grace, splashed the news across the front page with the headline, 'La Reine est Mort', a bitchy comment the keyboard player would have revelled in. As tributes poured in from around the world, a number of his favourite restaurants on the Côte d'Azur held a minute's silence in his memory. It was a sign of affection for a man who might criticise their décor but never their food.

When the coroner eventually filed her report, there were few on the Riviera surprised by its findings. Why would they be? They'd seen plenty of young stars perish needlessly behind the wheel of a fast car. It was just another case of 'Death By Misadventure', wasn't it?

Sat alone in his London apartment, Symes switched on the television to catch the latest news bulletin on the accident.

As old footage of David flashed up on the screen, he wiped away a tear.

What he saw was his and the band's once rosy future disappear behind a dark cloud, before the cloud itself disappeared over the horizon. Why, he asked, do so many great artists and bands leave us when, all things being equal, they should be savouring their finest hour? Where were Jimi, Kurt and Freddie when their fans needed them? Still coming to terms with David's untimely death, Symes was mystified. Despite his sexual excesses, David had always been one of the more sober, clean-living members of the band.

Simon howled like a banshee when he heard the news, regretting having teased David simply because he was gay.

"I can be so stupid sometimes," he confessed to Marcella, in a rare reflective mood. "We're all made from the same flesh and blood after all."

"Calm yourself now, honey."

"I loved the guy, even if he didn't know it," croaked Simon, a series of violent visual images of David's last moments on earth bombarding his senses.

They were images that would continue to haunt him for some time. The Mercedes taking off before hurtling over the cliff edge. Torn limbs flying out of it in different directions, on separate trajectories. His severed head rolling down the hillside before deep undergrowth finally halted its path. These terrifying images replayed constantly inside his head.

In a plot worthy of Torquay's most famous daughter, the crime writer Agatha Christie, Calum had given his bounty hunter the slip along the seafront.

The opportunity had arisen as the latter wandered off to make the telephone call claiming his reward for finding the singer. Much to the Devonian's dismay, when he returned with an ice cream in each hand, Calum was nowhere to be seen.

The singer, coming to the conclusion he wasn't ready to be 'found', had darted across the road to the Grand Hotel. Here, behind the hotel at the town's railway station, he'd hopped on a London-bound train standing stationary at the platform as if it were waiting for him.

Five hours later, when the train pulled into Paddington Station, light drizzle had turned into a torrential downpour. For Calum, soon drenched to the bone, there were other priorities and matters of a more pressing nature.

Reduced to wandering around London's West End in his never-ending quest for the next high, Calum needed to lay his hands on enough horse to stop him shaking uncontrollably. It was something that had begun to happen with alarming regularity.

"'Excuse me," he called out, addressing another junkie sat on the steps of the drop-in centre on Covent Garden's Endell Street. "I hate to bother you, man, but do you know where I can score?"

The junkie stared back, their two sets of hollow eyes cancelling each other out. Calum tried again.

"Do you have any idea where I might be able to score something, my friend?"

When this failed, Calum climbed the steps and began to tug at the torn, frayed hem of this other sad human being's jacket. His delicate equilibrium disturbed, the other junkie keeled forward gently, his upper torso folding on to his lap to assume what had become a normal position for him.

"Jesus," muttered Calum, watching as the wretched man OD'd in front of him after his latest hit from another filthy syringe.

Failing to score after his third attempt in as many minutes, despondent, Calum shuffled off in the direction of Denmark Street.

Still completely in the dark about David's death, Calum had read about Jay in the papers. Feeling pangs of guilt, he'd yet to visit the ailing guitarist, someone he regarded as his best friend.

On his way to make amends, he passed the same guitar shops he'd frequented with Jay in Tin Pan Alley, before he disappeared down the steps into Tottenham Court Road Underground station. After taking the first Central line train west, Calum changed trains at Oxford Circus to pick up the Bakerloo line. Five stops later, it spat him out at Paddington and St. Mary's Hospital.

"'Scuse me," he accosted the duty nurse behind the desk, his slur betraying substance abuse.

"How can I help?" she asked, convinced the bedraggled young man standing in front of her looked in urgent need of some himself.

"It's my friend. My best friend. I've come to see him."

She looked at him quizzically. "We do have specific visiting hours, you know?"

"I do understand, but I've been out of town in Devon on urgent business most of this week. I just got back," he added breathlessly.

"What's the name?"

"Mine?"

"No, the person you've come to see."

"Oh, sorry, it's Jay Jackson. He's in one of your wards – which one, I don't know. As I said, I've been out of town and haven't seen him since he was shot in Brixton last week. I can't remember the name of the club where it happened," he offered, before the duty nurse cut him short.

"I'm afraid close relatives and members of his band have left strict instructions that Mr. Jackson is not to be disturbed for the next forty-eight hours."

"But I am a member of the band," he protested. "The bloody singer. T-H-E key member."

"Good heavens," exclaimed the devoutly religious West Indian woman.

She'd recognised his face from the 'WANTED'-style poster in today's newspaper that was still poking out of her handbag.

"Is this you?" she asked, after retrieving it to check she was talking to the man in the picture.

"That's me alright," he beamed, pointing to his picture.

"So you are Calum James?"

"Yes," he confirmed, breathing a sigh of relief as she picked up the telephone to speak with someone briefly.

"Follow me," she directed, putting down the receiver.

"It's me... Calum," he hissed, addressing the prone figure with wires attached to it, lying in the bed beside him.

"You've got ten minutes," said the nurse, checking the chart at the end of the bed. "Fifteen minutes tops," she added brusquely.

Ignoring whatever she'd just said, Calum leant over the side of the bed to take a closer look. They'd told him that his stricken friend was lucky to be alive. Seeing Jay in his current condition, Calum begged to differ. Was his friend not as good as dead already?

"Why are we so fucked up?" he demanded of the lifeless body. "Why does it have to be such an almighty fucking hassle getting through every day?"

Still experiencing breathing problems, wired up to a life-support machine, the man he was talking to would likely have given half his fortune not to be. He would have been delighted to deal with whatever the world could throw at him. But that window of opportunity, as Calum could plainly see, was closed to him – for how long, nobody could say.

"It's the pressure I can't handle," he confided in his friend, still lying motionless. "All that fucking pressure. Everybody wanting a piece of you, day in, day out. People wanting me to live up to their expectations. Well, what about my fucking expectations? They say I'm some kind of messiah, but I'm not.

How could I be? How could I possibly be? Are you fucking listening to me, man?" he babbled, prodding the body carelessly to drive home his point.

There was something else he couldn't come to terms with. The man lying in front of him hadn't elected to inhabit another world. Calum, though, had chosen the narcoleptic demi-monde he currently inhabited.

"Follow me," motioned the nurse, who'd shown the 'WANTED' man to her patient's room while somebody had called the police.

"So where is he?" asked the policeman, as baffled as his colleague in Torquay had been when the singer disappeared into thin air. "He's not under here either," he concluded, taking a swift peek under the bed.

"He was here ten minutes ago, of that I am certain. May God strike me down if I'm lying," declared the nurse, tilting her head towards the heavens.

"Well, he's not here anymore. He must have scarpered before we got here. Bugger's been eluding us for weeks. And if I'm being brutally honest with you, the country's hard-pressed police force has more important matters to deal with than tracking down pop stars with personality disorders."

"My husband," the nurse said, glaring at the WPC accompanying the cooper, "he says their music is the work of the devil."

"Do you really think so?" replied the young policewoman, quite fond of a bit of techno herself.

"He's always telling me the Rolling Stones are responsible for everybody taking drugs today," she said, offering a unique insight to the Met.

"He may have a point," nodded the policeman. "Your husband sounds like a wise man to me," he added, unaware Calum had helped himself to a stash of methadone from the trolley when the nurse had her back turned.

CHAPTER SEVENTY-THREE

It was a meeting he'd been dreading since Jack Weisberg called to warn him in advance. Symes consoled himself with yet another glass of champagne. At least it went according to plan – their plan, if not his. With one member of the band dead, another in a coma and one a full-blown junkie who'd gone missing, SSB's record label wanted out. When they met to discuss what was already a done deal, they tore up the band's contract right in front of the manager's eyes. "Feel free to approach another record company" was the parting shot.

As of now, all future ties with the company were severed, the relationship dissolved. Outside their back catalogue, which was still in high demand, there would be no more new albums. The band's work would continue to sell well until the following year, when sales would rise as a result of fans mourning the anniversary of the day Jay was gunned down so cruelly.

"Heartless fucking bastards," Symes cursed, replaying the disastrous meeting in his mind as he helped himself to more champagne. "It's over," he admitted. His cash cow was gone.

If the circumstantial evidence had been flimsy, the ballistics report was seriously flawed and, in places, totally fabricated. The police had also lied consistently throughout the Old Bailey trial that was currently making front-page news – a point that was not lost on the presiding judge. After days of summing up, the foreman of the jury was ready to deliver their verdict by mid-afternoon on the final day of the trial.

Waiting for the charge to be read out, the man accused of shooting Jay stood silently in the dock, head bowed, prepared to go prison for a crime he hadn't committed.

"And how do you find the defendant?"

"Not guilty."

There was uproar and ecstatic cries of relief almost immediately from the public gallery, where members of the defendant's immediate family were sitting.

Understandably, this less than satisfactory verdict was greeted with stunned silence from Jay's family, sitting quietly on the opposite side of the courtroom. They'd got the wrong man. Jay's would-be assassin was still at large, free to roam the streets of London commanding respect from his peers and enforcing it down the barrel of a gun.

There were hard-hitting headlines the following day: *'Justice For One Man'*, *'Police Humiliated'*, *'Racism Runs Deep In The Force'*. The most accurate of these – *'Not On My Watch'* – was a savage indictment of Lambeth's Chief Constable, now on permanent gardening leave. It was he who'd backed his comrades to the hilt when he knew half the evidence they'd given under oath was inaccurate and in many cases false.

Born into a family of mechanics and with revenge uppermost in his mind, it hadn't been too difficult to know what to do. And after studying the Mercedes manual he'd found in the car's glove compartment fresh and untouched, it had taken just half an hour to make the necessary adjustments. Loosening a bolt here, a bolt there, then severing a cable, the job was done. But his handiwork hadn't fooled investigators attending the scene of the accident.

Passengers looked on in astonishment as three armed *gendarmes* stormed their late-evening flight bound for Tangier before hauling the former houseboy off the flight. Wanted for questioning about the murder that had dominated the headlines in the south of France, Aziz al-Fasi was placed into custody immediately.

When his day in court arrived, Aziz was not as fortunate as the man tried for murder in London. At the mercy of French prosecutors, he was found guilty on all charges, receiving life imprisonment for the premeditated murder of David Edwards.

Once an internationally famous keyboard player, David had been downgraded to one more murder statistic on a police file. It was a file that could now be closed to their satisfaction, if not that of the deceased man's family.

It hadn't been half as difficult as Symes had imagined. In fact, it had only taken one phone call to find himself back in the world of the employed – a phone call to a man who could boast even fewer scruples than he could.

"Andrew, my old son, long time no hear. I was absolutely fucking gutted to hear about the demise of your band." As indeed the slippery Danny Gosling might have been. "You know as well as I do, my son, and I've always said it: rock is hard. Rock is fucking hard," he guffawed, laughing tactlessly at his own joke. "Anyway Andrew, what is it I can do for you today, my son?"

"You can stop patronising me – and you can stop calling me son," growled Symes, in no mood for the conciliatory cockney crap Gosling dispensed.

"What would you like me to call you?" sneered the promoter. "Successful? It's not as if you're quite the powerful man you once were, Andrew. Certainly not to the likes of me. But as I was saying, at risk of repeating myself, what would you like me to call you? Today, that is," he added sarcastically.

"For the time being, 'partner' will do just fine," Symes assured the man who was one step away from becoming his new business associate.

"Partner?" the king of the counterfeiters choked, dropping the ham sandwich he'd been gnawing at. "You're not my fucking partner, you piece of shit!"

"No, but I'm about to be."

"The fuck you are!"

"Allow me to elucidate."

Over the next fifteen minutes Symes spelled it out in ten foot-high capitals.

After hiring a private detective, Symes had discovered that Gosling had been ripping off the band, and by implication himself, rather comprehensively with his own counterfeit merchandise. Rather than shut him down, Symes had been biding his time, waiting for a moment such as this to arrive.

"Well? What's it to be? The choice is yours."

"Choice? I haven't got a fucking choice. What fucking choice?"

"I could, if you prefer, and quite legitimately if I may say so, go to the police," Symes said, reminding him of his fate should they fail to reach a mutually acceptable agreement, the boot on the other foot now. "They're having a huge clampdown on counterfeiters at the moment. I suspect they'd love to meet you. In person," he added cockily. "I think they'd like to know all your secrets, Danny."

"I'll bet they would," acknowledged the disgruntled counterfeiter.

"Whereas I know all about them already. Certainly enough to get you banged up behind bars for the next twelve months. Despite what they say in the papers, I can tell you, from personal experience, prison is no picnic – and if you don't play your cards wrong, Danny, that's exactly where you'll be going."

"It's blackmail," argued Gosling. "Fucking blackmail, that's what it is."

"Blackmail, counterfeiting, call it what you like," pooh-poohed Symes, cut from the same cloth as the man he was persecuting for his misdeeds. "At this point," he pressed home his advantage, "I'd say it's purely academic from your perspective. As I already said, Danny, the choice is yours."

"You cheeky pompous jumped up twat. You two-bit fucking crook. I'd rather stick pineapples up my fucking arse than make you my partner."

"Danny," Symes voice boomed down the line. "You can take it, leave it, or shove pineapples up your arse for all I care. But as your new silent partner I want fifty per cent of the business – that, or you're history. Brown bread, as you would say," he mimicked his cockney prey. "And that would be fifty per cent of the gross, too."

"I'll give you twenty-five per cent. Best I can do."

"You're nowhere near, Danny. You're going to have to do a lot better than that. Shall we say forty-five per cent and call it a day?"

"You poxy fucking thief," swore Gosling, forgetting he was one too. "Thirty per cent sounds nearer the mark," he rasped, fighting one of the toughest battles of his long if undistinguished career – one that could end at any moment.

"Not enough, Danny."

"Thirty-five per cent," Gosling continued, chipping away.

"Because I'm in a benevolent frame of mind, Danny, today for one day only, I'm prepared to settle for forty per cent of the gross."

"Forty fucking per cent!"

"That or you, my old cockney sparrer, are fucked," Symes reminded him, intimidation his weapon of choice at this delicate stage in the negotiations. "And I'll be the one to fuck you."

"You mean it, don't you?"

"That's fucked with a capital 'F'," his new partner pointed out, in case Gosling hadn't fully understood the terms of this truly stellar piece of negotiation.

"OK," the counterfeiter relented. "You win. Forty per cent."

CHAPTER SEVENTY-FOUR

Stretched out on top of the sea wall, Calum was back in Torquay again for the hot summer months. Except this time, he really was staying at the YMCA.

Suddenly, he recognised something faintly familiar about the person standing at the front of the queue, yards away from him buying himself an ice cream.

"Excuse me," he called out to the man as he walked past the bench he was sitting on. "Don't I know you from somewhere?"

A quizzical look on his face, hair slightly thinning, it was Ashley Page, another rock star who'd fallen on hard times. The one he and Jay had shared a bottle of red wine with on Carmine Street in New York's Greenwich Village. The man who'd predicted their downfall.

In many respects he'd been spot on: the drug dealers, vintage guitar dealers, lawyers, journalists, promoters, dishonest managers and even more dishonest record companies.

"What a small world we live in," Page greeted him, licking his ice cream feverishly as it began to melt under the heat of the midday sun.

"Great to see you. How are you, man?"

"Could be better," Page replied, shrugging his shoulders, fixated by Calum's drug-ravaged complexion. "I hear life hasn't been too good for you guys since we last met."

"That wouldn't be a million miles from the truth."

"I was pretty shocked when I heard about your keyboard player. What was the guy's name?"

"David," replied Calum, who'd learned of his demise after visiting Jay.

"And what about the other guy we were drinking with that night? Your guitar player, if I remember correctly."

"His name was Jay."

"What happened to him was something else. Poor bastard. Condemned to spend the rest of his life in a hospital bed wired up to a life-support machine. And you, my friend, how are things for you?"

"Mmm," Calum mumbled in feeble acknowledgment.

"Was the price you paid too high a price to pay for fame?"

"I may not have thought so at the time. Now, I'm not so sure." Without warning, he slumped forward unconscious, his head coming to rest on his lap.

Page shook his head in sympathy at the sight of this sad, broken individual. Before he continued his walk along the promenade, he tucked a five-pound note and some loose change into Calum's threadbare trouser pocket. He thanked his lucky stars. He knew in different circumstances it could have been him.

For two former members of SSB, life actually did turn out better. For one of them, life turned out better than they could have imagined in their wildest dreams.

Grant had retired from the business altogether. Finding his true vocation, he'd carved out a more fulfilling life and career for himself running his charity for the homeless.

Simon, reduced to playing the occasional pub gig with the new band he'd formed, was having more fun than he'd ever had in his life. Gone were the days of hectic recording schedules and gruelling world tours, replaced by a new life with none of the associated pressures.

"This will be our last number of the evening, we hope you enjoy it," he beamed at the audience, as he counted in the band on his hi-hat.

Simon had, against all odds, and anybody's expectations, become an exceptionally wealthy man. With a helping hand from Marcella, he'd been able to turn his passion for exotic automobiles and speed into a thriving business – and made himself the real winner in the race to get rich in the process.

Today he rented out the kind of flash vehicles that his chiefly rock-star clientele adored. Future plans included leasing a super yacht and the purchase of two Gulfstream jets., which he intended to hire out to his newer clients: businessmen, famous movie stars and an assortment of extremely wealthy European footballers.

As if this wasn't enough, he'd also had the foresight to make a series of astute investments in the property market. He now owned a series of rentals in Manhattan and Brooklyn, which Basil managed for him, while the childless couple maintained a second home of their own in Florida.

Built as a replica of Southfork, South Park was identical in every detail.

"Thank you for being a fabulous audience, we love you!" Simon shouted into the microphone as the last power chord of the evening faded to ecstatic applause. "God bless and be lucky."

Lightning Source UK Ltd.
Milton Keynes UK
UKOW06f1426160316

270280UK00001B/24/P